IN HISTORY'S
SHADOW

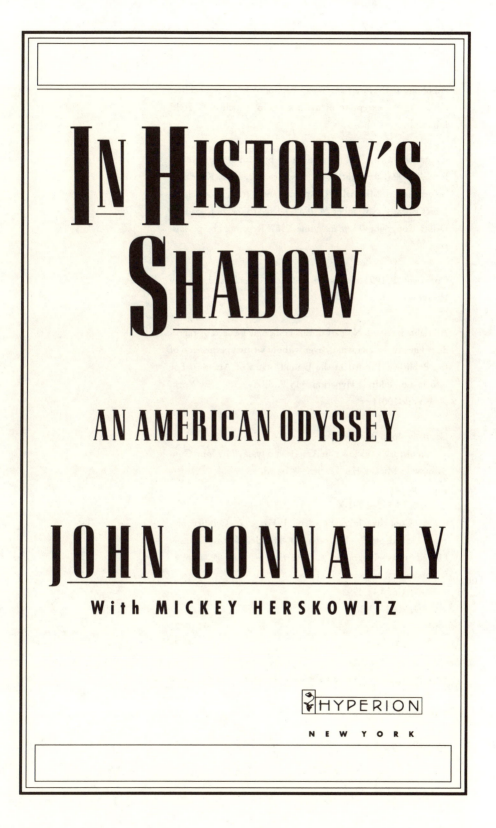

In History's
Shadow

AN AMERICAN ODYSSEY

John Connally

With MICKEY HERSKOWITZ

HYPERION

NEW YORK

Connally, John Bowden.
    In history's shadow : an American odyssey / by John Connally, with Mickey Herskowitz. — 1st ed.
       p. cm.
    ISBN 1-56282-791-X
    1. Connally, John Bowden, 1917- . 2. Cabinet officers—United States—Biography. 3. Presidential candidates—United States—Biography. 4. Governors—Texas—Biography. I. Herskowitz, Mickey. II. Title.
    E840.8.C66A3 1993
    973.926′092—dc20
    [B]   93-10472
                                       CIP

BOOK DESIGN BY BARBARA M. BACHMAN

FIRST EDITION

10 9 8 7 6 5 4 3 2 1

To Nellie, our sons John and Mark, our daughter Sharon, and the new generations of Connallys they have given us—They have been there to share the joys, and when times were hard to bear, to make them bearable.

ACKNOWLEDGMENTS

Throughout my three terms as Governor of Texas, I was blessed with as talented and reliable a political staff as any ever assembled. The opinion may be biased, and should be, because I saw them perform and benefited from their loyalty.

Many of them came together to encourage this book, to prod my memory and lend their impressions. I am indebted to them now, as I have been over the years: Howard Rose, Larry Temple, John Mobley, George Christian, and Mike Myers. This group also included three who were not officially on my staff: Julian Read, a valued adviser through his Austin-based public relations agency; Wayne Gibbens, who headed the state's Washington office; and Ben Barnes, one of my earliest supporters and later my lieutenant governor.

Rose, Temple, and Christian later went to the White House to work for President Johnson, who used my staff as a sort of farm club. I took it as a compliment. They continue to be close friends, these former members of the Connally team, and we still meet each year at Christmas for a reunion.

My former secretaries, Dorothy Jones and Joan Kennedy, were largely responsible for the preservation of my guber-

ACKNOWLEDGMENTS

natorial papers, which are now at the LBJ Library in Austin. Others who helped manage my offices, my papers and my time, are Joe Moore, Terrell Blodgett, Clara Jean Sherrill, and Maureen Ray. My special thanks are owed to Bob Tissing, Jr., the library's archivist, for his timely assistance.

The insistence of Barry Silverman, whose instincts I have always respected, played a part in my undertaking this project, and pushed it along. His advice and counsel over the years have been invaluable.

Marilyn Poole, my present secretary in the Houston offices of the Maxxam Corporation, tracked down long-lost names and numbers and kept the files in order, no small task.

As he did so often in the past, Robert Strauss, Esq., former chairman of the Democratic party and the last U. S. ambassador to the Soviet Union, made available his wit and insights. Over a hundred interviews were conducted for this work, providing material and confirming or clarifying significant details and stories. Many are friends of long standing, too many to list. But they know who they are—and they are appreciated.

Especially, I must acknowledge former Presidents Richard M. Nixon and Gerald Ford, who were very generous with their time and recollections.

Finally, I was fortunate to have an editor with the insights and perseverance of Pat Mulcahy.

CONTENTS

CONTENTS

In History's
Shadow

THE MOTORCADE

I heard what I thought was a rifle shot. I turned my head in the direction of the sound, which seemed to come from behind my right shoulder. My eyes saw nothing unusual, but I felt an icy chill of anxiety. I turned to the left, toward President and Mrs. Kennedy.

In the middle of my turn, I felt a thud, as if someone had pounded me on the back with a fist, a blow so hard I doubled over. My eyes were still open. I could see blood drenching my shirt and I knew I had been hit.

The car jerked into another speed. My wife, Nellie, pulled me to her lap and said without panic, "Be still." I blurted out the words "MY GOD! THEY ARE GOING TO KILL US ALL!" In the microsecond it took for that cry to leap from my lips, two things happened. Nellie's action saved my life, and the conspiracy theorists had the first peg on which to hang their endless webs of intrigue. John Connally, the governor of Texas, had referred to the collective They, the mysterious They, the ever-present and all-powerful They.

It would be a conceit to think, much less claim, that a spontaneous outburst from a wounded man touched off the cycle of conspiracy plots that have spread like crabgrass and whose numbers continue to grow with each passing November. If my phrasing encouraged anyone, and apparently it did, I resent and deplore being used in any way to turn the tragedy into a cottage industry.

I suppose the conspiracy rumors began that day, the first of the books within months, or weeks. We have had the two Oswalds, the two guns, the two John Kennedys, conspiracies sponsored by the Soviets, by Fidel Castro, by the Mafia, the FBI, the CIA, and the oil cartel. Anyone with a theory could find an audience or a forum. The wackier the theory, the stronger the response.

At least one book—probably more—argued that Lee Harvey Oswald was a Russian spy. I believe you could make a better case that his wife, Marina, was the lost Princess Anastasia.

I am angry, and at times incensed, over the seriousness with which these fantasies are taken, because they exploit a sickness and keep renewing the nation's most haunting ordeal. The assassination of Lincoln and the death of Franklin Roosevelt left their marks on America's soul. But television did not bring either into our homes. Lincoln was the President of a divided land; FDR was old and sick.

Of course, none of this was on my mind as our motorcade, traveling on Main Street, approached Dealey Plaza. Commerce forms the south side of the plaza as the roadway curves east from the underpass. Elm Street is on the north, and after we turned right on Houston, Elm was the road we took, past the grass-covered slopes that rise above the gray Texas asphalt. The plaza is a parklike setting with pavilions, which were built by the WPA during the Depression, and parking lots. A wooden picket fence bordered a grassy knoll on Elm.

On the northwest corner of Elm and Houston Streets was the Texas School Book Depository, an ugly brick building— once a dull red, but now sandblasted to a shade of rust. In 1901 it had been erected as the offices of the Southern Rock Island Plow Company. It looked like a factory.

I had driven past that spot many times. It was just another

roadway whose only purpose was to move you along to a prettier section of town. That day it would join Ford's Theatre in the history of the nation. The fact that it did will be a source of pain to me all of my life, both for the tragic act that happened there and for the shadow it cast on Texas so unfairly. A twenty-four-year-old misfit named Lee Harvey Oswald, who had been dishonorably discharged from the Marines, had gone to work as a clerk in the School Book building on October 15.

The day was brilliant and sunny and crisp, and the President had made the decision not to use the bulletproof top that came with the car. We were all smiling and waving to the crowds. I was, frankly, relieved, pleased with how lovely the day had turned out and by the size and enthusiasm of the crowds that lined the curbs.

Then I heard the first shot, and felt the second, both the sound and the impact like a loud smack. In such a moment of helplessness, of total alarm and confusion, your mind races. You have perhaps a fragment of rational thought left before the pain or the fear or both take over. And I knew, with a terrible certainty, that all of us were players in a major tragedy.

A third shot was fired and the President's brain tissue and blood were splattered over the blue velour of the limousine, over Nellie's clothes and my own. By then my head was resting in my wife's lap and she was whispering to me, "Be still. You're going to be all right." From a distance, as if in an echo chamber, I heard Jackie Kennedy cry out: "I have his brains in my hands!"

As I was losing consciousness, I heard one more voice, a Secret Service agent screaming at the driver: "Get out of line! Get us to a hospital quick!" I was vaguely aware of the motion of the car jerking into high speed, pulling away from the rest of the motorcade. I may have heard the sirens, I can't be sure. I felt frozen, and my ears rang with the echo of the gunshots or the sirens of the police or an inward wail that said Jack Kennedy was dead--of that I was sure—and I was dying.

It could not have come to this. The trip had gone so smoothly, so successfully, through the first two stops. I had been governor for less than eleven months and this was the first time I had been host to the President of the United States. It had all the responsibilities, I thought, of having him to one's home. There is a great air that surrounds the Presidency, of excitement and even glamour, and I think this infected us all.

From Houston we had flown to Fort Worth Thursday night, somewhat subdued, everyone on the plane suddenly tired. It was close to midnight when we landed at Carswell Air Force Base, and there was a light drizzle. Even so, there were knots of people standing in the darkness and waving as the closed Presidential car passed. At the Texas Hotel, the lobby was packed with cheering people. The President worked his way through them smoothly, smiling and nodding, and led Jackie into the elevator.

After I had taken Nellie to our suite, I went down to the coffee shop for scrambled eggs and a glass of milk. Fort Worth was like home to me—I had been in business there before joining the Kennedy cabinet in 1961—and I knew most of the people in the coffee shop. They were all discussing the "Yarborough incident." Twice that day, in San Antonio and again in Houston, Senator Ralph Yarborough had refused publicly to ride with Vice President Johnson—just the sort of lively, petty clash that attracts the press. I knew there would be a stir in the morning papers.

It was still drizzling in Fort Worth Friday morning, but the President appeared in good spirits. He seemed to have slept well. The Secret Service had selected his suite, one that was rather plainly furnished and had only one door. Contrary to reports made later that it was dingy and worn, the hotel had redecorated it. A committee had gathered from private homes all over Fort Worth a collection of great paintings to hang in the suite—a Picasso, a Monet, a van Gogh among them. Before he came down that morning, the President called Mrs. J. Lee Johnson III, who had assembled and arranged the art, and thanked her.

Before breakfast, I saw President Kennedy waiting to make his entrance after everyone else was seated. He beckoned me over. "John," he said, "did you know that Yarborough refused to ride with Lyndon yesterday?"

I said I did. "What's the matter with that fellow?" he asked.

I said I didn't know, and a cold, exceedingly firm look came into Jack Kennedy's eyes. "I'll tell you one thing," he said. "He'll ride with him today or he'll walk."

A few minutes later, the President was seen in earnest conversation with Senator Yarborough. The President was doing all the talking and the senator the listening, and when we left Fort Worth at midmorning, Yarborough rode with Johnson. They rode together again in Dallas. I'm fairly sure you could have fit into a thimble the number of words they exchanged.

It was an unpleasant incident, but quite minor. After the assassination, when everything that had happened became important and magnified and much talked about, it came to seem significant. I think there is no doubt that this fed the gradual growth of a public impression that the President went to Texas to settle a feud. He did require Senator Yarborough to pay the Vice President the courtesy of riding in a car with him, but there was no more to it than that. It was a case of bad manners, not bad politics. Kennedy was astute enough to know that one can lead to the other.

He apologized to his breakfast audience—mostly members of the Fort Worth Chamber of Commerce—because Jackie wasn't down yet. "Mrs. Kennedy is organizing herself," he said. "It takes her longer, but, of course, she looks better than we do when she does it." After his speech, he walked outside in the mist to greet the overflow of people who had been unable to buy tickets. Before we left the hotel, he took a few minutes to place a phone call that was sure to please Texans, who put a heavy store on respectfulness. He called Uvalde to wish a happy ninety-fifth birthday to John Nance Garner, Vice President in the first two terms of Franklin Roosevelt.

That gesture took me back to my political roots. When FDR decided to run for a third term, Garner and Lyndon Johnson wound up on opposing sides. I was with Johnson. From then on, I had no illusions about how fast and hard Texans chose sides.

We took off for Dallas at about 11 A.M., and while we were still airborne John Kennedy looked out the window and said, with a smile, "Our luck is holding. It looks as if we'll get sunshine."

And, indeed, when we landed, Love Field glistened with sunlight on the puddles left by an overnight rain. The clouds were gone and the air was soft and the sky powder blue. In this most crucial of Texas cities, we were being favored. There was an overpowering sense of success and I knew that President Kennedy felt it, too.

At the airport, someone wheeled up an elderly lady who had never met a President. John F. Kennedy leaned over and gently spoke to her. The Secret Service was waiting to move everyone toward the line of cars, looking as if their shoes were too tight, the way Secret Servicemen often look.

But the Kennedys exchanged glances and then walked over toward the fence where a crowd was waving and cheering. They walked along the fence, touching the hands and smiling and cooing at the babies that young couples were holding aloft. This went on for eight or ten minutes, and you never thought about exposure, or threats, or danger.

I had been worried about Dallas, fearing not violence but embarrassment. An ugly advertisement had run that very morning in the Dallas *Morning News*, signed "The American Fact-Finding Committee," demanding to know, among other things, why the President had "ordered . . . the Attorney General to go soft on Communism." It was stupid, and only a ripple on an otherwise calm sea, but I couldn't forget that Dallas had been the scene of other episodes. A month earlier, Adlai Stevenson, the ambassador to the United Nations, had been nicked on the head by a picket sign. There had been a 1960 attack on then Senator Johnson, in which he was jostled and spat upon by Nixon supporters.

My fears had to do with insulting signs and rudeness, crowds that might be hostile or sullen, or—just as bad for a politician—apathetic. I had objected to the parade route being announced well in advance because that lends itself to organized heckling. My concerns had been rejected by the White House staff.

But as we neared downtown about noon, my misgivings began to fall away. The people were friendly, waving, smiling, calling the Kennedys "Jack" and "Jackie." Americans have generally been possessive about their first couples, but the Kennedy's represented something else: a new generation come of age, the essence of being in the right place at the right time. They were young, athletic, and raising a family. They represented the best years of our lives.

In most of the cities the President had visited, crowds stood on the sidewalks, barely venturing into the streets. Downtown Dallas was different. So many people lined the man-made canyon that they surged in on the motorcade from either side. Secret Service agents clambered out of their open touring car, just behind the President's, and tried in vain to shoo the more enthusiastic away.

At Lemmon Avenue and Lomo Alto Street, a group of schoolgirls frantically waved a sign: MR. PRESIDENT, PLEASE STOP AND SHAKE OUR HANDS. He grinned, and the limousine glided to a halt. The girls swarmed forward, giggling, and clutched at his outstretched hand.

The big clock on the Mercantile Bank had just moved past high noon. We were falling a few minutes behind schedule, traveling at ten to fifteen miles an hour. The sun was causing Jackie to squint, but she was too busy waving to search her purse for her sunglasses.

We saw only one negative sign. I believe it said, simply, KENNEDY, GO HOME. He nudged my shoulder and motioned with his thumb. "See that sign, John?" I said that I had, and hoped he had not. He smiled and said, "I see them everywhere I go." With an edge of sarcasm, he added, "He's probably a nice guy."

At a point where the crowds and the noise slackened momentarily, he asked how I thought things were looking in Texas. He had been pumped up by the reception and his political interest was quickening.

"There will be a Houston *Chronicle* poll out tomorrow," I said, "which should give us some ideas."

"What is it going to show?" he asked.

"I think it will show that you can carry the state, but that it will be a close election."

"Oh? How will it show you running?"

"Mr. President," I said, "I think it will show me running a little ahead of you."

"That doesn't surprise me," he said, and those were the last words we exchanged. By now, Mrs. Kennedy had managed to slip on her sunglasses; when the President noticed, he said, in a low voice, "Take off your glasses, Jackie." She had not campaigned with him since 1960, and was making her second appearance in public since the death of their infant son, Patrick, in August. She may not have realized it, but you might as well put on a mask as dark glasses, which have the same effect of hiding one's face and emotions and making it almost useless to take part in a parade like this one. Several minutes later, in perhaps a forgetful moment, she had slipped them back on, and I heard him say, in exactly the same tone: "Take off the glasses, Jackie."

He was watching the crowd, waving at them steadily with a stiff forearm, his right hand moving only a few inches out from his face and back. It was a small movement and struck me as curiously formal, but I could see it was effective. I kept hearing a rumble from behind me—I was on the right jump seat, in front of the President, and Nellie on the left side, in front of Jackie. It sounded like a low monotone, and then I realized he was responding to the crowd, "Thank you, thank you, thank you." Over and over, he repeated himself to people who could not possibly hear him, but who could sense that he was answering them, and who knew that a contact had been made.

And then he turned his head slightly and said, "Jackie, take off your gloves."

Up to that very day, I had thought—and the polls showed—that John Kennedy's re-election was no sure thing. Observing him on that trip, riding with him in the car that morning, I knew he would get a second term. Kennedy would run against Barry Goldwater, who had not yet learned to lighten up in public, and he was going to so captivate the people that his record wouldn't much matter. And up to that point, the record was rather thin. But Kennedy would make Goldwater look and sound like a hardcase, pinched and crabby.

The week before, I recalled, Senator Goldwater had asked for labor's support in a speech "to two thousand cheering businessmen in Chicago."

The crowds were going wild, swelling larger and larger. We passed a school and the children poured into the street, so excited they were shaking my hand, too. As we neared the center of town, people were packing the sidewalks clear back to the buildings. They were hanging out of windows ten stories up, waving banners and signs. They were smiling, laughing, pointing, waving, shrieking. Some of the schools had let out early and girls were jumping in front of the limousine, creating pandemonium for the Secret Service agents. It was an incredible show, directed as much at Mrs. Kennedy as the President. I had the distinct feeling she was unbending, relaxing, learning to accept and enjoy this outpouring of affection.

The last of my worries had evaporated. I felt exuberant. The people on the street were his. The business community, whose help he would need in 1964, had found him sincere and unthreatening. He would charm more of them at the luncheon— for which we were already late—and at the dinner that night in Austin. The President looked hearty and confident. Nellie leaned sideways between the jump seats and said proudly, over the roar of the crowd: "You can't say now that Dallas doesn't love you, Mr. President."

He smiled and nodded. At that instant, the big dark blue car turned off Main Street and slowly negotiated the turn under the looming School Book Depository building, and dipped down the hill into the bright sunshine.

It was almost exactly 12:30 P.M., November 22, 1963, when we followed the motorcycle escort onto Houston Street and past the ugly brick building where Lee Harvey Oswald waited with his scrambled egg of a mind. People were still jostling for a better view. The noise of the motorcycles, the clearing of the mechanical lungs, b-r-r-o-o-o-m, competed with the rising cheers, and at first many people thought what they heard was the back-fire of a motorbike.

I knew it wasn't. I had been to war, hunted, handled guns all my life. And even if there had been time to wonder, within seconds the evidence was all over us. The first shot struck the President in the neck. His hands flew to his throat, a reflex. I turned, and felt the blow against my back. My body was aligned in such a way that the bullet passed through my chest, shattered my right wrist, and lodged in my thigh. It is remarkable, over the years, how many people have tried to tell me where I was shot, and how. I never argue with them. I only need to consult my scars.

I was still conscious when the third shot blew off part of John Kennedy's head. It is no longer possible to say with certitude how much of the race to Parkland Memorial Hospital I remember, and how much I have been told by Nellie, or picked up from watching the news films or reading the official reports.

My images are the same most people have: a motorcycle cop veering to the curb and almost falling off; another dropping to the ground, gun drawn. People running in every direction, some holding or dragging their children. Jesse Curry, the Dallas police chief, who had been riding at the head of the motorcade, ordered his officers into the Texas Book Depository. The federal agents, who had been assigned to their own car (called "the Queen Mary"), jumped out and headed for the front entrance even as some in the crowd were still waving to the President. Once the motorcade began to speed away, and the police and

Secret Servicemen drew their weapons, no one had to be told that something had gone terribly wrong.

Photographers closest to the building began aiming their cameras at the window at the southeast corner on the sixth floor.

The Presidential limo, a 1961 Lincoln, whose bulletproof bubble was packed in the trunk, spun around corners on two wheels at speeds up to seventy miles an hour. The hospital was three and a half miles away. Nellie cradled my head. Clint Hill, the special agent assigned to the President, jumped onto the car and pushed Mrs. Kennedy, who was reaching toward him, back into her seat. The question the film doesn't answer is whether she was trying to get out of the car, or frantically reaching back to pull him in. No matter. She was in shock, and yet still sustained by some incredible inner discipline.

In the car behind us, I would learn later, an agent named Rufus Youngblood had shoved both Lyndon and Lady Bird Johnson to the floor and covered their bodies with his. In the press-pool car, the gentleman from the United Press International was wrestling with the gentleman from the Associated Press for the one mobile phone.

Twice during the race to the hospital, Nellie admitted, she had thought I was dead. I was in and out of consciousness. I came to just when the car jolted to a stop at the emergency entrance to Parkland Memorial. How strangely the mind works. I knew I was badly wounded and I thought fatally so. I knew the President was dead. Yet it made sense to me that the hospital orderlies would want to get him out of the car before they could think of treating me.

The back door was beside the jump seat I was in, and I realized I might be blocking the way. Arms snaked across Nellie to reach the President. Subconsciously, I suppose, I struggled to raise myself from Nellie's lap to give them room. I half stood, then collapsed and passed out again.

They reached over me and lifted the President out of the back seat. Minutes later, they lowered me onto a stretcher—I didn't know then that one of those attending me was Dave

Powers, one of the President's oldest friends.

I had been unaware of any pain up to that moment; an adrenalin block, I guess. Suddenly, I was revived by a pain that was excruciating. I cried out, "My God, it hurts . . . it hurts!"

Inside the hospital, a young doctor named James ("Red") Duke was the first to reach me. He began barking out orders. It may be true of most lives, but I do believe mine has been marked by an uncanny knack for the way people and events keep connecting. Red Duke is now the chief of surgery at the University of Texas Medical School in Houston. I bump into him from time to time.

They wheeled me into Trauma Room 2, and Dr. Duke probed the hole in my chest. Another doctor examined my wrist. They spotted more blood on my trousers, and someone fumbled with the belt and tried to wriggle them down my legs. I cried out sharply, "Cut them off!" When I spoke, people jumped back as if a coffin lid had moved. I hadn't been given a sedative because it hadn't occurred to them I would be conscious—if I was alive.

I don't know which, but fear or stubbornness kept waking me. I heard someone say, "Let's turn him over and see if he was hit somewhere else." With that, I spoke up again. I said, "No, I was only hit once." The sound of my voice would shock them into a more feverish round of activity.

Red Duke was then a protégé of Dr. Robert Shaw, who had been home barely a month after a year's sabbatical in Afghanistan. Shaw was driving along Hines Boulevard and arrived at the hospital about the same time we did. He was a world-renowned thoracic surgeon, who had performed literally a thousand chest operations during World War II.

I could not have been in better hands. The bullet had taken out part of two ribs (I was relieved to learn that they would grow back). I had what the doctors called a sucking air chest wound. When Nellie pulled me onto her lap, the pressure of my arm closed off the hole and kept me alive. Otherwise, they said, I would not have lived another eight minutes. The bullet had struck the fifth rib and shattered the end of it. Splinters of bone had pierced and collapsed a lung, and when we pulled up to the emergency entrance at Parkland, I had only a few minutes of air to breathe. I was close to either bleeding or strangling to death.

The exit wound in my chest was the size of a baseball—Dr. Duke's description, not mine. My head was smeared with blood, causing the doctors in the trauma room some brief, early confusion. Then one of them realized the blood wasn't mine. It was John F. Kennedy's.

I knew many, many years ago that I would never be able to give people what they wanted or needed about that day. I have felt rage and grief and helplessness, as tens of millions of Americans did. What else I can share I have shared with Nellie because the lasting, bitter emotion of that day is numbness. Many of my memories are secondhand. I am missing the most historic minutes of my life. There are blank spaces in an unbearable scene; perhaps I could not have borne the scene otherwise.

There was no modesty in my struggle for life. Whatever I knew, whatever I thought, was shaped by the darkest reality. The drama was in the room next door, in the President's death. In my lucid micro-moments, I knew he was gone. I was detached from the chaos that touched every corner of the hospital. I was almost impatient with the time it was taking for me to die; I had made my regrets, that I would leave Nellie alone to see our children and grandchildren grow up.

This was what I missed, what I would put together from the accounts of those who survived that day in Dallas.

It was the noon hour, and several of the doctors, if not most, were in the cafeteria. They looked up from their lunches and stared at each other when the nurse's voice said over the paging system: "Dr. Tom Shires, STAT." The "STAT" meant emergency. But Dr. Shires, the chief resident in surgery, was out of town and they rarely called him for an emergency.

A doctor named Malcolm Perry put down his fork and

went to the nearest telephone. "This is Dr. Perry," he said, "taking Dr. Shires's page."

The operator said, "President Kennedy has been shot. They are bringing him into the emergency room right now."

Perry and Duke and a dozen other doctors started heading quickly out of the cafeteria and down a flight of stairs. They pushed through a brown double door, and a nurse pointed to Trauma Room 1. Perry walked into that one. Someone else steered Red Duke toward Trauma Room 2.

Malcolm Perry found the President of the United States on his back, on an aluminum hospital cart, with a huge lamp beaming down on his face. He had been stripped of his coat, shirt, tie, and undershirt, and Dr. Charles Carrico was already at work, lowering a tube down his throat. Perry did a tracheotomy and put another in his windpipe. They didn't give him an anesthetic. There wasn't any need for one. The President wasn't breathing. He had no heartbeat. The damage a 6.5-caliber bullet can do to the back of someone's head is unbelievable. The car seats and flooring had been soaked in blood. Now more blood covered one side of the floor below the aluminum table.

The room was narrow and had gray tiled walls and a cream-colored ceiling, just like the one I was in. But a few minutes before they brought in the body of the President, a Secret Service agent had burst into the emergency room, his face contorted with emotion, waving a submachine gun. Everyone in the room hit the floor.

When a man in a business suit ran in, the agent slugged him on the jaw, and as he slumped to the floor, the man pulled out the card that identified him as an agent of the Federal Bureau of Investigation.

I had no sense of what was happening around me, or in Trauma Room 1, but I knew all I needed to know. Later, little by little, Nellie and others filled in the parts that were missing.

In no time the hospital had turned into a scene of stark confusion. Secret Service agents moved through the halls carrying tommy guns. The Dallas police were there with revolvers drawn, unsure if a massive and and ghastly plot was unfolding, but ready in the event that terrorists stormed the building. Other agents shouted into their walkie-talkies or guarded the pay phones. The security people threw out one Dallas reporter who was found hiding under a sheet on a table in the operating room.

They say that within minutes fifteen doctors had squeezed into Trauma Room 1. John Kennedy was dead and they all knew it, but no one wanted to be the first to admit that it was hopeless, and speak the words that would confirm the fact that the 35th President was dead.

The wound in the back of his head told Dr. Perry that the President never felt the bullet that killed him. Still, he began to massage the President's heart on the surface, hoping that there would be some jiggle on the screen of the electrocardiogram. While he was doing this, Dr. William Kemp Clark, the hospital's chief neurosurgeon, walked in and looked at the machine, looking for some sign of life. There was none. The line was flat. His eyes caught Malcolm Perry's.

Dr. Perry's fingers stopped moving, and he got up from the stool the nurses had shoved under him when he began to tire from the massaging. Another doctor, M. T. Jenkins, who had been regulating the flow of oxygen, picked up the edges of a white sheet and carefully pulled it over the handsome face of John Fitzgerald Kennedy, age forty-six. The IBM clock on the wall of the room read 1 P.M.

Three policemen swept through the corridor and ordered everyone out of the way, which was unnecessary, really, because instinctively everyone moved closer to the wall when they saw the priest arriving. Dr. Perry left the room as Father Oscar Huber, the seventy-year-old pastor of Holy Trinity Church in Dallas, walked in. They actually brushed each other at the door.

Father Huber expressed his deepest sympathy to Mrs. Kennedy, and then he began the chant that Roman Catholic priests have recited over the dead for centuries.

The prayer said: "If you are living, I absolve you from your sins. In the name of the Father and of the Son and of the Holy Ghost. Amen."

Meanwhile, I had been prepped for surgery. Red Duke said later that when he opened my chest and cleaned out the wound, he thought, I've never seen anything like this. As they wheeled me toward the elevator, a member of my staff hustled alongside the gurney and asked if I was going to make it. One of the doctors said they wouldn't know until I came out of surgery.

There was a certain amount of disarray in the matter of handling personal effects. While I was in the operating room, a nurse handed two brown paper bags to Cliff Carter, an aide to Lyndon Johnson. They contained my bloody and ragged clothing. She told him, almost routinely, that I was not expected to survive.

A nurse spotted Nellie and handed her one of my gold cuff links. We never found the other one.

But the most curious discovery of all took place when they rolled me off the stretcher, and onto the examining table. A metal object fell to the floor, with a click no louder than a wedding band. The nurse picked it up and slipped it into her pocket. It was the bullet from my body, the one that passed through my back, chest, and wrist, and worked itself loose from my thigh.

There was enormous significance to that scrap of metal, but I can't be certain how many years later I understood the importance of it. I have always believed that three bullets found their mark. What happened in the hospital demonstrated how easily a bullet could have been swept aside and lost. (Three spent cartridges were found on the sixth floor of the Texas School Book Depository, near the southeast corner window. They matched a bolt-action rifle with a telescopic sight abandoned near the back staircase.)

The Warren Commission, and many of the forensic experts, feared it would weaken their conclusion to simply state that one of the bullets was never found. This led to their reliance on what became known as "the magic bullet," which supposedly went through the President's neck and throat and then caused my multiple wounds.

Everything I saw, heard, and felt is consistent with what was visible in the frame-by-frame analysis of the film taken by Abraham Zapruder, a Dallas merchant who became an accidental historian: The first shot passed through the neck of John F. Kennedy. I saw him clutch his throat. The second shot was the one that struck me; of this I have no doubt. Nellie had pulled me to her when the third bullet blew across the car a spray of the President's brain.

Nellie later told me that she and Jackie sat in the narrow hallway outside Trauma Rooms 1 and 2, facing each other on straight chairs, in the midst of this terrible confusion, with FBI agents and doctors and strangers pushing one way or another. Hysteria had taken over and yet, in a way, order reigned.

The two women, believing that one husband had been killed, and the life of the other hung by a thread, faced each other with little to say. The sorrow, the horror, the shock were evident on the face of each.

I was in surgery for the next three hours, while the Dallas police fanned across the city looking for the assassin, and Lyndon Johnson had been sworn in as the 36th President, and Air Force One lifted off the runway, carrying Jackie Kennedy and her husband back to Washington, D.C.

I slept through the rest of Friday, unaware that Officer J. D. Tippit had been killed by Oswald, who was then arrested a few blocks away in the Texas Theater. I slept through all of Saturday, and was not fully conscious and alert until Monday morning. I am not sure that I understood at first what Nellie was telling me when she said a man named Jack Ruby had killed Lee Harvey Oswald in the basement of the Dallas police station.

Oswald had been arrested, jailed, shot and killed, and I may have been the last man in America to know it.

The Heart of

Texas

Rangeland has a character all its own: hard and open, begging to be ridden, but unsparing to those who do. The land the Connallys worked and eventually owned rolled south toward the Rio Grande. Fields for grazing and farming were cleared the old-fashioned way: a man or a boy behind a plow pulled by a mule. Dirt trails wound around the scrub oaks and cactus and mesquite that tore at a horseman's chaps.

This was Wilson County in the first quarter of the twentieth century, storied land. Here the Spanish conquistadors fought the Comanche, the Tonkawa, and the Apache, and drove them in bloody battles from their hunting grounds. In 1830, a Mexican cattle baron named Francisco Flores de Abreyo built the first hacienda in the area. His descendants are still my neighbors in the town named after him, Floresville.

The county was named in honor of an Englishman, James Charles Wilson, who settled there in 1837. He missed the Texas

Revolution, but in 1842 went to Mexico with a raiding party and was captured and imprisoned. He escaped and returned to Texas, where he was received as a hero and elected to the legislature. It isn't clear if his military adventure or his imprisonment qualified him for politics—possibly both.

Wilson County was in the middle of the range wars of 1883. The early cattlemen had been accustomed to grazing their herds wherever there was grass. No one worried about the ownership of the land; much of it was unclaimed. But barbed wire came to Texas in 1879. In the category of mixed blessings it ranks up there with the necktie and television. Settlers in Wilson and other counties began fencing in their lands. The cattlemen had their cowhands cut the fences at night. The landowners repaired them by day. This ritual was accompanied by a certain amount of gunplay, until the legislature passed a law in 1884, requiring fence builders to put in gates every three miles. The same law made it a crime to cut a fence. The open-range ranchers and the homesteaders learned to live with each other.

The county courthouse was completed in 1885, surrounded in its original design by a whitewashed wooden fence. The bell that sits atop the old building has rung only three times: once when World War I ended; again when the county celebrated its centennial in 1950; and the last time on the day a native son was sworn in as governor of Texas in 1962.

I am a part of the last political generation in this country tested by World War II, and an even more dwindling breed shaped by the soil of rural America. As a condition of government service, neither experience is essential. But you don't survive that kind of war without gaining a respect for the processes of peace and diplomacy. You don't engage the land, let it punish and feed you, and not understand the cycles of life.

The three cultures of Texas are Western, Southern, and Latin. Texas shares 889 miles of border with Mexico. Originally, she was a province of Mexico; she fought her first war with Mexico. The language, attitude, servitude, and political traditions endured for decades in South Texas. Mexican culture played a prominent role in my career, and that of Lyndon Johnson. To miss that point is to miss the truth of the mystery of Box 13 in the Senate race of 1948.

Floresville is less than thirty miles from San Antonio, in the upper coastal plains. Much of South Texas is called the brush country for the endless miles of bushy mesquite trees and cactus clumps that cover it. Once, in the day of the buffalo, this was grassland with streams that ran sweet and clear.

Yet for all the facets that condition the Texas mind, all the size and diversity of the state, there is one quality that overrides every other. That quality is the inherent hardness of the land itself. There is beauty here, but it appears in random and distant places. Texas always was, and is today, a hardscrabble land that had to be broken and held by the pure strength of man and woman. It was on that strength always that it was made to produce and prosper, never on the bounty of its own natural endowment. And that sense of strength which the land demands comes down still to condition the people.

The Connallys were a textbook example.

They came to the United States from their native Ireland with the great swell of immigrants escaping the Irish potato famine in the nineteenth century. The first American Connally, Charles P. Connally, my great-grandfather, migrated to Texas from Alabama. He was a neighbor and close friend of a man named Hardin, and when sons were born to both, they named them John Wesley, after the Methodist churchman.

John Wesley Hardin went on to become one of the renowned gunslingers of the Old West.

John Wesley Connally settled in his adult years on farmland in Wilson County. His first son, John Bowden Connally, my father, was born there in 1889. He was given the middle name of his maternal grandmother's family.

It was the custom then in rural Texas, as in Mexico, to marry young and hope for several sons to help you work the land. My father was nineteen when he married Lela Wright, who taught at the country school and had picked cotton as a girl after her daddy died. They were a striking couple.

I was the fourth of their eight children, all delivered at home. So far as I know, my mother never spent a day of her life inside a hospital.

Their first child, Wyatt, died as an infant. After Stanford and Carmen, I arrived on February 27, 1917. Then came Golfrey, Merrill, Wayne, and Blanche, each two years apart. I still remember Carmen, my older sister, chasing the five boys out of the house when the doctor came to deliver Blanche. I didn't really know what was happening, except that there was a sense of excitement and activity. A few hours later, I learned that I had a baby sister. I was too young to be aware of the anticipation when my younger brothers came along, but I knew this was a wondrous moment.

We were then renting a house in Floresville. We lived not far from a Rufus Johnson, whose sons, William and Edward, would be part of my University of Texas years.

We kept a horse in town called Buttons, and the Johnson boys owned Shetland ponies. They kept haranguing me about a race, me riding Buttons against their ponies. I was about six, giving away at least two years to the younger of them, but I finally accepted the challenge. We picked the dirt street that led to town for a track, and Buttons left them in the dust. I could ride a horse quite well for my age, and I knew even then I would never like the taste of losing.

It is difficult, if not impossible, in the 1990s to imagine what the texture of that world was like. It was part Huck Finn and Tom Sawyer, and part Charles Dickens. The First World War had recently ended. Lean times were getting leaner, and people talked about jobs the way nomads crossing a desert talk about water. Soon the times would be given a name: the Great Depression.

My father was, in turn, a tenant farmer, a bricklayer, a barber, butcher, and bus driver. In one respect, the Depression never touched us. We were so far down on the economic ladder we hardly knew it happened.

We moved from the house where I was born to the Griffith place, three miles east of Floresville. In those days, a piece of property was called by the name of the original owner, no matter how often it changed hands. Right across the road, on a little gravelly hill, was the county poor farm. No national welfare system existed then, but the county had a farm where people with no other means of support were sent, given shelter and a place to raise their chickens or a cow, and do a little farming. Basically, they did as well as they could to provide for their families, with some modest support from the county government.

It wasn't a life sentence. People coped, waited for better times or a break, and moved on. But I can't recall a more chilling phrase from my boyhood than hearing that a family had been put out on the poor farm.

My dad tried everything he could think of to raise a crop that would support his family. We had chickens, turkeys, hogs, milk cows, goats, horses. That part of Wilson County is weak farming land, but we raised peanuts, cotton, and a little corn. One unforgettable year we grew turnips. My brothers and I had to get up early in the morning to go pull those turnips and wash them at the pump. Of course, turnips were a winter crop and it was so cold—we had no hot water—that your hands would freeze. Many a morning I rode into town with my father in a horse-drawn buggy, with those turnips in the back, trying to sell them door to door. That may explain why most of my life I have hated the thought of turnips, much less the taste.

At the old Griffith place, even the most common chore sometimes took a twist. One day my younger brother Golfrey and I went with my father to slop the hogs. We would put all the leftover milk and scraps from the table into a five-gallon lard can. We carried it down to the pen, climbed in with the hogs, and tried to distribute the contents into the trough so all the hogs had an equal chance of getting something to eat.

We had to fight off an old boar, which weighed nearly 400 pounds, while we emptied the slop bucket. (This was not a pretty sight.) Suddenly, the boar reached up and bit my father in the elbow, cutting a nerve and sending an enormous shock to his nervous system. He finally beat the boar over the head with the empty bucket and crawled out of the pen. We held his hand and led him back to the house; he was shaking all over, just quivering. We went inside and immediately called the doctor, who drove out to the house and gave my father a sedative to put him to sleep.

My father was a big man who stood six feet five and weighed anywhere from 230 to 250 pounds in his prime. He and my mother slept in an iron bedstead, and you heard it rattling all over the house that night. He couldn't stop shaking, and he had a terrible time with that arm for years to come. He eventually got over it, but he bore an ugly scar across the width of his elbow for the rest of his life.

The Griffith place would have been a good setting for a Hitchcock movie. For some strange reason, we were constantly having accidents with the animals. Once, my mother went into the fields to bring in a cow that had recently dropped a calf. We had a big bulldog named Major; he had one black and one blue eye, and everyone in the county feared him. He had been trained to fight by the former owner who gave him to my father. But he was wonderful around our family, and in particular around the children. He would not allow any harm to come to us, nor any stranger to approach us.

Major was an intelligent dog, and he followed my mother that day when she went to fetch the cow and her calf. Mother knew the presence of the dog would upset the cow, so about halfway through the field, about fifty yards from the wire gap, she told him to sit and she left him there.

She got a rope around the cow and led her back to the gap, which isn't to be confused with a nice wooden or metal gate. It was just wire stretched around the top and bottom of a pole, hard to open and close, a traditional country gap. She maneuvered the cow to the other side and was trying to push the calf through when the cow turned, charged my mother, and knocked her down. Enraged, the cow started hooking—she had not been dehorned—and stomping my mother on the ground. Mother, fearing she would be maimed or even killed, cried out for Major. "Sic 'em, Major!" and the pit bull immediately leaped to her aid. He jumped on the cow and, in an attempt to pull her away from my mother, chewed off both ears and then got his teeth lodged in the cow's nostril, which is the way he had been trained to fight.

The force of his bite pulled the cow's head over her shoulder and Major lowered her to the ground. He just sat down on her while Mother scrambled away. Bruised all over, and with a deep gash in one foot, she limped back to the house.

Meanwhile, Major continued to sit there, his teeth clamped on the cow's nose. She was bawling her head off, bleeding and in pain, but he would not turn her loose. By then, the noise had attracted some of our farm help, and they tried to coax Major into releasing her, with no success. They finally had to get an iron bar and pry open his jaws to free the cow. I guess he would have sat there forever, or until my mother returned, if they hadn't used that iron bar.

Ours was a small and rugged patch of earth, but we learned from it. The cow was afraid for her calf. The dog knew only that his mistress was in trouble. Had it not been for his devotion, she might have been killed.

My mother was a gentle soul who led a robust life, active almost to the day she died, just short of her ninety-second birthday. Longevity was a characteristic of her family. There were nine brothers and sisters, and all survived into their nineties. My Grandmother Janie Wright lived to be ninety-four, and my maternal grandfather, known to everyone as Grandpa Haddox, made it to one hundred and two. He died during my senior year in college, in 1938.

Grandpa Haddox was born in Chattanooga, Tennessee, in 1836, so he had lived through more than half the life of this nation. He had been a cabin boy on a Mississippi steamboat when he was fifteen, later enlisted in the Confederate Army and fought under General Green. After the War Between the States, he migrated to Texas and reared his family there.

One of my lasting regrets is based on two omissions of my youth: (1) that we didn't have the recording and dictating equipment available today; and (2) that I did not have sense enough and a sufficient reverence for history to sit at his feet and take notes while Grandpa Haddox talked. What a shining opportunity I missed!

My father used to visit with him at length, listening to his tales of his early days on the Big Muddy, and during the Civil War, and of settling on the frontier of Texas. He had many stories to tell, and I consider it a tragic family error that all have been lost to history. At least two Sundays a month, we gathered for a big reunion at Grandma Wright's house—all the uncles and aunts and cousins on every side. The boys were out hunting or riding donkeys or playing at games, way too restless to sit around and enjoy an old man's stories.

The one thing we were all very attentive to, however, was the warning that no one fooled with his axe. Until he was past one hundred years old, Grandpa Haddox chopped every stick of wood that went into the stove and fireplaces of his daughter's house. He had a double-bitted axe that he kept on the porch, right outside his bedroom, and none of the kids dared touch it. He kept the blade razor sharp and no one used it but him. That is how vigorous he was, and proud.

I have not tried to romanticize the rural life I knew as a child, and to some of which I remain partial today. I followed a pair of mules many a mile, breaking the land with a turning plow. That is a fine sensation. You get under a layer of turf and it sort of crackles as it breaks loose. I used to take off my shoes because the soil behind the plow felt so good to walk in. There is no formal education that can equal the experience of planting the seeds, cultivating the crops, and helping to harvest them. You see the corn spring forth from the ground, see it nurtured by the sun and rain, see it mature.

Mostly, we lived off what we were able to produce. I

chopped cotton, hoed the peanuts, and pulled the corn, and for many weeks in the summer I went to the farm of my cousins, the Wrights, and helped in the fields. Uncle Tom Wright's oldest son, Phlemon, and I were in the same graduating class at Floresville High School.

My energy and my drive came out of the struggles of my boyhood. No argument. But I have no unpleasant memories of having been poor, and by today's standards we surely were. But we were not as poor as the Wrights. They lived on what we would describe today as a subsistence level, in a house with three rooms and no indoor plumbing, a one-plank house with all the two-by-four studs exposed on the inside. We made home-made glue so that my Aunt Annie Wright could paper the walls to keep the winter winds out of the cracks. She used pages torn out of mail-order catalogues from Sears Roebuck and Montgomery Ward.

I don't see how anyone who grows up on a farm or a ranch can be anything but an environmentalist. You want to conserve everything you have—the soil, the trees, the grasses—because your very life depends on it.

At a very early age, any rural boy or girl learns about nature and the mysteries of procreation. You see the calves and the pigs born, the chickens lay and hatch their eggs. You watch this day to day, and your respect grows for the patterns of life, the workings of nature. It gives you a certain philosophy, a depth of understanding, that I doubt can be found in the asphalt jungles of society today.

These impressions would be reinforced decades later, when I was fortunate to go to East Africa on safari. I saw the wild dogs attack and kill a gazelle, the lions make a kill, and the rush of the hyenas and buzzards that came to prey on the remains. These were raw and graphic scenes. (One might even see in them a metaphor for America's political wildlife.)

Nature teaches you humility, and to appreciate the inevitability of the things you cannot control.

I always had the example of my father, a decent and enterprising man, who had never gone beyond the eighth grade. He always wanted to be more than a tenant farmer. He enrolled in barber college, but he was too tall to keep stooping over a barber's chair. He opened a butcher shop when I was a child, and he and a lawyer borrowed money for cattle feeding—to fatten a bunch of steers. The market crashed; they lost everything and were unable to repay a $5,000 loan at the bank, a hefty sum in those days. He was broke, but he didn't quit.

He borrowed fifty dollars from a friend, and spent twenty-five to buy a permit to operate a bus between San Antonio and Corpus Christi, over the largely dirt roads that existed in 1926. With the rest he made a down payment on a used Buick with room for seven passengers, including the jump seats. He started his own service, the Red Ball Bus Line, competing with older and bigger companies. Agents for the other lines were known to drag the independent drivers and their passengers from the buses and beat them. But Dad did well in the business simply because he worked hard, unsparingly, and saved his money. Even though he was a large man, he would sleep in the Buick to save a dollar a night, then go to a public washroom and shave and clean up for the return trip into San Antonio and then to home.

We were still living on the Griffith place, in Floresville, and we had no luxuries and few clothes. We went to school barefooted most of the year and wore overalls, the kind that buttoned at the shoulder and had big pockets. I was eight or nine years old and formed at least two habits that lasted a lifetime. I always had a pocketful of peanuts. I'd go up in the hayloft and pick the peanuts that had escaped the thresher. I ate them raw, in season, and acquired a taste for peanuts in any form that I indulge to this day.

During that time, I started carrying a pocketknife. Those were the days when a good pocketknife was a young boy's first serious possession. I don't recall a day of my life that I have been without one. It has been almost an obsession, and over the years I developed quite a collection, some elaborate, a few useful for little more than cleaning your fingernails.

There wasn't much among the Connallys that passed for leisure. I cut kneepads from old tires to wear while dragging a sack between the rows of cotton. We were obedient sons and daughters, and I welcomed the responsibilities that I was too young to fear. I was a quick learner, so they said. One day, when my father left on his bus run, my mother and I rode into town with him in the old car we kept on the farm. At the edge of town, he swung the car around and pointed it back out the dirt road. That way I could get behind the wheel and not have to turn the car around. My mother hadn't yet learned to drive. I could, in a manner of speaking.

At nine, I was almost too short to reach the clutch and the brake in those high-strung old motorcars. By sitting on the edge of the seat and lying almost flat, I could operate the pedals and see over the hood, peering through the steering wheel. The road was narrow, all dirt and sand, but straight and normally without peril.

Just before we reached the first of the two entrances to the farm, we saw two motorcycle riders heading toward us from far down the road. In those days, the highway patrol almost exclusively rode motorcycles. My mother was in a near panic, and said, "Hurry, Johnny, hurry!" The reason for the urgency was that we had no license plates on the car. We couldn't afford the few dollars for the plates and so the car was unregistered. And, of course, even in the 1920s they didn't issue driver's licenses to nine-year-olds. The '20s may have been roaring in places like New York and Chicago, but not in Floresville.

I immediately pulled up to the first entrance, while my mother jumped out to open the wire gap just as the two motor-cycle riders roared by us. They were not the law after all, and we looked at each other with a shared sigh of great relief, knowing that we were not going to get ticketed.

That was the year I first learned to drive a car, and I have been driving ever since without ever having a single moving violation on my record. I consider myself a prudent driver, but a lucky one nonetheless.

When my father started driving his bus line, it became increasingly difficult for him to maintain the farm out in the country. So we moved into town and rented what we called the Knox place. It was right on the main road from Floresville, and our greatest thrill as children was to stand by the side of the house and wave to our father as he passed us, heading in either direction.

After a year it was obvious we needed to be at one end or the other of that particular run of his. So in 1926 we moved to San Antonio, making two intermediate stops before renting a house at 115 Bristol Street.

Money was still scarce. Both my parents worked in the fields, struggled hard, had almost no conveniences. My mother cooked three meals a day on a wood-burning stove, did her laundry in a black washpot over an open fire in the backyard. The children studied by kerosene lamps. We made our own lye soap, butchered our own hogs, cured our own bacon and ham, put up our own lard, ground our own cornmeal.

Yet we really felt no deprivation. We were a happy crowd of kids who grew up in a home where there was affection, love, and discipline. There were family squabbles, of course. The brothers had knockdown fights, as brothers will. One day, we were working in the back fields, and we started throwing ears of corn at each other. What started out as playful turned into anger, and my older brother Stanford and I got into it. We slapped each other around for a while, and then I walked two and a half miles back to the house. I was sitting there when my dad came in and asked what was wrong. I said, "That field isn't big enough for both Stanford and me."

Stanford waited as late as he could to get home, expecting to catch hell when he did. He waited until after dark, and by then we had all cooled down.

Otherwise, we competed in the ways that were healthy:

who picked the most cotton, or earned the best grades. Looking back, we measured the improvement in our modest circumstances by the kind of Christmases we had. In the 1920s and '30s, I suppose many American families did.

On the Griffith place, it was reason to celebrate when each of us found a stocking filled with fruit, apples and oranges and bananas. A Christmas that stands out is the year the five boys received the gift of a football—that is, one ball shared by five. None of us played sports at school because there were chores to be done at home.

Our first Christmas in San Antonio may have been the best of all. My father bought from one of his cousins a a secondhand bicycle, which he repainted and gave to the boys. We cherished that bicycle until Golfrey, who was never the most coordinated brother, ran it into a tree and bent the wheels beyond repair. It was a sad day for all of us.

Stories of this kind may strike some as pure American corn. My political aides often argued or pleaded with me to talk more openly of being a farmer's son, of knowing humble times. I wasn't comfortable with up-from-poor talk. I did not try to conceal my roots, I simply chose not to exploit them.

This is an area where you sometimes can't win. If I mentioned that my dad drove a bus, an opponent or a reporter was sure to point out, with sarcasm, that he owned the company. Never mind that his first "bus" was a used car with jump seats. They made him sound like a tycoon.

Like a great many other kids of that era, I worked at whatever jobs I could find. The most convenient of these was at a Triple X root-beer stand, located right at the end of our street, which was only about a block and a half long. I flipped hamburgers, which cost a dime, and poured root beer at a nickel a mug. One of the great memories of my boyhood occurred when Jack Hoxie, well known then as a maker of Western movies, made a personal appearance at a nearby theater. He came out between features and ordered a hamburger and root beer, which I served him. Lo and behold, he left me a five-dollar tip, which was in truth the most money I had ever seen at one time.

I went through the tenth grade in San Antonio and worked part time for the Robbins Dairy, south of town. Frequently, I would spend Friday night at the home of Henry Robbins and his father, who owned the dairy. I would get up at three o'clock in the morning and help milk about sixty cows. During the week, Paul Sanders, who lived around the corner from us and who was one of a large family, would hop the milk truck with me and make deliveries.

Those were the trucks with the big fenders. We would ride on either side, reach in the back and get out the milk, jump off while the truck was moving, run up to the front porch of the various houses, and leave the amount of milk we knew the families had ordered. We rode seventy-six miles through the streets of San Antonio every afternoon, delivering milk and occasionally butter and cream to the customers of the Robbins Dairy. We got very proficient at it, even though we were kids fourteen or fifteen years old, and in the summer were hopping the truck barefooted.

We could carry four quarts of milk in our two hands, dart off the truck at twenty-five to thirty miles an hour, and not miss a house. Henry Robbins did the driving, and on cold or rainy days Paul and I would rotate in the cab, taking turns in the other seat to get out of the weather.

This gesture was suspended whenever Henry, who was twenty-seven, invited one of his girlfriends to join him. This meant she occupied the inside seat while Paul and I sure enough had to ride the fenders. The arrangement was a continuing source of irritation, and we never understood how Henry could do that to us. It never bothered us when he would park the truck occasionally and stop at a girlfriend's house for fifteen or twenty minutes while we twiddled our thumbs. But it always annoyed us if he brought one along and robbed us of a chance to ride in that cab.

What made the long, bumpy rides through the streets of San Antonio worthwhile was a bakery at the end of the line, on

East Josephine Street. We would stop and buy a pie, each of us, a coconut or lemon or banana pie. I would perch myself on one of the big front fenders, hook a leg over the headlight for security and balance, and on the way home the three of us each ate a whole pie and drank a quart of milk.

My pay for this work was all the milk, butter, and cream that the Connally family needed. Every night, just as the route was ending, I stopped off at my house, and Paul at his, and we'd bring in six or eight quarts of milk and a couple of pounds of butter and cream. So I supplied all the dairy needs for a family of nine as a result of my hopping on and off that milk truck.

We wore shoes to school in San Antonio and felt lucky to own one jacket and a tie or two. That was the extent of our wardrobes—a word I doubt we knew.

My father kept his bus service going from 1926 to 1932, pushing himself to exhaustion and holding on long enough to sell out to Greyhound. From the sale, and savings, he had accumulated nearly $15,000, a small fortune to the Connallys—to most anyone—in those times. (A few miles to the north, Bonnie Parker and Clyde Barrow were burning up the roads in a variety of stolen cars.)

For the first time in our lives, we were about to become landowners. A year earlier, Dad had paid off his share of the $5,000 note that dated back to his losses in the cattle-fattening venture. So we moved back to Floresville in the summer of 1932, with a clean slate and money in the bank, right in the heart of the Depression. He bought one thousand acres of mesquite-infested land known as the Coughran Ranch. He paid fifteen dollars an acre, putting half the money down ($7,500) and using some of the rest to buy cattle and farm equipment. Very little of the land had been cultivated. Most of it was covered in mesquite brush and prickly pear.

We were not exactly thrown into the lap of luxury. There were no paved roads and no farm-to-market road systems. In wet weather, it was sometimes impossible to navigate the two or three clay hills that were between us and the town, five miles to the east.

We moved into a fairly large house, a homestead with an ample kitchen, a separate dining room, and a living room, which my parents converted into their bedroom and where my mother did her sewing. The house had no bathroom, but we enclosed a part of the porch and put in a bathtub, an optimistic step, considering that we did not yet have running water or electricity. We used kerosene lamps and Coleman lanterns for all of the light we needed inside the house and barn. We would not get electricity until 1940, eight years after we moved in.

In our earliest days at the ranch, we were rounding up cattle through the thick mesquite brush. One of my uncles, Harold Tobias, who was a Pennsylvania Dutchman married to my mother's sister, came over to help. We had herded most of them into the pen when out of the brush appeared one cow followed by Uncle Harold and his horse, which had been ridden so hard in the heat he was foaming, wet with perspiration. We helped pen the cow, and Uncle Harold turned around and started off again. One of us asked what he was doing, and he said, "I'm going to get another one."

He thought you could bring in the cows one by one, and I assure you he would have needed an armada of horses because he had ridden that one completely down. So from time to time we did have some inexperienced help in working the cattle.

Dad had bought some stock from a man named McDaniel, a rancher who lived south of us. None of the cows had been dehorned, and they were wild and ornery. He was going to sell them at auction—none too soon as far as we were concerned. It had been a real battle to get them into the pen. We had to actually rope some and drag them out of the brush. That time all the horses were exhausted, and so were the Connally boys.

The hauler, a man named Barney McCloskey, had a bobtail truck that he used to haul cattle for everybody in that area to the stockyards in San Antonio. When he came to get ours, Dad told him, "You better put some ropes across the top of that truck. If you don't, these cattle are going to get out."

McCloskey said, "I've been hauling cattle for thirty years and I've never had one go out yet."

"You've never hauled any like these, either," my father warned him.

We ran the cattle up the chute and they didn't even stop. One of them got into the truck, and the next instant she jumped, her front feet landing on top of his cab. The cab of his truck had a partial canvas top, and her hooves sliced right through the canvas, smashed the center post of his steering wheel, honked the horn, and turned on his lights. She did a complete flip, landed on her back on the hood, caving it in, and hit the ground on all four feet in front of the truck. She was gone.

For an instant everyone stood frozen with awe. Then all hell broke loose and it was coming from us, such cursing and complaining, because we had to climb back on our horses and take out after her. This was one dusty chase. She got to the brush before we could head her off. She was smart enough to make it hard for us to rope her, sticking her head up tight against a mesquite tree trunk. We finally got her roped, and dragged her all the way back to the house. In the meantime, Dad had put some ropes across the top of Barney McCloskey's truck. I assure you, it was a great relief to see that load of cattle finally leave the ranch. I'd get a flashback to that incident when I saw TV spots for movies such as *My Heroes Have Always Been Cowboys*.

That year, 1933, I was a graduating senior at Floresville High School. I had developed an interest in debate, discovered I had some talent for it, and won a number of contests. But I lost one that left an impression on me, to the son of a district judge. There was a lesson in that about political favoritism—the school superintendent needed the good will of that judge—and about working your way to the other side of the tracks. The reaction in the auditorium was one of disbelief when the other boy's name was announced as the winner.

My fifth-grade teacher, a Mrs. Lucille Lang Duffner, encouraged me to take up what was then called "declamation." I won one competition after another with a reading of Joaquin Miller's, "The Defense of the Alamo," and Patrick Henry's speech before the Virginia Provincial Convention. My sister Carmen would help me rehearse and, to this day, she claims I made the rafters shake with the immortal lines "I know not what course others may take; but as for me, give me liberty, or give me death!" With every reading, I took those words more deeply to heart. In today's idiom I was a square; the times were made for squares.

It begs the obvious to note that we were living in an age of not only innocence but inconvenience. I am appalled at the amount of work my father and mother did. My dad continued to drive for Greyhound for several years after he sold out to them, as a way to augment his income from the ranch. We had no tractors. We had walking plows, and pulled all our equipment with horses or mules. We had a riding cultivator, a riding one-row planter, and a horse-drawn wagon. We actually took our corn into town and had it ground into meal to make cornbread. My mother normally cooked biscuits for breakfast, cornbread for lunch, and biscuits again for supper. Not until many years later did I ever see a loaf of white bread in that house.

We heated our bathwater in the tank of the wood-burning stove, and carried it by buckets into the tub. In 1940, all the children chipped in and we bought my mother her first electric stove. When I think back upon the sacrifices that she and my father made in order to try to educate us, I can't ever be grateful or thankful enough.

Despite the limits of his own education, my father was a man of ideals. He was eager to participate in local affairs, and in 1936 ran for county clerk on a reform ticket. An audit had revealed a shortage in county funds, and the reformers were running against "the courthouse crowd."

My sister Carmen and I went from door to door handing out my father's card and asking people for their votes. Carmen did the knocking and I did most of the talking.

Wilson County had its share of suspicious voting procedures. During absentee voting, the son of the candidate for sheriff and I were sent by our fathers to the courthouse to keep an eye on the ballot boxes. The deputies confronted us and ordered us to leave. I told them I couldn't. "My father told me to stay here," I said, "and I'm staying until he tells me to go. If you want me to leave, you'll have to carry me out."

The reform ticket won. My father was elected county clerk and served until 1942. By then the war was on, and apparently he alienated many of the voters who were of German ancestry. He had three sons in the service—I was in the Navy, Merrill in the Marines, and Wayne in the Air Force—and a son-in-law, Speedy Hicks, fighting with the Army in Italy. So he may have been quite outspoken to those with the slightest sympathies for Germany.

He was as proud and independent a man as I have ever known. Sadly, he would die of a heart attack in 1950 at the relatively young age of sixty-two. The war had taken a hard toll on him, I believe. Merrill had left home at seventeen and enlisted in the Marine Corps after a spat with Dad. Merrill refused his offer to drive to town to catch the bus to San Antonio. The next time they saw each other was after the war, when Merrill came home on a hospital ship, having been seriously wounded at Iwo Jima.

My father's race was my first experience in real campaigning, although by then I was in my junior year at Texas, up to my eyeballs in campus politics. Years later, after Harry Truman left the White House, he made a speech to a college audience and one of the students asked how one went about getting into politics. Truman snapped back: "You're already in it. You're here on someone else's money, aren't you?"

A VERY SPECIAL
CLASS

I was sixteen years old when I enrolled at the University of Texas, in the fall of 1933—in retrospect, far too young for college or for the ambitions I brought with me.

I had made up my mind that I wanted to be a trial lawyer, and from that time forward I told myself whatever else I did was temporary until I returned to the law. Some of my friends regarded this goal with skepticism, but it has been one of the frustrations of my life that politics kept interrupting what I thought would be my career. I never tried a single case.

Other than my sister Carmen, no immediate member of my family, on either side, had been to college much less become an attorney. But I think what attracted me was having attended a case tried by Wick Blanton, a lawyer famous in our part of the country. He had been a Baptist preacher, recited from the Bible with authority, and was involved in most of our area's major criminal cases.

Whenever he appeared, the courtroom would be packed with people who just wanted to hear the eloquent orations he delivered in defense of his clients. The drama of the scene, the power of his speeches inspired in me that early desire to become a criminal lawyer.

In September of 1933, my father drove me to Austin and let me out in front of the rooming house where William and Edward Johnson, my boyhood neighbors, were staying. Two other fellows from Floresville were boarding there, Ole Donaho and Bill Sheehy. In what qualifies as a paradox, the lady who took in roomers was a Mrs. Smith, whose son C. R. Smith had been promoted in 1933 to the presidency of American Airlines. He served as the chief executive officer of the airline until 1968, when Lyndon Johnson appointed him as his Secretary of Commerce.

C. R. Smith would become one of my closest friends. Two paintings that I treasure most were commissioned by him—one by Tom Lea, the other by Ogden Pleissner—and still hang today in the state Capitol in Austin. They were gifts to the governor's office during my terms.

So my first experience in Austin was as a lodger in a rooming house run by C. R. Smith's mother.

As I told my dad goodbye that day, he looked at me for a long moment and said: "Johnny, I can't tell you what to expect. I can't tell you what to do because I've never been here and I haven't been through it. But you do your best, and your mother and I will help you any way we can." I was one lonely kid as he drove away—lonely but excited.

They helped me when they shouldn't have, helped me more than they were able. I am partial to a quotation from Henry Ward Beecher: "There are only two lasting bequests we can give our children. One of these is roots . . . the other, wings." My parents had truly given me the former; now they were making the most difficult gift a mother or father can provide, the gift of wings.

As overpowering as it seemed to me when I first stepped on

the campus, the University of Texas I saw that September day bore little resemblance to the school it is today. The old main building, erected in the 1880s, was still standing. The university tower that would gain so much notoriety was not yet under construction.

For years it has been a campus tradition to turn on the tower's orange lights after a Texas football victory. But, of course, this dominating campus feature is better known as the site of the Texas sniper killings, when the deranged Charles Whitman, firing at will with a telescopic lens, randomly murdered thirteen innocent people, and wounded thirty-one. Such bizarre contrasts, I regret, have become an inevitable part of the state's image.

In 1933, the university was just turning the corner into a time of intellectual change, and challenges and controversy. The president was Harry Yandel Benedict. V. I. Moore was the dean of men, and his assistant dean was Arno Nowotny, who would be helpful to me then and a friend well after college.

I must admit there was probably never a greener, less sophisticated kid to land on the Texas campus than me. I went to my first orientation program at the Geology Auditorium without knowing a soul other than those in the rooming house. I had no experiences other than those of a country boy. I had never played tennis or golf or ridden a train. Few students ever got more out of the university than I did, but I didn't set any new standards for scholarship. My grades were nowhere near my potential—if only I had spent more time on my studies and less on outside activities. But who can say what turns out to be the most precious in life?

In those days, you only needed two years of pre-law and three years of law school to obtain an LL.B. (Bachelor of Laws) degree. A Bachelor of Arts–LL.B. combination required three years of each. I was not in a position to stay in school any longer than I absolutely had to, so I opted for the two-year course, meaning that I would be able to enter law school in 1935.

In two of my courses, the instructors were recent graduate

students. One, Benno Schmidt, would leave both law and academia and become the managing partner of Jock Whitney & Company in New York. His son Benno Schmidt, Jr., has now retired as the president of Yale University. The other was Covey T. Oliver, from Laredo, later a distinguished professor of law at the University of Pennsylvania.

My university days were a uniquely exciting time for me. I had turned sixteen in February unaware that the world would soon be rearranged forever, and that watershed changes were already taking place in America. What I did know was that a new intensity had come to the University of Texas, attracting fresh, bold minds to the faculty. The students were filled with a sense of their own destinies, of going beyond the lives their parents had known. They were bright, hungry, unwilling to fail. We were the generation between the Depression and the war. We wanted to do everything, be everywhere.

If that sounds too sweeping, too lofty, it is the way I remember it, as a turning point for the university, for the law school, for myself and my classmates. Politics was the air we breathed. It was an easy time to find a cause, to choose sides and go off in all directions. We were young lawyers-to-be, judges, congressmen, movers and shakers: Jake Pickle, Homer Thornberry, Henry Wade, Joe Kilgore, John Singleton, Perry Pickett, Mack DeGuerin, Bob Strauss, Gus Garcia, Tom Law, Spec Logan, Nelson Rodgers, Eugene Talbert, Murff Wilson, Jimmy Nesbitt, and many more.

In military lore, the class of 1915 became known as "the year the stars fell on West Point," because of the impressive number of generals that were produced, including Dwight Eisenhower and Omar Bradley. I guess you might say that 1937 and 1938 were the years the lawbooks fell on Texas.

We had a group of young men with similar backgrounds, basically from poor families all over Texas. Some of them lived in the little campus dormitories. We all leaped at as many jobs as we could juggle, trying to earn side money to help relieve the burden our parents were carrying. I stacked books in the state

Supreme Court library for seventeen cents an hour and received free room and board as the house manager for the law school fraternity. As chairman of the Student Union, I was paid thirty dollars a month. At one point, I was the campus rep for Beechnut chewing gum, modest pay but a coveted job because of the access to free samples.

We sat up until all hours of the night, talking, planning, dreaming, testing ourselves with what we thought passed for philosophy. We made many fortunes in those sessions, and made many conquests. We enjoyed more in our imaginations than we could ever experience in a lifetime of trying. Those were exhilarating days and nights and we took full advantage of them.

The conversations were mobile, moving from the dormitory, or the rooming house, to the Night Hawk coffee shop, breaking up around two or three o'clock in the morning. I didn't drink or smoke, which made me one of the more popular fellows in that circle. It was reassuring to know that someone would be sober enough to drive them home after a weekend binge.

Austin was less than a two-hour drive from Floresville, but to me it was the future. The university was where you made the kind of friendships that last not for a week but a lifetime. Here, hard work and enthusiasm could take you at least as far as money could.

That was a fine proposition because, for certain, I didn't have the money. I joined just about whatever I could find that didn't charge an entry fee. I joined the Wesley Players, the Methodist Church drama group, and the Curtain Club. I was given a part in *Green Grow the Lilacs*, the play that the musical *Oklahoma!* was based on.

My drama teachers said that I might have had a career as an actor. Of course, some of my political foes said so, too.

In the 1930s, under the direction of James H. Parke, the Curtain Club had no shortage of people headed for Broadway and Hollywood. The list included Eli Wallach, Zachary Scott; Brooks West, who married the actress Eve Brooks; Elaine Anderson, who became the wife of John Steinbeck; Allen Ludden, and Betty White, one of the stars of the series "Golden Girls."

For the first time in my life, I was exposed to personalities, to types of people who were different from anyone I had known growing up in a rural community. They were creative, artistic, volatile. They did not believe in ceilings.

The line between dramatics and politics, I found, was a thin one. I became president of the Wesley Players, the Curtain Club, and the Athenaeum Literary Society, a debating society whose support was essential to any "non-Greek" candidate for president of the Student Assembly.

My favorite year up to then was 1935. Through the Curtain Club, I met a co-ed named Idanell Brill, who had graduated from Austin High and entered Texas that fall. I worked backstage; she was an understudy in one of the plays. On the publicity committee was a future newscaster named Walter Cronkite.

Falling in love with Nellie was easy to do. It was necessary only to let my heart follow my eyes. She was elected a Bluebonnet Belle and one of the Ten Most Beautiful as a freshman. From the moment she appeared on campus, she was among the best liked, and the most genuine. More honors kept coming her way, and there was little doubt where our courtship, which lasted five years, was headed.

That same year, 1935, Lyndon Johnson was appointed by President Roosevelt to head the National Youth Administration. Johnson had been the secretary to Richard Kleberg, the congressman whose district included Floresville. Johnson had visited the town often, and my father knew him well. But it was Sam Fore, Jr., publisher of the local newspaper, who recommended me to Johnson as one who needed help to stay in school. My job of stacking and dusting books in the Supreme Court library was arranged through the NYA.

I became involved, and embroiled, in campus politics through William Johnson, who was a Young Democrat. I started going with him to the meetings, and part of my philosophy began to take shape. I instinctively sided with the more moderate-to-conservative group within the membership. The opposition among the Young Democrats on campus were names that would become quite prominent in Texas politics, among them Herman Wright and Otto Mullinax, who became labor lawyers, and Bob Eckhardt, later a Houston congressman, and Chris Dixie and Sam Barberia.

They were eloquent spokesmen for their causes, great debaters. Eckhardt was a man of diverse talent, a cartoonist and humorist, and at one time the editor of the campus yearbook, the *Texas Ranger*. These men became mainstays in the liberal wing of the Democratic Party in Texas. Our paths crossed many times in my political career. Although I had a respect, and still have, for them as individuals, our views were never very compatible. We invariably wound up on opposite sides of the fence.

Their mentor on campus was Robert Montgomery, a professor of economics and a man of remarkable intellect. Later, when I began practicing law, I represented Trans Texas Airways (later Continental) before the Civil Aeronautics Board, and Dr. Montgomery was hired to do the economics study for the applications that needed to be filed.

Finally, over dinner one night, I said to him, "Doctor, I have been mentally adding up the length of time that you have spent in your various endeavors and pursuits, and I've calculated that you're now three hundred and twenty-three years old."

He said, simply, "Four hundred and eighty-nine." It was difficult to get the better of Dr. Montgomery in any kind of discussion—personal, political, or philosophical. I never had a course under him at Texas, but came to have a great attachment to him after I graduated.

In 1937, the legal fraternity, Delta Theta Phi—referred to by its members as "Dollar Thirty Five"—rallied behind the candidacy of Jake Pickle for president of the Student Assembly. I was his campaign manager. We campaigned against the "fraternity clique," and Jake was elected in a runoff.

The next year we switched roles. It seemed unlikely that a

person from the same "non-Greek" organization could win two years in a row, but we had a network now and I was eager to run. We divided the campus into sections, like precincts, and we swamped the students with leaflets and position papers. The campus *Daily Texan* suggested that we had built a "machine," but we were still attacking the Old Guard.

Coming out in favor of clean cafeterias sounds like baby stuff, but I can assure you it was effective training. On the evening of the day I won my election, the results of the voting for the Sweetheart of the University were to be announced at a grand ball in the Gregory Gymnasium. The vote was closely guarded, but I received a call from Arno Nowotny telling me in confidence that Nellie had won. To say that I was a happy young man would be the understatement of the decade.

Campus politics was a reflection of the struggle within the state's social hierarchy. The friends who supported me would reappear in the campaigns of Lyndon Johnson, and later my own. And some of our opposition over the years would continue to show up on the other side.

It is not absolutely clear to me why the friendships that survived the ups and downs of my life were the ones I made in college. Perhaps this is true of most people. We shared the joyful moments and the sad, the victorious moments and the bitter.

I matured late physically and only weighed about 155 pounds while I was at Texas. I was too light for football and, at six feet two, an in-between height for basketball. But I did play for the Delta Theta Phi teams, mainly a bunch of renegades who competed in every sport in season, and did well at that level.

Golf intrigued me, and I finally took up the game, but never played enough to become skilled at it. I suspect my sports activities mirror my life in general. I never concentrated on any one thing long enough to become an expert at it, although I enjoy all sports, love to hunt and fish, trap- and skeet-shoot, play golf and tennis.

I have been both blessed and cursed with an insatiable

curiosity about many different subjects. There is no sport or recreation I don't enjoy, none that I wouldn't try. But I have never been in a position to devote the time necessary to become proficient at any one activity.

But far more than my inability to play a superior round of golf or set of tennis, I am frustrated by a sense that there was so much else to learn, so much I missed, in my college years. I wish in a way that I could do it all over again, and devote myself almost entirely to the acquisition of knowledge. Is that a curious desire, or do many of us wind up feeling we took the turns too fast, didn't slow down for some of the best parts of our education?

I wish I had taken courses in astronomy. There are other courses I would like to repeat—history, for one. I never took a course in architecture or physics or chemistry and I regret it, because the world we now live in depends so much upon engineering, upon mathematics and the sciences. I never took enough of those courses to give me the background I would like to have to better understand the rhythms of today's world.

My life is made up of many frustrations, and there is not much one can do, at this point, to repair them.

I wonder, for every person who wishes he or she had studied more, is there someone who wishes to have studied less? As president of the Student Assembly, in 1938, I joined the manager, Charles Zively, and Sally Lipscomb, the secretary of the student body, on a tour of other colleges. We spent two weeks driving, and visiting the Universities of Nebraska, Wisconsin, Minnesota, Oklahoma, and Iowa.

A call from the Dean's office was waiting for me when I returned, and I was about to get a rude reminder of the number of classes I had missed. The Dean told me I had an unacceptable number of absences, and I would be dropped from two of my law school courses. This meant I could not graduate on schedule, and, instead of getting my degree in 1939, I had to make up the classes in summer school two years later.

This was a wound to my ego, but all it really meant was that my diploma would read "1941," even though I had passed the bar exams in 1938.

I was in the unfortunate class that for the first time had to take the bar exams. Prior to 1938, if a student graduated from the school of law at Baylor, SMU, or Texas, he or she was automatically admitted to the state bar. Beginning in '38, we all had to take the exams.

If you have ever seen those Japanese science-fiction movies, where the populace is scrambling in every direction awaiting the arrival of Godzilla, you get a sense of what that time was like for me and my classmates.

The seniors all signed up to take the exams in the fall, and it was, in short, a grueling experience. We were confronted with tests on courses that we hadn't even taken. We got all the canned briefs and notes we could get our hands on, but the inventory was thin. One woman we knew had been tutoring students who had not attended law school but had trained with private law firms and hoped to qualify to practice by passing the bar exam. We acquired all of her notes and studied those, as well as our own textbooks and the cases we had been quizzed on in class.

The exams lasted two and a half hours each, per course. We took four exams a day for four days, sixteen in sixteen different courses. I can say with no fear of contradiction that by the end of the last exam on the fourth day, few of us knew what we were writing or what we were reading or arguing. We were at the point of being just desperate to get it behind us.

Gratefully, I passed the exam on my first try and actually was licensed to practice law in December of 1938. In what I considered a poetic touch, the Texas bar notified me in 1988 that, having been a practitioner for fifty years, I was now exempt from paying any dues.

In my senior year, there were ten thousand students on the campus, and I honestly think I could have called at least half of them by their first, last, or both names. What came together was a network of friends who would be critical to my election as governor of Texas in 1962. There was no design to it, no clever motive. Who plans twenty-four years ahead?

Clearly, those were among the best and most productive times of my life. I was fortunate to be part of an unusually talented and aggressive group of people, most of whom would have exceptional careers.

Jake Pickle is to this day a United States congressman from the 10th Texas District.

Henry Wade became a legend as the district attorney in Dallas, the prosecutor in the Jack Ruby case, the Wade of Roe versus Wade (although he did not personally argue the landmark abortion rights case).

John Singleton, in Houston, and Perry Pickett, in Midland, retired after esteemed service as federal and state judges.

Warren (Speck) Logan, Scott Daly, Sherman Birdwell, Nelson Rodgers, Jimmy Nesbitt, and Mack DeGuerin all enjoyed long and successful law careers across the state. DeGuerin's sons, Mike and Dick, are today widely sought as defense attorneys.

Joe Kilgore represented the lower Rio Grande Valley in Congress for two terms after the war, retired, and was succeeded by Lloyd Bentsen.

Robert Strauss became the chairman of the Democratic National Committee, and a political analyst whose advice was sought by Presidents of both parties.

This is by no means a complete list of my contemporaries who made their mark in the legal and political system. Others, who were visible figures in Delta Theta Phi, left the practice of law to make it big in business. Norvell and Jim Jackson got rich with a family seafood company. No one was surprised by this, even though our nickname for Norvell, a tough, husky guy, was "Ironhead."

Perhaps the point should be made here that Delta Theta Phi was not a fraternity in the social sense. We didn't do the frathouse scene, and in theory, at least, were bonded by academic goals, not parties. But everywhere one looked on the Texas campus, one found the boundless potential of hungry minds. I had moved at one point to a rooming house on Nueces Street, run by a lady named Mrs. Rush. Her son Eugene, who had freckles and red hair, became my new roommate. He was a few years my senior, a Phi Beta Kappa, bright, witty, and obsessed with a love of poetry. He insisted that I sit for hours listening to him read and recite poetry.

After a while it was catching. I loved the works of Byron, Keats, Shelley, Lord Tennyson, and Kipling, and memorized a good many. My favorites included verses in Kipling's poems, as well as Tennyson's *Locksley Hall*, and *In Memoriam*. The sonnets of Byron became a part of my education.

From my first day, I knew I was ill-grounded to compete with students two or three years older, many from private academies, who had a broader, more fundamental schooling than mine. So this was a case of my benefiting from having been exposed to an older student who had diverse interests.

Nearly all of my friends at the university were short of funds, and we spent a disproportionate amount of time devising creative ways to save a buck. None of us had cars, so maybe once a month we pooled our money and hired one for a Saturday night from a fellow who had opened a rental office on Red River Street.

An occasional salesman would befriend us on the theory that as law students we had prospects of future employment. The most persistent of these was a fellow named Bob Dalton, who represented the Hamilton Tailors, out of Ohio. Bob was quite a salesman. He would pounce on us and sell us slacks, and sometimes an entire suit, that we couldn't afford. He knew the condition we were in, knew we couldn't pay for them. When the suit or pants or sports coat came in, we would go to great lengths to hide from him; it was like a cartoon. He was having a hard time making a living, and when we told him we were broke, he would say, "Well, just give me a down payment and a couple of dollars when you can, and I'll carry you."

Those of us who owed him money would pass the word

that he was around, and we kidded about dodging the "Dalton Gang." But I felt sorry for Bob. The knees in some of those slacks would be worn out long before the bill would be marked paid in full.

I was widening my horizons, but all the offices I held were of no value to me in class. In truth, they may have hurt. Ira Polk Hildebrand was the Dean of the law school when I enrolled and, unluckily for me, taught the course in contract law. This was his favorite subject, and a first-year course one had to take. He used to ride me unmercifully, as well as Jimmie Brinkley, with whom I would frequently sit in the back of the classroom. Brinkley was president of the Student Assembly in 1936, the year before Jake Pickle, and was elected as an independent with the help of our crowd.

To a large extent, we took over campus politics for four years running, and Dean Hildebrand would use this to get my attention in class: "Oh, Mr. Connally, you might as well go back up on the hill," the hill being the Arts and Sciences Building, or any place other than the law school. "You'll never make a lawyer. You and Brinkley are just going to be little ole campus politicians who stick together like germs."

I thought I was a pretty fair student in contracts, but my grades didn't reflect it under Dean Hildebrand. His son Hildy and I became good friends. I understood why the Dean gave me fits. He was a jealous custodian of the law school, and he did not see in me the seriousness he demanded. I did care, and wanted to prove myself to him, but there were indeed distractions.

Or maybe he just had my number.

Back then, local elections were held in the summer, with the runoffs generally in August. So I was able to campaign for my father in the county clerk's race in 1936, and a year later I was reunited with my benefactor from the NYA, Lyndon Johnson.

In 1937, Congressman James P. Buchanan, who had represented the 10th Texas District for twenty-four years, dropped dead of a heart attack at seventy, and Johnson ran in a special election to fill that seat. I helped out by licking the stamps, folding and mailing letters, tacking up posters—all the things a young gofer is expected to do. My impression of that campaign was exactly the same as that of every campaign I later engaged in: it was frenetic. I was drawn to the noise and the urgency.

Johnson had been encouraged to run, at twenty-nine, by a wise and visionary man named Alvin Wirtz, a retired state senator who was then practicing law with a Judge Powell in Austin. Wirtz had been impressed by Johnson during his work on behalf of the Colorado River Project.

The Colorado River was subject to terrifying floods, with devastating effects on Austin and other cities downstream. Wirtz had pushed the idea of damming up the Colorado, and Johnson was there to carry it forward. He had left Washington in 1935 to direct the Texas office of the National Youth Administration, and in that job met and worked with many of the leading citizens across the state. Wirtz liked what he saw: a rising star, intelligent, dynamic, tireless.

I am unsure how those born in the age of laser technology can relate to what Johnson accomplished back in times that now seem almost primitive. I don't know how I can reconcile the contemporary image of him with the Lyndon Johnson who wanted to bring the twentieth century to a land that barely knew it existed.

As virtually his first footstep in government, Johnson had adopted the goal of damming the Colorado River, of building a simple, rural electric line to the farmers who lived in his own native Hill Country. I wonder, can this be interesting to a generation that grew up with images of men walking on the moon? I don't know. I only know it was important then, and historic now.

No one thought then in global terms. You thought of whatever was just over the county line. Johnson thought in terms of flood control, irrigation, cheap power, of conserving land and putting in new grasses that would hold the soil and prevent excessive wash-off. He knew that electricity could do all this, but the power companies fought him at every turn. He didn't know, as a young congressman, that he would need their permission. He soon learned that he would. In desperation, he went to see Roosevelt. The President had put out the word to his people. Work with that young congressman from Texas, Lyndon Johnson—he's a comer.

He was in those years, the mid- and late-'30s, far more liberal than he voted. But he recognized that to be an effective politician you have to survive. "There is nothing in the world more useless," he said, "than a dead liberal." As the representative from the 10th Texas District, he was a true New Dealer. He wanted water, dams, all the rural electrification he could get. He fought for the farmers.

His objective was a relatively simple one: to float a loan for a project that would be known as the Pedernales Electric Cooperative. He never forgot that meeting with FDR, who would usually allocate fifteen minutes to any loyal Democrat with a problem. He listened patiently for the first few minutes, then asked him, out of the blue, "Did you ever see a Russian woman naked?"

Johnson said no, he hadn't, but then he had never been to Russia. Roosevelt told him of the impression Harry Hopkins, one of his closest advisers, had brought back from the Soviet Union. Hopkins had told him that Russian women had physiques dramatically different from American women because they were so accustomed to heavy work, which, as a consequence, had an effect on their muscles. FDR was fascinated by this information. Johnson was nonplussed.

"Before I knew it," he would say, "my fifteen minutes was gone, and old Pa Watson [another FDR aide] was tugging at the end of my coattails, and I found myself in the west lobby without ever having made my proposition. So I had to go back and make that damned appointment all over again. I went over and consulted with Ben Cohen, Tommy Corcoran, Jim Rowe, Harold Ickes, and all the various close friends of Roosevelt."

I was in awe of these men. They WERE the New Deal; they were the government.

Corcoran told Johnson: "Roosevelt likes pictures, the bigger the better. That's where you made your mistake. You should have gotten a picture of some dam, and pictures of your transmission lines and of the big cities, Houston and Dallas and San Antonio. That would have caught his attention."

Johnson obtained photographs of the Buchanan Dam, and of the electric lines that led into Austin and on to Houston and Dallas. He ordered a print three feet high, and then went to see Roosevelt again. He pulled out his picture map and showed the President the transmission lines, and the charts of power consumption, and even a picture of the shacks of the tenant farmers who lived directly below the lines but had no power.

"Here," he said, "we have the largest multiple arch dam just built, and here is that big transmission line just wheeling with power. But it's all going to the big-city big shots, the light-and-power companies, and the poor people living in the shadow of the line can't get any."

With that, Roosevelt called John Carmody, the head of the REA (Rural Electrification Administration), who had earlier virtually thrown Johnson out of his office. His position was that the population density did not meet the standards. There were only one and a half customers per mile.

And Roosevelt said: "John, I know you've got to have guidelines and rules and I don't want to upset them, but you just go along with me—just go ahead and approve this loan and charge it to my account. I'll gamble on those people—I've been down in that country. They'll catch up to that density problem because they breed pretty fast."

The loan was made, and in a way that happened once, and can't happen again, there was light. In those days, in most of rural America all anyone expected or wanted from electricity was a droplight in the middle of the house. No one dreamed then about air-conditioning and feed mills, machines that milked and washed, radios or television, and so many other things.

So in Wilson County and across South Texas the voters liked FDR and they liked Lyndon Johnson, who won easily over a field of seven opponents.

I was uncertain what I would do when I finished school, but in 1938, while I was president of the student body, I gained my first experience in statewide politics.

Ernest O. Thompson, who was then the chairman of the Railroad Commission of Texas and a former mayor of Amarillo, was running for governor. He had been the youngest colonel in the American Expeditionary Force in Europe in World War I. Redheaded, feisty, a bright and aggressive man, he had assembled a team of heavyweights to back his campaign. J. R. Parten, of Houston, was a successful, independent oilman, tall and suave. J. S. Abercrombie, also of Houston, founded the Cameron Iron Works. Myron Blalock, from Marshall, Texas, was the latest in a line of distinguished lawyers, and had been chairman of the state Democratic Party. I worked with an Austin attorney named Claude Wild, helping to organize first-time voters, who, like myself, had just turned twenty-one.

These men were masters at the political art, which included a certain skill at fund-raising. All of them would play a role in my own campaigns, twenty or more years in the future. Major Parten was active and alert until his death at ninety-two, in 1992. I called him Major, his rank in the first war, all my life. In 1989, he was named a distinguished alumnus of the University of Texas, an honor long overdue.

I spent a great deal of time with Claude Wild, and occasionally had an opportunity to accompany him to Suites 1602 and 1604 at the Stephen F. Austin Hotel. There Mr. Abercrombie, Major Parten, Myron Blalock, and Grover Hill mapped their campaign strategy and analyzed the candidates. It was obviously an exciting time for me to see how the maneuvers unfolded. I saw four masters at work. Abercrombie, who had built a machine shop into one of the largest companies in the world, was in a class of his own as a fund-raiser.

Nearly everyone expected Colonel Thompson to win his race over a tough field whose least regarded entry was W. Lee O'Daniel, a hillbilly singer known as "Pappy." O'Daniel had no experience in politics and not much in the way of formal schooling. What he did have was a name and a voice. A Fort Worth native, he had been on the radio for years with his band, the Light Crust Doughboys, on the air every day at high noon, sponsored by Light Crust flour. His catch phrase, known to people all over the state, was "Pass the biscuits, Pappy."

I later heard, and believe it to be true, that O'Daniel had been persuaded to run by Jack Burris, the owner of Burris Mills, and Clint Murchison, the conservative oilman whose son, many years later, would own the Dallas Cowboys.

Pappy campaigned from the back of a flatbed truck, with his band providing the music and Pappy the words, always an attack on those "nasty old politicians" he intended to run out of Austin. We paid no attention to him at all until I went to Waco for a big rally he had planned in the spring, and got the shock of my life. He had drawn a crowd of 25,000, and they were passing around miniature flour barrels. People were pitching in half-dollars, ones, and fives—whatever they could afford. He had brought rural America, or at least rural Texas, to its feet. W. Lee O'Daniel swept the field in the primary, without a runoff, to become governor of Texas.

It was not the first or the last time that the voters of the state would rally behind the least sophisticated candidate.

In 1939, Johnson needed a replacement for his first assistant. I learned that he had begun a background check on me from an older friend, Eddie Joseph, the owner of a men's shop on Guadalupe Street. I patronized his store on those rare occasions when I had the money to buy anything. One day, during my senior year, he asked me what job I had applied for with the federal government.

Startled, I said I hadn't applied for anything, anywhere, and why did he ask?

"You must have," he said. "Congressman Johnson called and asked me for a reference on you. I figured he was trying to help you land a job."

I shrugged. "Nope. I've not applied for any federal job at all and don't expect that I will."

I was puzzled by what the call meant, but my plans were still uncertain. I had worked on two statewide campaigns in 1938. Colonel Thompson had lost his race for governor, but I had worked in the runoff for Gerald Mann, who was the state's new attorney general. Mann had been a football hero at Southern Methodist University with the colorful nickname of "the little red arrow," a reference to his skill as a player. The phrase applied to his character as well. I thought I might enjoy working in the office of the attorney general.

Not long after my chat with Eddie Joseph, I received a call from Lyndon Johnson, and then a visit from one of his staff, Jesse Kellam, who would eventually run LBJ's radio station in Austin. Kellam, I learned, had recommended that the congressman not hire me, on unusual grounds. "He's too able," he said. "You won't be able to keep him."

That was probably all Johnson had to hear. He flew down himself to see me, and offered the job. I agreed to go to work for him after I completed my studies in the summer of 1939. Jobs were not that plentiful for young lawyers.

I was to be his congressional secretary, the same position he had held under Richard Kleberg. I arrived in Washington during what came to be known as "the neutrality session" of Congress. President Roosevelt had called it for the purpose of arming the Merchant Marine, and to provide armament and ships to our allies. He foresaw, as many did, that the United States would become more and more involved in the widening conflict in Europe. Those were electric times, heightened by the endless speculation over the American role.

On the first day of September, 1939, the telephone in

Roosevelt's bedroom in the White House rang at 2:50 A.M. Ambassador Bill Bullitt was calling from Paris to tell Mr. Roosevelt that World War II had just begun. Adolf Hitler's bombers were dropping death all over Poland. Now, in Washington, speculation centered on one echoing question. How long could America stay out of it?

FDR went on radio to tell the world: "This nation will remain a neutral nation, but I cannot ask that every American remain neutral in thought as well. Even a neutral has a right to take account of the facts. Even a neutral cannot be asked to close his mind or his conscience."

Although it was not clear to me then, my life changed on that day. The thoughts I had entertained about practicing law in Texas were put on hold. I entered into a whole new era that was exciting, informing, and disturbing. I stayed in the basement of the Dodge Hotel, by the Union Station, up until then known as a residential hotel for mostly elderly widows. They rented rooms on the two lower floors to young gentlemen who were not quite broke. Our floor became a gathering point for the Texans then flocking to Washington, such as Henry Wade, Jim Langdon, and others who arrived to take government jobs in the waning prewar months.

I lived at the Dodge for the six weeks that Congress was in special session. The work went on as usual in the office of the congressman from the 10th Texas District. Johnson was nearly unbearable as a boss. Those who stayed did so because he was hardest on himself, totally consumed by and committed to politics. We worked ten- and twelve-hour days, took constituents on tours of the Capitol, with maybe a side trip to Mount Vernon. If anything was undone at the end of the day, we stayed at our desks to return calls and process the mail to and from the various agencies and departments.

The congressman insisted that every letter that came into the office be answered that same day. The people back home were a little dazed by the service they were getting. A man in Bastrop wrote about a claim he had filed with the Veterans

Administration five years earlier. The man told a reporter that he had an immediate reply telling him that Congressman Johnson had received his letter and was at work on the problem. The next day he had another letter, saying he was still working on it and hoped to have results quickly. On the third day, he heard again: the case was looking good. The fourth letter was from the VA, saying his claim had been accepted.

We were getting bags of mail in 1939 about pensions for veterans of World War I, and about patronage jobs, and from worried farmers. Johnson drilled it into us that we were always to take the position of the constituent, never the government. We worked hard at establishing relationships at all the agencies with clerks or people down in the ranks who could get us the information we needed.

There were lessons Johnson passed on that he had learned as an intern with Dick Kleberg. When Senator Tom Connally (no relation) arranged a federal project for Texas, he would have apoplexy if the news appeared in print before he could announce it. On occasion, the release quoted "Lyndon B. Johnson, secretary to Congressman Kleberg."

One day, the senator stormed into the office and demanded an explanation of why the stories were reaching Kleberg's district "before my message gets out." Curious himself, Kleberg turned to his aide and said, "Now, Lyndon, tell us how that happens." Johnson said, "When I came to Washington, the first people I got well acquainted with were the Western Union boys."

We were hearing from people desperate for jobs, and we badgered the departments all day long. We fought with them, trying to get everything we possibly could. Today the rules have changed, and I suppose you might get in trouble for calling an agency on behalf of a constituent. Back then, we thought that was our job. Those were the days before Civil Service, when the agencies and departments were filled with patronage appointees who were willing to help find answers, not throw up roadblocks.

After six o'clock, when the office closed, we started answering the mail. Some of the secretaries had been working at it during the day, but I frequently stayed until nine—some nights as late as midnight, actually typing up to fifty letters on an old upright Underwood typewriter.

By and large, the staff was exceptional. At the core were Walter Jenkins, Dorothy Jackson (soon to marry a Harvard lawyer named Philip Nichols), and Herbert Henderson, an absolute whiz as a typist and a competent speech-writer, with one weakness. He would disappear for a week at a time on an occasional bender, and then the whole staff turned out to hunt for him.

In time, Mary Rather joined the office, and others passed through: Jake Pickle, who came to Washington as a policeman; a Beaumont lawyer named O. J. Webber, who was raised in Stockdale, Texas; and John Singleton, the future federal judge in Houston, and a lifelong friend from my college days.

I see them now—at the end of the decade and in the early 1940s—as members of a golden age of national politics. The times were tough and uncertain and romantic. Young people were particularly attracted to the idea of government service. I was the first of my contemporaries to join Johnson's staff, and I began getting calls from classmates. Thinking people could see the coming of the war. They wanted to join the Air Force or the Marines or the FBI—even the Internal Revenue Service.

MOST OF THE WAY
WITH LBJ

He was a man of contradictions: generous and selfish; compassionate and cruel; thoughtful and neglectful; charming and crude. He was Lyndon Baines Johnson and, like a fine actor who seems to grow larger the moment the spotlight locates him, he could be whatever he wanted to be.

Few men or women knew him better, longer, than I did, or argued with him so loudly, so often. I was, at twenty-two, his congressional secretary—in turn, his protégé, his campaign manager in five races, his friend and adviser.

If one were asked to construct a stereotypical Texan, I suppose you would wind up with someone close to Lyndon Johnson. Early in his career, he was labeled a Texas wheeler-dealer. If that means knowing where the levers are, how to use them, how to get things done, I suppose he was. I have been called one myself, a time or two.

He came to high office under the most traumatic conditions

of any President since another man named Johnson—Andrew—succeeded the murdered Abraham Lincoln. Lyndon Johnson began his Presidency with a whirlwind of major legislative achievement. But he ended it by announcing he would not run for a second full term, in hopes of healing the nation's wounds and reuniting those who had become so polarized over a war he did not start or want, a war he could not shed.

Vietnam was his curse. We knew it then and more so today. It kept the country from knowing Lyndon Johnson, from accepting and recognizing his other works, his efforts to improve the quality of life for all.

Few Presidents more fully reflected the promise and risk of that office. He was a unique man, but the richness of his character was too often obscured by the bitterness of a war that came to dominate our lives. His manner and language were colorful, his sense of humor earthy. He should have been a popular and admired President, but he was turned upon by the young, scalded by the press, and abandoned by his party.

No one ever said he was easy to describe. His critics were never quite sure if he was a liberal, a conservative, or an opportunist. He came of age as a Franklin Roosevelt New Dealer. He sought power and found it. He relished exercising it. Many have said that if the parliamentary system had existed here, he would have been a gigantic figure as a prime minister, perhaps one of a century, a man to stand with Pitt and Disraeli and Churchill.

One man who felt that way had supported him for President in 1960 and opposed him in 1968. Eugene McCarthy once said that LBJ would have been a great prime minister, but there is no one to tell a President when he is wrong. Except, of course, the people.

In my lifetime, no one helped me more than Lyndon Johnson, no one to whom Nellie and I owed a larger debt for many of the good things that happened to us. Yet in time, I did not hesitate to tell him when I thought he was wrong. (Nor did he to me.) I believe I can write about him, his times, his impact on the rest of us, objectively. I would not lie for him in the heat of a political campaign, and I won't now.

Like so many who felt they had earned his closeness, I have wrestled with the jigsaw puzzle of his life, and felt frustrated by the attempts of others to reveal what they herald as the "truth" of Lyndon Johnson. He was surely not the Satanic figure some have painted. They missed the fun that people around him often shared. They missed the very genuine beliefs that motivated him. They missed the best part of him.

Not that any of us can capture it all. He alienated conservatives by passing massive social programs. The liberals rejected him because they thought his reasons were not their reasons. You study the many different pictures of Lyndon Johnson. You try to put them together. It is like trying to lift an untiled bay of hay. No handles. It comes apart in your hands.

He was, by most standards, qualified as few others were to ascend to the Presidency. He had moved up the ladder—congressman, senator, majority leader. Yet there was this paradox: for all of his ego and self-confidence, he felt a sense of inadequacy. He was a man who hungered for everyone's affection. One of his weaknesses, in my view, was this desire to be loved by everyone. To this end, he too often courted his enemies and abused his friends. He thought he could convert every foe into an adherent. He was unwilling to believe that there were people who just didn't like him, and never would, and that he was better off if they did not.

He was a man who was accused of wanting to rewrite his past, yet never felt secure about the forces that shaped him: his birthplace, his schooling, his odd brand of graces and manners. He never really decided how, or if, he could use them.

Born in the Texas Hill Country, a graduate of Southwest Texas State, a small teachers' college in San Marcos, he bore the unmistakable stamp of a leader. Bill Deason, who had run his campaign for president of the student body, was one of his early political aides and later served in the Navy with him.

They were among the leaders of a new campus fraternity called the White Stars, organized to compete with a fraternity dominated by the school's football players called the Black Stars. The names had no racial meanings, it ought to be noted. Along with every other school in the state, Southwest Texas was segregated.

The White Stars soon outhustled the jocks for most of the campus concessions, including the candy machine in the cafeteria. Many years later, a reporter asked Johnson if it was true that the White Stars swept aside their competition. He laughed. "I don't know," he said, "but I'm sure we took everything we could."

Oddly—to me, at least—this episode has been cited as an example of Johnson's ruthlessness in bloom. It was what it appeared to be. Kid stuff. Jesse Kellam, a football hero and one of the leaders of the Black Stars, a year ahead of Lyndon's class, became one of his closest aides.

In the spring of 1990, in Austin, I moderated a symposium on the life and political times of LBJ. Bill Deason was there, in his eighties and going strong. Johnson's nickname in school, he said, was "Bull," although not for the reason you might expect. "He was always bulling his way across campus," Deason explained. "The phrase that described him best was 'a young man in a hurry.' He had two jobs, working in the president's office and sweeping out the education building. He was a young man in a hurry, and later he was a middle-aged man in a hurry. All of his life he was in a hurry. He could see around a corner. He knew, by God, what was going to happen long before it happened."

Even then, what set Lyndon Johnson apart from most people was the way he poured himself, every ounce of energy, into whatever he was doing, right or wrong. He held nothing back. He pounded and pounded. Then, of course, he cultivated everybody who could be of help to him.

Making electric power available to the common man remained one of the passions of Johnson's career. Long after the problem had been solved in Texas, the importance of it stuck in his mind. It provided a common ground for his later discussions, as Vice President, with the heads of underdeveloped countries. In a sad and curious way, the connection was there in his judgments on Vietnam when, as President, he talked of "rural pacification" in the Mekong Delta.

To describe now what his hopes were for that besieged land will sound unaware and naïve. But the experts at the Rand Corporation and other think tanks agreed with him. To encourage a truce, he offered Ho Chi Minh $100 million with which to build his (LBJ's) idea of a bountiful Mekong Valley. He could not understand how the North Vietnamese dictator could refuse. "George Meany would have snapped at it," he complained. He saw the Vietnamese farmer in terms not unlike the Texas farmer or the Oklahoma farmer. We, the United States, would provide them with roads and water and improve the rice crops.

Again his instincts clashed. His idealism was frustrated by his inability to make a deal. Yet his motives were genuine, and they could be traced to his first job out of college, as a teacher in a small Mexican-American school in Cotulla.

He was not born into poverty, but it was around him. In many ways the urban poor led a meaner life; there was no harvesttime on the streets. In the city, if you had a home and food and clothes, you were middle class. Cotulla was a border town and few of his pupils could speak English. Neither could the janitor, an old man, but Johnson taught him to read and write, meeting with him in the early mornings for nearly a year.

His own Spanish was poor, but he taught three grades, math and history, and he gave his pupils songs to sing. Most of them came to class hungry; they dug through garbage for orange peels. During recess, the other teachers retreated to the rest room and smoked, while the students went outside and fought. Johnson organized them into softball teams. "They knew even in their youth the pain of prejudice," he would recall. "They never seemed to know why people disliked them, but they knew it was so, because I saw it in their eyes.

"I often walked home late in the afternoon, after the classes were finished, wishing there was more that I could do. Somehow you never forget what poverty and hatred can do when you see its scars on the hopeful face of a young child."

He meant it, and the memory shaped him. This was poverty of a different sort and it shocked him. He didn't discover poverty, but he sometimes sounded as if he did. His critics didn't hear the pain; they only heard the twang.

In December of 1937, he went through the black slums of Austin for the first time, and the effect was much the same as in Cotulla. In a radio broadcast in Austin, he advocated slum clearance and public housing. He called the speech, "Tarnish on the Violet Crown." The writer William Sydney Porter, better known as O. Henry, lived in Austin and had once referred to it as "the city of the Violet Crown."

Later, one of his supporters challenged Johnson's stand. He was upset because he had heard that such programs would bring the government into competition with private business. He demanded to know if this was true.

Johnson said it was. "The government is competing with shacks and hovels and hog sties," he said, "and all the other holes in which the underprivileged have to live. The government is attempting to wipe out those wretched excuses for American homes. If you object to that kind of government, then I'm disappointed in you."

These feelings were always in him, and yet he picked his times and his places to voice them. There were those who wanted nobility, and settled for action, but for too long they remembered only Johnson's silences. What was necessary politically exposed him to charges of being cynical.

He believed in voting rights, fair housing, equal education. Yet in twelve years in the House, he never made a speech during any civil rights discussion. The advocates reproached him bitterly. "You're dead right," he agreed, "and I'm all for you. But we ain't got the votes. Let's wait until we got the votes."

Intuitively, he knew how to build a base. He quickly became friends with other young Southern New Dealers, such as John Sparkman, of Alabama, and Albert Gore, of Tennessee. They were not liberals about civil rights, but then there were no civil rights.

He was a particular favorite of Tommy Corcoran: "He always knew what he wanted and who could get it for him. And he got more for his district than anybody else."

In 1938, when the U. S. Housing Authority awarded the first three grants to cities for low-rent housing, the projects went to New York, where the need was the most urgent; to New Orleans, where Roosevelt had to counter the threat of Huey Long; and to Austin. No one understood how Austin had qualified. Johnson did it by walking the corridors, wearing them down. And the political gain was nearly zero. Few urban blacks and Mexicans ever registered to vote. Many could not pay the poll tax. And Johnson had voted against legislation to end state poll taxes. It must have made sense to him; he was the one with the plan.

His father, Sam Ealy Johnson, Jr., had won a seat in the state legislature at twenty-seven. Soon after his election, Sam was interviewed by a young woman who worked for the Blanco County *Gazette*. In time, he married the reporter, Rebekah Baines, the daughter of the man who had previously occupied the office. She had just graduated from Baylor College, where her grandfather, George Washington Baines, a renowned Baptist minister, was the president.

Teaching was what Lyndon Johnson thought he was ordained to do. Every politician, I think, starts out as something else. His mother convinced him to enroll in Southwest Texas State Teachers College, at San Marcos, thirty miles from Austin.

But, in 1931, Richard Kleberg, newly elected to Congress and acting on the recommendation of a friend, offered to take him to Washington as his secretary. Johnson jumped at the chance. He was soon doing not only his job but the congressman's.

Kleberg was the son of one of the owners of the fabled King Ranch, the largest in the world, a million acres or more—larger, as Johnson was fond of saying, than the state of Connecticut. Dick Kleberg enjoyed winning the election, but didn't care much for what Lyndon kept referring to as his "obligations." As a boy, he traveled in a private railroad car. He was a good man, of limited imagination, who was mainly interested in fast horses, bird dogs, and golf.

Typically, Johnson's workday started at 7 or 7:30 A.M. and often lasted until midnight. He not only took care of any matters related to the constituents, he even dictated personal letters to Dick Kleberg's mother—for Kleberg to sign.

It was only a matter of time before Johnson ran for Congress, and was elected, on his own. When he won the seat left vacant by the death of Buchanan, in 1937, Lyndon was in a hospital on Election Day, recovering from an attack of appendicitis suffered two days earlier. The belief was widely held that Johnson won because of his unconditional support of Roosevelt, including the President's plan to "reorganize" the Supreme Court.

As luck would have it, three weeks later FDR began a ten-day fishing vacation on an island in the Gulf of Mexico, with the White House staff quartered in Galveston. Along with Governor Jimmie Allred, the congressman-elect arrived on the island on May 11, where he accepted congratulations on his victory and his loyalty to the President.

Had he followed the news accounts, FDR might have known that five of the ten candidates also ran as diehard New Dealers. But Roosevelt, like Lyndon, was not very interested in losers. Nor was Jimmie Allred, an extremely handsome man who had been elected governor in his early thirties. Johnson called on him early in the campaign, wearing a new, narrow, snap-brim Dick Tracy hat. The governor looked at him and said,

"You'll never win in Texas with that kind of hat. I'm going to give you one of mine." He gave him a cowboy hat, a white Stetson, and Lyndon wore it the rest of the race.

I learned one of my earliest, most vivid, and most lasting lessons in taking orders from Lyndon Johnson not long after I joined his staff. He was going away for the weekend, he said, and I could reach him in the event of an emergency at the St. Regis Hotel. Under no circumstances was anyone else to know of his whereabouts.

I followed his instructions to the letter, until a call came in from the one man I believed would qualify as an exception: Charles Marsh, the Austin publisher, who had supported his career financially as well as editorially. He said he *had* to talk to Lyndon "and no one could find him." Almost proudly, realizing his importance to the congressman, I shared with him my secret information.

"He isn't where he wants to be disturbed, Mr. Marsh," I said, "but I am sure this doesn't apply to you."

As I soon discovered, to my chagrin, it applied to Mr. Marsh above all others. Johnson was spending the weekend in New York with Alice Glass, who had been the publisher's mistress for five years and would become his wife.

Alice was tall, nearly six feet, red-haired, statuesque, beautiful by any man's standard. But I believe her particular appeal to him was the cultured and sophisticated aura in which she moved. She was a graceful hostess, extremely well read, intelligent, politically sensitive. She knew the rarest wines and the most obscure books and how to set the perfect table. He had never known anyone as cosmopolitan. Few politicians of that period did.

Later that day, I heard from Johnson, his voice like cold steel. "Do you have a brain in your head?" he asked tactfully. I said I thought I had. "Well," he continued, "the next time I tell you not to let anyone know where I am, I mean exactly that.

And the last person on earth I want to hear from is Charlie Marsh. Can you remember that?"

I did not repeat that mistake. Nor was it necessary for me to ask any questions. Johnson and Alice Glass had been lovers since the mid-1930s, and continued to be after he married Lady Bird Taylor in November of 1935. Without question, Alice was already involved with Marsh, who had introduced them.

Moral judgments are always risky. To speculate on what was inside another's heart is an indelicate business at best. But Lyndon Johnson's relationship with Alice Glass Marsh was unlike any other I am familiar with. He guarded the secrecy of that relationship. He never talked about her, never revealed his feelings—this alone set it apart. That she loved him seems clear from the testimony of her sister and her friends. He loved Lady Bird, but was enamored of Alice. I have no doubt that it was the most intense and longest-lasting of any affair he engaged in.

Contrary to the pictures sometimes drawn of him, Johnson was not indiscreet in his pursuit of women. Nor was he given to boastfulness about his conquests. Whether he ever considered marriage to Alice, I can't say. Those who knew her well, who saw them in the same room, believe it was what she wanted and, for a time, thought possible.

She was the hostess for Charles Marsh at his Virginia plantation, called "Longlea," eight hundred acres of lush and rolling hunt country. It was European in the quality of its art and furnishings and company. Johnson was a frequent visitor, Lady Bird less so.

Yet they kept the relationship very quiet, limited to an intimate circle that clearly did not include Charles Marsh or Lady Bird. It is my own conclusion that Alice believed that Lyndon would eventually leave political life, divorce Lady Bird, and marry her. Ultimately, she decided none of the above was ever going to happen, and she married Charles Marsh. In 1942, a few months after the war had started, and a year or so after her marriage, she ended the affair with Lyndon. I doubt that any more than half a dozen people knew the true depth of the relationship. It was certainly not a scandal. Alice never stopped supporting him politically.

I don't think Marsh ever had a clue about them. But the women who were part of the circle, who saw the way Lyndon looked at Alice when they were at Longlea, how he listened to her, are convinced that Lady Bird knew. If their readings are correct, one can only guess at the anguish of mind she endured.

She handled the affair, I suppose, as well as such things can be handled: by behaving as if there were nothing to handle. She had a wonderful capacity for accepting her husband just as he was, weaknesses and moral slips included.

Lady Bird was quoted once as saying of Lyndon's rumored eye for the ladies: "Lyndon was a people lover. It would be unnatural for him to withhold that love from half the people."

In the fall of 1942, I helped the Johnsons settle one common domestic issue. Lady Bird had come into a small inheritance, around $20,000, from an uncle in Alabama. She wanted to buy a house, a two-story brick colonial, at 4129 30th Place, in the northwest part of Washington.

We were discussing office matters at his apartment one afternoon when Lady Bird walked in after another session with the real-estate agent. She was afraid of losing the house, and she was desperate to have it. Every woman wants a home of her own, she said. She had been pregnant, miscarried, and wanted to start a family. She was sick of living out of a suitcase, she said.

When she finished, Johnson, without another word, turned toward me and continued our conversation. Lady Bird burst into tears and ran out of the apartment.

Johnson, with a truly puzzled look on his long face, finally said: "What do you think I should do?"

I said, "Buy the damned house. She deserves it." They did, for a price not much over $18,000.

Politics, not unlike boxing, has always attracted the next generation of those fighting their way up from neglect or prejudice.

The Irish were feeling their political muscle as the 1930s came to a close, and the Jews were not far behind.

Tommy Corcoran and Ben Cohen wrote much of the New Deal legislation. I was intrigued by Tommy the Cork; he had been the law clerk to Chief Justice Oliver Wendell Holmes, who said of him, "His is the brightest legal mind I have ever encountered."

Corcoran had been responsible for bringing in Felix Frankfurter, who was later appointed to the Supreme Court. Because of Frankfurter, a lot of the bright young Jewish minds were being attracted to Washington. And Corcoran himself told of a conversation he had one day with Frankfurter: "Felix, we're getting too many Jews down here. We're going to have to stop this influx and save the Jews from themselves." Whether he was serious or not, it didn't go over well with Frankfurter and started a rift between them.

Looking back, I try to relate to that young man from the dirt roads and mesquite-infested lands of Floresville, Texas, who had never ridden a train until he was grown. I recall what it was like living in Washington, a part of that thriving, turbulent period in the life of the nation.

Roosevelt had lost in his attempt to stack the Supreme Court. Now the sides were dividing over the issue of the third term—no President, including George Washington, had ever been elected for more than two.

It was going to be an especially interesting year for Texans. John Nance Garner, then seventy-one, had decided he wanted Roosevelt's job. Largely through the maneuverings of Sam Rayburn, who wanted to succeed Garner as speaker of the House, "Cactus Jack" had landed on the ticket as the nominee for Vice President in 1932, when FDR was elected for his first term.

The pairing was a miserable one. Garner, though known as an enemy of Herbert Hoover, was no friend of Franklin Roosevelt. He opposed everything the New Deal represented. He said so in private and he said so in public. What they said of each other was unprintable. In those far-off days before investigative reporting, such matters were not considered news.

Now, in 1939, Garner again looked to Rayburn for support and Rayburn looked to Lyndon Johnson. There was a myth that Texans, confronted by an outsider, come together like freight cars. The myth was about to be proved wrong.

In July, John L. Lewis, the head of the United Mine Workers and still a Roosevelt loyalist, called the Vice President "a labor-baiting, whiskey-drinking, poker-playing, evil old man...." Garner was upset, even though most of his friends and supporters told him that any denunciation by Lewis should be considered a compliment and would win him votes.

Nevertheless, Garner got in touch with "Mister Sam," then the majority leader of the House, and insisted that he call the Texas delegation to order—there were twenty-three members—and pass a resolution defending him. In short, the resolution would say that none of the things said by Lewis were true. Reluctantly, Rayburn said he would do his best.

Rayburn had no way of knowing that the youngest Texas congressman was being bombarded by calls from just about everyone on the President's staff. Roosevelt did not want any such resolution passed.

Corcoran called him. Harold Ickes, Harry Hopkins, William O. Douglas called him. In the movement of his career, Johnson owed much to Sam Rayburn, as I would owe much to both.

But when Rayburn raised the proposition, one voice spoke out against it. Lyndon Johnson, of Austin, said he could not support any such language and, in fact, the delegation would look foolish if the statement were issued because everyone knew that Garner was all those things, a heavy drinker and more.

The argument lasted two hours. Mister Sam asked the members to excuse them and he led his protégé into a private room. Everyone assumed that the older man was about to administer a verbal spanking. But, according to both, these were the words they exchanged.

Mister Sam said, "Lyndon, I'm looking you right in the eye."

And Johnson said, "And I'm looking you right back in the eye."

No resolution was drafted and the issue was allowed to die. When Garner formally announced his candidacy for President, Roosevelt made a sly reference to the episode: "I see the Vice President has thrown his bottle—I mean his hat—into the ring."

In the congressional elections of 1938 and 1940, Johnson ran unopposed, but in the fall of 1940, we—his staff—found ourselves immersed in the election battles of many of his fellow Democrats.

The trends seemed to favor the Republicans, and there was a widening fear among the Democrats that they would lose control of the House. Johnson was eager to get involved in the congressional races around the country, and he sought to take over the campaign committee of the House. But "Cap" Harding was there and he had been running the committee nearly forever. Cap wouldn't surrender his control, no matter how ineffective he was. So, after consulting Sam Rayburn, he just set out to form his own group, a kind of subcommittee.

The President threw up his hands. The idea of giving this responsibility to a congressman in his second term struck FDR as absurd. He asked Rayburn why he would recommend him. Mister Sam said, "Because he can do the job, and no one else wants it."

After a week of checking around, and finding no one available, the White House gave in—which is often the way things worked then, and still do. We found an office downtown, rented, furnished, and opened it in a few hours. Johnson had us call every Democratic candidate in the country and find out what he needed. In those days, people running for Congress never had enough money. Johnson did something about it. We raised money from our friends in Texas, and some in New York, and we financed a lot of desperate House fights. The word went around that we had raised a tremendous amount of cash, and we had, for those times: $100,000. Candidates were calling from Indiana, Ohio, Oregon, all over the country. On Election Night, instead of losing the House, the Democrats picked up seats. Roosevelt was pleased, and from that day forward there were thirty or forty people who figured they owed their elections to Lyndon Johnson.

They had pleaded for as little as $200, but that was enough to make the difference in a particular race. We are talking about sums of money that in today's world would not keep a candidate in clean shirts for a week.

When we needed a major contribution, Herman and George Brown sent in a check for $10,000. There were cheers in the office that day. The money would become more substantial later, but the Browns were not yet Texas-rich. Nor were they indebted in any way to Johnson. It was Alvin Wirtz who saw that their company won the contract with the Lower Colorado River Authority to enlarge the Mansfield Dam, in 1937, and to build others.

The relationship between Lyndon Johnson and Brown & Root has long tempted the imaginations of investigative reporters, scholars, and LBJ's political opposition. It is fair to say that Johnson was very close to Herman Brown and, later, his brother George. They were helpful to him, and he to them. When war broke out, the Houston-based company was among the successful bidders for construction of a naval air base in Corpus Christi. Along with Columbia and Kaiser and Hughes, and other companies like them, they built air bases all over the world, and launched huge shipbuilding programs. In wartime, companies survived, and many flourished, on their defense contracts. There was not a great deal else.

The figures rumored to have been contributed to Johnson by Brown & Root over the years are impressive. A quarter-million dollars. Half a million. They are also grossly exaggerated.

Keep this in mind: in the races that were his most controversial, the cost of running for public office was minimal compared to what it is today. In checking records, I ran across a letter dated 1941 from the Stephen F. Austin Hotel, in Austin, asking for payment of a bill that had been overlooked (by the hotel). The amount was $381.00, and it covered the use of two rooms, a suite on the sixteenth floor that was one of our principal headquarters, for which we were charged $6.50 a day; and a room on the fourth floor whose rental was $2.50 a day.

A number of forces were converging to make 1940 an extraordinary year. To begin with, it was a battle not only for congressional seats, but for the Presidency itself. Opinion was divided over Roosevelt's decision to run for a third term, and he was running scared. His opponent, Wendell Willkie, was an appealing man, and their positions on national defense and aid to Britain (then undergoing the blitz) were virtually the same.

On the Democratic side, long-standing friendships would soon dissolve. Jim Farley, one of the President's oldest allies, broke with him over the third term. So did John L. Lewis. The names of Farley, Garner, and of Senator Millard Tydings, of Maryland, would all be placed in nomination.

The national convention in 1940 was to be my first. William Bankhead, of Alabama, the speaker of the House, had died. It soon became known that Rayburn, the majority leader, would be the new speaker. (Bankhead was the father of Tallulah, one of that era's popular actresses.)

The Texas delegation was badly split before the train pulled into Chicago. We were headquartered at the Stephens Hotel—later, the Hilton—and behind every door the debates raged. There were many who simply supported Texas' native son, Garner, and others who opposed a third term for FDR as a matter of principle. Indeed, an early national poll taken in May had shown only a third of the voters supporting Roosevelt, while 55 percent said they would vote against him.

But Hitler's invasion of Poland had changed all the equations. With clouds of war hanging over the convention, the Texas delegates took up their positions. We had the pro- and anti-Garner forces, conservatives, liberals, and the hard-line segregationists. It was not possible to conduct a meeting, or finish a breakfast prayer, without the most bitter feelings and denunciations erupting between two or more factions.

I am not sure that the political process has been harmed by the change, but conventions then were unpredictable and emotionally charged, as opposed to the sterile and tightly orchestrated productions of the TelePrompter age. One of the leading Texas delegates was Clara Driscoll, a determined and outspoken woman of considerable wealth, who had built the Driscoll Hotel and the Driscoll office building in her hometown of Corpus Christi. Her real legacy was having saved the Alamo for the people of Texas. As unlikely as it may seem, at the turn of the century the Alamo was in private hands, and about to be demolished, when she bought that historic shrine and turned it over to the Daughters of the Republic.

Clara could outdrink most of the delegates, and when she did she would take the floor during a caucus and upbraid anyone who disagreed with her. She knew four-letter words that a mule skinner would have envied, but all in all she was quite a lady.

Feelings ran so high that a number of fistfights broke out around the Texas delegation. I had to jump in between Lyndon Johnson and Bascom Timmons, a Washington newsman, and separate them before they came to blows.

Roosevelt was indeed nominated, and elected (over Wendell Willkie), but the divisions that surfaced among Texans would fester and spread through the rest of the decade. In truth, the feuds of 1940 were the foundation for the emergence of the Republican Party as we know it in Texas today.

Johnson came out of the campaign bearing Roosevelt's stamp, although fate, and the tangled fishlines of war and ambition, would render its value short-lived. One of the puzzlements of Johnson's record would come into play here. He was such a skilled embellisher of a story that people often chose not to believe him even when his version was closest to the truth.

Johnson claimed to have been in the White House, visiting with the President, the day FDR decided to fire Joseph P. Kennedy as ambassador to England. Kennedy's flight had taken him from London to Lisbon and now, safely, into New York.

Roosevelt invited him to the White House for a meeting the next day. Then he turned to Johnson, according to those who repeated the story, and said, "I'm going to fire the son of a bitch."

The ambassador, it was no secret, had been an early isolationist. He warned that England was unprepared for war—he was right, of course—and that the United States should avoid being drawn into Europe's quarrel with the Nazis.

Johnson left his meeting convinced that the diplomatic career of Joe Kennedy was finished. Several people, including Hugh Sidey, the respected political columnist for *Time* magazine, were amused by his claim that FDR had taken him into his confidence in such a way. "I think he put himself into many, many imaginary situations," said Horace Busby, a longtime friend and adviser. "As a young man, he identified with him, and he put himself in there talking to Roosevelt, and thirty years later he believed the fiction."

The Roosevelt appointment book for October 27, 1940, showed that Lyndon Johnson was in the Oval Office when the President took a call from Ambassador Kennedy after his arrival in New York.

Television was never to be Lyndon Johnson's medium. The telephone was. Coupled with his well-known disdain for clocks, his calls inspired some with energy, others with dread. Nellie once teased Jack Valenti about an often quoted statement of his: "I sleep better at night knowing Lyndon Johnson is my President." Nellie retorted: "Jack may have slept better at night, but a lot of nights I didn't sleep at all because he was my President."

In 1940, Nellie moved to Washington during the final months of our engagement and was working on Johnson's congressional campaign, out of the offices in the Munsey Building. One day she didn't react quickly enough to a question and he threw a flowerpot in her direction. His aim wasn't that good. Nellie's reflexes were quite keen, and everyone went back to work. He intimidated her, as he did many others, when he thought he could. Nevertheless, you made allowances for temperament in people you judged as special, and I asked him to be the best man at our wedding.

He agreed. Nellie went back to Texas to make the arrangements, and a small but lingering problem developed. Johnson could not or would not find a time when he felt we both could leave the office. I finally told him that if one of us had to stay behind, it was going to be him. I had a wedding to attend. I brought most of the staff and a good deal of the workload with me, and Jake Pickle, my old fraternity brother, stepped in as best man. Nellie and I were married on December 21, 1940, in the First Methodist Church in Austin.

In our final months in Washington, Nellie and I entertained in a small apartment close to town. The refreshments were simple and usually homemade, and the guests included the Texans Jake Pickle, Bob Strauss, and Homer Thornberry, all later to assume national political identities. And Tommy Corcoran brought his accordion and his inventory of sweet, festive Irish ballads, songs that endeared him to Franklin Roosevelt.

My own early political values, like Lyndon's, were shaped by FDR and the men around him. They passed the acts that provided hope to a generation of the poor and disenfranchised. My social skills were polished by the people who, in the years just before America entered the war, dropped by our tiny apartment for snacks and conversation. Others among them were Alvin Wirtz and Abe Fortas, two of Johnson's close friends and advisers. That was where these relationships began to form.

We were living in an entirely different era. The Depression had crippled the country. The great Dust Bowl of the 1930s had hit Oklahoma, Kansas, and the Texas Panhandle, and the migration from those states to California was in full swing. Government service was viewed differently than it is today; men in public life were viewed differently . . . with hope and respect.

I thought Roosevelt was a great President, and my opinion has hardened with time. First, he knew how the government functioned. He knew about people. As assistant secretary of the Navy and governor of New York, he had gained experience that served him well when he came to the Presidency.

He also had a certain ruthlessness about him. He understood human nature. He played one man against another, one cabinet officer against another, in order to get the most out of them. He was not above being ruthless in getting rid of people who were incapable of doing the job, or reflected poorly on his administration. He was imaginative, he was innovative. He was doing everything in his power to bring about change, to revitalize the country. Of course, many say he exceeded his powers.

By the spring of 1941, I had a wife, a new law office in Austin, Johnson's re-election campaign to run, and a commission in the Naval Reserve. I owed that status to the persistence of a Commander Quigley, a recruiter whose primary target had been Lyndon Johnson. The United States, he kept insisting, would enter the war within the year, and the Navy would need its best men as commissioned officers. The Naval Reserve was offering every member of Congress, regardless of age or background or experience, the rank of lieutenant commander. Johnson finally succumbed to Quigley's pitch, accepted his commission, and we thought not a great deal more about it.

Soon after, I signed up as an ensign, the highest rank that a twenty-two-year-old was entitled to hold. In September of 1941, I was called to temporary active duty to attend the Naval Intelligence School in New York, at 90 Church Street. Across the Pacific, the Japanese fleet was getting ready to sail for Pearl Harbor.

My experiences in the war would not much differ from those of many thousands of other young Americans, meaning that I would not care to repeat them, but I would not trade those years for all the oil in Arabia.

ANCHORS AWEIGH

I understand that I will be identified forever as the man who was wounded by the gun that killed John Kennedy. I cannot escape that connection and I have never tried. But I am also aware of another of the ironies of my life. I would not have been there to be remembered at all if, in the midst of war, a plane I was aboard had crashed.

By ordinary odds it should have. That plane, as it happened, carried a passenger with a famous name: Elliott Roosevelt, the son of the President of the United States.

In December of 1943, when I was based in North Africa, Elliott invited me to hitch a ride on a reconnaissance plane heading Stateside for Christmas, with refueling stops in England and Labrador. It was a stripped-down B-24 bomber, with bucket seats in the back for the few passengers who could squeeze aboard.

An hour or two over the North Atlantic, I was invited into the cockpit. The pilot asked if I knew anything about navigation. Startled by the question, I replied that I knew very little. "Well," said the captain, "our radio is out and our instruments are down and we're uncertain where we are."

I said, "If you need help from me, we're in even worse shape than you think."

All I knew about navigation was how the old-timers did it. I asked the pilot, "Can't you take some celestial fixes?"

"It's too cloudy and overcast," he said.

Directly below us was the icy North Atlantic. The temperature was below freezing and we had a long night ahead of us to think about what that meant. We had been lost for six hours, running with two engines shut down to conserve fuel. We knew time was running out. I talked to Elliott. He said he had parachuted twice, the second time to convince himself he couldn't possibly be as terrified as he was for his first jump. But he wouldn't do it a third time, he said, and whatever came he was going down with the plane and take his chances.

We all felt the same way. There wasn't one of us aboard who was prepared to parachute into the frigid North Atlantic waters. So we contemplated what courses and options were open to us, and there were none. None. The pilot decided that we would go on until the fuel ran out or until we sighted land.

That was a night as harried as any I could possibly imagine. It was the kind of night where you conjured up every conceivable thing that could happen to you, none of them good, and during which you have a chance to relive your life, bit by bit, the good and the bad, wondering if you would do the same things over, make the same mistakes, the same choices. I had more time than I needed to reflect, at that young age, knowing in the back of my mind that we couldn't last long in the freezing waters.

We were still airborne as dawn broke and it occurred to us that we would at least be able to see around us when we went down. We began to scramble for life jackets, rubber rafts, anything that would float. The pilot had the flaps and wheels down and was ready to ditch into the sea when we saw in the mist what appeared to be a small landing strip. Then, a few miles ahead, he spotted a beacon light flashing—an airport beacon. He gunned the engine, gave it full power, and we followed the landing lights and touched down.

Blind luck had brought us to a British airfield, and by the

time we were on the ground half the base turned out to greet us. Through the night, we now learned, the word had been broadcast that a plane was missing with President Roosevelt's son aboard. We had been overdue by five hours at Gander.

We had landed at St. John's, Newfoundland, a thousand miles off course. And what we thought was a small strip, where we first started to land, turned out to be a fishing pier.

Of the men I knew personally, I can recall none who went off to war burdened by fear or gloomy premonitions. We were, for the most part, volunteers, if not eager at the idea of joining the fray, at least unwilling to be left behind. If you had any interest in politics, you knew that some military experience would be essential. For many of our generation, the future would be determined to some degree by what you did in the war.

It was acceptable to have a normal amount of forebodings, and these were often justified. But there wasn't much serious talk about death, except among Marines on the eve of a landing, or airmen flying a mission over well-fortified targets. They assumed they were going to be mauled. Their work called for it.

My naval career started slowly, had its ups and downs, and in the end provided enough action to keep me from feeling deprived.

On the first Sunday in December, 1941, Nellie and I were entertaining guests, including Jake and Sugar Pickle, at the guest lodge on Lake Buchanan. We were having coffee in the living room when I heard a screaming and wailing so wild I couldn't imagine what had happened. One of our friends, Marjorie Ransom, had been in her room, listening to the radio, and she had just heard the news that Pearl Harbor had been bombed. Her husband, Colonel Kormeier, had just recently reported to the Philippines, and she was deathly afraid for him.

This was where we were and how we heard the news of the attack on Pearl Harbor. In that instant, of course, all our lives were turned upside down. It would mark the beginning of years of uncertainty and turbulence. Nellie and I drove back to Austin and closed our home. I wired the Navy Department that I was en route to Washington, D.C., to await my orders.

I was soon assigned to the office of the Undersecretary of the Navy, the Honorable James Forrestal. President Roosevelt had persuaded him to leave his position as the head of one of the largest investment houses in New York, and assume the post of Undersecretary to Frank Knox.

As a young ensign, I was in awe of the brass who trooped through our doors—men like Admiral King, the chief of Naval Operations. Most impressive of all was the opportunity to shake hands with the old sailor who had the office across the corridor from ours in the days before there was a Pentagon. His name was known to all—Admiral Richard E. Byrd, the Antarctic explorer whose brother Harry would have a long political reign as the senator from Virginia.

I created every opportunity I could to cross his path and to exchange a word or two. He understandably paid little or no attention to a young ensign, but I must add parenthetically that one never knows what the future will hold. Nineteen years later, in 1961, as Secretary of the Navy, I would have the honor and privilege of delivering the address when Admiral Byrd's statue was dedicated on the Avenue of the Heroes, leading up to Lee's home and the Arlington Cemetery.

One of the admiral's relatives was D. Harold Byrd, of Dallas, who was a strong supporter of mine when I ran for governor a year later.

From Forrestal's office, I was assigned to the Lend-Lease program, which was then the lifeline to Russia, with the embattled coast of Africa as the jumping-off point. Edward Stettinius headed the operation and under him had been assembled a team of rising stars.

They included: Philip Graham, later the publisher of the *Washington Post*; Oscar S. Cox, a future solicitor general; Lloyd Cutler, who would head a powerful Washington law firm and serve as Jimmy Carter's legal counsel; Eugene Rostow, Dean of the Yale Law School and later Undersecretary of State; Walter Thayer, a partner of Jock Whitney and later editor of the New York *Herald Tribune*; and George Ball, Undersecretary of State to Presidents Johnson and Kennedy.

That particular group, I believe it is safe to say, left a mark on the American political landscape.

In 1943, I was shipped to North Africa and assigned to Allied Force Headquarters, where the basic planning was under way for the invasion of Sicily. We made the trip in a DC-3, which I can assure you is a slow way to cover four thousand miles. Our flight path took us from a base in Florida to Georgetown in British Guiana, then to Brazil and across the ocean to Dakar, the capital of Senegal on the west coast of Africa. As a result of that journey, I formed a lasting friendship with a man who was to achieve notoriety later in life. He was then a Marine captain named T. Coleman Andrews, from Richmond, Virginia. He later became commissioner of the Internal Revenue Service and was active in the Third Party movement during the Presidential campaign of 1948.

Everything about Dakar fascinated me. It had been the capital of the slave trade in the nineteenth century, a strange city on the edge of the Sahara Desert. We were there only a few days but saw some amazing sights. It was a crossroads of the world, and a strange assortment of people passed through from every point of the compass, as I suppose they had since almost the beginning of time.

We left Dakar in our DC-3 flying north to Mauritania to refuel. The air was so clear, the land so flat, that we could stand on level ground and see mountains fifty miles away. We flew hour after hour over barren desert, until we saw ahead of us the outline of the Atlas Mountains. I wrote Nellie about those mountains because they were stratified with the most vivid colors I have ever seen—rust, reds, shades of orange and yellows and purple, all in magnificent contrast to the starkness of the desert. We dropped down into the Valley of Marrakesh, which would have made any Californian or Floridian or South Texan green with envy at the endless and bountiful citrus groves and vineyards.

For the first time, we were billeted in sumptuous quarters, a luxury hotel with a glass-enclosed dining room overlooking gardens brilliant with tropical plants. We moved on to Algiers, and there I would spend the greater part of 1943. General Eisenhower had launched his invasion of North Africa with the objective of challenging Rommel and his Afrika Korps in Tunisia.

I had arrived at a time of particular intrigue. The week before, Admiral Darlan, who had succeeded Marshal Pétain as the leader of the Vichy French, had been assassinated; General Giraud became head of the Free French movement—all this before Robert Murphy, the brilliant American diplomat, brought Charles de Gaulle out of France in a submarine. De Gaulle, of course, went on to London, where he established himself as the spokesman for the French Resistance and, after the war, became the dominant figure in French politics.

The grand strategy for both the Atlantic and the Pacific had been settled in the Casablanca Conference between Churchill and Roosevelt in January, 1943.

Algiers was to be the staging area for the landing at Sicily, code-named Operation Husky. Rommel had already met his major defeat at El Alamein, and had been repulsed by General Montgomery and the combined British forces in their drive to reach Alexandria and then Cairo. The vaunted Afrika Korps was in retreat, with the bloody battle of Kasserine Pass still to be fought.

Through dispatches and word of mouth, we were able to keep up with the fierce battles that seemed to be waged so near us. In the port of Algiers, Admiral Henry Kent Hewitt was in charge of the greatest naval armada ever assembled, for the invasion of Italy. Charles de Gaulle rode into Algiers on May 30, 1944. In July, the invasion was launched.

I can't say that my education suffered any during this period. Algiers was being bombed almost nightly by the Luftwaffe, and I had been able to rent an apartment owned by a wealthy

Frenchman. He had moved his family to what he felt would be a safer location, his home in the countryside. He was apparently a fine sportsman, judging from the trophies on the mantel that identified him as the best pistol shot in all of North Africa.

The family had left the apartment intact, with all of the furnishings, glassware, and a Victrola with a superb collection of Caruso records. That was when I first began to acquire an awareness and appreciation of the incredible voice of Enrico Caruso. They had the original recordings of Caruso singing arias, and duets with other artists of the time. Those were thrilling sounds and, having very little to do at night, I would sit there hour after hour and listen to those matchless recordings. I have been a devout Caruso fan ever since, and there are only two voices that I would compare with his. One is the late Swedish tenor Jussi Bjoerling, and the other is Luciano Pavarotti.

In times of difficulty or danger, cut off from your family and your roots, you tend to remember little things that pleased you. Right down the street from the apartment was a bakery, set up the by the U.S. military forces. Every night at midnight, they brought the first loaves of bread out of the ovens. And nearly every night at midnight I was down there to buy a fresh loaf of that bread, because the aroma was so absolutely delightful that I could not resist. I would return to the apartment with that fresh-baked bread and eat it, still warm, with butter and jelly, while I listened to the voice of Caruso.

At Tunis, one of the wing commanders, a Colonel Dunn, turned out to be a former classmate of mine at the University of Texas. He invited me to visit him at headquarters and to take a ride in a British Mosquito they had stripped down for reconnaissance flights. This was a twin-engine night fighter and light bomber, developed by the de Havilland Aircraft Company, with all the armor and heavy equipment removed, so they could install their cameras and gain maximum speed. Behind the pilot, there was a little shelf where the radio gear had been stored. There was a vacancy now just enough for a man my size to bend over and huddle in; you couldn't hold your head up, but you could at least see out with your head held halfway down on your chest.

When Dunn asked if I wanted to take a ride and see part of the country, I heartily agreed. I almost wished I hadn't because he turned that Mosquito every which way but loose. Among other things, he took us on a hair-raising dive down into the Roman Amphitheater at Sousse. It appeared that we went right down to the bowl of the amphitheater—I believe we were really below the seats—before he did a dramatic climb.

On the return hop from Tunis to Algiers, I booked myself on a more conservative model, a World War I biplane with wooden wings. We were making about eighty miles an hour, and at takeoff some natives had simply climbed aboard. The plane didn't even have a door and some of the passengers were carrying chickens in wire cages.

This was one of the wildest flights I have ever taken in my life. There were about four of those planes in existence in that part of the world, and one by one the other three were lost in crashes. If I never take another strange or scary flight, I will not feel shortchanged.

In the late fall of 1943, I received my orders to return to the States and that was when I hooked up with Elliott Roosevelt. We had met at the Democratic Convention in 1940, and again after he moved to Fort Worth to manage a chain of radio stations for the Texas State Network. By the time that B-24 landed safely in Newfoundland, we were bonded.

After we refueled, rested a bit, and drank some coffee, we continued on to Washington. We ran into a rain and hailstorm between New York and Washington, and the plane pitched and bucked until we were all singing "Nearer My God to Thee."

After I returned from a brief leave, my commanding officer said he had several openings for a naval attaché at bases around the globe, and asked if I wanted to choose one. I told him I really wanted to go to sea. I wanted to catch up with some of my friends. Jake Pickle was already in the Pacific. John Singleton was on a destroyer escort. Burleson Smith, of San Antonio, and

Henry Wade were in Fighter Director's School on St. Simons Island, Georgia, being trained to control fighter planes at night.

The idea appealed to me as a way to get to sea. My next stop was Georgia and three months of intensive training. A Fighter Director Officer is responsible on a carrier for aircraft from the moment they are off the flight deck and airborne. He controls them both in combat and on their attack missions until they are back aboard the ship. That is a simple explanation of the duties, and it is simple until the skies are crowded and the bullets are flying and the bombs are falling.

I was doing quite well in school until about a week before we were to finish. One night I suddenly felt ill, vomiting with sharp stomach cramps. I was rooming with Henry Wade, and about midnight he called the doctor, who quickly diagnosed my problem as appendicitis.

He said, "You need an operation."

I said, "Fine. I'm going to be in Washington in a week and I'll have it then."

He said, "Like hell you will. I've already ordered the ambulance. You're going to Brunswick and you're going to have that surgery tonight."

So they bundled me into an ambulance and hauled me off to Brunswick, an hour's drive from the base. I underwent surgery at around two o'clock in the morning. My appendix was just short of bursting, and I was still in a hospital bed when I graduated from the Fighter Director's School. Finally, I was transferred to Beaver Tail, Rhode Island, for additional night training, with a few days off to visit Nellie and our young daughter Kathleen.

Night controlling had taken on a new urgency because of the persistence of the Japanese pilots, who were trained to spot our aircraft carriers at night and radio back their location. The night controllers could guide our fighters until they made a visual sighting of the enemy aircraft.

I had my orders to embark with a Night Fighter Group. We had given up our apartment, and I had arranged for a friend to drive Nellie and Kathleen back to Texas. I was back in Beaver Tail, packing for my trip to the West Coast and Hawaii when Henry Wade and Burley Smith walked in and asked me what I was doing. I said I was packing to get out of there.

They looked at each other and, almost in a chorus, said, "You're not going anywhere. Commander Taylor changed your orders. You're going to Martha's Vineyard as officer in charge of a training unit."

I said, "Like hell I am." This went on into the night. I was due to leave the next night. That morning, I was waiting for Commander Taylor when he opened his office. I begged him to reinstate my original orders. I said, "Commander, I have just sent my wife and baby home. I want to go to sea. There are other officers here whose wives haven't left, who would be happy to have this assignment. I don't want to stay. All I want is to go to sea."

He said, "So does everybody else."

I said, "Commander, I respectfully disagree. There are a lot of officers who would be happy to stay here and accept those orders to Martha's Vineyard."

He said, "Lieutenant, I'm not asking for your opinion. We're not running this service for your benefit."

I said, "Sir, I understand that. But I am pleading with you to let me go to sea. I have a brother who is in the Marine Corps. He's getting shot up all over the Pacific. I've got a brother-in-law who is with the Army in the Mediterranean, and another one with the Army in Europe. I've got a younger brother who is with the Air Force in the Aleutians.

"I don't want to be the officer in charge of a training unit at Martha's Vineyard. I want to go to sea."

He said, "Well, that's too damned bad. You're going to Martha's Vineyard."

The conversation was over. I snapped off a salute, did an about-face, and walked out of the room. I had steam coming out my ears. He had been totally unyielding and not only unsympathetic, I thought, but arrogant in the process. He seemed to have made it a personal point to deny what was really a rather basic request. I was a naval officer trained for sea duty. And that was what I wanted.

I called Lyndon Johnson and, for the first time in my life, I made a deliberate effort to use political influence on my own behalf. I was livid. I remember telling him what happened and I said, "Congressman, I am either going to sea or I am going to the brig for insubordination. What I am NOT going to do is go to Martha's Vineyard for the rest of this war."

Johnson said, "Well, you just be quiet. Don't say anything and don't do anything more until you hear from me."

I later found out that he called Nellie and said, "If I didn't know that John doesn't drink, I'd swear he was drunk when he called me just now. He sounded like a raving maniac."

I suppose I probably did. By noon of that day, I had gone down to a remote radar unit and was running some exercises—trying to keep my mind occupied—when a lieutenant pulled up in his jeep and said, "John, you've got to detach yourself immediately."

I said, "What for?"

He said, "Admiral Durkin is waiting to see you at Quonset Point."

I said, "What about—?"

He cut me off: "All I know is, you have orders to be there by two o'clock and it's already past noon. Hank and Burley are packing your gear and you need to get going."

I jumped into the jeep, went to my room, changed clothes, grabbed all my gear, and made it to Quonset Point a few minutes before two. The admiral looked at me and said, "Connally, I understand you want to go to sea."

I said, "Yes, sir."

He said, "Well, that's a commendable wish. When do you want to go?"

I said, "At your convenience, sir."

He said, "What about this afternoon?"

I said, "That would suit me fine, sir."

He said, "Good. We are cutting orders for you to proceed immediately to Hawaii for further assignment."

I thanked him and was gone. I later learned that Admiral Durkin was a Navy hero who had been in the South Pacific in the early days of the war and had lost a foot in battle.

In time, I heard from Hank Wade and Burley Smith that Commander Taylor was beside himself over what had happened. He called them in and asked what they knew, what I had done, and with whom I had talked. They said they didn't know a thing, but they warned me that I had better hope I never crossed Taylor's trail again in the Pacific. He tried for weeks to find out how I got my orders changed, and how I got out of there so fast.

No matter. I eventually heard that he came to the Pacific on another aircraft carrier, but I never saw or heard from him again.

In June of 1944, I sailed out of San Francisco on the U.S.S. *Franklin,* bound for Honolulu. The ship was obviously transporting all the men and equipment it could possibly carry. The flight and hangar decks were stacked tip to tip with aircraft. We were also carrying an additional 2,500 men, meaning that there were probably 6,000 troops on board. They were sleeping under the planes and in the passageways, anywhere they might find a space of cool air. We were all shut in, with no light showing because complete security measures were in effect. All the portholes were closed.

It was dank, damp, humid, smelly with human sweat, and not a breeze stirring. Those of us who were officers had to walk security watches during the night. I drew the late watch one night down on the third deck. The heat and the odor were just repulsive. I felt weak with nausea and, fortunately, was walking past the head (lavatory). I ducked in, threw up, washed my face, and kept walking my post until I was relieved of my duty. That was the only time I took sick during my tour of sea duty, notwithstanding that I later went through two typhoons.

We reached Hawaii and within a week I had my orders: I

was assigned to the U.S.S. *Essex*, the aircraft carrier bound for torrid action in the Pacific and whose crew would proudly label it "the fightingest ship in the Navy."

We did not know then that we were entering a new phase of the war—indeed, an era of military tactics so fluid that the results could be historic and obsolete at almost the same time. No young officer could board the *Essex* without feeling an immediate burst of pride. This was the flagship of a new and faster class of carriers, state of the art.

The *Essex* would be in the thick of the last great air-sea battles. Land-based planes had engaged in the heroic dogfights of World War I. The so-called "limited" wars of the next fifty years would be fought in jungles, swamps, or deserts, not the ideal settings for sea power.

By the early summer of 1944, eleven of the *Essex*-class carriers had been launched, with all but one joining up with Admiral Halsey's Pacific fleet. The U.S. carrier groups were moving westward, landing the divisions of Marines who had begun the struggles to take the Marianas, Iwo Jima, and Okinawa, among the dramatic datelines of the war's later, desperate weeks. I had met no one in the staging areas who expected those to be anything but bloody and disagreeable. It was easy enough to be swept along, trying to find the *Essex* and report for my new assignment, but I had a family interest in these invasions.

I made my way down through Kwajalein, in the Marshalls, and, seeking word of my brother Merrill, I wandered into a tent where a Marine was sorting mail. Merrill had been a sniper on Guadalcanal and again at Bougainville, where he tracked the Japanese in the jungle with native scouts. Once, leading a patrol through the jungle, he came upon four Japanese who were just finishing a meal in a little clearing. The Emperor's soldiers immediately jumped to their feet and grabbed their weapons. Whereupon, Merrill drew his pistol, fired four shots, and killed all four. He had seen enough action to script a dozen John Wayne movies. At Guam, he became a forward spotter, flying

in light fabric planes that were catapulted off the decks of battleships and were retrieved upon their return, if they did return,
with a boom and cable.

The Marine postal clerk told me that Merrill was resting
not a mile away. I burst in on him and woke him from his nap.
My memory of that moment is not of a tearful, emotional
reunion. It was like a grand practical joke; we hugged and
laughed like fools. Later, Merrill suffered terrible wounds when
a Japanese shell exploded beneath his feet as he scouted for
targets over Iwo Jima, from an OS2U aircraft. A Japanese artil-
lery shell exploded under him, and ripped up both his legs.

He was operating off the battleship *Idaho*, and when he
opened his eyes three days later, he was in the ship's sick bay.
He had no memory of how or when they fished him out of the
water, or how he survived. He was in and out of the naval
hospital at Corpus Christi for years after the war ended.

I finally went aboard the *Essex* as it lay off Eniwetok Atoll.
All hands were preparing for the assaults on Guam, Tinian, and
Saipan. I was relieved just to be there. The *Essex* was a magnifi-
cent ship, and a happy one, with a splendid crew.

I had been aboard a relatively short period of time when
our senior flight controller, my roommate, had an accident during shore leave on one of the smaller islands. He had consumed
more than his share of whatever beer or libations had been
available. When I got back aboardship and walked into our
room, I was stunned to find it splattered with blood. I had no
idea what had happened. The bed, the towels, the floor, the
washbasin—the place looked like a butcher shop.

I went looking for him and found him in the dentist's chair.
The dentist was wiring his jaw. He had returned to the ship a
little tipsy, and had fallen into the Number 2 elevator well,
driving a reinforcing rod up through his jaw—broke his jaw and
knocked out some teeth. For a fellow whose job depended on
his mouth, and his ability to talk into a radio, he was not going
to be of much use to us. His commanding officer immediately
detached him and sent him back to the States. That was how I

became the ship's Fighter Director Officer. Later, I was given that responsibility for the whole task force.

My battle station was in the Combat Information Center (CIC), and on my immediate right was the executive officer, Commander (later, Admiral) David L. McDonald, seated at a horizontal plotting board. We became lifelong friends. He was awaiting orders back to the States, and was anxious to go after three or four years away from his family. The *Essex* had been at sea the entire war and I, of course, had joined her late.

He loved to play bridge, so when we were refueling away from the battle areas, four of us—McDonald, the air officer, the dentist, and myself—would have a game of bridge. This went on every night to the point where I couldn't even find time to write letters home. Immediately after dinner, we would sit down to the bridge table and stay there until I was ready to fall asleep.

It reached a point where I tried hiding out. I would eat early and go back to my room, but there was no escape. The word would come over the speaker system for Lieutenant Connally to dial 002. That was the executive officer's extension. I had to call, and McDonald would say, "Where are you?"

"In my room."

"Well, get down here. We're waiting on you."

"Commander, I just have to write some letters back home tonight."

"You can write them tomorrow. Get on down here."

This went on night after night, but we formed a great friendship. He was a magnificent officer. I never shall forget his words the day we took our first kamikaze hit, late in the war. The plane crashed into our flight deck and skidded across the edge of an elevator. It shook the entire ship, and dust settled on all the cables and telephone wires overhead in the CIC. It just left a thick powder all over the room. I thought it was unbelievable that a Japanese Zero, a relatively small plane, could shake a ship a thousand feet long and as big as an aircraft carrier. But it sent a tremor through the whole ship.

Commander McDonald got up very calmly from his stool,

and said, "Well, they finally got our cherry." This was the first real hit that the *Essex* had taken, and it came when the Japanese were reduced pretty much to sending out the kamikazes—suicide attacks—to defend the mainland.

The nature of great naval battles has changed since the *Monitor* and the *Merrimack*. In the Battle of the Coral Sea, in May of 1942, carriers from the U.S. and Japan did not fire a shot at each other, but each lost a carrier in the first all-air naval engagement.

Combat on the seas was exciting and exhausting and exhilarating, and at times frightening. We went through nine major battles while I was on the *Essex* and, briefly, the *Bennington*.

There is no reason to feel sentimental simply because wars will not be fought this way again. All ways are repugnant. Now, and in the future, air duels will be waged between warplanes miles apart, using heat-seeking missiles. Or their duels will be not with each other but with missiles on the ground, fired from fixed or mobile launchers, guided by lasers. It isn't likely that a pilot will ever again see his enemy's face as they attempt to kill each other.

But men—and women—find it hard to let go of what they felt or learned or lost in combat. The adventure of war changes you, although perhaps not as much as the inhumanity of war. It is one thing to watch on your television screen as the bombs fall, another to see the blips on radar, and yet another to see the burning planes plunge into the sea, or the gray and black plume of smoke from the beach, where men are measuring their lives an inch at a time. Once, on the *Essex*, a bomb fell so close that a geyser sprayed the flight deck, and a pilot complained of smelling fish for a week.

On the eve of what is expected to be a major engagement, it is hard to judge whether one man is more apprehensive than another. Most are too busy to care. There are always the brave or the curious who want their full share of combat. I felt that way for a while. I also like ice cream; I just don't want it shoveled down my throat by the gallon.

But there was something special about the last dozen days of October, 1944. General MacArthur was about to keep his promise to return to the Philippines, and the *Essex* was responsible for providing much of the air cover.

The shelling from the big guns in the convoy began on October 19, softening up the Japanese positions. The next day, with the beach secure, MacArthur waded ashore on Leyte, with his officers and troops, his khaki trousers wet up to the knees. A photograph captured the moment, a symbol of American resurgence second only to the flag-raising on Iwo Jima.

The ground battle raged for two days, when the Japanese launched a counterattack with all they had. Our radar was the first to pick them up, three waves of sixty planes each, from Luzon airfields. Led by Commander David McCampbell, the Navy's foremost air ace, seven Hellcats scrambled and were the first to intercept them. I was the control officer as McCampbell and his wingman scrambled to meet the first wave. Between the two of them, they broke the Japanese formation—sixty fighters, bombers, and torpedo bombers.

The Japanese were holding nothing back. Of more pressing concern, their pilots were committed, literally, to flights of no return. We had heard throughout the war of the act of kamikaze, pilots low on fuel or bombs or determined to die for the Emperor, who crashed their planes into American ships. Now the suicide mission had become an essential part of their last-ditch air-and-sea strategy.

In the first wave, the *Essex* came under direct attack. McCampbell, now joined by other Hellcats, scattered a nest of bombers and fighters. "They're falling like leaves," I heard him say over the radio. The sky was crisscrossed by twisting white vapor trails and black puffs of smoke from the guns of our battleships. A lone Japanese Judy dive bomber slipped past the defense net and headed for the *Princeton*, which had launched its own air group. Every available gun was trained on it, but somehow the plane staggered on and smashed through three decks. Bombs and torpedoes exploded. In flames, the *Princeton* sank quickly, 2,000 yards off our starboard bow.

We were into the wind, taking on the fighter planes as fast as we could get them back. We were rearming them, regassing them, and launching them as fast as we could.

The kamikaze mission had now emerged as a deliberate and menacing Japanese tactic. I made the distress call that signaled the fighter planes to abort all missions and return to the carrier; the base was under serious attack. There were air battles all over the sky.

The last to return were David McCampbell and his wing-man—seven planes in all. Normally, you don't launch anything less than a division, consisting of four planes. They always went in pairs, two to a section. We were launching everything we could. There was a huge raid coming in from the west. I could see it clearly on the radar screen, a blip as big as your thumb.

Commander McCampbell, his wingman with him, led the other five planes and instructed them to stay together, to fight as a unit. He and his wingman went up to 20,000 feet to take on the fighter cover over the bombers. Under our procedure, I gave them their heading and altitude until they spotted the enemy. McCampbell said, "Tally-ho," which meant he had visual con-tact with the aircraft. We could hear him talking; then the control passed from our hands to his. We heard him say, "We're up above them . . . you take the one on the right, I've got the one on the left."

Only eighteen of the sixty Japanese planes were still in formation when the action broke off.

Those seven planes turned that whole raid. McCampbell and his wingman shot down fifteen aircraft without losing one; he got nine kills himself, his wingman six. They were shooting them down until they were about to run out of ammunition and fuel. Just as a pilot landed and caught the barrier cable, his plane was completely out of gas. The seven pilots that day performed almost a miracle. At the time, we were already under attack and had been for hours.

Each of the Japanese planes, known as the Betty, had a tail

gunner. They would stalk us all night, so that when dawn came they could launch their land-based planes against us. Of course, we also tried every night to knock them out. I frequently went up to the flight deck and ran interceptions with our night fighters. When we got an enemy contact—called a bogey or a bandit until we identified it—our planes tried to shoot it down before it could render any more positions on the fleet.

I was on duty one midnight when we picked up a bogey about 160 miles out. So I took control of the contact, and sent a young ensign out to make the interception. Normally, the technique is to turn the intercepting fighter 180 degrees, 500 feet below, and two to three miles behind. I turned him from a heading of roughly 360 to 180 and said, "Steady on, your bogey will be twelve o'clock, three miles." He said, "Contact," and from that moment he was in control of his own destiny.

I got off the radio and maintained radio silence until I heard him shout, "He's firing on me from a tail gunner position!" I said, "Roger, are you still in contact?" He said, "Negative," and then: "Can you put me on him again?" I said I would try, and gave him a new heading. He said, "Tally-ho," and again he closed. As a rule, they would close and start firing. But the Betty obviously was picking him up on the tail gunner's Japanese radar.

I put the young ensign on the Betty four times, and each time the Japanese saw him from the tail-gunner turret, gave him another burst, and he fell back. The Betty came within thirty miles of the task force; obviously, with his naked eye he had spotted us streaming across the ocean in the wake of the ships of this great fleet.

I noticed the young ensign was losing altitude. I told him our information was poor, and he said, "Put me on him one more time." Which I did: "Starboard zero, one, zero, steady on." He sang out, "Contact," and that was the last word we heard. I had sent up some other fighters to see if they could raise him if he was out of range.

I assumed the Betty had shot him down, and it was now

past two in the morning. I spent most of that night talking to a radio operator on the nearest island. Sometime around dawn, I realized that I was talking to Henry Wade, my law-school and naval-training classmate, who was on the beach at Okinawa.

Those nights were heartrending for us. I gave Hank the downed pilot's position, latitude and longitude, in code. I didn't learn what happened until about three days later, when the pilot came back aboard the *Essex*. I looked him up and said, "What the hell happened to you?" He said, "I made up my mind if you put me on him one more time, he was gonna get me or I was gonna get him. I went in with all guns blazing, hit him, saw him explode just as he hit the water." It was almost two o'clock in the morning, and he bailed out, climbed into his rubber raft—with no injuries, not a scratch on him—flashing his mirror. A sub surfaced and pulled him in.

We often broadcast the downed pilots' position over open radio circuits, and from time to time the submarines had amazingly good luck. Along with the ensign, four pilots had been picked up right after first light the next day by submarines commanded by Admiral Chester Nimitz.

It is heartwarming when you see them come back aboard. In the meantime, you live a life of anxiety and worry because it doesn't always turn out that well. Our air group commander had been out leading a raid and had been badly shot up. We turned in to the wind to take them all aboard, and the commander radioed that his plane was in such bad shape he couldn't make it; he would have to ditch in the ocean.

We dispatched a destroyer to get him and told him where to land so the men could throw him a life raft. He grabbed the rope, and they were pulling him up the side of the ship when he suddenly just turned loose, and that was the last we ever saw of him. He had been wounded, hadn't been able to tie the line around himself, and had blacked out. And we lost him, seconds away from being pulled aboard the destroyer.

That was a demoralizing time for the whole air group, and

a pall of gloom settled over the ship whenever something like that happened. You see men you live and work with every day and then, suddenly, they are gone. You never get used to that.

So there were moments of jubilation and joy and glory, but also moments of depression and fear. At one point, we had been in the South China Sea caught in a fog so dense the planes couldn't fly. We were all listening to Tokyo Rose, who was telling us that they knew we were in the South China Sea but wait until we started going back into the straits; they were waiting for us, the Japanese planes and submarines.

We lived a couple of days with some trepidation that, indeed, Tokyo Rose knew what she was talking about. This was Christmas Eve and God only knew what would happen to us, but we got through those straits unchallenged. We were operating then under Admiral "Bull" Halsey in the Third Fleet, and he came aboard with his call letters. He said, "Now hear this—" And he wished everybody a Merry Christmas and concluded with "Keep the bastards tired." We frankly didn't know whether he was talking about the Japanese or us, because we were so weary and exhausted.

Our particular task group, under Admiral Frederick Sherman, was the last to be relieved of duty. We reprovisioned and took a few days of rest when we were operating between Okinawa and the Japanese mainland in the latter part of the war. In early April of 1945, I found myself on duty for fifty-two consecutive hours. We were under attack around the clock, and had tried to track down the Japanese spy planes at night so they couldn't radio back our exact positions.

American submarines spotted the super battleship, the *Yamato*, with an escort of six destroyers and two cruisers. The largest battleship ever built, low on fuel, she was on a suicide mission: to shell our defenses on Okinawa, agitate the American fleet, and sink, if possible, one or more of our carriers.

A reconnaissance plane from the *Essex* spotted the *Yamato*. Some two hours later, wracked with repeated hits, she began to sink. One of the poignant stories of the Pacific war was how her captain gave his crew the order to abandon, then lashed himself to a beam and went down with his ship.

During this and the surrounding action, I had a little stool that had been built aboard ship, about as big as a piano stool but with longer legs and a ring around the middle where I could hook my heels. That was as comfortable as I could get during those fifty-two hours at my post. We had nothing but sandwiches and coffee and cigarettes, and it was then I learned to smoke, mostly to help me stay awake. My feet were so swollen I couldn't get my shoes on, and I was totally exhausted.

Commander McDonald, who would go on to command the Sixth Fleet, ordered me below. He said, "You've got to get some rest. I don't care what else is happening, you go below and get some sleep." So I went down to my cabin and fell asleep. I left the portholes open, and my cabin was right under the 40-mm guns on the port side of the ship.

While I was down there, the ship went to general quarters and I heard absolutely nothing. We were under attack from Japanese aircraft and the five-inch guns started roaring, the 40-mms started roaring, and the planes came closer and closer. My porthole was open—the sounds were all around me—and I slept through every bit of it.

About this time, the admiral sent for me and, of course, I wasn't at my battle station, which is a serious offense. Fortunately, Commander McDonald was there when the admiral asked, "Where's Connally?" And McDonald said, "Admiral, he has been on duty for fifty-two hours, he's exhausted and I ordered him below. With your permission, I'd like to leave him there."

The admiral said, "Fine," and that was the last I ever heard of it. That was the kind of man Dave McDonald was; without his sympathetic defense, I could have been court-martialed.

There were a lot of medals won during those air-sea battles. McCampbell deservedly was awarded the Congressional Medal of Honor. I was awarded a bronze star, then the Legion of Merit with the combat ribbon.

In mid-1942, Congressman Johnson had been decorated by General MacArthur himself, in a gesture that would become more controversial over the years. Johnson had received orders to the South Pacific to MacArthur's command, and volunteered for a bombing raid. A Colonel Stephens, I believe, actually took Johnson's place on one plane, and Johnson was diverted to another aircraft on the same raid. Stephens's plane was shot down and he was among those who died in the crash. Johnson's plane made the raid, was badly shot up, but came back safely, and General MacArthur bestowed the silver star on him.

Johnson was criticized for the decoration he got, but he was very proud of it. The silver star is a significant award for bravery. Like any military man, Johnson didn't ask for it; if he had, it wouldn't have been granted. He voluntarily cast himself in harm's way, agreed to go on this mission, and MacArthur wanted him to have it.

Years later, Johnson wore the pin in his lapel and was derided for it. Some of his detractors painted a picture of Johnson cowering in the plane and getting a medal for it. But he was neither a physical nor a moral coward, and those who wrote or said so would not have dared in his lifetime to suggest it to his face.

Shortly after the raid, President Roosevelt said to members of Congress, they either had to leave the service and return to the post they were elected to, or resign their seats in the Congress if they stayed in the military. Nearly all of them resigned their commissions and resumed their congressional and senatorial roles.

Meanwhile, all through the spring and early summer of 1945, the *Essex* remained at sea. In June, Admiral Tommy Sprague came aboard the *Bennington* with a new command, looking for an experienced Fighter Director Officer for his task group. So I was detached from the *Essex* and assigned to the

Bennington, which was the flagship for Admiral Sprague.

He invited me to eat in the admiral's mess, which I did, but that kindness was short-lived. The *Bennington* had a new crew and had not been seasoned in battle. The admiral wanted me to stay in the Combat Information Center, which was below the double bottoms of the ship, at all times when we were at sea.

He suggested that I instruct the ship's carpenter to build a bunk in the CIC, suitable for my twenty-four-hour-a-day duty. I didn't bother. I found a toolbox that was about five and a half feet long with a one-inch leather cover, wide enough for me to sleep on; I picked up a blanket and pillow and used it as a bed, night after night, week after week, whenever the ship was at sea, until the admiral gained confidence in the crew.

After general quarters every morning, a Filipino steward would walk down the many levels of ladders to bring me my breakfast, lunch, and dinner. I would go topside once a day, in order to bathe and shave and change clothes. Then, when the ship was not in a forward area—when we returned to port to refuel or reprovision—I would emerge from my hole and eat in the admiral's mess.

The first time I did so, after having been below for more than a week, he greeted me with, "Well, well, well. Look who's joining us—the Mole." Thereafter, he often kidded me about being "the Mole." It was a nickname well earned, although not one I would have chosen for myself.

My tour of duty on the *Bennington* turned out to be a flawless one—my unusual station notwithstanding. From the time I joined her in the summer of '45, the ship's guns never had to open fire on enemy aircraft. Our own fighter planes either intercepted them or they were shot down by the guns of the battleships, cruisers, and destroyers traveling in our task force.

I was aboard the *Bennington* when we received orders from Admiral Nimitz to stay two hundred miles from the Japanese mainland. Under no circumstances were ships or planes to move inside that distance on August 6, 1945. Our curiosity ran amok, but all we could imagine was a massive air strike. None of us understood the caution. The B-29s had been flying over us for weeks on bombing raids over Japan.

Then came the astounding news of the explosion of the atom bomb on Hiroshima. We were totally ignorant about the bomb and its destructive force. But when the second one fell on Nagasaki, it became clear that the war would soon end. Japan surrendered on the fourteenth of August and within days I was making my way to Pearl Harbor and home to Floresville, where Nellie and Kathleen were waiting. It was a giddy, joyous reunion, with one minor distraction: a mustache I had grown out of sheer boredom at sea.

After we embraced and kissed, Nellie stepped back and pointed to the shrubbery above my lip. Almost her first words were *"That* has got to go!"

ELECTIONS LOST
AND FOUND

his is about political realities before the term "hardball" was ever applied to the process of electing a United States senator. It is also about having votes stolen, and supposedly stealing them back. It is about the making of a myth.

The largest and most enduring stain on the name of Lyndon Johnson is the accusation that he won his seat in the Senate in 1948 by cheating, buying votes, and stealing the election from an unflawed Coke Stevenson. By any measurement, Stevenson is not a major figure in Texas political history. He had two claims to fame: (1) as governor, he left the state no worse off than he found it; and (2) he lost the election that sent Lyndon Johnson to the Senate. The notoriety of that race became a convenience: his critics could shrink Johnson in size by elevating Coke to a state of saintliness few who knew him could fathom.

It is not possible to draw any final conclusions about the campaign of 1948, how or why Lyndon Johnson won it, without understanding the roots of that race, which go back to 1941—or beyond.

My knowledge of what happened in those years comes from the fact that I lost the '41 election. I know who stole the votes that cost Lyndon Johnson that 1941 victory: the crowd that backed Pappy Lee O'Daniel and Coke Stevenson. I vowed that it would not happen that way again, and I kept that vow.

I had attracted my first few law clients, in Austin, when Senator Morris Sheppard died. He had been in office since 1913, and very quickly a scramble developed to succeed him. Lyndon Johnson announced he would run, and he asked me to plunge in and organize his campaign.

Governor O'Daniel declared his intention to run, and Martin Dies, a congressman known as a reactionary, but one of the best stump speakers I ever heard, joined the list. After them came the deluge: the final ballot would contain twenty-nine names, including twenty-five Democrats, two Republicans, one independent, and one Communist.

O'Daniel kicked off the race by announcing Andrew Jackson Houston—General Sam Houston's last surviving son—as the interim senator. The son of Sam was eighty-seven years old, in ill health, and a lifelong Republican. But he had a glorious name and one other strong credential: he didn't want to run in the special election, set for June 21. It was just as well. Andrew Jackson Houston went to Washington on June 2, over the objections of his family, and died while the ballots were still being counted.

It was, as everyone expected, a closely fought election. We had our headquarters in downtown Austin and I practically lived there. Charles Marsh, owner of the Austin newspaper, gave his editor Gordon Fulcher a leave of absence to head up our press section.

In the middle of the race, Johnson took ill with a very high fever and had to leave the campaign trail. He asked Everett Looney, a distinguished lawyer and a partner in Looney and Clark, to take over his speeches across the state. Gordon and I drove out to the candidate's home at 4 Happy Hollow Lane, went upstairs to his bedroom, and told him we were going to issue a press release saying that he was ill and would be admitted to the Scott and White Clinic, in Temple. At that moment, Dr. Arthur Scott was on his way to see him.

Johnson was nearly out of his head from the fever, not rational, and bellowing that we were not to put out a press release under any circumstances. I said, "Congressman, you can't be gone for a week. You can't hide for a week. You can't check into one of the finest hospitals in Texas and expect people not to notice. You can't cancel out a week's schedule, have a substitute give your speeches, and not have every newsman in the state wondering where you are.

"We are not going to lie to the press and we are not going to withhold this information from the public. We are going to tell them where you are."

He said, "Well, if you do, I'll never speak to you again. And you can get the hell out of my house."

Which is precisely what we did. Even by Johnson's later standards, this was a major confrontation. Lady Bird came down the stairs behind Gordon, tears in her eyes, saying, "You know he doesn't mean that."

I said, "Well, maybe he doesn't, but that's what he said. He told us to get the hell out and we're getting. But I still intend to put out that release." And we did.

After a week in the hospital, Johnson went home feeling better and wanting to talk. I refused. I was being about as childish as he was. Finally, Charlie Marsh came to me and said, "You have a campaign to run and you have to talk to each other whether you like it or not." After a few more days, we began to talk again about the campaign and what needed to be done. But that was one of the first serious encounters we had, and there would be others as the years passed.

The irony was that Johnson, who had started the race far behind O'Daniel, cut the lead in half in the week he was out of sight.

Meanwhile, we were building a superb organization across the state, primarily of young people, many of whom had been in school with Johnson—men like Bill Deason, Sherman Birdwell, Jesse Kellam, and his brother Claude. There were others of my vintage, young lawyers just out of college, starting in small towns, with time to spare and little to lose. Cecil Burney, Jr., Jake Pickle, Bob Strauss, Joe Kilgore, my brother Merrill, John Peace, and John Ben Shepperd fanned out across the state.

Their efforts would help elect Lyndon Johnson to the U.S. Senate in June of 1941. Or so I thought. And so the votes indicated as they began to be tallied on Saturday and into the night. Five hours after the polls closed, Johnson led by 3,000 votes. The next morning the Houston *Post* had him ahead by 5,000. Two days after the election, on June 23, a headline in the Dallas *Morning News* declared: ONLY MIRACLE CAN KEEP FDR'S ANOINTED OUT.

What happened next was less a miracle than a case of simple larceny. And I allowed it to happen through my own inexperience. We had the election won, in large part because we had the support of most of the South Texas counties which represented the so-called "controlled vote." Of course it was controlled and, to a lesser extent, still is today. But in 1941 there was no question about it. A number of those counties, from San Antonio to the Valley and up the Rio Grande, went the way their political bosses told them to go. Sometimes it was the sheriff, sometimes the county judge. Many of them were Hispanic. Historically, they delivered the vote of their workers, their farmhands and laborers, as a bloc.

When the calls came in from South Texas around midnight Saturday, election night, asking what they should do with their returns, I said, "Tell me what they are and then report them." And one by one the county leaders phoned in their actual count to the Texas Election Bureau, which they were under no obligation to do. The bureau was simply a totally owned arm of the Dallas *Morning News*, an unofficial reporting agency they had built up over the years. It was a convenience to the paper and a service to the public—but the bureau had no legal status.

By having our fieldmen provide a prompt and accurate tally, we played into the hands of the opposition. That night, in the Driskill Hotel, in Austin, Governor O'Daniel, Coke Stevenson, and James ("Pa") Ferguson met and plotted the exact number of votes they needed to snatch the election.

Ferguson led the clique of men who were behind O'Daniel and Stevenson. Pa Ferguson was a former governor of Texas, the first ever impeached, found guilty in 1917 of ten counts of taking bribes and misappropriating funds. Now he was backing these two spotless citizens who were committed to driving the politicians from the temple.

The numbers kept changing in East Texas, and Johnson's lead kept shrinking. On July 2, O'Daniel was declared the winner by 1,311 votes out of more than 600,000 cast. Pass the Biscuits Pappy was the new junior senator from Texas, and Coke Stevenson, his lieutenant governor, succeeded him in the statehouse.

A state investigation into voting irregularities, controlled by the new governor, produced a whitewash. In my mind there is no doubt that Lyndon Johnson won that election. We decided not to contest the outcome, knowing that the process would take months to complete and the regular race would be rolling around in 1942. Of course, something happened that would rearrange everyone's schedule. World War II happened.

When I went off to war, the Democratic Party in Texas was torn and in turmoil. By 1944 the split had grown wider and deeper, the enmities sharper and meaner. The anti-Roosevelt forces, mobilized by Senator O'Daniel, supported by Governor Stevenson, and financed by the more conservative element, organized what was known as the "Texas Regulars." They conspired to accomplish two goals: sabotage the national ticket and destroy, personally and politically, the reputation of Lyndon Johnson.

Although neither effort succeeded, the libels spread about

Johnson would plague him the rest of his career, would be repeated and recycled and offered as gospel by his enemies, would discomfort his friends, and would go unchallenged by some who were neutral.

As their instrument, the Regulars recruited a man named Buck Taylor to run against Johnson for Congress in 1944. Buck Taylor was your basic lobby sitter, what more genteel circles referred to as a ne'er-do-well, who hung around the hotels cadging drinks and an occasional lunch. He had no semblance of a chance to be elected, and no obvious self-worth, which gave him one advantage. He could say anything his sponsors wanted him to say without fear of being dishonored. But he could indeed leave a record for others to quote, and no fingerprints.

So Buck Taylor accused Lyndon Johnson of everything except stealing the pennies from a dead man's eyes. He accused him of owning most of the city of Austin, including a lumber-yard and apartment houses that belonged to Gordon Fulcher. What he did was throw a handful of mud at the ceiling to see how much would stick.

He tried to create the impression that Johnson was so rich and greedy that he needed to use someone like Gordon to front for him. Johnson didn't campaign, because of the war, and won easily, but at a cost. This was the beginning of the whispers about how wealthy he might be, and what the sources were.

The talk came back to haunt him in 1946, when Hardy Hollers, an Austin lawyer who had been discharged as a colonel from the Army, and a more responsible man, opposed Johnson. Hardy was the beneficiary of a lot of the trash Buck Taylor had started, and Johnson had to win a tough and nasty campaign to return to Congress. A pattern had been established that would be a part of every race he ever ran.

In an article in the *New Republic*, Stanley Blumenthal reviewed the events that led up to what became the most famous of all Senate races, the 1948 contest between Lyndon Johnson and Coke Stevenson. The Texas Regulars were thwarted in a plot to throw the Electoral College votes to the Republicans in the national election of 1944. At a second state convention, the Democrats loyal to Roosevelt produced a majority, whereupon:

"The right bolted. . . . Its platform clarified the meaning of their 'Jeffersonian' self-designation. Among its points was 'Return of state rights which have been destroyed by the Communist-controlled New Deal.' And: 'Restoration of the supremacy of the white race.' The Regulars filled the state's newspapers with full-page ads that exhorted, 'Let's keep the White in Old Glory.' And they widely distributed a poster in which Sidney Hillman, a liberal labor leader who had organized a political action committee on behalf of Roosevelt and who was Jewish and clean-shaven, was depicted with a rabbinic beard knocking down Uncle Sam.

"On election day, in Texas, Roosevelt won 822,000 votes, Dewey 191,000, the Texas Regulars 135,000. Devastated by the immensity of their defeat, the Regulars disbanded themselves as a party. Sam Rayburn . . . remarked that 'this election will prove the death knell of certain mountebank politicians in Texas,' meaning specifically O'Daniel and Stevenson. Tarnished by their association with the Regulars, neither won office again."

Roosevelt died less than a year into his fourth term. Harry Truman was in the White House when they fired the starter's gun for the '48 elections. Truman was an unpopular and to many an unattractive President. His handicaps were obvious: he was not Franklin Delano Roosevelt, lacked the rich radio voice and the elegance. The mood of the country was moving to the right.

Johnson entered the race reluctantly, and as a distinct underdog. He didn't like the omens. He was about to turn forty and believed that his prime years were behind him. Some of his younger friends, among them Jake Pickle and myself, had returned from the war and gone off on our own. Johnson talked about quitting public life, going back to teaching or running the radio station. He was good for at least one such drama a year.

By March, Johnson had still not made up his mind to run. The polls showed Stevenson's lead down to three to one. Even if he lost, Alvin Wirtz pointed out, he would gain valuable exposure for a campaign in 1954. Johnson's face froze. "In 1954? he repeated. "By 1954 I'll be forty-seven years old."

Five or six of us met with him in early May to discuss whether he should be a candidate. He kept raising objections, then declared he wasn't going to run. We agreed. That was the only way to deal with him when he was in one of those moods.

There was a chorus of voices: "Congressman, that's really the right decision. We really think you ought to step aside and let us put forward a younger man who can carry on this great tradition."

He said, "Who do you have in mind?"

Someone said, "Well, if you step aside, we're thinking of running Connally."

Johnson said, "Well, just a minute. Let me think about this a little bit." He announced his candidacy the next morning. My guess is that he had already made up his mind, but he wanted to be persuaded.

By the June filing deadline, ten candidates had announced for the Senate race and Pappy O'Daniel was not among them. It was generally agreed that Coke Stevenson, the slow-moving, slow-talking, pipe-smoking former governor, was the man to beat. He was sixty-one. The author John Gunther, doing the research for his 1947 book, *Inside U.S.A.*, had asked Coke to recall his greatest decision. "Never had any," he said.

All during the war, Stevenson had the luxury of presiding over a state where there was no money to spend, little to spend it on if you had any, and a public that had no interest either way. Everyone was focused on the war, on young men leaving home and some not returning, and young women taking jobs in factories or themselves serving in the armed forces, here and overseas.

So few demands were made on the state, and no taxes were raised, all to the benefit of Coke's reputation as an advocate of sound, frugal government. Of course, to his credit, he believed in that philosophy. He was from the Hill Country, around Junction, rough land that produced hardworking people.

Stevenson maintained his lead, but the first statewide polls showed the margin now at two to one. It is unclear whether Coke's lead would have been greater or smaller if he had not previously fired the president of the University of Texas, who had expressed his support for academic freedom, and if Coke's racist views were not so strongly held that he felt no need to conceal them.

Stevenson campaigned in what had been the traditional way. He shook a lot of hands, spoke to crowds on the courthouse steps in various towns, and posed for photographs smoking his pipe and looking reflective. Johnson, running like the underdog he was, correctly sensed that the times were changing. He rented a helicopter and dropped out of the sky in virtually every county in the state, drawing attention and throngs of curious voters with each stop. Anyone who ever questioned the physical courage of Lyndon Johnson should have talked to the pilot of his helicopter, an aircraft not then regarded as the transportation of choice by those who prized their safety.

Johnson was then giving a classic demonstration of his boundless energy, his drive and persistence. He could charm a handkerchief out of a silkworm if he wanted, but he knew, and so did everyone around him, that he was gambling his political future on this race.

And damned if we didn't have a blowup in circumstances almost identical to those in the campaign of '41. Alvin Wirtz had all but predicted it. Lyndon thought he was going to lose, and the idea depressed him, and when he was depressed he had a way of taking ill. I hadn't realized it, but Wirtz was right. There had been the appendectomy at the end of his first race for Congress, and then pneumonia in 1941.

Sure enough, he became ill again—in the Adolphus Hotel, in Dallas—and had to cancel a speech in Wichita Falls. He was contorted with pain, and his symptoms seemed to indicate an attack of kidney stones. Warren Woodward was traveling with him as an aide, and we arranged to have him flown to the Mayo Clinic in Rochester, Minnesota.

These were not everyday arrangements. His pilot was to be Jacqueline Cochran, the famous aviatrix, whose husband, Floyd Odlum, was head of the Atlas Corporation in New York and a friend of Johnson's. Jackie Cochran was flying down to Dallas in their company plane.

Again he wanted no word disclosed about his condition. Bracing myself for the storm I knew was coming, I said, "Congressman, there is no way you can have one of the most famous fliers in the world swoop down here in a plane, pick you up and fly you to Rochester to the Mayo Clinic, and not have the press find out about it. We can't do that. We have got to put out a release."

"If you do," he threatened, "I'll withdraw from the race."

I said, "Well, you better get ready to withdraw."

"Dammit," he said, "why can't you help me instead of always working against me?" That was one of his favorite techniques. I don't believe anybody had yet coined the phrase "guilt trips."

I called Woodward and said, "Woody, here we go again. He's sick and he doesn't know what he's saying. You get hold of the supervising operator at the hotel and have all the calls, incoming and outgoing, transferred to you. Just don't let him talk to anybody except through you. He's threatening to withdraw from the race and we've got to put out this release."

Jackie Cochran flew Johnson to the Mayo Clinic, where he passed the kidney stones after several days of intense pain. When he flew back to Texas and was feeling better, he started calling headquarters and I wouldn't talk to him. So for two crucial weeks of a race so close it would be decided by 87 votes, the candidate and his campaign manager communicated through third parties.

The best indication that the race was tightening came when Stevenson flew to Washington, having decided that he needed to get a flavor of national politics. He had never been involved in a national race, and knew nothing about national issues or foreign policy. So his managers scheduled a trip to Washington, where he would be briefed on national affairs, on the budget, foreign relations, and more.

Johnson's vote in favor of the Taft-Hartley Act led labor to oppose him for years to come, including 1960 at the Democratic Convention. But it may have won the election for him in 1948. Coke Stevenson, although opposed to unions in principle, avoided taking a stand.

It was, in truth, a complicated piece of work. Although most unions had agreed not to strike during the war, once the hostilities ended, there were frequent walkouts affecting steel, coal, and the railroads, among others. The Taft-Hartley bill allowed people to work without having to join a union; it was a political response to so much unrest.

While Stevenson was in Washington, Marshall McNeil, a very tough reporter for the Scripps-Howard newspapers, decided to interview him. Stevenson had been avoiding the press. McNeil tracked him down to the men's room at his hotel, and asked him where he stood on the Taft-Hartley bill.

Lamely, Coke answered that he left his notes back in Texas, "and I'm not in a position to comment on that." The Scripps-Howard papers had a field day with McNeil's story, and the fact that Stevenson couldn't give a position on one of the vital issues of the day because he didn't bring his notes.

Of course, Johnson used it against him. On Election Day, all of our indicators told us the vote was going to be too close to call. We wound up the campaign in San Antonio, going from precinct to precinct largely in the Hispanic and black neighborhoods. I had planned on driving back to Austin, but the candidate wanted company, and the two of us spent the night in Johnson City.

I was confident and told him I thought we were going to win. He was pessimistic: "No, I think we've lost it."

I made a prediction. "It's going to be the reversal of 1941,"

I said. "You carried the big cities and lost the election in the rural areas. The people who cost you the election in 1941—if indeed you lost it—will be the very ones who elect you this time. You are going to win it with the rural vote."

He gave me a long, probing look and said, "Well, I hope you know what the hell you're talking about." We went to sleep, and the next morning drove into Austin.

All that day I felt my spirits soar. I could not think of a detail we had overlooked. A very effective organization had been put in place, reaching into every one of the state's 254 counties. We were keeping up with developments on an almost hourly basis. I had a cadre of young lawyers all over Texas, monitoring the returns, watching the polls, prepared to call us immediately as the tabulations were made. I would keep a running tally.

And most crucial of all, contrary to what happened in 1941, I had instructed all our precinct leaders in South Texas that we needed every legitimate vote they could cast: to run the car pools, to do whatever they had to do to get their people to the polls. Then we emphasized a final point: they were *not* to call in their precise voting totals to the Texas Election Bureau. They were to understate their returns. We had been bitten once. It would not happen again.

I knew what the exact totals were, and I knew the difference would be razor thin. This procedure, I well understood, was sure to give rise to charges that votes had been changed, the ballot boxes stuffed.

At midnight on Saturday, August 28, the Texas Election Bureau's unofficial returns gave Stevenson a lead of 1,894 votes. At 3:30 the next afternoon, the lead was down to 315 votes, and by midnight Sunday, Johnson had moved ahead by 693 votes out of nearly a million cast.

At one point, I called a fellow in West Texas and asked what the results were. He said, "I don't know. We don't have the box. Someone took it home."

I said, "Well, go get it and call me with the totals."

He said, "My God, he lives forty miles from here."

"I don't care if it's a hundred and forty miles from there. Go get that box."

He jumped into his car about ten that night, drove the eighty-mile round trip, and brought in the box.

In the end, as any political junkie will tell you, Johnson won the disputed race by 87 votes, inspiring a nickname he initially enjoyed but came to detest, "Landslide Lyndon." My figures showed, and I always believed, that he won by 376 votes.

What made the story a great deal more colorful were the reports out of Jim Wells County that 203 signatures, all for Johnson, showed up on the voting list for Box 13, all in a different-colored ink (blue) from the names preceding it, and all in alphabetical order.

Now, this is not to say that no illegal votes were cast in Duval County, or Jim Wells County, or dozens of others. In point of fact, the recounts revealed that there were irregularities in twenty-six counties, fourteen of which heavily favored Coke Stevenson.

There may have been invalid votes that were cast for Lyndon Johnson. But they were not bought and they were not stolen.

In April of 1948, Warren Woodward had been present when George Parr offered Johnson his support in the Driscoll Hotel in Corpus Christi. The votes Parr controlled in South Texas had in the past gone to Coke Stevenson.

But Parr was disenchanted with Stevenson, who he felt had reneged on a promise to appoint Phil Kazen, of Laredo, as district attorney. When Parr said he was for him, recalled Woodward, Johnson asked, "What do I do next?"

"You don't do anything," replied Parr. "When I say I'll support you, I will." No cash changed hands, no promises were made, no quid pro quo. In states all over the land, where machine politics once flourished, this was the way it worked. In Tammany Hall or Chicago or Philadelphia or Boston.

The controlled votes were not just in Box 13 in Jim Wells County, where the last votes came in that decided the 1948 election. The townspeople always had done what George Parr, the local political boss, known as "the Duke of Duval," told them to do. If his candidate needed 4,000 votes, he marched 4,000 of them to the polls. But George was a sportsman. He didn't round up any more votes than were actually needed.

There were controlled votes all up and down the Rio Grande River. Johnson lost one precinct by nearly a shutout, 3,200 votes to less than a hundred.

The 1948 election marked the end of an era in Texas politics, politics that exists today, unchanged, only in parts of Mexico. But there is a rather quaint footnote to this piece of history.

Around the turn of the century, there was a man who was the sheriff of Duval County named Buck Buckley. His son graduated from the University of Texas, and his daughter became the official translator for the state land office, translating Spanish documents into English. She worked there for forty years. The son went to Mexico, was one of the founders of the oil fields in Tampico, and later a pioneer in developing the Venezuelan oil fields. Eventually, he moved his family to New York and then Virginia.

The sheriff of Duval County was a Democrat, but his grandsons became rather prominent in conservative political and literary circles—William F. Buckley and former New York Senator James Buckley.

It must have been reassuring to the Buckleys to know their family was part of a tradition that helped send Lyndon Baines Johnson to the United States Senate in 1948, in an election that was truly incredible.

There has been so much pure drivel about the Senate election of '48 that it has driven out the impure drivel. I can't say with absolute certainty who tampered with what—no one can. But I can offer a theory or two at least as credible as those that have been so gladly accepted.

There is a recurring story about Johnson proudly showing

off a photograph of himself and a few of his friends standing around the hood of a Ford, on which sat a cigar box with the number "13" written on it. I wonder how anyone could have taken the picture seriously. They didn't collect votes in cigar boxes, not even in Jim Wells County, and the missing box—not uncommon after an election—never had a number on it. None of the boxes did.

As for the 203 signatures in alphabetical order, and in different-colored ink from those that preceded them, it was clearly an affront against democracy. But, in fact, there were still state poll taxes in 1948, and George Parr paid them for his farm workers. The lists were alphabetical. I doubt that he marched them through the voting hall in any particular order. Nor could many of them, if any, sign their own names. A clerk, one of Parr's men, followed the list in front of him.

As for the voters, I doubt if they knew who was the beneficiary of their ballots. Nor did they know in 1941, when they cast them for Pappy Lee O'Daniel.

As far back as the 1920s, there was an investigation by the state senate into irregularities in Duval County, where Archie Parr, George's father, exercised his feudal control. A random number of voters were brought in to testify and were put on the witness stand under oath.

One was asked if he had voted in the election.

"Sí, sí, señor."

"Did you vote for a President?"

"Sí, sí, señor."

"Well, who did you vote for?"

"Señor Archie Parr."

"Did you vote for a governor?"

"Sí, sí, señor."

"Who did you vote for?"

"Señor Archie Parr."

"And who did you vote for as state senator?"

"Señor Archie Parr."

Everyone gave the same statement; all said they were voting

for Archie Parr. That broke up the hearings, and everyone went home. It may not be the example you would offer a civics class about honest government and democracy in action. But it was a part of the system in Texas. What it proves is mighty little, except that Lyndon Johnson didn't steal that election. Nor did anyone steal it on his behalf.

There was at least one other interested party who knew there had been no theft. His name was Coke Stevenson, and in the late 1970s, some thirty years after the election, he said as much to Joe Frantz, the University of Texas historian.

"I'd always had George Parr in my pocket," Joe quoted Coke as saying. "But George had been after me to name a rascal as state judge, and I kept telling him: 'The guy's no good, he'll land us both in jail.' To which George said, 'All right, if you don't name him, you'll be sorry.' And by God, I was sorry!"

The inference was clear to Joe Frantz, who wrote about the interview years later: "LBJ did not steal the election in Duval County, Parr gave it away out of spite."

When we returned to what Nellie and I both hoped would be a normal life in Austin, after the Senate race, I loved to attend the University of Texas football games. Johnson never cared a lick for football, or any sport, but when he was in town he called every Saturday morning. One way or another, he always had good tickets and invited us to the games.

Nellie and I went a number of times, but we wouldn't watch the game. That is, we tried. You would concentrate on what was happening on the field, and Johnson would be pounding your ear, talking about politics. It drove me batty. It got to a point where, on Saturday morning, I left the house early so he couldn't locate me. Nellie and I would buy our own tickets and go ahead to the stadium.

It was the same scene in Washington during the summer. When he was in the Senate, he learned that Senator Dick Russell, of Georgia, had a passion for baseball. He was from Ty

Cobb country. I doubt that Lyndon Johnson had been to a baseball game in his life until he heard that Dick Russell enjoyed the sport. He would get Washington Senators' tickets and the three of us started going to the ballpark. And before long, Russell began avoiding him because he was exactly the same as he was at a football game. He just wouldn't let you watch the action.

He was single-minded in his pursuit of politics. Everything else was secondary. Everything. He loved Lady Bird and he loved his daughters, but his time and energy were devoted to politics.

Through it all, there was a genuine and permanent affection between us. It was never father-and-son, more often he treated me as one would a bright, headstrong younger brother. Even after I left Washington, in 1949, if I went back on business, he would insist that I go with him to his meetings. One day, he had a luncheon in a little private room he kept for the use of the senior members of the Senate. There were about twelve of us, including myself and Skeeter Johnson, the secretary of the Senate. The other guests included Alben Barkley, Stuart Symington, Walter George, Richard Russell, George Smathers, and Carl Hayden, who had represented Arizona from the time it joined the Union. He had been a sheriff of the territory before it was a state. They all got to reminiscing and talking about the old days, and the colorful characters, and they settled on the topic of Huey Long, the Louisiana populist known as "the Kingfish."

Alben Barkley was saying that he would never forget in 1932, when the Bonus Marchers were advancing on Washington, how he and some others were in the cloakroom when Huey Long came rushing in. His hair was askew and his eyes were wild as he burst through the swinging doors in the cloakroom. He said, "Fellows, there's a mob in the streets. I'm trying to make up my mind whether to stay with you and defend this Capitol, or go out there and lead them against you."

Hayden said, "I think he meant it as a joke, but none of us

was ever quite sure because Huey was quite capable of doing either one."

How Johnson operated backstage was never more skillfully shown than in the events that led to the fall of Senator Joseph McCarthy, whose name in the 1950s became a synonym for witch hunts. Nor did Lyndon receive the credit he deserved for exposing McCarthy as the dangerous knave he truly was.

When Eisenhower swept a Republican Congress into power with him, in 1952, a vacancy was created for minority leader of the House, a position formerly held by Wayne McFarland, of Arizona. He lost his seat to Barry Goldwater.

The Southern Democrats swarmed to Johnson the moment they learned that Dick Russell didn't want the job and Hubert Humphrey did. Humphrey had alienated the South by making an impassioned civil rights speech in 1948 at the national convention, and later by calling Harry Byrd, of Virginia, a son of a bitch.

Johnson won easily, as the liberals put up a token candidate, a respected but obscure Midwesterner named Jim Murray. Later, Humphrey recalled being invited to the office of the new leader and being told: "Let me tell you something. You and I can get along fine. I know we don't agree on a number of things, but at least we can get along. You're an open-minded man. Now, who do you want on the policy committee?"

When Humphrey said "We ought to put Jim Murray on there," Johnson nodded. "All right," he said. "That's a damned-fool selection, but if you want him go ahead."

Humphrey asked, "Why is it a damned-fool selection?"

"He's too old," replied Johnson. "He's going to go along with me on everything I want. You know that. You ought to pick somebody who if you want to have somebody stand up and fight with the leader will do it."

Until Johnson took over, no one had known what to do

with the policy committee, a toothless group given to academic thinking. Johnson used it to shape legislation and work out compromises. He applied the "unanimous consent" rule, which required a bill to be endorsed by all the members (or, at least, 90 percent of them). In his opinion, a minority party should not bring bills onto the Senate floor that it was not solidly behind. He overcame the opposition of such senators as Herbert Lehman and Paul Douglas and Albert Gore, whose bills were popular back home and who wanted to force the Republicans to go on record against them.

But Johnson was using the Eisenhower years to restore the Democratic Party, and he believed there was more mileage to be gained by the appearance of unity, even when there was none. Seeking a consensus was not for him a negative act. It was the art of finding the most that you could get a majority to support. He saw little benefit in taking on a popular President, a war hero, and getting bloodied in losing skirmishes in the Senate.

In the political game of chess, Johnson made a brilliant move in 1953 when the Republicans, some of whom had waited eight years to control Congress, saw an opportunity to punish the Democrats for "selling out" to the Soviets at Yalta and Potsdam. What had been frequently overlooked was the role Eisenhower had played in these agreements as the Allied Supreme Commander. He was, not unnaturally, in some discomfort over the calls by Robert Taft, who was seriously ill, for a resolution that strongly suggested that these treaties might be legally invalid. Always there was the implication that the country had been betrayed.

The White House offered instead a resolution that did little more than object to Soviet enslavement of Eastern Europe. Johnson came down hard on the side of Ike, pleasing Democrats on the left, the supporters of Yalta and Potsdam, and at the same time aligning the Democrats with the President against the Taft conservatives. He would dare not treat this as a partisan issue, said Lyndon, and "jeopardize the President's prestige before the country and the world."

The death of Joseph Stalin in March, and the lingering illness that sidelined Taft, allowed the matter to fade from public view. But Johnson had won recognition in a new public role: as defender of the President against the majority of his own party.

A climate had been established. Senator Joseph McCarthy, of Wisconsin, would begin to monopolize the political news as did no other figure of that time. He made anti-Communism his personal crusade, and his motives and his methods were not easily questioned. For a long time, no one did. Public sentiment was with him, and the money cascaded into his office. Some of his backers were very rich, and many were fanatical. In the most hawkish states, Texas included, it wasn't prudent to criticize him. Ordinary people liked what they were hearing. McCarthy warned that the Communist conspiracy was all around us. He was going to get the Reds out of the State Department, and off the college faculties.

There is no way to overstate the danger of McCarthy. He had the power to inflame people, to divide them, to set neighbor spying upon neighbor. Among his supporters, he created a combination of rapture and hysteria, as Hitler had done in his ascent in Germany. McCarthy's weapons were words, not force. He followed his imagination, not a plan. His influence was frightening because he was a man without discipline, a man whose ways were casual and reckless.

Where McCarthy's ambitions were headed, no one could be certain. It may not have been ideology that even drove him; he was an arsonist whose satisfaction was in the spreading of the flames.

I am not certain that these thoughts were my thoughts at the time. I believed, as Lyndon Johnson believed, that Joe McCarthy would be the engineer of his own defeat. As a professional, I was impressed with how far he had come, and how quickly. I was practicing law in the early 1950s, and by 1954 I was involved in the extensive holdings of Sid Richardson and his nephew Perry Bass, primarily oil and gas but including real estate and ranching. I was a frequent visitor to Washington during the decade in connection with their varied interests.

Johnson was pressed from several directions to cut down McCarthy. One who pleaded with him was the author William S. White, who feared that if he was left unchecked, McCarthy would leave our civil liberties in ruins. In Merle Miller's oral biography *Lyndon* and in tapes made for the LBJ library, White revealed Johnson's explanation of why he intended to wait. It had everything to do with political logic.

"If I commit the Democratic Party to the destruction of McCarthy," he said, ". . . first of all, in the present atmosphere of the Senate we will all lose and he will win. Then he'll be more powerful than ever. At this juncture I'm not about to commit the Democratic Party to a high school debate on the subject 'Resolved, that Communism is good for the United States,' with my party taking the affirmative."

Added White: "Now, later on, Johnson did indeed go after him and he got him in the sense that he brought about the creation of the select committee that investigated McCarthy. But he waited until the atmosphere was right."

No one in my memory was more addicted to reading the political weather than Johnson. In Vietnam he read it wrong. Until then his record was almost uncanny. He considered himself gifted, in an almost mystic way, at understanding the nature of people. The truth is, he worked at it.

McCarthy, as a type, may have confused Johnson. At least, this was the early view among Lyndon's Texas circle. We had all dealt with the classic Southern demagogue; he might be detestable, but you could make a deal with him. But McCarthy was not simply a Northern version of the Southern demagogue. There were no deals to be made with him. He had no goals. He wanted power, of course, but what kind and for what means no one could be sure. Those who analyzed him closely doubted that he had a plan, that he seriously believed he might someday sit in the White House.

For two years after McCarthy had found his issue, no one

moved against him. He began waving around his famous list of 205 or 206 "known Communists" still working in the State Department, and no one openly challenged him. Not Lyndon Johnson. Not Eisenhower. Not his logical adversaries in the Senate. They were not frozen by fear, although you couldn't blame Joe for thinking so. There was a reluctance in the Senate, then and now, to attack even the worst among them. According to the code, if the people of a state send to the Senate a sorry lump, that was and is regarded as their business.

The Democrats, and others, were waiting for a signal from Lyndon, who was never more liked or respected or feared than when he was selling behind the scenes. The guile, the intensity, the cajoling that were part of his salesmanship did not endear him to the voters, and the harder he tried the more they resisted him.

Still, Johnson was a worthy opponent for McCarthy, whose threat he understood. "If you're going to kill a snake with a hoe," Miller quoted him as telling Humphrey, "you have to get it with one blow at the head." Sons of farmers learn that lesson quickly.

The House minority leader did not shape the events that brought down McCarthy, but he helped herd the cattle into the pen. In fairly rapid order: McCarthy became chairman of the permanent subcommittee on investigations in 1952. He hired as his chief counsel a sleepy-eyed prodigy of twenty-six named Roy Cohn. His legal staff briefly included Robert Kennedy, then twenty-seven.

McCarthy seemed to have carte blanche so long as his targets were primarily the men who had been around Harry Truman and his Secretary of State, Dean Acheson. Then, as he grew more arrogant and reckless, he attacked the friends of Senators Harry Byrd and Carl Hayden. Even more stunning, he questioned the loyalty of General George Marshall, a hero of the victory in Europe, a postwar statesman, and a man Dwight Eisenhower held in special esteem. Then, he literally picked a fight with the U.S. Army. He accused General Ralph W.

Zwicker, who had led one of the landings on Normandy Beach, of promoting a suspected Communist and concealing acts of espionage and subversion. Coincidentally, he accused the Army of neglecting and misusing a dear friend of Roy Cohn's, and one of McCarthy's former staff members, G. David Schine. An Army spokesman countered that McCarthy had sought favored treatment for Schine.

It sounds now like bad satire, but these were explosive times and one headline begat another in 1954. The country was fascinated, and the charges and countercharges led to what became known as the Army-McCarthy hearings, and to one of the dramatic, early demonstrations of the coming power of television.

For Johnson, the moment he needed, and predicted, had arrived. The weather had changed. He concluded that television coverage was essential to any effort that would resolve the Joe McCarthy problem. Both NBC and CBS had refused to consider the idea of broadcasting the hearings in their entirety. Johnson then sent Senator John McClellan, of Arkansas, one of the three Democrats on McCarthy's subcommittee, to make an appeal to the American Broadcasting Company, known then—and until the success of something called Monday Night Football—as "the third network." ABC agreed to televise the hearings every day, all day, as long as they lasted.

No one really knew what to expect. People who were accustomed to being put to sleep by school board meetings were in for an electric shock. But going in, the Democrats had the better draw; they were on the Army's side. One other factor was critical. If nothing else, Lyndon Johnson understood that if a man was a snake, that would come through the TV camera as it zeroes in on him day after day.

And it came to pass. The hearings were held in the Senate Caucus Room. It was riveting drama, the best and most dramatic use of the television medium up to that time. McCarthy played to the audience sitting in living rooms across America. He interrupted constantly—his use of the phrase "point of order" became a comic punch line in the months ahead. He mugged, he objected, he trotted out fake photographs and wild new allegations directed at people whose names no one recognized.

The hearings continued into June of 1954, and everyone knew Joe McCarthy was finished when he earned the open contempt of the Army's chief counsel, an elderly and proper Boston lawyer named Joseph Welch. McCarthy dropped into the record a reference to a young lawyer in Welch's office who had once belonged to an organization whose name appeared on one of the Senator's famous lists. Welch had disclosed this connection to McCarthy, along with the fact that he had excluded the young man from the Army's legal team so as to spare him any embarrassment.

McCarthy was left naked after Welch spoke the words that have become among the most memorable in television lore: ". . . Have you no decency, sir? At long last, have you left no sense of decency?"

The applause that greeted that anguished question was reflected in the reactions around the country. A Senate committee was appointed to recommend a punishment of McCarthy, if any. There were three members from each party and all six were conservatives. Johnson knew that if he seated even one liberal, he would invite cries of pinko, Commie-sympathizer, kangaroo court. In the end, the Senate passed a resolution to condemn him, allowing McCarthy to avoid the harsher penalty of censure.

In time, "McCarthyism" would become a political deadly term. Joe himself never recovered from the outcome of the hearings and the Senate vote, and his weight and drinking problems lurched out of control. Still, the vote was a difficult one for several of the senators, especially the Southerners.

The Democrats took back the Senate in the mid-term elections of 1954, by forty-eight seats to forty-seven. Lyndon Johnson became the youngest majority leader in Senate history.

Around that time, it had become the fashion to refer to

Johnson as the "second most powerful man" in Washington, giving Eisenhower a reasonable benefit of the doubt. Historians would decide many years later that Ike, in his diaries and correspondence, revealed himself as a far more forceful President than was believed at the time. Yet the indications were few that he enjoyed the job.

He disliked the company of politicians, went out of his way to avoid controversy, didn't miss many days of golf. Nor was the image of the benevolent "Uncle Ike" a true one. His opinions of people were often pithy and well aimed; he kept his philosophical side hidden, but his ideas have worn well. His distaste for the tedium of governing, and Johnson's talent for compromise, made Eisenhower's years relatively smooth. A virtual partnership existed between them. Johnson decided who was to serve on which committees, and who would not. He decided when a bill should come to the floor and, once on the floor, when it should come up for a vote. He decided which of the President's bills the Democrats should back, and which to oppose, and when a stand was worth risking defeat.

To press his agenda, Johnson could call on a reliable circle of people for advice, help, and, whenever possible, their votes. Although mostly Democrats, the network included an influential Republican or two, such as Styles Bridges, of New Hampshire. There was the conservative Robert Kerr; the liberals Hubert Humphrey and Wayne Morse; and the South's man of distinction, Richard Russell.

When necessary, he would appeal to the outsider, to the sentinels, with a special disposition toward those in the media. Most of my adult life, I have been asked to explain what constituted "the Johnson treatment." I am partial to a description given by Ben Bradlee, once a reporter for *Newsweek*, who worked his way up to editor in chief of the *Washington Post:* "When Johnson wanted to persuade you of something, when you got the 'Johnson treatment,' you really felt as if a St. Bernard had licked your face for an hour, had pawed you all over.

"When he was in the Senate, especially as majority leader,

he never just shook hands with you. One hand was shaking your hand: the other hand was always someplace else, exploring you.

"And of course he was a great actor, bar none, the greatest. He would be feeling up Katharine Graham and bumping Meg Greenfield on the boobs. And at the same time he'd be trying to persuade you of something, even if you knew it was not so. And there was just the trace of a little smile on his face."

Once, when Lyndon needed the vote, and Hubert Humphrey's plane from Minnesota was stuck in the traffic pattern over Washington, Johnson called the control tower at National Airport and told them to get Humphrey's plane on the ground. They did, and a car was waiting to rush him to the Senate to cast his vote.

For the first time, Johnson was being talked about by totally impartial observers as a potential candidate for the Presidency. But a toll had been taken. In my talks with him, in late June, he complained of feeling constantly tired, so much so that he had decided to do the unthinkable: take a vacation. He was going to spend the Fourth of July weekend at the estate of George and Herman Brown, near Middleburg, Virginia.

The drive took only two hours, and not long after he left his office, on July 2, he began to have difficulty breathing. By the time he reached the estate, he felt nauseated, but insisted it was only indigestion. Finally, over his objections, a doctor was called and his symptoms confirmed—he had suffered a heart attack. Hours after he felt the first severe pains, he allowed himself to be admitted to Bethesda Naval Hospital. He was in shock when they whisked him into the cardiac care section. The doctors rated his chances of surviving at fifty-fifty.

As soon as I heard from Lady Bird, I could guess what had happened. He had tried to ignore the heart attack because the *Washington Post* was about to run a story on his Presidential prospects. His vanity, if not his ambition, nearly killed him.

By the first week in August, he was discharged from the hospital and on his way to a remarkable recovery. In the meantime, he had enjoyed the kind of extravagant praise often paid to people we think are about to die. Senator Lehman, of New York, described him as "beloved by his colleagues."

Soon the attack and any attendant doubts were behind him. That fall, he was at his ranch when Joe Kennedy phoned to tell him that he and his son Senator Kennedy wanted to support Johnson for President in 1956. He was asking Lyndon's permission to set the wheels in motion. Johnson replied that he thought it would be a mistake for him to be a candidate. He did not volunteer a reason, although there were several, including his firm belief that Eisenhower would run for re-election despite health problems of his own.

The conversation was the kind he loved, providing him with endless hours of speculation. Joe Kennedy hung up, no doubt wondering how sincere was the denial. Lyndon hung up wondering what Joe Kennedy's real motive had been.

The Democratic Convention opened in Chicago in August of 1956, with Adlai Stevenson primed to accept the nomination after a brief battle with Estes Kefauver. Johnson disliked Kefauver, a troublesome man who drank too much and was suspected of accepting bribes. As a final indictment, he was an inattentive senator and a loner. For a long while, Johnson was puzzled by Kefauver's popularity. He had gained fame as chairman of an anti-racketeering committee, and was fond of posing for pictures wearing a coonskin Davy Crockett cap. But Kefauver was a rare bird in American politics. His ambition really was to be Vice President.

On the morning the convention opened, Johnson called a press conference to announce he was a candidate for President and John Connally was his campaign manager. It was a classic Johnsonian gesture and, on the surface, made no sense to anyone, myself included. But Johnson hoped to influence the convention, and he needed to be more than just another favorite son.

We were nearing the end of that era when politicians believed in spontaneous forces, that delegates could be stampeded,

in the eleventh-hour draft, in a deadlocked convention turning
to a compromise candidate. Most of us—in the Texas delegation, at least—hoped that something of this sort would happen.
The party was reluctant to again nominate the literate Stevenson. Truman had tried to block him by supporting Averell
Harriman. But we all knew the odds.

The junior senator from Massachusetts, John Kennedy,
gave the nominating speech for Stevenson. I nominated Lyndon
Johnson, and the rousing demonstration that followed made the
delegates, and television commentators, wonder if they had
missed something. The show was Sam Rayburn's doing. Almost
every state paraded under an LBJ banner; whether Johnson won
or lost, Sam Rayburn would still be speaker of the House, and
no one wanted to offend Mister Sam.

Stevenson won easily on the first ballot. The real contest
was for second place, between Kennedy and Kefauver. For the
first time in history, Stevenson opened the nomination to the
delegates. Johnson quickly expressed his support for Kennedy.
Sam Rayburn praised "all the fine young men" in the party, but
clearly put a hand on Kennedy.

Then Johnson arranged for a delegate from the Valley, a
Mexican-American, to make a moving speech on Kennedy's
behalf—and he had Texas. Johnson enjoyed the role of king-
maker. He also honestly liked the gangly Ivy Leaguer and
thought he might be useful to him in the battles ahead.

They might have brought it off if Johnson had been able to
swing the votes held by Raymond Gary, the governor of Oklahoma. But Gary was opposed to Kennedy, who had voted
against the farm bill. Kefauver was nominated and went on to be
buried, with Stevenson, by the Republican ticket of Eisenhower
and Nixon.

Adlai became the kind of martyr figure Democrats love, the
man too good to win. Kefauver just dropped through the trap-
door reserved for politicians who are no longer interesting.

In politics, one can drive oneself mad by wondering how

the course of history might have been changed if this or that had happened. But the fact is, if Johnson's effort had succeeded, John F. Kennedy would have been the running mate of Adlai Stevenson in 1956. And he would have been tarnished as just another defeated Vice-Presidential candidate.

RISKY BUSINESS

fter Eisenhower was elected and the Korean War ended, there was a tendency to believe that this country just sort of dozed through the rest of the 1950s. Ike was popular, many said, because the people liked a President who didn't meddle in the affairs of government.

But time would prove that he was wiser than we thought. In his farewell address, Ike left us with two warnings: not to let American troops get bogged down in a ground war in Asia, and to beware of the influence of the military-industrial complex. We disregarded both at great cost.

We have a national habit of picking a decade and selling it back to ourselves as the good old days. We wallowed in the nostalgia of the '50s longer than any other era, and a lot of that had to do with the fact that those were boom years and we thought they would never end.

A million young men went to college on the G.I. Bill, and it was a fine time to start a small business or a career or a family. No one thought less of you for trying to build a net worth before setting out to save the world.

I was among the many in that position after the war. I had spent four years with Lyndon Johnson and over four in the

Navy. Running a campaign every four years didn't qualify as steady work. I had seen the desperation that comes with being a man of modest means in politics, the despair of losing and knowing that everything you have done or thought or believed in, or worked for the past two years or so, had been wasted. I was therefore still able to contain any political ambition I might have had.

I turned down three offers in New York. One was the powerful law firm in which Edwin Weisl, Sr., was a senior partner. The others were with the Hearst Corporation in publishing and with Lehman Brothers in the investment banking business. This may put a dent in the image of the overconfident John Connally, but part of the reason was my feeling of inadequacy and insecurity about competing in the New York environment. I knew my limitations, and I lacked experience in those circles.

However, the stronger factor was my desire to remain in Texas. I did not want to uproot my young family from a state and an area and a people that I knew, understood, and loved.

I had left Washington to join the Austin law firm of Alvin J. Wirtz, one of LBJ's original political advisers. When Wirtz died of a heart attack in October of 1951, at a University of Texas football game, I lost a friend and a mentor. I had to decide whether to stay with the firm or make a move. I made one that would have a profound influence on my life and career.

The word "legendary" takes a fearful pounding when people write or talk about Texas oilmen. But Sid Richardson was the genuine article, a colorful, fearless, and eccentric Texas wildcatter, whose discoveries led to one of the country's great family fortunes. Richardson called and asked me not to make a decision until we had talked.

He flew me from Austin to Fort Worth in his private plane, and talked far into the night about my goals and his operations. Then he offered me a job as bluntly as one can be offered. "I can hire good lawyers and good engineers and good geologists," he said, "but it's hard to hire good common sense. I'm not going to let you set up any fancy law firm. But I'll pay you twenty-five thousand dollars a year, enough so Nellie and the kids won't go hungry, and I'll put you in the way to make some money."

I accepted on the spot, with this condition: we agreed that we would give it a try and see how we both felt. If he didn't like it, he could let me go in the morning. If I didn't like it, I could leave in the afternoon.

We moved to Fort Worth in 1952, and rented a house our first year there. In the meantime, Perry Bass, Sid's nephew and partner in all of his investments, had built a new home and sold his old one, at 53 Westover Terrace, to a lady who never moved into it. We bought the house from her.

I spent nine extraordinary years working for Sid Richardson and Perry Bass, and through them had frequent, if casual, contact with the dominant figure of American intrigue: J. Edgar Hoover. J. Edgar was a guest every summer at the Del Mar Turf Club, the racetrack Richardson owned with Clint Murchison at La Jolla, California. Hoover had his own bungalow and was always comped. He tried to avoid the mobsters who also enjoyed their afternoons of horse racing, but a few of them he got along with quite well.

There is a story, and I believe it to be true, about a small-time gambler named Swifty Morgan, who once spotted Hoover in a restaurant and tried to sell him a hot gold watch. Hoover offered him a hundred dollars. Morgan looked aggrieved. "A hundred dollars!" he objected. "Hell, the insurance reward is worth more than that." Damon Runyon based his character the Lemon Drop Kid, in *Guys and Dolls,* on Swifty Morgan.

Sid Richardson and Clint Murchison, Sr., were two of a kind, part of a unique and rugged band of individuals who grew up in and around Athens, Texas, east of Dallas. There were the Wynne boys, Angus and Toddie Lee. Amon Carter came to Fort Worth to strike oil and became a newspaper baron. Major J. R. Parten, from Madisonville, supervised the Big Inch pipeline that fed an ocean of vital Texas oil to the East Coast during World War II.

But Sid and Clint were the two who stuck together, and always competed and tried to one-up each other, the way real friends do.

Clint was the son of the town banker. He was an entrepreneur in a time when ordinary people were still trying to figure out what a tycoon was. He bought cheap and didn't always stay long, but he eventually owned and operated over two hundred companies, ranging from the Daisy Air Rifle to *Field and Stream* magazine. His sons John Dabney and Clint, Jr., were quite young when their mother died, and he didn't remarry until the two boys were educated and grown. Father and sons were private men, publicity shy, and the Murchison name wasn't widely known until Clint, Jr., became the owner of the Dallas Cowboys in 1960.

Sid Richardson and Clint Murchison shared the same values and the same rigid work ethic, but Sid was more likely to enjoy a drink and a card game. He was five years older, self-taught in the ways of trading cattle and oil leases. When his first well came in, he bought a long black Cadillac, drove home to Athens, and circled the Courthouse Square twice so all the old nesters could see him.

Clint Murchison saw him, too. They headed west and eventually turned up in Wichita Falls with $50,000 between them. Then Murchison heard about a well coming in near the Oklahoma border, yanked Sid out of a card game, and drove close enough to the site to actually smell the oil. They bought every lease they could, an investment that increased in value 300 percent the day the news got out.

Later, Richardson leased land in what became the Keystone field in West Texas. His partners in this one were Charles Marsh and Amon Carter, and Keystone became one of the first hundred-million-dollar oil fields. He had made a fortune, lost it, made another. In the early 1930s, the price of crude oil dropped briefly to ten cents a barrel, cheaper in some places than water.

That was a wild and heroic and reckless era, the Texas version of the California gold rush. Prospectors worked out of their cars, followed their noses, their instincts, and at times the prostitutes, who often had better information than the geologists.

Richardson remained a bachelor all his life. He was far from handsome, stocky, had almost no neck and thick shoulders. Women found him interesting but elusive. "They're all wanting a landing field," he told me, "but mine's fogged in."

He was a man of modest habits who lived most of the time in two rooms at the downtown Fort Worth Club. His suits had to be custom-made because of his peculiar build, but I knew of no other extravagance he engaged in. For most of our years together, he drove a used car and rarely entertained. He spent less money on personal things than Nellie and I did, and we were fairly frugal ourselves.

I formed a deep attachment and affection for him, and for Perry Bass, who was about my age and had grown wealthy from his uncle's partnerships. We saw a lot of Perry and his wife, Nancy Lee, as our children grew up. Their four, Sid, Ed, Bob, and Lee, were approximately the same ages as ours, Kathleen, John, Sharon, and Mark.

I doubt that Sid Richardson had any idea what he was actually worth. He was a billionaire, or close to it, when that species was extremely rare. At one point, Murchison talked him into buying his own private island, St. Joseph, off the Texas coast near Corpus Christi. Clint had one, farther north at Matagorda; it had become a Texas thing to do. They had to look for new and creative ways to spend or invest their money, or else give it to the government, an alternative both men by nature resented. In 1957, Bob Young, then the president of the Allegheny Corporation, called and asked for their help in taking control of the New York Central Railroad, built by the Morgans and the Vanderbilts. They were successful, and that was how I came to be on the board of the New York Central, as Mr. Richardson's representative.

I doubt if it would have made any difference, but Sid misunderstood the deal. He thought he was putting up $5 million, half of their combined investment. The commitment turned out to be for half of $20 million. When Clint explained it to him, Richardson had only one question: "What was the name of that railroad again?" I was the first to hear the story and probably the first to repeat it. He wasn't being witty or absentminded. It was a matter of priorities.

The line was profitable and the stock went up, but for the first time I saw the deadly troubles that loomed ahead for the railroads. The featherbedding of the unions and political pressure from the government made it impossible for management to control the industry. They couldn't contain costs or improve conditions.

The next deal was never very far away, and occasionally an interest in a new venture was made available to me.

I was involved in every area of the Richardson-Bass operations, and they ran the gamut, from crossbreeding cattle, raising grass, and mining for uranium, to running a radio network and racing horses. Their oil and gas holdings had made possible everything else, but Richardson also financed a chain of drugstores, and with Amon Carter he owned the Texas Hotel in Fort Worth, where John F. Kennedy and I, and our wives, would spend the night before driving to Dallas in November, 1963.

It fell my lot to inspect uranium mines Richardson, Bass, and Murchison had bought in Oregon and Colorado. I made a number of trips, and on each one I put on the miner's hat with the flashlight and went crawling through those underground shafts. This was my first such experience, and I wasn't saddened when we later sold the mines to Kerr-McGee. I found no great joy in groping around beneath the earth.

Richardson's investment in the horse-racing business was one he made with his heart, not his head. A man named Browning, who had befriended Richardson during one of his down cycles in the 1930s, was down on his luck and in debt to Sid for thousands of dollars. As collateral, Browning pledged the papers on several racehorses. Then he died, leaving his widow with nothing but a stable of mortgaged horses.

Knowing she had nothing, Richardson tore up the notes and paid her an additional, generous sum. He turned the horses over to a trainer named Bill Finnegan. A few had potential, but they were always breaking down. Sid was constantly being told by Finnegan that this one was being blistered, and another was being treated for colic, or whatever. In one of his moments of frustration, he mourned for the late Mr. Browning. "The old son of a bitch shouldn't have died," he muttered.

There were some good brood mares we owned jointly, but I was stunned when I learned he was paying $5,000 to breed one mare to the great Kentucky Derby champion Swaps, which was owned by Rex Ellsworth.

We finally got out of the breeding business and sold off all the horses, to my relief. During this time, Richardson came up with an idea that he knew would please J. Edgar Hoover. Whatever anyone thought of the FBI director, especially in his later years, he had an abiding, almost innocent belief that one of the cures for crime was more support for underprivileged boys. Not long after Sid Richardson bought the Del Mar track, he created a foundation called Boys, Inc., with the goal of acquiring more tracks and dedicating the income to boys' clubs around the country.

Perry Bass and I were on the board of Boys, Inc., which received about 90 percent of the profits from the Del Mar track. Still, there was a constant hassle with the private interests in California, who disliked the idea of a nonprofit foundation owning a racetrack, and feared that the idea might spread. The animosity that developed over the ownership killed the long-range plans and the benefits they might have produced.

Of all the tasks I performed for Sid Richardson, the most inevitable was my role as a political troubleshooter. I had, in fact, first met him at the Democratic Convention in Chicago in 1940. He was there not as a delegate but as a personal friend of President Roosevelt. He had to some extent financed Elliott Roosevelt's stock in the Texas State Network, then based in Fort Worth.

Sid was a student of political affairs. It has been my observation that most of the truly wealthy are. Think of any of the great American family fortunes—Rockefeller, Du Pont, Mellon, Carnegie, Hearst, Getty, Hunt—and you will find a record of political involvement, though much of it behind the scenes. No mystery here. They made noble acts of philanthropy, but these mandarins and their heirs had a deep and, I think, healthy interest in the system that made their wealth possible.

By the 1950s, the oil industry had joined the defense establishment, big business, and labor as the major forces that drove the political system. This was no interlocking network, but gradually the power passed from the hands of those who controlled the rails, the coal mines, and the steel mills of old.

The year 1952 would represent a watershed for Texas, for the future of energy in America, and for Presidential politics. That national election would divide the state as it had not been divided since the Civil War.

Clint Murchison was a Republican most of his life, certainly before there was an effective Republican Party in Texas. He and Richardson were both conservatives, but Clint was somewhat farther to the right, an early admirer of Senator Joseph McCarthy. Richardson stayed a Democrat, but crossed over when he felt the need.

Murchison backed Robert Taft for the Republican nomination in 1952. Richardson's first choice to head the Democratic ticket was Richard Russell, of Georgia. Shortly after I went to work for him, Richardson sent me to Chicago to help Senator Russell's campaign in the primaries, but it was soon apparent that he lacked the national appeal to head off the party favorite, Adlai Stevenson.

Sid Richardson had a second option, and that was to personally implore Dwight Eisenhower to run as a Democrat. He also had a third option: if the Republicans prevailed upon Ike, and Russell somehow rallied to become the Democratic nominee, he would have supported *both*. Richardson regarded Russell as one of the greatest public servants this country ever developed, and the better I came to know him, the more I agreed.

I suppose there is the appearance of a contradiction here. In their political preferences, Texans can be willful and obsessive. They can also be quite flexible. What was already obvious among the oil producers was the fact that Stevenson, the eventual nominee, would lose Texas on the Tidelands issue. He opposed claims by the individual states to oil deposits submerged off their coasts. Billions of dollars hung in the balance if the offshore lands could be shifted from federal to state jurisdiction.

Early in 1952, Sid Richardson sailed on the *Queen Mary* to Europe, then flew to Paris to meet with Eisenhower, who was winding down his command of the postwar allied forces. Richardson had known Ike since 1941, when they had a chance meeting five days after Pearl Harbor on a train bound from Texas to Washington, D.C. Richardson was traveling with Bill Kittrell, of Dallas, a protégé of Sam Rayburn. Kittrell and I would later serve together, briefly, in Algeria.

Eisenhower was still a colonel, flying on a military plane that had been forced down not far from the railway line. He boarded the train in the Midwest and joined Richardson and Kittrell in their drawing room while his berth was being prepared. Richardson had no idea who their guest was, nor did he catch his name—not at all out of character for him. Later, he entertained Eisenhower and Mamie on his private island.

In their meeting in Paris, Richardson begged Ike to return to the States to run for President on the Democratic ticket. He assured him that there would be substantial oil and gas money behind his candidacy. He explained why the Tidelands should be returned to Texas. Twice, Congress had passed legislation to do so, and both times Truman had vetoed the bills.

In truth, the Democrats were responsible for bringing Eisenhower home, so alarming were the numbers of those disaffected with Truman. The popularity of the man from Missouri had plunged again after his 1948 upset over Tom Dewey, and the country awaited his retirement with a relief that went beyond party lines.

At that point, I believe you could have flipped a coin as to which party would win Eisenhower's affiliation. For reasons known only to himself, he picked the Republicans. In any event, Richardson pledged his support if Ike entered the race. "General," he told him, "there's no way out. You've got to do it. I'll go along with you any way you go, but if you go as a Republican, it's going to be hard."

He meant that it would be a harder sell in Texas, but as matters fell into place that pessimism turned out to be unjustified. Ike carried Texas easily, and his popularity there may well have been the turning point in his campaign against Adlai Stevenson. At the Republican Convention, I met with the Texas delegates at Richardson's request to try to convince them that Eisenhower would be better for Texas than Taft. That convention was bitterly fought, and it was there that I met John Wayne and Ward Bond. The two heroes of so many Western epics were vitally interested in what was going on when they were not expressing themselves at the hotel bar.

Texas turned out to be the crucial state in swinging the nomination to Eisenhower. A few months after his election, Ike signed the bill returning the Tidelands to the states.

Sid Richardson could be coarse and stubborn in some of his dealings, but his political instincts were often subtle and shrewd. Many of the Democrats who supported Eisenhower (twice) were among the first to back my candidacy for governor in 1962. And the same ones, conservatives and moderates, led Texas into the Republican column for Richard Nixon ten years later.

In my various duties for Richardson, in the 1950s, I was flying to Washington often enough to justify keeping a suite at the Mayflower Hotel. My responsibilities during this time would be questioned later when I was nominated as Secretary of the Navy and, again, as Secretary of the Treasury. An effort would be made by Senator William Proxmire and others to portray me as a hired gun for the oil and gas industry.

The battles over oil rights were not, in my mind, along the traditional conservative and liberal lines. They opened old and new wounds, North and South, rural and industrial. The Sun Belt, especially Texas and Oklahoma, had the large reserves of oil. The rest of America, but notably the North and East, had the bitter, freezing winters.

In mid-1955, President Eisenhower approved a bill that had passed in the House by six votes to end federal price controls at the wellhead. Lyndon Johnson, back on his feet after his heart attack, announced that the Natural Gas Act would be his top priority as Senate majority leader.

A massive lobbying effort was soon under way in the Senate to pass the bill sponsored by Oren Harris, an Arkansas Democrat. I can't think of a more formidable array of advocates than those who lobbied for the Harris bill. The coalition reached into every corner of the energy field: producers, independents and the majors, the pipeline and distributing companies, and the coal miners all were involved.

The negotiations just within the industry were long and intense, trying to resolve provisions of the Harris bill that would satisfy—or at least be acceptable to—the various interests, whose views were so frequently divergent.

A special committee was organized and Robert Windfohr, of Fort Worth, was chosen as the chairman. He was a close friend of Sid Richardson, as was his wife, Ann Burnett Windfohr, the heiress to a large fortune from her father, Burk Burnett, for whom the town in Texas was named.

Every heavyweight connected with oil and gas was involved in some way to support the bill, including William M. Keck, who founded Superior Oil of California. I had not yet met Mr. Keck, whose son Howard, years later, after I returned to Houston to practice law, would ask me to serve on the company's board. But during the months in which the Harris bill worked its way through the House and Senate, our paths didn't cross.

Sid Richardson asked me to stay in Washington and monitor the progress of the legislation. A classic confrontation was shaping up between the oil-producing states and the oil-consuming states. Leading the opposition was Senator Paul Douglas, of Illinois. My responsibility was to maintain contact with Oren Harris, Speaker Rayburn, our Texas senators, Lyndon Johnson and Price Daniel, and Bob Windfohr. I did no lobbying as such, but it was a full-time job trying to keep up with what the various companies and their lobbyists were doing and saying. Sid Richardson and I used whatever contacts we had within the industry to see that no mistakes were made.

Then in early February, a moment of drama, dreadfully timed, took place. With a favorable vote virtually assured, South Dakota's Francis Case, a supporter of the bill, rose in the Senate chambers to announce that an envelope had been delivered to him containing $2,500 in hundred-dollar bills. The cash had been characterized as a campaign contribution, but in a manner that he felt amounted to a bribery attempt.

Overnight a cause célèbre had exploded. The lawyer who had left the cash, a man named Neff who was employed by the Superior Oil Company, denied that any bribe had been intended. Even though the bill passed the Senate, the furor cast doubts on whether the President would approve it. Sid Richardson had heard that George Humphrey, the Secretary of the Treasury, was furious; that he had been quoted as calling the oil and gas lobby "greedy and selfish," and complaining that the coal people had gotten "nothing." He had threatened to recommend that Eisenhower veto the legislation.

Even before the Case disclosure, I thought that a veto was a distinct possibility. After the incident had broken wide open, I went back to see Secretary Humphrey. I tried to convince him that the bill represented a compromise that was fair to all the parties; all sides had given up something. I implored him not to urge Ike to kill it. He was adamant.

He was bright, articulate, and strong-willed, unquestionably one of the dominant two or three people in the Eisenhower cabinet. He could be as cold as a bishop. Shortly after my meeting with him, Humphrey invited Eisenhower to his Georgia plantation to go quail hunting. And that was where the President announced the veto.

That decision broke a lot of hearts in Texas and Oklahoma. A tremendous amount of effort had been expended, all of it wiped away with the stroke of a pen. The Case affair had been seized to make it appear that the effort had employed tactics that were at the least unsavory. My personal conviction was that no attempt had been made to bribe anyone. A contribution that would have been given routinely was handled clumsily, with atrocious timing.

But this was, unfortunately, one of the quirks of character of people who lived and died in an industry where fortunes were made and lost almost overnight. Many oilmen of that period carried with them staggering amounts of cash, and they treated it as though they were tossing around chips in a Las Vegas casino.

Richardson was disappointed in Eisenhower's veto, but they did not fall out over it. This was the other side of the coin—oilmen knew how to accept a defeat.

Right after Christmas of 1958, Richardson asked me to join him at the Thunderbird Hotel in Palm Springs, where he had now transferred his winter allegiance. It was not unlike any number of visits we had shared over the years. He had called and asked what I was doing. I said, "Nothing I can't drop." He told me to have his chief pilot, Ed Armstrong, fly me out to Palm Springs on his best aircraft, the DC-3, and to plan on staying a few days.

Each morning I would join him in his parlor. He would be sitting there in his pajama tops and an old gray sweater, boxer shorts and a robe. He never wore the bottoms of his pajamas. We drank coffee and talked all morning and through lunch. Then he would adjourn to what was called "the Snake Pit," where the gambling took place. At times, Phil Harris was there, or Ray Ryan, a high-stakes gambler and oilman, or many others who came and went.

After he finished playing cards, we had dinner, talked some more, and went to bed. The next morning the routine started anew. It was never changing, never failing.

The only difference in this trip was the result of a second call I received just before my departure. The call was from Perry Bass, Richardson's nephew and partner, asking me to raise a matter of delicacy with his uncle. Sid, in his will, had bequeathed nothing to the family except $200,000 to his sister, Perry's mother. The rest was going to a foundation.

I told Perry I would be glad to bring up the subject while I was in Palm Springs, and late one night I did. I just said it to him without any embroidery: "Mr. Richardson, you need to leave some substantial money to your family and Perry's children."

He seemed genuinely startled by the suggestion. "Why should I?" he asked. "Bass is rich. He could leave them plenty."

I said, "I don't know exactly what you're worth, but it is certainly in excess of a hundred million dollars." I briefly recounted the very full life he had lived, and added, "Yet you keep trying to find another mother lode. What for? Even if you tried, you couldn't spend the money you have now."

"I have it set up so I won't have to pay any taxes," he said.

I almost laughed. "What difference does that make? You won't know it. You'll be dead. You have spent your entire life accumulating money. Now you're preparing to leave almost all of it to a foundation that ultimately will be controlled by strangers. They will determine how your money is spent and, in the long run, you'll get little if any of the credit.

"Did it ever occur to you that you might have as much fun giving your money away as you did making it?"

He looked at me with the slightly worried expression of the first barber in a good barbershop. I had planted a thought that he needed to chew on. We had established a relationship over the years, on these various trips, where I felt completely at ease. He discussed with me all of the top people in his organizations. Obviously, he trusted me to be totally candid with him. I could talk as frankly with him as I would with one of my brothers. We went over the estate in great detail. The day he returned from Palm Springs, he called his tax man, Harry Weeks, and changed his will.

As a result, he left $2 million each to his sister (Perry's mother) and $2 million to Perry and each of his children, plus the island and the stock in several of his corporations. By the time the children were old enough to take control, their inheritance was worth in excess of $50 million. These millions in 1959 became the basis for the fortunes that the Bass brothers, Sid, Bob, Lee, and Edward, amassed into the billions. In no way does this diminish the tremendous success the brothers and their compatriots have achieved from their own endeavors.

I was at the Fort Worth Club the day the will was changed. Harry Weeks and Mr. Richardson were looking around for witnesses, and I said I would be glad to witness it. Harry said no, you can't sign. That was the first clue I had that I was mentioned in the will.

Sid Richardson died of a heart attack in September of 1959, removing from the Texas landscape one of the last of his breed, and ending for me a relationship that had been close to paternal. He was sixty-eight. His body was flown from his private island off the Gulf of Mexico for services, with Billy Graham giving the eulogy. He was buried in his hometown of Athens. At his death, he was worth more than the entire town.

His nephew Perry Bass, his brother-in-law Hal Smith, and I were named as co-executors of the estate. As executors, we had the authority to pay the bequest in either cash or equivalent property. Obviously, at the time, Perry's children didn't need the cash. We had the oil properties evaluated and gave them the equivalent interests. Oil was $2.40 a barrel then, and even by 1993 prices they have quadrupled. They are still producing.

The estate taxes alone totaled $42 million.

There were two interesting footnotes to this story. As a co-executor, I was entitled to a third of the executor fees. Given the size of the estate, the fees would have been easily in excess of $5 million. When I was offered the position of Secretary of the Navy in 1961, we had substantially completed the work of the estate. Instead of seeking the full amount, I reached an agreement with Perry to receive $750,000 and for this sum to be paid by the foundation over a period of ten years. I deferred the monies to relieve the tax burden, but at the same time waived any interest on the unpaid balance.

Under the circumstances, I felt fairly compensated, and I am raising it now not as a whimper but as the first public explanation I have made of the implications that surfaced during my political career. My opponents in the race for governor, and at the hearings on my nomination as Secretary of the Navy, tried to make something evil of the fact that I was to collect money from "these oil interests in Texas," as if it were a retainer carried on some company payroll. I resented it then, and I do now.

I have seen the Bass brothers, Perry's sons, on many occasions since they reached maturity. I never mentioned the source of their inheritances, nor did they. To this day I don't know if they are even aware of the role I played in persuading Sid Richardson to change his will. There is no doubt in my mind that he would not have done so otherwise.

I had an enormous respect, which grew into affection, for their Great-Uncle Sid. There was little about his life that I didn't become familiar with, and the more I learned the greater my respect for him grew. To his dying day, I always addressed him as "Mr. Richardson," even when we were alone.

I never saw him do or say anything that I thought was out of line or inappropriate or unfair to anyone, with a single notable exception. He had one failing in his relationship with his nephew Perry Bass. Their approach to problems was entirely different. Richardson was a generalist and never got involved in details.

Perry, given his background and education, was just the opposite. They shared the same secretary, and she kept an elaborate calendar and diary for Perry. I never saw Richardson so much as ask to make a note. Perry delved into the intimate details of any problem that had his attention, whether it was the drilling of a well or designing the interior of an airplane. He loved to work with his hands, and in his home in Westover Hills he built a woodworking shop that was adjacent to, but separate from, the living room. There he could do his woodworking while visiting with his wife, Nancy Lee, and the children through the open doorway.

Richardson was often critical of Perry even in front of others. I thought it was unwise, certainly unnecessary, and undoubtedly resented by Perry. I was uncomfortable when he derided Perry in my presence. That practice may have resulted in some degree of resentment against me from Perry, and I can understand it. If I had received such treatment, I probably would have been more visibly upset than Perry. I never really understood it, except that it may have been a reflection of Sid's attitude about their backgrounds.

Where Perry had graduated with honors from Yale, Richardson never pursued any education beyond a couple of semesters of college at Hardin-Simmons, and Baylor. He had come up through the school of hard knocks as an oil-field roughneck to achieve his success in life. He obviously loved and trusted and worked well with Perry, yet he took some peculiar pleasure out of needling him. I thought it was so uncharacteristic of the man I had come to know so well.

We spent countless hours together on trips to Washington, New York, and California, a different quality of time from our days in the offices in Fort Worth. Leaving town seemed to unlock Sid Richardson's memory bank. He had opinions on everything, and told earthy stories of his days when he was a lease hound for Gulf and other oil companies.

Typical of him was a gesture he made when he was dug in at Ranger, where the only telephone service available was a land office with a central switchboard presided over by a very, very plump lady, who sat on a small stool with no back. She was obviously ill suited for that type of chair, so Mr. Richardson went to Fort Worth on one of his trips and brought back to Ranger a large, heavy, swivel armchair. She accepted the gift as gratefully as if it had been a car.

Thereafter, when he walked into the office where the lease hounds were lined up trying to make or receive a call, the operator would immediately sing out: "Sid, your call is just coming through." That was his cue to move to her side, and she would whisper, "What number do you want?" Then, while everyone else stood in line waiting to get their connections made, she put through Sid Richardson's calls.

The Bass brothers turned their legacy into a fortune awesome even by modern standards. But I can't forget that their Great-Uncle Sid was the one with the clout at the switchboard.

8

KATHLEEN

She was sixteen, intelligent, popular, and beautiful in the eyes of others more objective than my own. We had been given a glimpse of the woman she would become, heard a bar of the music she would make.

All of which served only to make our daughter Kathleen's death harder to accept. I cannot say with honesty that I ever have accepted it. She didn't die on a highway, or on an airplane, or as an innocent in war—a place beyond anyone's control. She died in the living room of the tiny apartment she had rented, alone with the boy she loved and married, and whose child she was carrying.

None of this has anything to do with politics. It has everything to do with being aware of the frailties of life.

By the late 1950s, I was busier than ever as the legal counsel and adviser to Sid Richardson and his nephew Perry Bass. I was spending considerable time traveling between Fort Worth and Washington.

Toward the end of 1957, we began to notice a subtle change in Kathleen, who had been bright and sometimes headstrong, but never difficult. There were disagreements over what seemed to be little things: going out, how late she could come in, how long she stayed on the phone, her clothes, her makeup, her schoolwork. I think Nellie and I recognized the signs of a teenager in love, and I don't believe that we took them lightly. We just did not know how to deal with them. We were living in a 1950s world: Elvis and hula hoops and backyard bomb shelters, penny loafers, 3-D movies, and McCarthyism.

When she could, Nellie traveled with me to Washington and her mother came in to stay with the children. After one of these trips, Nellie and I received a phone call from one of Kathleen's teachers. We went to the school, and were dazed by what the teacher told us. Kathleen had been having morning sickness. The teacher thought she was pregnant.

We thanked her sincerely and returned home to talk with Kathleen. She denied emphatically any such conclusion; she had been ill a morning or two—probably a virus, nothing else. She was certainly not pregnant.

Not many days later, Nellie and I traveled again to Washington. We had barely arrived when we received a call from home telling us that Kathleen was in the hospital. We immediately flew back to Fort Worth, only to find that she had checked herself out. We were told that she had been admitted after hyperventilating. The records also showed a puzzling description: she apparently had been rolling over and over in the grass. Her clothes were covered with burrs and grass stains. The hospital had no information as to her whereabouts.

It was soon clear that she had been taken in by the family of Bobby Hale, her boyfriend, and by now had returned to our home. We again confronted Kathleen, as gently as we could, with concern, not anger. We begged her to tell us what the trouble was. We told her there was nothing that could possibly be so wrong that we could not help her, if only she would let us. We asked if she was pregnant. Again she insisted that the answer was no.

I called Bobby and asked him to come to our house. He was eighteen, a senior, a star of the football team. His father, I. B. Hale, had been a Hall of Fame linebacker at Texas Christian

University in the 1930s, and was chief of security for General Dynamics in Fort Worth.

We spoke to them separately, and each denied that anything was wrong. Then we faced them together as they sat next to each other on a couch in our study. I asked Bobby if Kathleen was "in trouble." He denied it. I said, "Well, something is wrong. The two of you are not being truthful and this has gone on long enough."

I might have reworded the question a dozen ways. But it was certain that something wasn't right. I was close to the edge of my patience and my temper. During these few weeks when we were groping for answers, Nellie and I were both perplexed and agitated. We could hardly talk about anything else. We knew her behavior was irrational. We tried to be supportive, not oppressive or demanding. I repeatedly told her there was nothing so wrong that it could not be corrected one way or another, if only she would confide in us and let us help. She would not share with us the pressure she felt or the secret she kept.

I had told Kathleen that I did not want her going out. She did, and that night Nellie and I waited and waited until she appeared, at midnight. I was furious at her behavior, as I suppose most parents would have been. I knew she was confused and upset and concealing the truth.

I accused Kathleen and Bobby of lying to us. She repeated once again that nothing was wrong. And then I slapped her. Even as I did it, I wished that I hadn't. A thousand times since— maybe more—I have wanted to call back my hand. She was silent. The slap echoed in my ear. She turned and went to her room.

That was in March of 1958. I left for Washington on a business trip the next day. I had told Kathleen I wanted to talk to her when I returned. But that night she loaded her clothes into our station wagon, while her mother pleaded and cajoled and raged. She drove off with her mother begging her to stay.

As much as any child, Kathleen had been open and sweet and wholesome, a daughter to be envied by anyone who raised a child, watched her bloom. She had never caused us the least of worries. But suddenly a wall had gone up that we could not penetrate. She was almost defiant in her repeated statements that nothing was wrong. Nellie and I had no control over her, no clear way to help.

Nellie called the police and gave them the license number of the car. Then she phoned me and waited for me to arrive at 3 A.M. Of course, it developed that Bobby was missing as well. Neither we nor the Hales were rich, but both children had been reared in nice surroundings, in an atmosphere of plenty. In truth, we lived in an area that was somewhat beyond our means, so that her friends had more than she. That never seemed to be a problem.

She and Bobby had dated each other almost since they first met. We liked him. Everyone did. There was no reason to think that their relationship was anything more than a yearbook romance.

We heard nothing for several days; I suppose it seemed like weeks. Then we learned that they had eloped, had driven to Ardmore, Oklahoma, and had been married by a justice of the peace. Our first direct word was a letter Nellie received from Tallahassee, Florida. They had taken a small apartment in a boardinghouse, and Kathleen—we called her "KK"—described the magnolia tree she could see out her window. Bobby had taken a job at the shipyards for seventy dollars a week.

At that point, I.B. Hale and I got into my car and drove straight through to Tallahassee; the wives stayed behind with the younger children. We wanted to see how Kathleen and Bobby were, how they were managing, and if we could persuade them to come home.

They were living in two rooms, with a combination kitchen and dining room, and a bedroom. The surroundings were grim, almost pathetic, compared to what each of them had been accustomed to.

When I saw them, what I felt was simply heartache. I tried not to show it. Kathleen and I greeted each other with hugs and a holiday of kisses. Reconciliations are often more emotional than the disagreements that cause them. I assured her that her mother and I loved her, that we wanted her to come back and finish school.

I.B. and I told them both we would help support them. We did not ask or want them to divorce. We thought they should consider living apart until they at least had their high-school diplomas.

Kathleen was obviously glad to see me, nervous but relieved. She appeared to be reassured that we truly loved her, wanted her to have an education, and did not want them living in hardship. Together, they indicated they wanted to stay in Tallahassee a while longer, and would think about coming home in the fall. I pulled out several hundred-dollar bills from my wallet and told them to find a better apartment.

Kathleen was determined to prove that what she had done was not a mistake, not a fiasco. I knew she did not want to come home until she had shown they had worked through the rough spots. She had taken a job at a five-and-dime store.

Before we left, I talked with the lady who owned the boardinghouse, and what she said troubled me. She said she thought Kathleen was afraid—of what she did not know. But the landlady had seen her slip into the station wagon at night, and sit there listening to the radio. She wasn't tuned into a rock-and-roll station. She was listening to Oral Roberts preach.

I can only guess at what torment was going through her young and immature mind. She felt guilty, that was apparent. She felt that what she had done was wrong, that she had disappointed us, but she would somehow make it all turn out right.

Hale and I spent most of that day visiting with them, and even went out to the shipyard where Bobby had his job and looked around. Then we pointed the car west and drove back to Fort Worth.

We knew the truth now. Kathleen was expecting a child. We had offered our help and our support, and beyond that I didn't know what to say or do. I had no high hopes for their marriage, but neither Nellie nor I wanted it to fail. The landlady had told me there were spats, the young-lover quarrels, which were to be expected. Those are not limited to only the young and newly wed.

I still have a sense of disbelief at how quickly the events moved. Two or three weeks later, on the morning of April 28, 1958, I was sitting at my desk when I received a phone call from the sheriff in Tallahassee. He said clumsily, "Mr. Connally, your daughter has been shot in the head."

I said, "My God! How bad is she?"

He said, "Couldn't be worse. Half her head was blown away."

There is no good way—no magic words—to deliver that kind of message. I was too stunned to fault him for his insensitivity. I hung up the phone in shock, in an anguish that was a kind of seizure. I stumbled into Sid Richardson's office to tell him about the call, and ask if I could borrow one of his corporate planes so Nellie and I could fly to Tallahassee.

He said certainly, and picked up the phone. He called Ed Armstrong and told him to prepare the DC-3. Then I went home to tell Nellie the news that no husband ever expects, or knows how, to tell his wife: that their firstborn child is dead.

She had just returned to the house after sitting for three and a half hours in the dentist's chair. The daily nuisances of life have a way of intruding even on our tragedies. We held each other and wept. Then Nellie called the Hales, and they met us at the airport.

Somewhere during that time, it occurred to me that the sheriff had never actually said that Kathleen was dead. But I knew she was. We made the trip on automatic pilot—meaning the passengers, not the plane.

When we landed in Tallahassee, we took a taxi straight to the funeral home. Bobby was there. The story he told was jumbled, almost incoherent. He said they had quarreled and Kathleen had walked out. He went looking for her, with no success, and when he came back to the apartment, she was sitting in a chair with his loaded shotgun pointed at her head, her finger on the trigger.

At the coroner's inquest, he said that she told him, "Bobby, I'm sick in my mind and I need help. I know now that no one can help me." He said he tried to talk her into putting the gun down. She kept threatening to use it. He made a grab for it, he said, and the gun went off.

Exactly what happened in that room, what was said, what was done, we will never be completely sure.

A deputy in the sheriff's office told us there may have been a suicide pact, and Bobby backed out. That was one of the stories, one of the speculations.

The inquest was held the next day, and obviously no amount of testimony could show clearly what led up to the shooting. I was one of the witnesses, asked to testify to Kathleen's state of mind. The whole process to me was immaterial. She was gone. Nothing could revive her. Whatever blame or fault or innocence might have been attached to anyone else was of no consequence in my mind. The inquest, and all the circumstances that preceded and surrounded it, passed as a bad dream.

I only wanted it to end. I was ridden with regret that the two of them had not confided in us. I could not shake my doubts that Kathleen would never have taken her own life if her young husband had been mature enough to be kind and considerate to her in the dark moments she must have experienced. I remembered the landlady saying that she seemed afraid.

I tried to put all those thoughts behind me. I have not spoken to Bobby since then. Over the years, he has attempted to call me. I have never taken his call, nor will I. If this seems flinty and cold, so be it. Our daughter was gone and so was Bobby Hale, as far as I was concerned.

We did not take her body home with us on the plane; an autopsy had to be performed in the county where she died. The funeral was at the First Methodist Church in Fort Worth, and she was laid to rest a few days later in our family plot.

Like any parents who have raised a child, Nellie and I are

left with our private recollections. We watched her grow, heard her laugh and cry, lived with her anxieties, felt pride in her beauty and sweet nature. She was a brunette, at sixteen taller than her mother, active and vivacious, able to dance and sing and playact, all with ease.

I don't think you ever recover from the loss of a child, especially one who was not allowed to be an adult. There is no exercise more pointless than trying to compare the pains of death. Why would one, except to search for meaning? When Kathleen died, we searched and found none. This is the pain that never leaves. You go through the period of the what-ifs. What if we had done this, done that. Maybe if, maybe not. Eventually, you are able to push it far enough back in your mind so it doesn't just roll constantly through your thoughts. "Even today," says Nellie, "I can start thinking about Kathleen, and from deep inside me there wants to emerge a terrible wail that would relieve me of my misery."

For the most part, we grieved inwardly, silently, trying to shield the other children, trying not to magnify for them the loss of a beloved older sister. As Nellie put it: "We just went on. We had three little other pairs of eyes looking up at us. You go on from there."

Kathleen left no letter, no note, no diary. In the apartment in Tallahassee, we did find the notice of her doctor's appointment for the next day.

Misfortunes have befallen us: the assassination of a President, at less than an arm's length; my bribery trial; my bankruptcy. All were traumatic, devastating events that eat away at your soul. However sad or grievous, none of these can equal the burden of sorrow we will carry with us to the grave over the death of Kathleen.

This is the first time I have ever discussed it in any detail, and it will also be the last.

WRONG ROADS
TAKEN

O f all my roller-coaster rides with Lyndon John-son, the one that remains the most perplexing was his abbreviated bid for the Democratic nomination for President in 1960. The race ended with his joining John Fitz-gerald Kennedy as his running mate, but just barely.

We ran a halfhearted campaign to win the nomination in 1960 because we had a halfhearted candidate. Johnson was the choice of the party elders, including Adlai Stevenson and Elea-nor Roosevelt, but by the time he decided to become active, he was too late. He wanted the nomination, but did not want to be tarred with having lost it. He would gamble on the win if he could avoid being responsible for the loss.

By the time we reached the convention in Los Angeles, it was too late. Kennedy by then pretty well had the nomination wrapped up. But to the question of whether LBJ was interested in the nomination in 1960, the answer is, we started too late, did too little, and did it the wrong way.

Few winning campaigns ever started out with so many negative reactions. The Texas delegation was already feeling mis-
treated. We had been put up at the so-called New Clark Hotel,
in Los Angeles, which was new about the time of the San Francisco earthquake. The delegation was disgruntled to begin with
because of the accommodations—it was a third-rate hotel—and
further aggravated when Jack Kennedy's nomination became
official. I was in my room shaving when Johnson called to me
from the adjoining suite. He said Bobby Kennedy was on his
way down to see him and what did I think he wanted.

I said, "He's going to offer you the Vice-Presidency."

Johnson looked startled. "Oh, no, he's not going to do
that."

I said, "Yes, he is.

"Well, what do I tell him?"

"The fact is, you don't have any choice. If he offers it to
you, you have to accept."

In the few minutes we had, I analyzed his options very
quickly. I said, "Well, there are four possibilities. Let's assume
that you take it and you lose the election. You're still a senator,
you can still be the majority leader. You will have been a good
soldier, and you won't be blamed for the defeat. It will be
blamed most likely on the religious issue or some other issue,
and you will continue to have a very viable position.

"Now let's assume you take it and you win. Then you're
the Vice-President of the United States, for whatever that's
worth. Now take the reverse side of it. Let's assume that you
turn him down, that you refuse to take it. And Kennedy wins.
Where are you then? You're the majority leader, but you don't
have any power left because the policies of the party are going
to be dictated by the White House and you're going to wind up
an errand boy, carrying out those policies. You're not going to
be the kingpin of the Senate that you are today. Sure, you'll still
be a senator, you'll have power, but you will also have incurred
the disfavor of all the people who supported Kennedy because
word will get out that you were offered the Vice-Presidency and

you refused it. So they'll have their pound of flesh.

"Now let's assume you decline and he loses the election. Then you're going to get much of the blame, because if you're not on the ticket, Texas probably will not vote for Jack Kennedy. Texas will probably go Republican, as it has in the last two elections. And then you're going to be blamed for Kennedy and the Democrats losing the White House. Frankly, it may cost you the majority leadership. But, in any event, it's going to cost you an enormous amount of prestige in the Democratic Party. I don't think you have any choice but to accept it."

This was a blunt, rough reading of what was on the table, but I sensed this was no time for table manners. The decision would be complicated enough.

"Texas is going to be very unhappy if I take it," said LBJ.

"Yes, they sure are," I agreed. "But Texas is going to be unhappy whatever you do." There was a knock on the door and I ducked out.

Kennedy arrived, and about fifteen minutes later Johnson called me back into the room. He was sitting there, stunned. "You were right," he said. "He offered me the Vice-Presidency."

I said, "Well, what did you tell him?"

"I told him I would take it."

I said, "That's what you should have done."

So began a long and serpentine day. Instantly, the word started to circulate around the hotel and the convention floor, and all hell broke loose. Sam Rayburn appeared, and he was upset . . . about Lyndon accepting the offer, and what he felt was a betrayal of all the principles Texas held dear.

"Lyndon, you can't do this," he said. "You promised us [and he had] you wouldn't settle for the second spot on the ticket. You just cannot accept this."

And, finally, Lyndon said, "Mr. Speaker, wait a minute. Let's just calm down. Let's talk about it. John, tell him what you think."

I repeated my outline of the options, and concluded with

"Mr. Speaker, he doesn't have any choice. He has to take it, for better or for worse."

At that moment, Bob Kerr, the senator from Oklahoma, came storming in. The news was already circulating. "Lyndon, what's this I hear about you taking the Vice-Presidency? If you do, I'll shoot you right between the eyes."

We went through the whole exercise again. Next came James Rowe, then Phil Graham, the publisher of the *Washington Post*, and soon the room was filling with people in varying stages of discontent. Then there was a call telling us that Bobby Kennedy was on his way down, and Johnson said, "Whatever it is, I don't want to see him."

Rayburn said, "John and I will see him." When Bobby appeared, we went into the bedroom and closed the door. He got right to the point. He said that they were in danger of losing control of the convention. Walter Reuther and labor were in revolt. "Lyndon just can't accept this nomination," he said. "It was a mistake."

Sam Rayburn, who had done a complete turnaround, looked at him and said, "Aw, shit!" And walked out of the room.

I said, "Bobby, Mr. Rayburn is absolutely right. If you're trying to convince us that Jack Kennedy can't control this convention, that's ludicrous."

"Reuther is threatening to revolt," he repeated.

"Then you'll have to tell your brother to call Senator Johnson and ask him to decline."

Ten minutes later, Bobby Kennedy was back. The second time, Rayburn refused to see him, and I met with him alone. We went through the same story, and the same problem. Johnson was unacceptable to Walter Reuther and big labor because of his vote for the Taft-Hartley bill.

I said, "Bobby, there is no point in your talking to me, or to Lyndon. Your brother came down here and offered him the Vice-Presidential nomination, and Johnson accepted. Now if he's changed his mind and doesn't want him to have it, he's going to have to call and ask him to withdraw, because Johnson is not going to do it himself. Don't try to kid us that you can't control this convention. Those are your delegates out there. They're going to do whatever Jack Kennedy wants them to do."

He left again, and now word had spread across the convention hall that Johnson might not stay on the ticket. Meanwhile, Texas delegates were coming and going, some angry and some just confused. They had supported Johnson against the young senator from Massachusetts, and they believed him when he said he wasn't interested in being Number 2.

They were all coming from different angles. Senator Kerr was upset, I think, because he was a very devout Southern Baptist and the religious aspects of the campaign were already looming large in his mind. Kerr was also a wealthy oilman, a conservative who saw in Kennedy a man whose philosophy didn't coincide with his own. He felt that Johnson would strengthen the ticket, and he really didn't want that to happen.

Even amid all that commotion, I thought it was quite remarkable that we had succeeded in finding a combination that the conservatives and the liberals equally disliked. Sounded like a winning formula all right.

Bobby Kennedy came back a third time. I met with him again, and said, "Bobby, you and I can sit here and talk all day, but there is no way that Lyndon Johnson is going to change his mind unless Jack Kennedy calls him and withdraws the offer. If your brother doesn't want him to be his running mate, then he has to call and tell him so. Absent that, the ticket is going to be Kennedy and Johnson, and there's not a damned thing you or I can do about it."

By now, exercising his political right to be contrary, Rayburn was determined to see Johnson hold firm, and even Bob Kerr had done a reluctant about-face. Both men resented the idea of the Kennedys trying to take back the offer—even though they themselves might have wanted Johnson to refuse.

I tried every way I could to analyze what might have prompted the curious Kennedy change of heart. Had Jack

Kennedy gotten cold feet? Had he expected Johnson to turn him down and then, having gotten credit for making the gesture, planned to name someone like Stuart Symington? On the other hand, I sized up Jack Kennedy as a very practical fellow who wasn't about to offer the Vice-Presidency unless he was prepared to have it accepted. I concluded that Bobby might have made the move on his own, a suspicion Lyndon Johnson shared, and one that soured the relationship between those two men from the start.

There the matter rested, and the Democratic ticket, like it or not, was in place. It is hard now to imagine the depth of the emotion among the Texas delegates. It was as though there was a shroud hanging over Johnson's suite. Lady Bird was in tears. Nellie was upset. The gloom, like a winter chill, seemed to penetrate to the bone. Many of the delegates literally left and checked out of the hotel and went home. Nellie and I saw friends who had been Johnson supporters forever but were now livid with rage, and cursed him as a double-dealer, a liar, and a hypocrite.

It was a bitter experience, and the minute the convention ended we left Los Angeles and drove to Las Vegas. We were sick at heart. We knew that divisions had been created that would never heal, and friendships of a lifetime had been severed that would never be rejoined.

Johnson considered Jack Kennedy a brilliant and attractive guy. But he saw him as someone having a good time, who did not take himself or the Senate too seriously, and in his heart he doubted that Kennedy deserved to be President.

For his part, Jack treated Johnson warmly, and with respect. Clearly, that was not the case with Bobby.

The Democrats carried Texas by 46,000 votes in a very close election. Obviously, putting Johnson on the ticket was the key to Jack Kennedy achieving the Presidency . . . in fact, to both of them achieving the Presidency.

—

There is no doubt in my mind that the Democrats would have lost in 1960 without Lyndon Johnson. At home in Texas, however, this fact had a paradoxical result. Texas was, and is, essentially a conservative state. General Eisenhower carried it twice. It had become fashionable to vote Republican nationally and Democratic locally. A great many Texans had been for Nixon for President and Johnson for senator—and their favorite senator had tipped the scales against their Presidential favorite.

Johnson actually ran two races in 1960, one for Vice President and the other for his old Senate seat. He polled 138,000 votes more for senator than he did for Vice President. The Old Guard had not forgiven him for joining a man they considered his junior in experience and ability. They continued to resent his having relinquished real power in the Senate for the weaker Vice-Presidency.

In the spring of 1961, Texas had sent a Republican, John Tower, to the Senate for the first time in eighty-four years. I had returned to private business in Fort Worth after the 1960 campaign, and then President Kennedy appointed me to head the Navy. But in late 1961, I came home to run for governor.

My opponents immediately tagged me with their taunting slogan: "L.B.J.—Lyndon's Boy John." The irony here was that the Vice President had urged me *not* to run. He was always oriented to federal service and I remember him saying bluntly: "I think you're crazy to give up a cabinet post."

He predicted that I would be branded a tool of the administration and, indeed, in the general election, in the fall of 1962, so unpopular was the Kennedy administration in Texas that my Republican opponent hardly ran against me at all, but against Washington.

With a campaign to run, there was no appropriate time in 1962 for me to host a Presidential visit. I had continued to ignore, as best I could, the barrage of hints coming down from Washington that the President wanted a Texas pilgrimage. They began early in the year, when I had just started campaigning in the first primary, with six candidates, including the incumbent governor, in the race. My first poll showed me with a meager 4 percent support. In Texas, in the day of one-party politics, we didn't have a powerful party structure that raised funds and focused support. Every Democrat ran on his own, built his own organization, raised his own funds. I was desperately trying to pay for my campaign and to rally support, and the last thing I wanted was a national foray for votes or money.

The urgings from Washington had continued through 1962. I finished first in the primary, and won the runoff and then the general election. Then I had a bare sixty days to assemble a staff and prepare a program that I had to maneuver through the legislature in early 1963.

I had not intended to stall President Kennedy indefinitely. We admitted the obligation, and he knew we would honor it eventually. Of course, there was nothing to prevent him from visiting the state; he could have come whenever he chose. But he wanted me to plan the trip, and wanted me deeply involved in the money-raising. I think he felt that I was more in touch with the elements from which he needed help than any other man in Texas.

And he did need help. Though it is largely forgotten now, the country did not yet consider President Kennedy a roaring success. The disenchantment with the administration was not limited to Texas. The President had recovered somewhat from the Bay of Pigs, but the blood on the beaches of Cuba had not been forgotten. He had stirred people with his élan and his eloquence. He had inspired a renewed sense of national purpose and a quickening of interests in culture and government. But his programs were stuck in Congress, which felt no mandate from the people to pass them. That meant that although his goals were fine, his results were slight.

This was widely recognized then. A Gallup Poll in October of 1963 put him at his lowest ebb and David Lawrence quoted the President's own fears of defeat. James Reston, of The New York Times, thought those fears unreasonable, but reported "doubt and disappointment" among the voters, adding that "people don't quite believe in him."

And he had alarmed business. This was a reaction partly to his handling of a rollback in steel prices, but even more to his concept of the need for change. People are cautious of change in comfortable times, and businessmen particularly so. They were suspicious of him, and though it irritated him to hear this and he thought the concern was unwarranted, that was the political reality.

What's more, while the trip represented work, trouble, and some risk for me, I also knew that I could expect little of the benefit that state officials usually get from a President's prestige. Many of the people who were Mr. Kennedy's most active supporters in Texas also tended to support my opponents. Many of my most active supporters did not lean toward JFK. To rally new support for him and to raise funds, therefore, I would have to appeal to my supporters—literally, to spend my political capital—while knowing that in the election of 1964, in which I too had to run again, many of Kennedy's backers would be fighting me.

On the other hand, if I couldn't rally support for my own party's ticket in my own state, it would be a political embarrassment that I would not be allowed to forget.

In short, it was shaping up as a lose-lose situation for John Connally.

This was the picture in June of 1963 when I went to the President's suite in El Paso, knowing I had exhausted my running room. Most of my reasons for delaying the proposed trip were past. I had successfully gone through three elections and healed some of the wounds. I had stepped into the governorship and had seen my program pass through the legislature.

I did not know Jack Kennedy well, but I respected him, had served as Secretary of the Navy early in his administration, and counted him as a friend. He was cordial, as always, with that reserve which was characteristic of him. He seemed to be in a good mood. He had flown from Washington for visits in Colorado and New Mexico and had stopped off in El Paso; there had been a motorcade, and now he was turning with easy relish to one of the most practical aspects of domestic politics.

When I walked into the room, he was smiling and it was obvious to me that he had been ribbing Vice President Johnson gently and, I thought, with some affection.

"Well, Lyndon," he asked, "do you think we're ever going to have that fund-raising affair in Texas?"

The question was directed to Johnson but the bite was intended for me. Texas was honored to have a native son on the national ticket, and by the same token we were obligated to support the ticket financially. I know that my delaying tactics, though valid, had caused the Vice-President some badgering. Now he threw the potato to me.

"Mr. President," he said, with a side glance at me, "you have the governor here. Maybe now you can get a commitment out of him."

Both men were looking at me, and though they were grinning and it was cordial and relaxed in the room, I was fully aware of the force of the White House, and the seriousness beneath the smiles. "Mr. President," I said, "fine—let's start planning your trip."

The President said that he had been thinking about *four* fund-raising dinners or meetings—in Houston, San Antonio, Fort Worth, and Dallas. I was still gulping at the idea of four dinners when he said casually that he thought Johnson's birthday, August 27, might provide a logical date and reason for the trip. I am sure Johnson appreciated as well as I did the futility of the early date, but I think he was prepared to let me carry the ball.

"Well, Mr. President," I said, "you know my feelings for Vice President Johnson, but I must tell you that the very people you will want to reach are likely not to be here—Texas gets mighty hot in August."

"If you don't like that date," he pressed, "what date do you like?"

I wasn't prepared to offer an immediate alternative, and the President said, still friendly but not quite hiding his impatience, "Well, let's get on with it. We've been talking about this for a year and a half."

From that point on, I gave a great deal of thought to the President's visit. Once we began, I was fully committed to going ahead. But I was anxious to see that it went off well, and the first move to that end was to drop the plan for four dinners.

I felt there should be one dinner and that it should be held not in any of the cities the President suggested but in Austin, the state capital, a smaller city, centrally located, and traditionally considered neutral ground in Texas. It was the only place that people from other Texas cities would come to with no feeling of rivalry. Fort Worth people would resist supporting a Dallas dinner, or Dallas a Houston dinner. But they would all come to Austin.

On October 4, 1963, I was to be in Washington, and now, with firm ideas on what the visit should be, I sought and received an appointment with the President. He rose from behind his desk in the Oval Office with outstretched hand, then sat down in his rocker, gestured me to one of two small couches, and moved immediately into the subject.

"How about those fund-raising affairs in Texas, John?" he asked.

"Mr. President," I said, "I think it would be a very serious mistake." He didn't answer and I went right on. "In the first place, I don't think four will raise appreciably more money than one properly organized affair—certainly not enough to make up for the political cost to you. You haven't made a real visit to Texas—except to El Paso—since you became President. You've made no speeches and no appearances. If you come down there and try to have fund-raising affairs in four cities on one trip, they are going to think you are trying to financially rape the state." I used just those words.

"I'm inclined to agree with you," he said.

"Mr. President," I asked, "what do you really want to do on this trip?"

In addition to the fund-raising, he said, he wanted to see and talk to some of the Texas people who opposed him so sharply. I think it galled him that conservative business people would suspect that he, the wealthy son of a father who thrived as a capitalist, would do anything to damage that system. He added with some heat, "They don't have any reason to fear my administration."

I had a strong conviction that if the business community in Texas could see President Kennedy in the flesh and talk to him, it would find quickly enough that he was not their enemy. I told him, "If you come down there and try to convert some of the more conservative people who have opposed you—or at least have been lukewarm—you are going to have to be with them and talk with them, and it is going to have to be done in a basically political meeting. What's more, these are the people who are going to supply the funds you need."

Texans are a courteous and hospitable people. The segment that distrusted President Kennedy would have felt neither desire nor obligation to attend an event centered on support of the national party. But I knew those same men would count it a point of pride and honor to entertain and welcome him if he appeared as President of the United States, instead of just another politician.

And I went on: "Now, I hope you can give us two days—time for an affair in Houston, something in San Antonio, a breakfast in Fort Worth, a luncheon in Dallas, and then the dinner in Austin. This dinner will be at one hundred dollars a plate and will be strictly political—but the rest of it should be nonpartisan. It will leave a good taste in everyone's mouth, it will enhance your prestige with all of Texas, and it will help you with the business element you're interested in reaching."

"I'll accept your judgment on that, John," he said. I told

him I believed he would carry Texas in 1964, though it might be close.

He nodded. "Lyndon thinks we'll carry Texas, but he says it will be hard." That thought irked him. He thought of the state as the safe haven for Democrats it had been for so long. "We shouldn't have a hard race in Texas," he snapped.

I suggested that if the trip was successful, his problems would be considerably eased. Then I ventured the thought that it would help if Mrs. Kennedy accompanied him. She had not previously gone on essentially political trips. But she had captured the imagination of the country, and particularly of the women. She had come to stand for culture, beauty, and fashion—her hairstyle and her wardrobe were news. The wives of the men he wanted to attract would be interested in seeing Mrs. Kennedy, and her presence would make the trip seem less politically oriented.

The President nodded. Mrs. Kennedy was in Europe then, he said, but on her return he would ask her. He said, almost wistfully, "I agree with you. I would hope that she would come."

I had dinner that night at the home of Vice President Johnson. When I arrived, he already knew that I had been with the President. He was visibly irritated. He greeted me with "Well, did *you-all* get the trip worked out?"

I said yes, and he said, "I guess you think I have no interest in the state of Texas or in this visit?"

I pointed out that I could hardly instruct the President as to his White House guests, but Johnson was not mollified. "I hope you know that I've got a *slight* interest in Texas," he said, "and in this trip, too." I regretted my thoughtlessness in not discussing the plans with him, and I apologized.

I went back to Texas, called in my staff, and began the extraordinary planning that a Presidential trip demands. There is no end to the detail that must be mastered, always with the knowledge that a single point overlooked can snarl a trip so hopelessly as to ruin it. A rule of working politics is that if a candidate falls an hour behind schedule, he might as well not have gone. The people who waited to see him will be irritated and resentful, and his message falls flat. Then the effort is all for nothing.

Soon the Secret Service men were in Texas and behind them came the President's own advance team, sent down by the White House to oversee all the arrangements. Just as I had anticipated, the troubles began almost immediately. They were of the political kind, not matters of life or death. So we thought.

JFK: Six Seconds
in Dallas

Nellie sat on the edge of the bed next to me in my room in Parkland Hospital that Monday morning, three days after the assassination, watching the images on the television screen. We did not talk, silenced by the sheer magnitude and the intimacy of the tragedy we had seen unfold.

It was unfolding still, before our eyes. We followed the caisson every slow, measured step it took down the broad avenues, from Hill to home to earth. The simplicity of that box with the flag draped over it, the great loneliness of each one among the many, would not have been bearable except for the dignity and beauty of the procession.

We were grateful every inch of the way for these traditions, for the awful solemnity of the muffled drums. There was a comfort in the rhythmic beat that broke the stillness, and the grief it echoed.

Tears rolled down our cheeks. It was an incredibly moving experience; indescribably sad. In my mind's eye, I can see as clearly today as I did then the riderless black horse with the boots turned backward, fretting and rearing, followed by a single sailor extending the President's flag.

Mostly I saw an immense longing, an aching need for people to express their grief in a moment that will be forever embedded in the mind and memory of all those who witnessed it. I have traveled to lands around the world, and I have yet to find any people approaching maturity who could not tell you where they were and what they were doing when they first heard the news of the assassination of John F. Kennedy.

The only dates in our modern history that had the same kind of impact were Pearl Harbor and the death of President Roosevelt. Some might add V-E Day (Victory in Europe): I don't. Too many of us were in places we didn't want to be, doing things we'd rather not have been doing.

Kennedy's death was a tragedy not only in the loss of a young President but a tragedy for the nation and the ages. As I watched the funeral procession from my room in Parkland Hospital, I couldn't help but reflect on what a thin sliver of time is required to transform triumph into tragedy. Six seconds changed the nation. That was all: six seconds. The thought stayed with me the rest of the day, Monday, November 25, 1963, as John Fitzgerald Kennedy was laid to rest. It is with me still.

I had been awake off and on that day, vaguely aware of Nellie tiptoeing into the room. She had brought the younger children and my mother with her. Unbeknownst to me, Nellie had sent our son John to Washington to attend the funeral on our behalf; he was in the company of President and Mrs. Johnson. He carried with him a personal letter from Nellie to Mrs. Kennedy. John was seventeen, solid and serious beyond his years, and we were confident he would represent the family well. Sharon was fourteen and Mark eleven, and each had been told by officials at their schools of the assassination and my having been wounded. They had faced the death of a sister bravely. Their strength came from Nellie.

I didn't realize until I woke up for the first time Sunday morning that my arm had been hit and the bones in the wrist splintered. Half-awake, I felt myself restrained. I looked up and saw my right arm suspended above my head in a sling. Thanks to Dr. Gregory, a brilliant orthopedic surgeon, I regained almost the full use of my wrist even though there was no bone intact. He told me at the time that I might regain 95 percent of my normal mobility, and that he would probably have to rebreak and reset it to attain the full use.

I closed that issue right there. I said there was no way I was going to let him break my wrist again to pick up the last 5 percent. Thinking back, I would not have injured the wrist at all if I hadn't been wearing a Stetson hat during part of the parade. I took it off and was holding it in my right hand across my chest when the bullet blew through it. The leg wound was little more than a puncture and of no consequence.

John Kennedy had been given a cowboy hat at the breakfast in Fort Worth, but he had declined in a good-natured way to wear it. A famous photograph of Calvin Coolidge in an Indian headdress had made an impression on him, and he was shy about any headgear that might make him look foolish. He said if anyone wanted to join him for breakfast Monday at the White House, he would put on the cowboy hat for them. Monday never came.

I knew my medical injuries would heal in time; the emotional trauma was somewhat more complicated. In the weeks after the assassination, there was a powerful paranoia loose in the country. No one could be sure what might happen, so the Texas Department of Public Safety installed steel plates over the windows in my hospital room.

Then the nightmares began. Every single night without fail, for the next two months, I found myself being shot at . . . under a never-ending series of scenarios. At times, I was in a war. At others I was being held up, robbed. Every dangerous human activity the imagination can manufacture paraded through my mind. And as those who have experienced such nightmares may recognize, I would try to outrun and escape the hail of bullets, only to find myself immobile, paralyzed with fear, unable to move. Then, suddenly, they stopped. The nightmares were gone, and in the intervening thirty years only the sobering sorrow of the tragedy itself recurs in my mind.

I can't be clear enough about those days to describe my state of mind. Surprised to be alive, I suppose, but with utterly no sense of relief or elation. There was a lot to like about Jack Kennedy. We were not kindred spirits, but I believe we might have become allies, even true friends. Others always stress his style and personal charm. I admired his judgment and sense of distance. Wit can be risky for a politician. Adlai Stevenson's humor flew over the ordinary person's head. Bob Dole and Alan Simpson are known to have a flair for the one-liner, but both have been accused of being caustic.

Kennedy had compassion, which lets humor rise above comedy. He was so mightily at ease with himself. He didn't trot out Caroline or John, Jr., for votes, but there they were: she wobbling around in her mother's heels, he crawling under the Presidential desk. The little boy who snapped off the salute turned three Monday, the day of his father's funeral. Caroline turned six two days later. The trip to Texas had been scheduled so he wouldn't miss either of their birthday parties.

There are other aspects of the trip that require a more detailed explanation.

I was not anxious for President Kennedy to come to Texas. For a year and a half he had sought the visit that ended so savagely on the afternoon of November 22. The national anguish that followed his death produced the Kennedy legend, and I suppose it is natural that in the growth of the legend, the real purpose and circumstances of the trip have been obscured. Once and for all, let me try to set the record straight.

The fact is that President Kennedy wanted to travel to Texas with two distinct purposes in mind. The first was to raise funds. The second was to improve his political position in a state that promised to be critical in the election of 1964. He wanted me, as governor, to arrange the trip for him, but for what I considered solid personal reasons, I had been trying to stall him.

To understand what was at stake, some background is in order. The genesis of President Kennedy's trip was pragmatic and quite natural. Campaign funds are the fuel of politics, and it was important to begin raising money before the heat of the 1964 race began. The Democratic National Committee was four million dollars in debt, and yet Texas, a key state because of Mr. Johnson's place on the ticket, had contributed little since 1960. As we talked in El Paso that evening, I recall the President saying, "If we don't raise funds in another state, I want to do so in Massachusetts and Texas." This was a point of both pride and concern to the President. The national ticket had taken Texas's 24 electoral votes in 1960 by only a slender margin—46,233 votes out of more than two million cast—and its position had hardly improved since.

Kennedy and Texas enjoyed a special relationship, beginning with the move to push him as the Vice-Presidential nominee in 1956. That support helped convince him that his religion need not be an insurmountable barrier in the great Protestant states. There had been the day in 1960 when Kennedy offered Lyndon Johnson second place on the ticket. With breakfast forgotten, coffee cups stacked high, and the air stale with tobacco smoke, I had helped justify that deal as Johnson's campaign manager.

I would not give it great thought at the time, but during those negotiations Johnson had been calm and almost somber. I had not seen him before so deeply in this mood, but I would see it often after he became President. Normally, he dominated any conversation, and all his listeners. He was restless, confident, persuasive. But when faced with a great decision, he changed. He fell silent, almost brooding. He questioned without revealing his thoughts. All his energy appeared to be focused on the decision.

As the discussion wore on, we came to understand that

Senator Johnson had no alternative but to accept the nomination. He agreed, and thus had forged another link that bound Jack Kennedy to Texas. But it had not been an easy decision. Lady Bird Johnson was in tears at one point. She knew the dismay their friends and supporters would feel.

Some of these feelings were at the root of the troubles I had sensed and dreaded about Kennedy's trip. They lay in the great schism in Democratic politics in Texas, in a personal feud that grew in turn from a political feud that was even older. It had nothing whatever to do with the trip, except that in a tiresome fashion it complicated the arrangements. Only later, after the tragic ending, would the feud assume larger and distorted proportions.

For a number of years, Ralph Yarborough, then the senior senator from Texas, had been embroiled in violent controversy with Lyndon Johnson and with the majority of the state's Democratic leadership. The senator's support came generally from devout liberals and labor, and he had run three exhausting, expensive campaigns for governor in the 1950s before he managed to win his seat in the Senate. It is hard to do justice to the bitterness that such campaigns generate in a state where each candidate must rally and hold his own support, instead of relying on a party structure. I would not attempt to chronicle here the claims of betrayal and counterclaims of perfidy that infested those times, but it was clear that Senator Yarborough was and remained the enemy of Lyndon Johnson while they were both in the Senate and after Johnson became Vice President.

Nor, I must add, was I exempt from or outside this endless cycle of infighting. My identification with LBJ, alone, assured that I would be viewed with open hostility by the Yarborough side. Nor did I feel any urge to send candy-grams to Ralph and his backers, candor requires me to admit.

Since there was a constant clash between these sides on patronage matters, President Kennedy was entirely aware of the situation. Much later, it was suggested that the purpose of the President's trip was to settle this tiresome old feud. Simply as an

An American century had begun as Lela Wright, a schoolmarm, married John Bowden Connally, Sr., on January 27, 1908.

The original Connally homestead, paid for with profits from the family "bus line" in 1932, still stands today in Floresville.

All the world was a stage to these University of Texas Curtain Club players: John Connally, Idanell Brill, and Don Jackson.

Young Mr. Connally goes to Washington; greeted by LBJ campaigners Claude Wild, Sr., and Ray Lee (1939).

President John F. Kennedy has Defense Department firepower behind his desk: John Connally, Roswell Gilpatric, Bob McNamara, Vice-President Lyndon Johnson, Elvie Starr, and Eugene Zuckert.

New Secretary of the Navy John Connally is piped aboard the Sixth Fleet flagship, and welcomed by Admiral David L. McDonald. Connally had served under McDonald, then the executive officer on the U.S.S. *Essex*, during the war.

Texans Johnson and Connally, pictured with the Vice-President of
the Republic of China at a luncheon in 1961

The Connallys at home on the range: Nellie, John, Sharon, John
Bowden III, and Mark. The governor was a hands-on rancher at his
beloved Picosa.

The Presidential limousine approaches the underpass in Dallas in this clip from the famed Zapruder
film; the expression on John Connally's face seems
almost apprehensive.

President Lyndon Johnson has the attention of Governor Connally aboard Air Force One; Nellie and Lady Bird look on, side by side.

The 38th governor of Texas, John B. Connally, Jr., and Nellie savor the moment on Inauguration Day, January, 1963. Their younger son, Mark, squints into the bright Texas sunshine.

Vice-President Johnson and Secretary of Defense McNamara congratulate the new First Sailor and his lady.

Richard M. Nixon and Connally, silhouetted against the window of the President's Camp David retreat in December, 1972

The Texas Ex-Governors' Club: from left, William F. Clements, Jr., Dolph Briscoe, Preston Smith, John Connally, and Price Daniel

A classic kind of love, shared through trial and triumph. "I can't remember," said Nellie, "when I didn't know John Connally."

exercise in logic, this was ridiculous. First, both men operated in Washington, not in Texas; one was across the street from the President and one was less than a mile away, and Washington would have been the place to settle it. Second, Presidents never inject themselves into such quarrels, for they can only get hurt. Third, the President couldn't have settled it anyway; the quarrel was implacable.

The trouble began when Senator Yarborough started to recommend changes in planning to the President's advance men, who, in turn, tried to force them on me. They wanted to give the President more crowd exposure and less of the exposure I believed he needed and, from our conversation in the White House, believed he wanted.

My focus on the businessmen, who hold power in politics through the money they contribute, but even more through influence in their communities, did indeed tend to cut out some of the President's most ardent supporters. He could have had, for instance, the type of trip that involves great public rallies, and receptions for labor, the state's liberal élite, leaders of the minority groups. But as a practical matter, I felt that his trip should primarily aim not at those who already supported him but at those who did not.

We went right ahead with the planning. A decision to dedicate the Aerospace Medical Center at Brooks Air Force Base in San Antonio, on Thursday, November 21, would serve as the non-political reason for his coming. In Houston, Fort Worth, and Dallas, the events would attract business and civic leaders—some of them nonpartisan—and provide the basic exposure he wanted.

Then, having shown the business community that the President did not have horns and a tail, he would move into straight politics. He would go into Austin for a reception at the governor's mansion, receiving the entire Texas legislature, and speak that night at a hundred-dollar-a-plate dinner.

The earlier tests had just a hint of the aura that surrounded his famous confrontation in 1960 with the Baptist ministers in

Houston. When he met these influential clergyman, whose beliefs, religious and political, were almost alien to his, and won
them over, he effectively put to rest the religious issue for all
time.

I had a particular interest in having the President see and
shake hands with all the members of the Texas legislature, the
150 House members and 31 senators, as well as the Democratic
state officials. I knew they would be impressed, and would return to every region of the state repeating what each said to the
President, and he to them, with some embellishment. They
would be our most direct link between Jack Kennedy and the
voters of Texas, and so I was anxious for the reception at the
governor's mansion to go well. I knew it would be of enormous
political value.

The plans for the Austin meeting suggest how complicated
these matters would become. Secret Service men had to check
out the hotel, the mansion, and the ballroom. The route the
President would drive was checked and timed. Arrangements
for the first reception were approved. The mansion wasn't big
enough to handle all the legislators at once, so we decided to
receive them in two shifts, which meant no refreshments would
be served. One group had to be herded out as the next came in.

A caterer took over the Austin banquet: 3,000 steaks, each
weighing 16 ounces, to be served hot approximately at once,
with potatoes, vegetables, several different kinds of wine, des-
serts, plus all the equipment and the people to handle it. Then
there would be the decorations, the sound system, the lighting,
the furnishings.

Those dinners were ticklish; they had to be well done, so
that the purchaser of a hundred-dollar ticket (top dollar then)
felt he had been entertained, but not so lavish that he decided his
political contribution was being wasted. Then there is the program—who will speak and for how long; and the seating arrangements—who will be at the head table, who will sit closest and
who farthest. Political contributors, in effect, are politicians,
too. They have their own influences to protect. Handling such

a dinner becomes an exercise in diplomacy.

Thus we came to the final week in a welter of detail, confusion, and change. Enthusiasm was weak and ticket sales lagged. I manned a battery of long-distance phones for two nights and personally sold more than fifty thousand dollars' worth. Frequently, I had to ask the purchaser to take them as a courtesy to me.

President Kennedy's own advance men continued to press for greater public exposure, in what amounted to a fundamental disagreement on the purpose of the trip. In Fort Worth, for instance, they scheduled an outdoor speech in a parking lot across from the President's hotel. The biggest change and, as it turned out, the most regretted, took place in Dallas.

The Washington advance men wanted a motorcade. I wanted to skip the motorcade and go directly to the Trade Mart for his luncheon. There was a heated argument over this between the President's advance people and my planning staff in Dallas.

My point was that motorcades are exhausting. This may seem surprising—doesn't the car do most of the work?—but it happens to be true. You sit there with all eyes focused on you. The wind blows and ruffles your wife's hair. You wave and smile, just enough to look interested, but not enough to look foolish. Block after block, you maintain this quality of giving yourself in what amounts to thousands and thousands of microscopic human encounters. I believe it has a powerful psychic drain.

On that single day, Friday, November 22, the President was scheduled to speak twice in Fort Worth, again at a luncheon in Dallas, then to appear at two receptions in Austin and give a major speech at a fund-raising dinner that night. People know when the speaker is tired and performing at less than his best. I wanted President Kennedy rested and in good spirits, not exhausted. But in the end I was overruled. The President's advance men, on the scene in Dallas, laid on the motorcade through the heart of downtown. Then they released the route itself for publication in the Tuesday newspaper—a full three days before the event.

All of these differences were settled or accepted and nearly forgotten by the early afternoon of Thursday, the 21st, when President and Mrs. Kennedy landed at San Antonio. I believed that the trip would be smooth and successful; that he would see an excellent cross section of Texas, would be warmly welcomed by the people, and would raise more than $300,000—half of which would stay in Texas.

The money may seem modest today. This was long before Ronald Reagan came along to make the three- or four-million-dollar dinner almost routine.

In the end, all we had to show for the trip, the planning, the anticipation was a nightmare at noon and a long period of national numbness. The food went uneaten, the music unplayed, the speeches unheard.

Every year, as the calendar draws closer to the third week in November, I hear from the television networks, the newspapers and magazines. I also hear from them whenever the latest outrageous conspiracy theory is introduced.

Before filming began on the movie JFK, I was visited by the director, Oliver Stone, and two of his assistants. We went to dinner and actually had a civil and undeniably interesting conversation. He started out by saying he had read many of the available books and found them persuasive, especially one authored by the discredited former New Orleans prosecutor, Jim Garrison.

They had picked the least plausible theory, from the least credible source, as the basis for their screenplay. Garrison all but plucked out of thin air the unfortunate Clay Shaw, a man of some distinction in New Orleans cultural circles. But Shaw was convenient prey because he was a homosexual, poorly positioned to defend himself against the onslaught. There was nothing else about him to raise suspicion. He was politically inactive, known among his friends as an admirer of Kennedy's.

Garrison had cast him as the mastermind of a very complicated plot, one that also involved an unemployed pilot, David Ferrie, who was distinguished only by his appearance—he was totally bald and had no eyebrows. Garrison later would be treated for psychiatric problems.

I said, "Well, Oliver, it's your movie and your story. But the general feeling at the time was that Jim Garrison was a publicity seeker and a buffoon, and that he fizzled completely in trying to build a case for a conspiracy. He was an embarrassment to the legal profession (which is saying quite a bit right there). As far as I know, he disappeared into the darkness. Beyond that, I have nothing to add. Obviously, what I say won't change your mind or the focus of your movie."

He said, almost in disbelief, "You don't think there was a conspiracy?"

I said, "No, I have never seen any credible evidence of a conspiracy."

He said, "I think there was, and I think Lyndon Johnson was involved."

I said, "What evidence do you have to support *that* claim?"

He said, "It is alluded to in several books."

I said, "I didn't ask what you found in the books. What evidence do you have?"

"Well," he said, "most people think there is a conspiracy."

Of course, I could agree with that statement. Most people do believe there was a conspiracy. The most recent polls probably indicate that over 60 percent hold that view. They don't know why, they just do.

Stone's movie was released, did great business at the box office, not surprisingly, and reopened a good many old wounds but no new ground. The Warren Report will continue to be attacked; yet I knew and admired every member of the Commission. Earl Warren was a courageous Chief Justice and a former governor of California. The panel included two senators, Richard Russell, of Georgia, and John Sherman Cooper, of Kentucky; two congressmen, Hale Boggs, of Louisiana, and Gerald Ford, of Michigan, a future President; and two lawyers, who had served Presidents of both parties, Allen Dulles and John J. McCloy. I find it unthinkable that their integrity in any forum, and particularly in this difficult and sensitive task, would be questioned.

Earl Warren, on the left, and Richard Russell, on the right, were then regarded as polar opposites of political thought. "What possible set of circumstances," mused Warren, "could get Dick Russell and me to conspire on *anything?*"

No one was obligated to accept all of their findings, including me. McCloy, who had been the U.S. High Commissioner for Germany after World War II, challenged my memory of being struck by the second shot. The Commission had embraced the theory that a single bullet had passed through the President's neck and into my back. McCloy recalled that while he was in Germany, he saw a young soldier standing on a platform hit by a stray bullet from some distance away. The shot was an accident, the soldier not even aware he was hit.

In rebuttal, I failed to see the analogy. I certainly knew when I was hit. And, in my judgment, it was virtually impossible, given the alignment of our bodies: for the bullet to exit his neck and go through my back, it would have been required to make almost a sharp right turn.

If that encourages the conspiracy fans, so be it. I can't tailor my memories to fit someone else's diagrams.

But the theories were fed initially by a series of strange coincidences, including the deaths of several fringe figures who either witnessed the assassination or knew someone connected to the case. Seen separately, none of the deaths were mysterious.

Still, people universally suspect the worst, and the Warren Commission was confronted with an impossible challenge. Even after interviewing thousands of witnesses, and compiling hundreds of pages of documents, how do you prove a negative? How do you prove there wasn't a phantom second or third killer, an Oswald double, a Manchurian candidate? You don't.

One of the theories that received early circulation paired Lyndon Johnson and H. L. Hunt, the eccentric, right-wing Dallas oil billionaire. They were supported by the oil cartel, and their objective was to get rid of John Kennedy so the Vice President could succeed to the nation's highest office. I don't believe Johnson had slept a night in the White House when this one was out in the open.

I think the charge is contemptible on the face of it, and even given the liberties taken in the name of art, Oliver Stone should be ashamed.

Johnson was well aware of the stories and so sensitive to them that he hounded Dick Helms at the CIA and J. Edgar Hoover at the FBI for any shred of evidence that might be disclosed. Some years later, as Secretary of the Treasury, I had authority over the Secret Service. I asked for every file, every report related to the assassination. I talked with every agent who worked on the case. There was simply no credible evidence that would lead any sane person to believe a conspiracy had succeeded for the past thirty years.

The rifle that killed John Kennedy and the handgun that ended the life of Officer Tippit were proved through receipts and deliveries to mailboxes to have been ordered and purchased by Lee Harvey Oswald, using at least two aliases. His fingerprints were on the weapons. A paraffin test on his hands and face showed he had recently fired a weapon.

Frequently, he took the rifle, a 6.5-mm Mannlicher-Carcano, out to the target range. Other shooters recognized his picture in the papers; they had admired his skill, how tightly he grouped his shots on the target. He had used the weapon at least once previously, when he stalked and shot at and missed the ultraconservative idol of the John Birch Society, General Edwin Walker, who lived in Dallas.

Oswald's wife photographed him holding the rifle. His landlord complained about his keeping it in the garage, wrapped in a rug. On the day the President was murdered, the rifle was gone from the garage. Oswald had ridden to work that day with a neighbor, carrying a long, bulky package that he said contained curtain rods.

But I believe we have gone way beyond the value of any point-by-point rebuttal of all the many and creative conspiracy theories. I believe they all become untenable when you consider one fact.

At the time of the assassination, Jack Kennedy's brother was the attorney general of the United States. Could anyone have possibly believed that Robert Kennedy would have tolerated for one second the possibility that others had been involved, and they were free, unpunished, walking the streets of a city somewhere in the world? It boggles the mind. Bobby would have moved heaven and earth to prove a conspiracy, to ferret out, indict, and prosecute anyone who had a hand, directly or indirectly, in the death of President Kennedy, to whom he was totally devoted. His grief never left him.

No doubt some of those who have researched the assassination for years, burrowing into old files like moles, are sincere and driven by a desire to prove that the young prince of Camelot was wronged not once but twice.

Yet I am convinced that most are in it for the money, or notoriety, or excitement. They exploit the public's disenchantment with official answers, and the need in most of us for complicated plots. Very quickly, it became unpopular to defend the report of the Warren Commission and its one-man, one-gun conclusions.

I happen to support the major findings of the Warren Commission. I believe there were errors, including the so-called "magic bullet." My ear and my body told me that I was not wounded in three places by a bullet that hit President Kennedy. I remain convinced that he was hit twice, and I once, by three separate shots.

I have no doubt, absolutely none, that Lee Harvey Oswald acted alone, obsessed with the idea of being an important person, a figure of history, and with no other means at his meager disposal than to commit this most cowardly and repellent of crimes.

It is puzzling to me that no conspiracy theories survive about the deaths of Bobby Kennedy or Martin Luther King, or the attempts on the lives of George Wallace and Gerald Ford and Ronald Reagan. Of course, the killing of Oswald by the unstable Jack Ruby eliminated our one hope of getting answers, and stoked the conspiracy fires. But in regard to any and all of the theories, my final opinion is this: I cannot believe that any department or agency of this government is capable of concealing a secret of that magnitude for so long.

Of course, one of the subplots to the assassination was the Wrong Target theory; namely, that Oswald really intended to kill John Connally. According to this scenario, he believed that I ignored a letter he had written to me, as Secretary of the Navy, in which he demanded that I rescind the dishonorable discharge he received from the Marine Corps after his defection to the Soviet Union. He wanted an honorable discharge and the restoration of his rights.

By the time Oswald wrote me, I had left Washington and was running for governor of Texas. The letter was never forwarded to me, and today it is in the archives of the U.S. Navy. I have never read it.

While the theory did not originate with her, it was Oswald's wife, Marina, who gave it currency. As the first witness to testify before the Warren Commission, she had been the source of the photographs, had disclosed the botched attempt to kill General Walker, and had revealed Oswald's preoccupation with President Kennedy.

Then, questioned for the third time, in Dallas in September of 1964, she announced that she had changed her mind, and now felt the President was not the prime target. "I think it was Connally," she said, a conclusion that led Senator Russell Long to mutter, "Baffling."

I do not entirely disregard the possibility that the second shot was a mistake: when Kennedy's body slumped, the bullet barely missed him and drilled me instead. But I have a conviction—less than evidence, more than a belief—that Lee Harvey Oswald wanted to kill both of us, the two men in the car who represented authority to him.

I can reflect now on the Kennedy trip to Texas, and see clearly the choices and the vagaries of fate that cost him his life. If the advance team had agreed to the safer parade route, rather than the one most traveled; if the President himself had not decided to have the bulletproof bubbletop removed; if the motorcade had gone another ten feet before the first shot was fired . . .

I accept the finding that Lee Harvey Oswald was a misfit, disturbed, compelled to perform an audacious and dastardly act to make himself a footnote in history. But the trail he left through Cuba and the Soviet Union fueled every type of speculation. All of which would go unanswered once Jack Ruby pumped a bullet into Oswald's belly.

No report created by mortal hands could overcome those handicaps. Yet it is worth remembering that the report of the Warren Commission was published initially to widespread critical acclaim. The facts haven't changed—only time and memories.

I have often wondered why my life was spared. I have made a conscious effort not to trade on being a presence at the assassination; to have done so would be indecent. I do know that in the aftermath I was accorded a sympathy and a respect that I could not have achieved absently. The Kennedys, especially Bobby, treated me with courtesy they could never show Lyndon Johnson.

On either side of the aisle, Richard Nixon and Bob Strauss suggested that my place in this tragedy might have served as a springboard to pursue the Democratic nomination for the Presidency itself. As strange as it may seem, though I later ran for the office as a Republican, I never planned, or sought, or wanted a long career in politics. I know that most people view me as a political individual imbued, as so many are, with a burning desire to hold office after office.

My motivation was different. I wanted to do good things for Texas. I say, not immodestly, that I could have been elected to the Congress or the Senate. I had cut my teeth on national politics as an aide to Johnson. I became fully aware of the badgering, the conniving, the bargaining that were so much part of getting legislation passed. I knew I would be intolerant of the process and therefore not very good at it.

But I wanted to tap into the imagination and resources of Texas, and so the sorrow I felt over the death of John Kennedy was compounded by the initial reaction. The whole country was prepared to denounce Dallas as the City of Hate. The feeling was fairly general that the political weather in Dallas was really responsible for this crime. I thought that criticism was terribly unfair. Oswald had lived in Dallas only a few weeks. What happened could have happened in any city in America. No such criticism was leveled at Los Angeles when Bobby Kennedy was killed; none at Washington, D.C., when President Reagan was shot; none at Maryland when George Wallace was wounded and paralyzed. So we witnessed a wave of anger leveled at a city and a state and many who lived there, which illustrates how irrational we humans can be in times of acute emotional stress and crisis.

As my own healing began, in late November of 1963, and my thoughts cleared, I saw the assassination as a story with no hope. But there was one: the preserving of the Constitution, the orderly transfer of power. Even in the worst of times, we cannot retreat to an attic. And so the torch was passed, from Kennedy to Johnson, from Boston to Austin.

On a personal level, the changes that were taking place were at best jarring and often bitter. Better than most, I could appreciate the feelings on all sides.

Fate and politics had brought us to that point on that weekend, and I had seen the potential of John F. Kennedy. My respect for him, and for what I thought he could achieve, had grown. I could not help but feel a surge of pride as the car rolled past the cheering crowds; we were born the same year, both of us Navy men, joined by what I believed were two of the most beautiful wives in the country.

The trip was the first time Nellie and I had been around Jacqueline Kennedy for any length of time. Like everyone else, we had been charmed by her—her poise, the excitement and the allure that she brought to the role of First Lady.

Nothing she did before or during the motorcade detracted from the impression we had of her. There was no reason for the relationship to exist after the death of the President, but we continued to feel a deep sorrow for her loss. These warm and almost protective feelings toward her continued right up until the moment she married Aristotle Onassis.

I suspect that Nellie and I felt what many Americans did. It was illogical to expect her to remain a grieving widow for the rest of her life, but her marriage to Onassis had all the sentiment of a hostile corporate takeover. It was unfair to feel this way, but the last of many illusions had been shattered.

I had clashed with the Kennedy brothers on political grounds. I was not a romantic, a candidate likely to embrace those fleeting times as Camelot. But I believe that Jack Kennedy epitomized, more than anyone since Washington, the idea of an American royalty. From the founding of this country, we could never quite make up our minds whether we wanted to have a king or a President. We decided against a monarch, but over the years the conflict has endured—witness our obsession with England's royal family.

President Kennedy and Jackie became the symbols of that indecision in ourselves. The lingering part of it now is what might have been. This is what those six seconds in Dallas left us with: what might have been.

THE JOHNSON
EXPERIENCE

The nation suddenly rediscovered Lyndon Johnson, and the many sides of him, in late 1963. I understood his weaknesses, and even the peculiar spell he had over those of us who were considered to be among his inner circle. I would grow irritated with myself for being irritated with him.

We argued vigorously, to the point of his ordering me out of his home more than once. The three disagreements we never resolved were over the war in Vietnam; his social legislation, not the merit or justice of it, but the volume and speed with which these acts landed on states ill-prepared to process them; and his failure of nerve when he needed to reconstruct the cabinet.

Johnson inherited everything from Jack Kennedy except his charisma. The generals were clamoring to send in combat troops to assure a victory for our allies in South Vietnam. The civil rights movement was gaining steam, driven by pictures of Southern sheriffs turning attack dogs loose on black demonstrators. Now Lyndon Johnson, a Southerner, was in the White House.

In the aftermath of the assassination, I tried to persuade him to fire John Bailey as chairman of the Democratic National Committee, and to ask for the resignations of the Kennedy cabinet. Such recommendations undoubtedly will come across as chilling and insensitive, but I felt then, and do now, that these steps were critical to the success of his Presidency and in the interest of the country.

"Why should I fire John Bailey?" he asked, the first time we discussed it.

"Because he hates your guts," I said.

He looked at me with disbelief. "What makes you think that?"

I said I happened to know that Bailey was at the airport in Austin with Frank Erwin, a political ally of both mine and Johnson's, when they received the news of the assassination. "Frank heard Bailey say," I told him, " 'Well, this means that son of a bitch Lyndon Johnson is going to be President.' He didn't grieve for John Kennedy. His first reaction was to express his distaste for you. I sure as hell wouldn't have a man like that heading the party whose label I had to run under in 1964."

Johnson said, "I just can't fire him now, and I can't ask any of the Kennedy staff or cabinet to resign. They are all in shock."

"I know that," I said. "But if you don't make the changes you'll live to regret it. These are Kennedy's people. And they're good people, bright, top quality. The only thing wrong is that their loyalty isn't to you. They were committed to him, as they should have been. You're the President now and you are entitled to have your own cabinet, people you know, people you trust. I respect McNamara and Rusk and O'Brien. I'm not saying they will be disloyal to you, but they obviously can't have the same feeling they shared for Jack Kennedy."

He kept shaking his head. "I just can't change them now," he said. "I promise you. I will make the changes after the election in '64."

Of course he never asked for anyone's resignation. He replaced the ones who moved on and he suffered, I thought, for the lack of devotion on the part of some who stayed.

He did not want to be seen as callous or uncaring, and he felt a very real obligation to the Kennedy appointees. Part of it, too, was his demeanor, his conviction that he could always convert foes or strangers into friends. He would work at it unrelievedly, courting them, trying to convert people who disliked or distrusted him. Many times it worked.

These were the situations that often left me feeling irritated. He would be tender—not timid, but tender—in matters that I thought demanded toughness. All of which was part of the enigma. Often his behavior fell short of what was considered Presidential: undoing his shirt to show his gall bladder scar, lifting his pet beagle by the ears. At a fairly formal dinner, he would reach over and finish the food on someone else's plate.

This was the crude, earthy Lyndon, and I may be to blame for some of it because I kept telling him to be himself, to let his actions reflect the kind of fellow he was. "You're terrible on television," I said, "because you want to be Roosevelt or Kennedy. Why did Harry Truman finally win over the people? Because they came to see him as someone who was real, whose emotions were his own."

He could be as coarse as a hanging rope, or he could be charming and suave and poetic. Harry McPherson, an astute Washington lawyer who served in several jobs, said he was "like a combination of Boccaccio and Machiavelli and John Keats."

The fact is, we may have seen the real Johnson in all the people he tried to be. Nearly twenty years after his death, I hear and read the descriptions. I remember the fun in being around him. We were, in a sense, like the blind men in the Indian legend describing an elephant.

Early in 1960, the young Bill Moyers was working right outside the office of the majority leader when Senator Olin Johnston requested a meeting. Lyndon frowned, knowing that visits from the South Carolinian tended to be on the windy side. Reluctantly, he said, "All right, but he always wants something and he takes forever to get around to it. Here's what we'll do. Before you let him in, tell him I can only give him ten minutes."

Moyers did, and Lyndon greeted him at his doorway. He talked for the next nine minutes without inviting him in; then he looked at his watch and said, "Oh, I've got to go now, but Bill will walk you to the elevator, Olin, and you can tell him what you want."

At the elevator, Moyers said, "What was it you needed, Senator?"

And a somewhat puzzled Olin Johnston replied, "My niece is going to San Antonio, and I just wanted to know how you get into the Alamo."

Moyers left after four years on Johnson's staff. At the time, some lamented his departure as the loss of a liberal presence in the White House. That evaluation begged the point. What the President would miss was Moyers's sensitivity. Bill gave Johnson credit, as few others did, for having a quality of moral imagination. "He rose to the top," said Moyers, "in a game where you do not get there on the wings of truth, candor, or conscience. I never felt he wanted to use his power for himself. He questioned, in conversations with me, the very institutions that he had ridden to the top. He was obligated to Brown & Root, but he wasn't owned by them. He came out of a racist culture, but was not a servant of it. He adopted the Southern wing of his party, but he was never its instrument.

"He really did believe that power was a social invention that democracy could enlarge, and that is rare in a person who has risen to the top playing the game as roughly as he played it. He was a man who had a moral imagination, and that was the ability to see life as it was lived by people who did not have access to the success he did . . . blacks, the poor, women, and others. It wasn't God's gift or his own nature that got him to where he was, but his ability to work a system that he was then determined to change. I still don't understand it, all these years later."

Once President Johnson took you into his confidence, it could be hell getting out. He refused to accept the resignation of Henry H. Fowler as Secretary of the Treasury in early 1967, explaining that "there was a lot on the griddle" and he would need his help. He extracted a promise that Fowler would stay on the job another year. "Henry," he said, "I'm going to have to decide if I should run for another term." Then he shared a thought so personal his visitor was unsure he wanted to hear it: "The men in my family die young. I don't know if I can discharge the responsibilities of this office for another four years. I'm troubled about it and I'm going to have to make that decision early in 1968." Fowler left the meeting guessing that he had just experienced another form of the "Johnson treatment," but he wasn't sure.

In his television speech of March 31, Johnson gave three reasons why he was removing himself as a candidate: in the time remaining in his Presidency, he had to deal with the war, with the domestic unrest, and with the economy. He didn't touch on the fourth and perhaps most pressing reason: whether he would be physically able to perform his job, or even survive another term.

Johnson longed to be seen as an ethical man. When he appointed Sheldon Cohen to head the Internal Revenue Service in 1963, he assured him that neither he nor any of his assistants would ever call Cohen to meddle in the substance of a case. Indeed, if anyone did, Cohen should report it directly to him.

That understanding worked flawlessly until early in what proved to be the President's last year in office. Johnson called and said, without explanation or preamble, "Sheldon, I want you to move the Dallas regional office to Austin. Now that," he added, "is *not* a substantive matter."

Cohen responded as Johnson lieutenants frequently did.

He said, "Yes, sir," while his mind began spinning, searching for an escape hatch.

He asked his deputy to prepare a memorandum on all the problems that would be created by moving the office and its staff of two hundred from Dallas to Austin. The next day, the memo went to the White House, and at 11:30 P.M. the phone rang in Sheldon Cohen's house, upsetting his wife. "It's the President," she said, handing him the phone.

"I don't want to know what problems it creates," grumbled the President, "I want you to move the damned office."

Yessir.

The following day, he prepared a memorandum on how much it would cost to move the office. And that memo was delivered to the White House, followed by another late night call to the Cohen home. He sat on the edge of his bed as the President commanded, "Sheldon. Do it."

Yessir.

The next evening, the Cohens were among the couples attending a White House dinner for the prime minister of Australia. As they walked through the receiving line, Johnson looked at Faye Cohen and said, "Did he do it yet?"

Playing dumb, she smiled and said she had no idea what he meant. Sheldon was next. Johnson grabbed him by the arms and lifted him up to his eye level: "Did you do it?"

Cohen said unhappily, "Mr. President, I must see you as soon as possible." Johnson said, "Call Juanita," referring to his secretary, Juanita Roberts.

The next morning, Cohen was sitting across from the desk of the President, who leaned forward and said, "What's the problem?"

Cohen replied: "Mr. President, I have been here over four years, and you have never bothered me on a substantive issue. If there was no office in Austin, I could move it in a minute. But I have to move two hundred people and I have to explain to them why I did it, and there is no earthly reason other than politics. Therefore, if you insist I do this, every judgment I have made in the past four years will be judged on a political basis. I don't want to live with that in the history books, and I don't think you want to live with that."

Johnson said, "Oh, shit. You win." That was the end of it. A few days later, Cohen and his wife were invited to have dinner upstairs with the Johnsons.

Henry Fowler, who became Secretary of the Treasury in 1965, enjoyed the international scene. He traveled often and it was left to Joe Barr, then the undersecretary, to deal with the daily emergencies of President Johnson. It may not be generally known, but soybeans were recognized in the Treasury Department as "the golden crop," the most important source of foreign exchange the United States had. The word came down that Orville Freeman, the Secretary of Agriculture, was going to raise the support price on soybeans. Barr set out to see the President, and found him in bed in his nightshirt. Winston Churchill had once recommended to him the salutary effect of putting on a nightshirt and taking a midday nap.

Finally, he picked up the phone and said, "Orville, Joe Barr is over here and he tells me you're farting under the bedsheets." Joe, who had never heard the expression before, doubled up with laughter. He never did learn Freeman's answer or the end of the story.

Once, a friend of his, André Meyer, a New York investment banker, complained that the market was being flooded with too many agency bonds, the Federal Home Loan bank, the Fannie Maes, the Farm Credit Administration. Johnson decided the way to slow them down was to make every issue subject to his approval. This meant they had to find him, convince him to sanction the bond, and sign off on it. One day, he was unavailable and a bond had to go to market that day. They called the Secret Service and learned that he was in the barbershop in the White House basement.

"My God," complained Johnson when Barr found him,

"can't I get any peace from you people?" He looked at the document and said, "I don't think I'm going to sign this thing."

Barr said, "Mr. President, Alexander Hamilton borrowed thirty million bucks from the Dutch in 1789. Since that time, the United States has never been late or defaulted on an obligation, and by God we're not going to do it today."

Johnson jumped out of the chair and said, "You can't talk to the President that way."

Barr said, "It's my ass on the line as much as yours."

Johnson blinked and said, "Oh, go do the damned thing."

He responded to that kind of blunt language, and that kind of commitment.

He was a man always checking his options. In 1968, he transferred Lloyd Hackler from his staff to the Johnson-Humphrey re-election campaign, explaining that he needed someone whose loyalty he could count on, someone who knew how to count delegates. A week later, he made his television announcement that he would not seek another term in office. Hackler heard the news at the same time the nation did.

It was said that Johnson lent less than his wholehearted support to Humphrey, and that if he had been more forthcoming, Hubert would have won the election. Orville Freeman was equally close to both men. "There were sensitivities between the two at that time," he told me. "I happened to agree that the President had done the right thing in Vietnam, and I tried to convince Hubert to follow the line of the administration. As we all know, he did not do so.

"The staffs of the respective men started chopping away at each other, which tends to happen under those circumstances. I got to be an emissary running between them, explaining things. President Johnson would take after Hubert something fierce on stands he wasn't taking. Tirades. But he never let me leave without grabbing my arm and saying, 'Now don't tell him I said that. I don't really mean those things, but I have to get them out of my system. Tell him I want to help him.' "

There was that kind of undercurrent throughout the campaign, but during the final days President Johnson appeared at an enormous rally in Houston and left no doubt of his support for Hubert.

After the March 31 speech, Johnson raised the question of whether an incumbent President was obligated to attend his party's convention. Franklin Roosevelt, of course, had not attended two of his. At one point, Johnson was willing to very seriously consider going to Chicago because he felt his appearance might help Humphrey. Not everyone agreed, and he made the decision not to go.

It isn't enough to say that he was ambitious. He had the ambition of the day, of the hour, of the minute. That was what obsessed him and everyone around him. While the convention went on, a flurry of legal activity was taking place. President Johnson had flown to San Antonio for his annual medical checkup. The doctors found what appeared to be a growth on his intestine. Whereupon his ambition of the moment was to prepare himself to die.

There were more codicils to more wills, more real-estate transactions than one can imagine. The doctors in San Antonio had the good judgment to look up his complete medical history, and they found that the growth had been there since his earliest X-rays, and had not changed in size.

So at the same time that some press accounts were speculating that Johnson was afraid of going to Chicago and being embarrassed, his doctors now had to assure him that he didn't have cancer.

I think it is fair to say that at probably no period in his life were more different signals sent than in the last eight or ten months before the convention of 1968. He and I had long discussions all through the year of 1967, after I made up my mind not to run for re-election as governor of Texas. He said, "You have to . . . we must have Texas in '68."

Then he said, "If you're not going to run, I'm not going to

run." There was no reason, of course, for our decisions to be connected. We were not joined at the hip. The truth was, he didn't need me in the governor's mansion to carry the state. I would have been in a better position to help his campaign if I didn't have one of my own to run.

In the fall of 1967, George Christian, my former press secretary and then President Johnson's, came to Austin. As he tells the story: "He had been talking that summer about not running again, and this posed a relatively new problem for him: how do you *not* run? How and when do you tell the people? Mrs. Johnson supported that position. Then the President sent me to Austin to see Governor Connally because he wanted his views and his language in whatever speech he gave withdrawing from the election. I drove to Austin, met with the governor at the mansion, and spent the rest of the afternoon taking down his stream of consciousness on what the President might say in a withdrawal statement. I took that back to Washington and shaped it in a way that he might present it to his party, which was his thought at the time because that was how President Truman had done it. He never could find a forum he felt was exactly right; he was uncertain about what he ought to do. He decided that maybe the best time to do it was during his State of the Union address in January of 1968."

Christian called at the President's request to ask what I thought about his making the statement that night. I told him he would never have a better audience. George wrote and Tom Johnson, later the publisher of the Los Angeles *Times*, typed the final draft of his speech, but history records that he decided not to announce his decision that night. George Christian waited in the back of the chamber, excited by the knowledge that he shared with only a handful of others, waiting for the dramatic moment that did not come.

On the way back to the White House, Christian gingerly voiced his surprise: "Well, I guess you decided not to withdraw . . . tonight." Unspoken was the question of whether the decision was off the table.

The President said, "Well, it was sort of difficult to lay out a big program for the Congress, and say I want you to pass all these things and then conclude with 'Okay, thanks and so long, I'm checking out.' It just didn't work."

What few were aware of at the time—and all but lost from the record since—is how fervently Johnson hoped he would be drafted by the convention in 1968. Larry Temple was at his side at the ranch, acting as a conduit for messages from myself and Marvin Watson in Chicago. In secrecy, he had sent Watson to assess his chances of being drafted as the nominee.

His withdrawal statement notwithstanding, Watson was there for that specific purpose, talking with as many delegates as he could reach. My assignment was to ask the governors of the Southern delegations if they would support a movement to draft Johnson. Whether or not he would have gone through with it, one cannot say with certainty. It may have been a ploy to force Humphrey to support his Vietnam policy. But this I know: I was sufficiently convinced to put the question to the governors, and their answer was a resounding no.

I believe in his heart he wanted that moment of drama, the emotion of a convention swept away as in olden times, and the vindication it would represent.

If all the trees in all the forests turned to paper, you still could not write enough words to heal the divisions caused by the war in Vietnam. Not then, not in 1990, not ever. Five Presidents were connected to it: Eisenhower, Kennedy, Johnson, Nixon, and Ford. And of these two were scarred by it.

Lyndon Johnson was vilified for enlarging the war, Nixon for continuing it. I have always felt that the most visceral of the criticisms—that Johnson created the war and that Nixon could have shut it down sooner—were unfair.

My argument with President Johnson over the war was not

that he escalated it, or somehow should have avoided it altogether. I came from a different direction. I felt it was nothing short of criminal—and that was how I put it—to permit American troops to do battle, and die, without a commitment to winning the war. He felt we were winning the war. I did not think we were. I told him he didn't have time to win it. This was the first war in American history where the American people were asked to make no sacrifices whatever in behalf of the war effort.

"You are promising that the nation is prosperous enough to have guns and butter both," I said, "and we aren't."

If President Kennedy had not been assassinated, no one can be sure what might have happened in South Vietnam. But in any event, Lyndon Johnson became President, and the war became his war, and the military advisers advocated sending more and more American soldiers into that Asian quagmire.

His advisers kept assuring him that the war was being won, and that a few more men and a little more time would make the difference, until finally we had committed over half a million troops. We were obviously fighting a defensive battle, and in spite of all our efforts the essential trails of the North Vietnamese remained open. In spite of all the defoliants, napalm, and other measures, nothing eliminated the continual supply of arms and ammunition and men into the South from the North.

The news coverage in the United States, particularly the television coverage, became greater and more personal, resulting in nightly portrayals of young American servicemen being maimed and killed in a war we were not prepared to win, for a cause most Americans did not understand.

I discussed the war many times with President Johnson, particularly on his trips home, when we would invariably get together and talk about a myriad of problems. "What is occurring as a result of these nightly telecasts," I tried to warn him, "is a sense of national guilt. Heretofore, when Americans were fighting, those at home were giving up certain comforts. We had women working in factories. We had rationing of meat and tires and gasoline. The American people felt they were making a contribution and participating in the war effort. In this war they were not. And they could not, night after night, see the mayhem that was occurring without a sense of guilt that they were safely removed from it.

"They can take this so long," I said, well before the protests had erupted, "and then they will turn against you, and the war, and anyone connected with it."

His response generally was "I'm doing everything I'm able to do. I've followed the advice of the Pentagon and my military advisers. We are making progress. We are winning the war. We won the Tet offensive even though the press played it the other way. What would you do?"

I had been waiting for that question. I said, "I would give Hanoi seventy-two hours to announce that they were withdrawing from the field and terminating their invasion of South Vietnam. If they have not done so at the end of seventy-two hours, I would destroy Hanoi."

He said, "We've been bombing Hanoi. It doesn't do any good. It doesn't even slow down the flow of supplies."

I said, "I'm talking about using nuclear bombs. I'm talking about destroying Hanoi."

Of course, I realize there is a danger in giving wing to these kinds of thoughts. Images are raised of the movie caricature Dr. Strangelove, or Bombs Away LeMay. But my argument was: give them ample warning to evacuate their people from the city, and then act—or, at least, use the threat.

The President replied, "Good God, I can't do that."

I said, "Why can't you?"

"I don't think the American people would stand for it."

I said, "The American people won't stand for what you're doing now much longer."

"I don't have an adviser who would recommend it."

"Then your advisers are wrong. You have no right to commit American troops to any battle they are not allowed to win. You might as well withdraw them and surrender."

We had many such heated conversations. The war was consuming him, and us, and I felt rage and frustration that we would allow the bleeding to continue. He argued that he did not want to nuke innocent people, and I responded, "Hell, you're killing them every day. Whether you kill them one by one or by the thousands, each person has only one life to give. If you can stop the war, as Truman stopped World War II, you can save millions of lives."

Certainly it was heartrending to think of the innocent women and children who died and suffered at Nagasaki and Hiroshima. But it is also heartrending to watch the flower of young American manhood blown apart, night after night, in living color on television. It is a scene that is totally unacceptable and unbearable to the American people.

He was Lincolnesque in his capacity to feel a personal burden of guilt for the lives lost in Vietnam. And I know that if these words seem now to be overly harsh and cold, it is because they were invested then with an anger that was fresh and full. But I recognized, too, that these were arguments, like the war itself, that would not be won.

Jack Valenti had been a partner in a Houston advertising agency, and was on Air Force One when Johnson was sworn in as President. He stayed on as a White House aide, the first person the President saw in the morning—with the exception of Lady Bird. He later left to become head of the Motion Picture Association of America.

Valenti sat in on every meeting from November, 1963, into 1966 that the President had on Vietnam: "I took notes on a lot of these meetings. I saw every piece of paper that crossed his desk. I saw handwritten notes sent to him by the staff and by members of his administration. I want to make clear one thing, and I am only being certifiably correct for the time I was there, not one single member of the White House staff, not one member of the administration with the exception of George Ball, ever in any meeting or by written memorandum, ever urged the President to get out of Vietnam. Not one.

"The record is there. I say that because, as Edmund Burke said, 'Retrospective wisdom does make us all quite intelligent.' But the only time an opinion counts is when that decision is taken. Not two weeks later, not two years later. But nine o'clock tomorrow morning, what the hell do I do? And all that time, not one single wise, brilliant mind that populated his administration ever gave him contrary information. Given that, if someone asked me, given the information I had at the time, given the accumulated wisdom that was provisioning the President's decision, I would have done exactly the same. I want history to record that during the time I was there, zero voices were raised against the war in a way that would tell this President he was doing something not only unpleasant and untidy, but something that would soil the future of this country.

"Having said that, I frankly didn't understand him, either. I loved him and I followed him, but I sure as hell didn't fathom all that made him tick."

Valenti met Lyndon Johnson in 1956, when Warren Woodward introduced him among a group of bright young men in Houston. "I pass along to senators now sitting some of the things Johnson did. About once a year he would make a foray into about forty counties in Texas, searching out young men and women under the age of thirty-five.

"Woodward called and said, 'I want you to meet the majority leader.' There were about twenty of us in a room at the Shamrock Hotel and in he stalked, all six feet four of him. From the first day I met him, my opinion of him never changed. It was like you were in the jungle and you meet this magnificent panther on a hillside, silken, silent, and ready to spring. And you're both a little bit afraid and at the same time totally fascinated by this jungle animal. And I never lost that kind of fascination, just being around him, because he was very exciting. He was also one tough son of a bitch. He was a hard, cruel man at times.

"I remember one time talking to him on an open car phone,

and he lashed into Bill Moyers like I had heard no man lashed into. I don't remember what it was about, but when I took Bill's side of the argument he lit into me, and damned near blew me away. This was symptomatic of the way he operated. But if you understood the moods you could handle it."

Valenti cited as an example "The Brick Wall Incident" that has become part of the lore of the Johnson White House. It occurred after he had left but was still a frequent guest in his role of Movie Mogul, the title the President teasingly gave him. Jack told the story during a symposium I moderated at the LBJ Library. It illustrated the difficulty any of us faced trying to read Johnson's moods and deflect the actions that were destined to get him in trouble if they proceeded.

The President was upset because a secret visitor had been spotted by the press entering through the basement. The entry was on West Executive Avenue, a narrow access between the White House and the Executive Office Building. This had happened before, so Johnson decided to do something about it. He instructed the General Services Administration to design a wall that would cut off the reporters' view.

At which point the story began to circulate through the press office and elsewhere in the White House. There was consternation all around, but no one wanted to argue with the President. Finally, a staffer enlisted Valenti's advice on what to do about the wall, before the bricks started arriving and the reporters saw what was going on.

Valenti called the President and coaxed an invitation to drop by for a cup of coffee. He turned it over in his mind, how he would raise a subject he knew to be touchy. And it came to him: "By the way, Mr. President, I see you're building a wall out there and by God it's about time you did that. That damned press, nosiest bunch of people in the world. I'm so glad you're doing something about it."

Johnson beamed. And Valenti continued: "Of course, you're going to have to put up with all the jokes. They're going to really ridicule the White House, and the Gridiron Dinner will probably have a skit on it, but I know you can handle that and laugh right along with them."

Johnson was silent. The next day Jack got a call and was told: "I don't know what you said, but the wall is coming down."

Power in Washington is determined by your access to the President: that's the coin of the realm. Before the plane took off to Washington on that nightmarish trip from Dallas, the President called Valenti aside and asked him to fly back with him. He wanted him on his staff. Jack said two things, both wrong. "I don't have any clothes, Mr. President." "You can go buy some." "But I don't have any place to live." "Well, you can live with me until your wife can join you."

Valenti moved into quarters on the third floor of the White House. Being within arm's distance of Lyndon Johnson meant being with him every hour of every day. The days were long and the nights were short. "He'd call me about five-thirty in the morning and ask, 'What are you doing?' What would anyone be doing at five-thirty? I wish I had remembered what Wayne Hays once said to him at a similar hour, 'Well, Mr. President, I've been lying here hoping you would call.'

"He'd say, 'Get out of bed, we have work to do.' I would groggily find my way to his face and we would get started at six in the morning, and work past midnight. His impact was all-embracing."

One question will not go away. If he was such a Satanic figure as some depicted him, why were so many so loyal to him?

Sixty miles west of Austin, the LBJ ranch is an oasis of green pastures, sparkling water, and majestic oak trees. The ranch house overlooks the Pedernales River. It was here that he spent his last five years, on the land he loved, withdrawing more and more into himself.

I saw him there several times after his return from Washington, and invariably I came away from those visits saddened.

It seemed to me that he was a lonely man who had—entirely out of character—resigned from life itself. He had entered into old age before his time, had gained too much weight, and punished himself by returning to old habits long buried. He smoked, drank, and ate to excess.

He knew exactly what he was doing, yet in an air almost of despair he continued to assault his own health. I believe he had convinced himself he didn't have long to live, and now he was like a race-car driver cutting the turns as sharply as he could. He would do whatever he wanted, whenever he wanted, without regard to his own welfare or anyone else's concern.

I was with him at the hospital in Fort Sam Houston after a flare-up of his heart problem. He said very little, and I had to choke back the impatience that welled up in me, the anger that clashed with the sympathy I felt. It was hard to watch this proud man I had known so many years, who had been vain of his appearance and fired with ambition, now suddenly devoid of a desire to lengthen his life. In a manner that was almost petulant, he had refused to develop any new interest, to dream any new dreams. He had consigned himself instead to days of defeat and despair.

Much of this, I think, was the lingering result of the way he left public life. He never fully recovered from his treatment at the Democratic Convention of 1968, when he fell so in disfavor as the outgoing President of the United States that he was made to feel unwelcome by his own party. In 1972, no one dared or cared to mention his name until Thursday night, when Senator Edward Kennedy did so in a gracious speech.

The convention backdrop featured portraits of Roosevelt, Truman, Adlai Stevenson, and John Kennedy, but none of the President who had done more than any other to protect civil rights, the right to vote, and the right to obtain fair housing for all. How clearly the picture was drawn: a party closed its eyes, and turned its back to him.

He had devoted his life to public service, and whether you liked him or disliked him, approved or disapproved of his poli-

cies, no one could claim that he did not give the ultimate in
energy and intellect and dedication to his task. Then, rejection
by his own party and, he felt, by the nation in general.

A lesson he knew well, he now relearned. When you are in
high office, you have many friends. When you are in a position
of power, the captains and the kings come courting. But when
you are sitting in retirement on the banks of the Pedernales, you
are no longer attended by the powerful, the beautiful, the rich,
or the famous. He found himself too often alone, and lonesome,
waiting for phone calls from old friends, many of which never
came.

A man who lived a life throbbing with activity and decisions, and interesting people who jumped to do his bidding,
now resorted to awkward phone calls asking others if they could
find time to visit him. It was a miserable and solitary time for a
man who had always found it necessary to be surrounded by
people.

He had never taken the time to develop a love of reading,
of sports or music, or an appreciation of any of the arts. Nor did
he ever attempt to acquire any other taste or talent beyond the
craft of statesmanship, and that was now denied him. Like the
captain of a ship who had spent his entire life at sea, he was
suddenly landlocked, never again to sail.

The deterioration of his health was gradual; by early 1972,
it was irreversible, a textbook case, I believed, of a self-fulfilling
prophecy.

Since his dramatic speech of Sunday night, March 31, 1968,
I have always thought that history would be kinder to Lyndon
Johnson than the public and the press and the academics of that
time had been. Twenty-five years have passed and it has not
happened yet, but I stand by that judgment.

That night, at least, he stirred the country with the crucial
sentence of a long and eloquent speech: "I shall not seek, and I
will not accept, the nomination of my party for another term as
your President."

He made no effort to gloss over the growing American

casualties in Vietnam. But he felt certain they had not been in vain. "I believe," he said, "that a peaceful Asia is far nearer to reality tonight because of what America has done."

One might argue that the emergence of *glasnost* and the retreat of Communism have less to do with, say, the invasion of Grenada and the arms buildup of the '80s than the stands taken by American Presidents in Korea and Vietnam. The political wisdom of those years was summarized by John Foster Dulles, who gave us the domino theory. While I am not an advocate of any policy that prefers containment to victory, I recognize the need to justify past sacrifices. As Harry McPherson, one of the President's top aides, wrote in 1972: "What had seemed inevitable four or five years ago—the rising of the Red Star over Asia—was no longer so. Indonesia, South Viet Nam, Thailand, Malaysia, the Philippines had at last been given time to strengthen themselves; whether they had made sufficient use of it only the future would tell."

It is often said that Johnson was in effect driven from office by mounting opposition to his policies. Anti-war protesters, young and not so young, should not flatter themselves. Their noisy protests may have been music to Communist ears from Hanoi to Peking to Moscow, but they had little or nothing to do with the President's decision to leave the White House.

Why, then, did LBJ decide not to seek another term? Certainly it was not for fear of Senator Eugene McCarthy and his student legions, or Bobby Kennedy, or Richard Nixon, his likely opponent and one he probably could have defeated. The reasons were different and distinctly so.

First, there was the President's overriding concern for keeping the nation's economy stable. Unlike Reagan, who engaged in a variety of reckless remedies, Johnson was determined to see the federal budget balanced in a time of foreign war, and balanced honestly. The solution he and his advisers finally agreed on was a 10 percent income-tax surcharge. Keep in mind that inflation was rising (from 1.3 percent to 3.4 percent per year) and so was the deficit required to pay for both the war and the Great Society programs.

In his March 31 address, Johnson left no doubt of the importance of balancing the federal budget and the trade deficit as well. ". . . Failure to act and to act promptly and decisively," he declared, "would raise very strong doubts throughout the world about America's willingness to keep its financial house in order. . . . Tonight we face the sharpest financial threat in the postwar era. . . . The United States must bring its balance of payments to—or very close to—equilibrium."

Second, there was the country's increasingly deep and bitter division on foreign and domestic issues. Far more than his political hero, Franklin Roosevelt, Johnson was and remained a consensus President. "Come, let us reason together" had been one of his favorite maxims for years. By early 1968, he recognized that he could no longer get the country to consider a variety of controversial and pressing problems seriously and with dispassion.

In these times, as Johnson put it in his address, "as in times before, it is true that a house divided against itself by the spirit of faction, of party, of region, of religion, of race, is a house that cannot stand." As the President saw it, there was only one possible solution to his dilemma. Let someone else attempt to restore the country's political and psychological tranquility.

Finally, and perhaps most telling, was the state of his health. For decades, he had driven himself unmercifully, and by early 1955—when he suffered his near-fatal heart attack—he was beginning to pay the price. Johnson was more prudent in the years that followed, but by the mid-1960s he was felled by one ailment after another.

I knew him to be increasingly fatalistic about his health. Few prospects worried him more than the possibility of a physical breakdown similar to Woodrow Wilson's in September of 1919, a collapse that left that wartime leader largely incapacitated the final sixteen months of his term.

As Johnson recalled in a little-noted passage in his memoirs: "Whenever I walked through the Red Room and saw the portrait of Woodrow Wilson hanging there, I thought of him stretched out upstairs in the White House, powerless to move, with the machinery of the American government in disarray around him. I frankly did not believe in 1968 that I could survive another four years of the long hours and unremitting tensions I had just gone through."

By the time he had written those words, and resigned himself to the seclusion of his ranch, Johnson had convinced himself that he never held out hopes of a draft in 1968, nor did he want to appear at the convention. And yet I know he did. I know he wanted to hear the accolades—hear the sound of applauding hands—which were denied him.

Based on reports from Marvin Watson and others, put as gently as possible, he understood that he would not be well received. There would be, at the least, boos and catcalls. He would be a disruptive force instead of a healing one, and that was an indignity he would not have wanted to suffer.

A point begs to be made here that so many have missed or ignored. His last months in the White House witnessed no weakening in his search for a just and lasting peace in Vietnam, nor in the economic and social legislation he felt was so needed at home. The most remarkable thing about his last year in office is not how embattled he was but how much he achieved under the circumstances—including a budget surplus of $2.1 billion, the last attained by an American President.

As it turned out, Johnson's concern about his health proved all too prophetic. Even freed of the burdens and pressures—but increasingly careless about diet and smoking and drinking—he survived barely four years after leaving office. On the afternoon of January 22, 1973, he died of a massive heart attack at the ranch outside of Johnson City. His last public appearance had been in December, at a civil rights symposium in Austin.

He was sixty-four years old.

His successor, Richard Nixon, paid him a fitting final tribute. They were the two most controversial figures on the American political stage in my lifetime, contrasting sharply in their natures, yet linked in the public mind as haunted men. It is not surprising that there would be a final empathy between them. "No man," said Nixon, "had greater dreams for America than Lyndon Johnson."

Invited to give the eulogy, I concluded with these words: "Along this stream and under these trees he loved, he will now rest. He first saw light here. He last felt life here. May he now find peace here."

THE GOVERNOR

My entry into the race for governor of Texas was unplanned, which is not to say it was impulsive. In one respect, I doubt that I would have moved when I did if not for what I had seen and learned in my year as Secretary of the Navy.

I had returned to Washington in January of 1961, fully expecting to stay there for the length of my appointment. We bought a house on Foxhall Road, and settled in after the children finished the school year in Texas.

Then a series of unrelated events occurred. John Tower, a Republican, won the Senate seat left vacant when Johnson became Vice President. Tower defeated Bill Blakeley, who had been appointed by Governor Price Daniel to fill the unexpired term and then won the nomination in a wide-open primary. I was irritated by the loss. Blakeley was a friend of mine, but he was far to the right, and a weak campaigner with no conspicuous interest in how government worked. What he had going for him was the gratitude of two governors—the other being Allan Shivers. Twice Blakeley had been appointed to open seats, and twice he had lost.

From Washington, I was watching the moderate-conservative wing of the Democratic Party in Texas self-destruct, and in danger of losing control of state government. The result would have been a legislature more fragmented than ever, almost leaderless, with continual sniping and obstruction by those on the fringe. I did not consider it in the best interest of Texas for this to happen.

At the same time, I had a ringside view of how and where the Defense Department spent much of its enormous budget. Hundreds of millions of dollars annually were funding research at such institutions as Harvard, MIT, Cal Tech, and the Rand Corporation. In turn, these think tanks were attracting the brightest young minds in the country.

It was apparent to me then that new industries would flow from this research, creating new products, new facilities, and new knowledge. I also envisioned that this culture and its clients would be located in proximity to the research centers. And so they were.

The clustering of the new technologies in Silicon Valley, California, and in the Harvard-MIT area of Massachusetts opened my eyes. I concluded that somehow Texas had to be awakened to the changes that were occurring, and that the state would need a revolution in its educational system in order to compete.

One other piece had fallen into place. During my years with Sid Richardson, I had been able to put aside some money for the first time in my life. I had made up my mind years before that I would never seek office until I had achieved a feeling of independence. That was the main reason I hadn't run for Congress in 1948. I was not concerned with being rich or even secure. The key was to not need the office, or a second job, to pay your bills. I had reached that point.

And so, late in my first year as Secretary of the Navy, I decided to run for governor. In making the decision, I relied more on my own instinct than any other factor, because by any reasonable standard I had no chance to win.

A handful of people who were closer to the scene urged me

to make the race. Bob Strauss, my former law-school classmate, organized a dinner in Dallas in my honor. In theory, the occasion was to recognize my role as Secretary of the Navy and the highest-ranking Texan in the Kennedy administration. Strauss, then practicing law in Dallas, feared that John Tower's election to the Senate meant more losses for the state Democratic Party. As he put it, the party elders wanted a candidate who could leave the Kennedy programs in Washington, but bring some of the Kennedy grace to Texas.

In November, I returned to my home state to speak at two more dinners. I had agreed to substitute for Sam Rayburn, who was gravely ill, at a Veterans Day program in Bonham. The next morning, I flew to Austin where I was to be honored that night as a distinguished alumnus of the University of Texas. A naval ROTC honor guard greeted me at the airport, and stood at attention to be inspected. I asked one midshipman his name, and the nervous young man thought I had called for "order arms." He brought up his rifle, and the bayonet struck me above the left eye and opened a bloody gash. I appeared at the banquet wearing a black eye patch, and the news of my injury preceded me. When I reached the head table, accompanied by Vice President Lyndon Johnson, I found that Harry Ransom, the University's chancellor, and Frank Erwin, later to become the chairman of the Board of Regents, had donned black eye patches. I took that display as a sign of tacit support.

To Vice President Johnson, the idea of my running for governor was pure foolishness. "Why in hell do you want to be governor?" he said. "This is where the action is, in Washington, in the federal government. You can have a great career here. This is where you ought to stay."

I suspected all along that he was being told by Ed Clark, the Austin lawyer and a savvy political analyst, that Price Daniel was going to run for a fourth term and I had no hope of being elected.

Indeed, when I did announce, in early December of 1961, my prospects appeared slim. The first polls taken showed me with 4 percent of the votes. Out of that dismal standing came the birth of the 4% Club. We ordered buttons with a blue background and nothing but the 4 percent symbol in white emblazoned across the face. Many of those buttons are still around, and even today I occasionally spot one when I appear at a public gathering.

The same polls showed Price Daniel favored by 50 percent of those surveyed, though Texas had never elected a governor to a fourth term. I called on Daniel twice to determine if he did, in fact, plan on running again. Our relations had been cordial, and I was reluctant to oppose him for the obvious reasons: my loyalty and his advantages. Daniel made it clear he didn't think I could win, but he said he had not yet made up his mind.

Our second visit was the first week in December, when I could wait no longer to declare myself. I was not well known and had to announce early if I hoped to compete. He was still deliberating, he said.

At the last moment, Daniel did offer himself for a fourth term, believing that he was the only candidate who could defeat Will Wilson, the incumbent attorney general, in the primary and win in the general election. He and Wilson had become bitter enemies after a long friendship, and his motivation was at least partly a personal one. In the grand Texas tradition—never settle for one feud when you can juggle two—Daniel had also fallen out with Shivers, who had served longer than any governor in the state's history. If Daniel served four full terms, he would eclipse Shivers's record.

I believe all of these points figured in his thinking. Then, too, people were telling him, as they tell every governor, things like "You're just as strong as horse radish. You can sure do this and you can sure do that and, yes, sir, whatever you say is right."

Daniel's big early lead in the polls did not discourage me. The voters held him responsible for a new 2 percent sales tax, and as he defended himself, his margin was going to shrink. There is a reason the pundits compare an election to a horse race—it works the same way. I'm not sure why, but it does.

You can watch the Kentucky Derby or the Preakness or any important race, and you rarely see a horse that breaks from the gate first finish first. This is true in politics. The candidate who is out in front early rarely wins.

Polls have probably defeated more politicians than the famous "incriminating photograph." To read one and try to project the results of an election six months away is pure folly. You have to go beyond the visible political positions. When you analyze their strengths and weaknesses, you include everything—appearance, size, age, looks, voice, mannerisms, dress, background, relationships, and the intangibles. Do they come across as forceful and sincere, or is the smile false and the manner bland?

You really don't know if a candidate can inspire people until he or she begins to campaign, if then. But the ability to lead and inspire can make the difference in the last two or three weeks. By then you rise or fall on the enthusiasm of the people in your organization.

Thirty years later, it may be hard to imagine that my being identified with Lyndon Johnson and John F. Kennedy could be a liability in Texas. But it was. Conservatives loathed the Kennedy brand of activism, liberals distrusted Johnson, and both felt betrayed by the circumstances that had put Lyndon on the Democratic ticket.

I knew the odds against me, but I felt a confidence far out of proportion to what the numbers showed. I still had the names of contributors and workers who had organized the state for Johnson's Senate campaigns in 1941 and 1948. They included many of my former University of Texas classmates, giving me contacts and a work force that the polls did not reflect. There wasn't a newspaper publisher in the state that I didn't know or couldn't call upon. This didn't mean they were committed to me, but at least I had an entrée.

With my "hard core" 4 percent support already in hand, I opened my campaign by telling the state's business leaders exactly what they did not want to hear. I told them that Texas was still in many ways a backward state, and they were foolish and shortsighted for wanting to keep it that way. I described how I had seen hundreds of millions of dollars in defense contracts awarded to states such as California, where sophisticated universities worked as partners with sophisticated industries.

"Industry follows brainpower," I told them. Politicians have a tendency to allocate funds for the construction of handsome buildings, where legislative pork-barreling and log-rolling are rampant. I was an advocate of more spending on faculty salaries and on research. Some of the business leaders nearly fainted when I said I wanted to double the salaries of teachers. Brains, not bricks, became a Connally war chant.

I also wanted the state to get into the tourist promotion business—I knew the dollars spent would come back to us a hundredfold. No one had run for the office in Texas with the kind of aggressive ideas I was proposing. Eventually, I would support liquor by the drink, parimutuel wagering, and a world's fair for San Antonio. I was described as a "cash flow" governor. I took it as a compliment.

As far as possible, I devoted the entire year of 1962 to the campaign. In a crowded field, I wound up in a runoff with Don Yarborough, the brilliant young liberal lawyer from Houston. We had eliminated an incumbent governor and an attorney general, a former chairman of the highway commission, and a list of fringe candidates that included retired Major General Edwin A. Walker. Walker had lost his post as commanding officer of the Twenty-fourth Infantry Division in Germany after it became known that he had indoctrinated his troops in the beliefs of the John Birch Society. He had resigned from the Army and settled in Dallas, unfortunately adding to the impression that the city was a hotbed of right-wing extremists.

I was proud of the fact that in the primary, I carried 83 percent of the vote of Wilson County, where my father had been county clerk from 1936 to 1942, and my brother Merrill had been a county commissioner and later a county judge. There is something uniquely satisfying about doing well where you grew up, where your family lived for generations. I understood that this degree of support was not so much of my own doing as a tribute to the reputation of my family over the generations.

My campaign manager was Eugene Locke, another Dallas lawyer and one of the smartest, most focused men I have known. He would later run for governor himself, unsuccessfully. But he had no seasoning in a campaign, and I wound up spending more of my time on fund-raising, public relations, and writing my own speeches than any governor elected in modern times.

All of which fit the image of the kind of campaign I planned to run. I wanted to bring new faces to Texas political life. I didn't think it was necessary to identify myself with the pros. And, besides, I didn't know where you could find one.

I defeated Don Yarborough by some 26,000 votes in the runoff, and then prepared to face Jack Cox in the general election in November. At the time Price Daniel was seeking a third term, Cox ran against him as a Democrat. Then Cox switched parties and ran as a Republican. He had served in the legislature, was articulate and well financed. Many regarded him as the first electable candidate the Republicans had nominated since Texas became a state.

All this switching around is part of what kept politics in Texas so lively. We were like a couple, each with children, who married and had more children of their own. One would look out in the backyard and shout to the other in alarm, "Your kids and my kids are beating the hell out of our kids!"

This was a confusing time for people who like their labels neat. The very liberal *Texas Observer*, which had been my most persistent critic, endorsed me. There were fears that Cox, if elected, would appoint General Walker to the University of Texas Board of Regents. At his party's state convention, Cox called for the United States to resign from the United Nations. Meanwhile, the Cuban missile crisis had turned my Washington experience into a more tangible asset.

In the *Observer*, editor Willie Morris wrote: "This nation needs as much moderation, restraint and understanding of the world power structure as it can get."

Still, this was not the perfect time or place to be running as a Democrat. Bob Strauss told me how his daughter came home puzzled one afternoon from Hockaday, a private school where wealthy Dallas Republicans sent their children. "Daddy," she said, "you and I are the only ones for Mr. Connally."

My campaign was a mix of old and new techniques. I whistle-stopped across Texas in a train; then made a late raid by air, sweeping through thirty-one cities in forty-nine hours. Nellie became the first candidate's wife to travel a thousand miles on her own and, as far as anyone knows, we were the first to hold morning coffees on television on "Coffee with Connally," a five-minute early- morning break during NBC's "Today" show.

With his attacks centered on the LBJ angle—"Lyndon's Boy John"—Jack Cox received more votes than any Texas Republican candidate for governor. The election was no runaway, but I won by 132,000 votes. When the results were official, I couldn't help but recall how Sid Richardson had picked up the phone and called me into his office ten years earlier. He turned to the Reverend Billy Graham, standing near him, and said, "I want you to meet a fellow who's going to be governor of Texas someday."

I was the 38th to take the oath of office. I had a salary of $25,000, an annual budget of $3 billion, and more than 200,000 employees.

I turned to the task of actually running the state, and began to lay out my program. I had definite ideas about where Texas should be headed and how to get there. About the future, I was proved right, which ought to count for something. I foresaw the coming of the sunbelt boom, and I knew Texas wasn't ready to take advantage of it.

I was as activist a governor as the state had ever had. I believed that leadership meant getting legislation passed, picking the right people for the right job, and keeping a self-serving bureaucracy in line.

As Jimmy Carter found out, and so will Bill Clinton, I could not please the liberals even when I championed issues that were dear to them. I called for sunset reforms, eliminating or consolidating a number of agencies that always seemed to have been there. The reforms would be enacted a dozen years later. I was the first Texas governor to call for the creation of a public-utility commission. I made the case for a revision of the state constitution six years before the legislature assembled itself for that purpose.

From the outset, my emphasis was on higher education. If we failed there, we could entertain no hope of unifying the state in the areas of race and social welfare. House bill Number 1 created a board to bring more intelligent direction to the role and scope of our colleges and universities. I hoped the board would husband and make more productive the monies that were to be funneled into higher education.

But it didn't stop there. We sought greater support for libraries, for research, for teachers' salaries, for vocational training. We developed a comprehensive water plan; created the Texas Tourist Development Agency and the Travel Trails of Texas. We combined the parks and wildlife commissions; their separate departments had constantly squabbled over such matters as which branch should pay for pencils. We merged the mental health and retardation agencies. We created the Texas Historical Commission. There was hardly an area of state government that we did not attempt to either reshape, reorganize, or create anew.

Having the right ideas is a part of leadership; selling them is no less important. I knew I would never persuade the business lobbyists to support my spending ideas, so I went over their heads. I talked to their bosses, to the chairmen of the boards, people I had come to know socially. I appointed twenty-five members to a Committee on Education Beyond High School, which was a virtual guidebook to power in Texas. It included H. B. Zachry, of San Antonio; George R. Brown, of Houston; the chairmen of Humble Oil, Texas Instruments, General Telephone, and Shamrock Oil & Gas; and the president of Ling-Temco-Vought.

To cover the costs of my education proposals, I submitted a bill that would raise $32.9 million in new taxes. For the first time in recent memory, such a bill passed the legislature without changes.

Still, I could not persuade the lieutenant governor, Preston Smith, and the speaker of the House, Byron Tunnell, to meet me halfway and allocate an extra $13 million for higher education. We met for two days and two nights, but they wouldn't budge. It was obvious that I was dealing with people in the statehouse who, however well intentioned, reflected the laissez-faire attitude that had prevailed in Texas government for too long.

The spending bill was adopted, and when I adjourned the legislature, I had a surprise for them. I announced that I had used a veto to remove more than $12 million from the bill, as a sort of layaway plan—a down payment on my plan to improve education. I promised the people of Texas, "I intend to let it accumulate as surplus to use for that purpose . . . and you may rest assured that I will guard that nest egg like an old mother hen."

For the first time since 1943, the legislature adjourned early. For the first time since 1955, no special session was required to finish the state's business. Within two years, the legislature had given me everything I had sought, including higher salaries and tenure for the faculty at the teacher colleges.

In 1876, in the post-Reconstruction era, the state constitution was crafted for the primary purpose of establishing as weak a government as possible. The governor has limited ways to exercise power, notably through his appointments, a worrisome process. For every appointment, you make one person happy and ten mad. On the other hand, the lieutenant governor and the speaker control the legislation.

When a vacancy occurred on the Railway Commission, the deceptively named but powerful body that regulates oil and gas, I thought it would be beneficial all the way around to appoint

Byron Tunnell to fill it. He was from East Texas and familiar with the workings of the petroleum industry. It was a perfect spot for him.

At the same time, the move gave me the opportunity to tell a young legislator, Ben Barnes, that he had thirty-six hours to line up the pledges (of support) he needed to become the new speaker. Ben had been one of my earliest supporters, and appeared with me in Brownwood, in January of 1962, when I made my first speech as a candidate for governor. I knew he would be more visionary, more progressive, and more loyal than anyone else in the speaker's chair and I needed that help.

Not all but most of the legislature had no particular interest in my vision of Texas, whatever it might have been. They were consumed by the things state legislatures almost always fight over: interest rates, tax breaks, keeping prisons and waste dumps out of their districts. They see trees, not forests.

It isn't much different, if at all, on the federal level. I have been told—at times by people who could have made it happen— that a seat in the U.S. Senate was mine for the asking. I never asked. Legislatures reward longevity, not productivity.

A turning point in my administration came when I appointed W. St. John Garwood, an eminent Austin lawyer and jurist, to the University of Texas Board of Regents. The Senate rejected him after Garwood said, "Any errors I make as a regent will be on the side of integration and academic freedom." The vote that sealed Garwood's rejection was cast by a disgruntled ultra-conservative who did so, he said, "just to let the governor know I exist."

That gadfly was Dorsey Hardeman, the senator from San Angelo, a legal scholar and historian. He was a pain in my neck from then on, and peacemakers kept trying to get us together. Finally, Edward Harte, a newspaper publisher, arranged a meeting at the Driskill Hotel, in the Jim Hogg suite, so we might bury our differences. Ben Barnes was there, a witness to Hardeman's charm and my generous spirit and how well we got along. A truce was declared. We all left the hotel beaming.

The next day, Dorsey was back on the senate floor opposing another of my proposals, and characterizing me as "arrogant" and "power mad."

I admit it. I called Harte and told him, "I never want to see that s.o.b. again."

My opponents won a few rounds. But there would be others. I appointed the Reverend C. A. Holliday, a black minister from Fort Worth, to the Board of Corrections. It was a sad reality that a quarter of the prison population was black. I thought it was certainly time for a black to sit on the board that supervises the prison system.

A number of senators quietly rebelled at the idea, and a delegation called on me to say that the appointment was unacceptable. I told them, in the frankest terms, "If you bust Reverend Holliday, I will appoint another black, and another, and another. You will have to bust every black man in Texas before I quit appointing them."

The Reverend was confirmed by a vote of twenty-five to four.

With that appointment, and others like it, I made enemies in the Senate and made my overall task more difficult. But it wasn't arrogance, as my critics claimed, that caused these clashes. I simply meant what I said about filling the boards and commissions with people who would provide the best supervision and the right direction.

The most sought-after appointment a Texas governor has is to the Board of Regents at the university. I had been hearing about a rabbi in Dallas who was described as a very wise and learned individual. I called Bob Strauss, who gave him very high marks. And I appointed Rabbi Levi Olan as a regent, having never met the man, not knowing whether he supported me or not.

Democracy is a wonderful form of government—most of the time. But when you have to deal with 150 house members and 31 senators every time you want anything accomplished, you pay a price. Every new move, every reorganization, every appropriation brought a demand for something in return.

I fully understood a legislator's desire to bring a prize back to his district. There is a thin line between pork and bringing home the bacon; the legislators have to please their constituents to get re-elected. But to accede to these demands more often than not is bad government. So much of your time is spent compromising, trying to persuade, trying to reason, trying to achieve your objectives without having a bill nibbled to death as it goes through the legislative meat grinder.

You witness the pride, the ego, the contempt, the greed, the selfishness of human beings to an unprecedented degree when you operate in a political environment such as state government. They practically hold you for ransom. Of course, it isn't fair to paint everyone with the same brush. I could deal with most of the members, but the chairmen of the major committees—appropriations and finance—had extraordinary power over the flow of monies. They were in a position, in effect, to extort almost anything they wanted.

In my six years as governor, I believe I fulfilled the promise of my first inaugural address: "We are all Americans. We are all Texans. Wearing these labels—and none other—let us be unified in our common purpose as we are united by our common heritage. Let it be heard wherever there are men of purpose and good will that here, on this day, Texas reaches for greatness."

Many of our programs would be completed after we left office: a Fine Arts Commission, tougher traffic safety laws, repeal of the poll tax, a student loan program. With state aid, San Antonio hosted the HemisFair in 1968. The Job Corps was going strong at Camp Gary. Our colleges and universities were attracting the country's brightest minds in mathematics and physics and in the arts.

I won a second term, again defeating Don Yarborough for the nomination, this time by a margin of three to one. I won virtually without campaigning and, frankly, felt that I should not have been opposed in the primary. I was still recovering from my wounds, and even the labor leaders tried to convince

Yarborough to stay out. The Republicans put up only token opposition in the fall.

I debated with myself up until the last moment before deciding to run for a third term. One word from Nellie—"no" —and I would have passed. But she thought I would have regrets if I left with so much business unfinished. In my race against the Republican, T. E. Kennerly, I received 72 percent of the vote, an indication that most Texans were not ready to run me off.

When to let go is an age-old problem. I would wrestle with that decision one more time. I came to terms with myself during a trip to East Africa, one that turned into a journey of the mind as well.

I was invited in 1967 to film a segment of what was then called "The American Sportsman" show, on ABC. I would be joined at intervals by four other guests from the entertainment world: Bing Crosby, Phil Harris, David Janssen, and Clint Walker. I readily accepted. We filmed on location in Tanzania, about fifty miles east of Lake Victoria. We drove past Mount Kilimanjaro and some of the world's most magnificent scenery.

What you never get used to is to be lost in the peace and serenity of this magnificent land, and then suddenly see it explode with some act of savagery. This is nature's process, the survival of the fittest, and it continues day after day.

You realize anew how beautiful nature is at one instant, at another cruel and deadly, but the cycle of life goes on. You realize humans are no different. I became quite philosophical about what life should mean, what can and should be accomplished. I made up my mind that you cannot predict how much time you have left; there is little time for pettiness, revenge, or selfishness. You have to use every talent available to you to leave any footprints at all.

At the conclusion of our hunt, we went north back to Nairobi and then to the Mount Kenya Safari Club, which is in the foothills of Mount Kenya, one of the most breathtaking spots I have seen anywhere in the world.

Ultimately, the experience of the safari was one that gave

me time to reflect, to ponder about what I should do. In the evenings, sitting, thinking, looking at the emergence of the stars, I finally decided that whatever I was able to accomplish in solving the problems of the state, there would always be new problems. I had served a year as Secretary of the Navy, and six as governor. I had no doubt I could be elected to a fourth term. The thought of losing an election never entered my mind, immodest as that may sound. I decided I had spent six years of my life trying to better the state, and upgrade the education of our young. However hard I worked or however long I stayed, there would always be problems, old ones to be solved, new ones to encounter. It was time for me to move on.

Shortly after I came back from East Africa, I told President Johnson I had made up my mind not to run for a fourth term. He objected strenuously. I said, "Mr. President, you're going to win Texas whether I am in or out of office. I will do everything I can to help you. In any event, I'm not going to run."

He was stymied by the war in Vietnam and beaten down by the protests. The idea of running again had left him torn, and he almost resented the ease of my own decision. We talked about it over many weeks. What started out as a bluff—I can take my ball and glove and go home, too—began to build in his mind as a real alternative, and an act of high drama and sacrifice.

How much my own actions influenced Lyndon Johnson, I can't honestly say. I believe the decision was one he did not intend to make—until he found himself bound by the momentum of it. He gave up the race, and the craft that made him feel most alive.

As for myself, I had seen the wonders of nature and heard its sounds, and I reflect on them still.

THE CONVERSION

In 1968, the new Republican President had begun looking for a high-profile Democrat for his cabinet. He had offered the job of Secretary of Defense to Senator Henry ("Scoop") Jackson, of Washington, who was known for his support of the military. Jackson declined, unwilling to give up his seat in the Senate.

Shortly, I received a phone call from the Reverend Billy Graham. He said that President Nixon was wondering if I would consider joining his administration as either Secretary of Defense or Treasury. Graham was then near the peak of his influence as an evangelist. He made an unusual political courier, but I wasn't startled by the call. He had Nixon's trust, and not many did.

The conversation was brief. After three terms as governor of Texas, I had returned to private life and accepted a partnership in the Houston law firm of Vinson and Elkins. And there I planned to stay.

My role in the 1968 campaign was not an active one until the final weeks and then, cranking up my own organization, we helped carry Texas for Hubert Humphrey. Though it came late, the effort was more in the form of sparing Lyndon Johnson's pride than electing Hubert. I would not forget the boos at the Democratic Convention that rang out with every mention of Texas, or the Texas delegation.

I was disenchanted with the party and therefore in a receptive frame of mind when Bob Haldeman called in the spring of 1969; President Nixon, he said, wanted to appoint me to the Ash Council, which had been assembled to study ways to reorganize the government. The goals were noble: eliminate inefficient agencies, reduce the bureaucracy, establish priorities. I accepted.

Roy Ash was the chairman of Litton Industries, whose headquarters were in Los Angeles, so our meetings with the President took place during his trips to San Clemente. I met Richard Nixon there for the first time. After the formal meetings, it became his habit to take me aside for a private chat. This was the beginning of what some of the President's men called the courtship of John Connally—a process not widely endorsed.

Contrary to other published accounts, I did not support him, did not raise money for him, did not vote for him against Hubert Humphrey in 1968. Four years later, I had not a doubt in my mind that the country would be in safer hands with Nixon than with George McGovern.

I had campaigned against Nixon in two national elections, the first in 1960, and both times he had lost Texas. The state and its politics intrigued him.

As I spent more time around him, I concluded that President Nixon was not just shopping for a token Democrat. To have a member of the opposition on one's team is usually good government, and nearly always good politics.

One month before I was offered the Treasury portfolio for the second time, Lloyd Bentsen defeated George Bush in the midterm Senate elections. It was a race I had urged Bentsen to make, and I helped design his campaign strategy. But the election was really won in the Democratic primary, when Bentsen upset the hero of the state's liberals, Ralph Yarborough. Bush lost because his campaign had been geared to running against Yarborough, not the dignified and moderate Bentsen.

There were two questions that greeted the news that Nixon had asked me to be his Secretary of the Treasury. Why had he offered it, and why had I accepted?

To the first, I can only repeat Nixon's own explanation: "I was impressed with his work on the Ash Council, the way he was able to go to the heart of an issue. I knew that just having a banker in that office wasn't enough. Many bankers had been Secretary of the Treasury, and many of them had been failures. It was a political position as well as financial. It was important to have a leader, a manager, someone who could deal with all the 'experts' in this huge bureaucracy."

As for my motives, the conventional wisdom was that I saw the job as an opportunity to improve my chances of running for President, in either party. Given the bitterness over the war in Vietnam, and the rejection of Lyndon Johnson, I doubted that another Texas Democrat could be elected President in my life-time. But to the extent that I thought about it, I would have been tempted not by the honor of the office but the power—the power to accomplish great deeds.

State has the glamour, Defense has the toys, but Treasury is and always has been the most powerful job in the cabinet. Great decisions were waiting to be shaped, and I did not fear them.

I never considered myself an economist, but I had the capacity to understand what the economists were saying. There were instincts that had to be applied and they were not mine alone. In the end, it was immaterial what position I took. My position was to sell the one the President took. My selection aroused interest because in 1970 there was little in my past to indicate what I thought or believed. I was a conservative who believed in an active government.

I was making my fourth political journey to Washington: with Lyndon Johnson in 1939 and again in 1949, and as Secretary of the Navy under Kennedy. But for the first time I would be serving in a major financial post, and as a member of what had been the enemy camp.

Hardened political observers were instantly curious about how Johnson had reacted to the news. The answer was, not well, and I didn't blame him. He had gotten the word from Nixon himself, who called from the Oval Office as I stood by his desk. Nixon said: "I want to introduce you to my new Secretary of the Treasury . . . he's an old friend of yours." Then, smiling broadly, he held out the phone, seemingly unaware of what an awkward moment had been created.

I would have preferred to be the one to tell the former President. Of course it was too late, and I was sworn to secrecy. My decision to join a Republican cabinet puzzled and infuriated him. I believed I could make a contribution, but he did not find that explanation sufficient.

President Johnson's reaction was a personal one; he felt he had a proprietary interest in me and I had no right to make a commitment without consulting him. By forming an alliance with Richard Nixon, I offended both his personal and his political values.

That was not the case with the average Texan. The state had made an even wider turn to the right, largely the result of a middle-class backlash against the years of anti-war unrest and social upheaval. On the editorial pages of newspapers around the state, a certain pride was evident: a Texan had been given a position of importance. The Republicans were probably more disturbed than the Democrats. President Nixon told me later that the shrillest complaints came from George Bush and Anne Armstrong, who were potential candidates for national office. They had toiled for the party in the lean years when the GOP often failed to run a candidate in some statewide races.

Actually, I had been more sensitive to the problem than the President. "We can't announce this," I said, "until you take care of a fellow down in Houston."

"What do you mean?" he asked.

"I mean George Bush. He's out of a job"—Bush had lost to Lloyd Bentsen in the 1970 Senate race—"and you had asked him to run. He has been very loyal. If I get a position in the cabinet, while he's sitting in Houston doing nothing, you're looking at a huge backlash."

"Well, what does he want?"

"I don't have no idea," I said, "but you have an opening at the United Nations. Give him that."

Nixon nodded, and said, "Fine." Bush was named ambassador to the U.N. in early December, and my announcement came three days later.

In Texas there were three points of view. Some thought the Republicans were using me to spread the blame if the economy crashed. Others thought I was using Nixon to advance my own agenda. The third group didn't care who loaded the truck, they just wanted it loaded.

When I took over as Secretary of the Treasury, I did so with feelings of trepidation. I was not an economist; I had really never studied monetary affairs. My experience with fiscal issues was limited largely to a familiarity with Congress in the matter of appropriation of funds. I knew that I would be supporting policies not because they reflected my philosophy but because they were necessary.

I also had a final concern because I was stepping midway into what could be considered a hostile environment. I was a Democrat stepping into a Republican administration, into a department already staffed by Republicans. When I talked to President Nixon, and accepted the job, I made a point of having a clear understanding that no appointments would be made in Treasury without prior consultation with me. I would not be presumptuous enough to expect to make his appointments, but under the circumstances I felt I had the right to ask that none be made without my prior consultation.

He readily agreed, and so informed Bob Haldeman and others on his staff.

I soon found that working with Charls Walker, Paul Volcker, Eddie Cohen, Sam Pierce, Eugene Rossides, John Hennessey, and other top people in the Treasury was not at all difficult. They accepted me and I certainly accepted them. We worked in a very harmonious fashion, I thought.

The first difficulty I faced stemmed from the fact that I was expected to appear before the Ways and Means Committee almost immediately after I took office on February 11, 1971. I knew Wilbur Mills, the chairman of the committee, and sent word to him that I would appreciate having a few weeks to get familiar with the Treasury and its policies before he called me to testify. He was kind enough to grant me that time, and so I started a crash course covering almost every aspect of the Treasury.

I took home large briefing books every night, read them until I fell asleep, studied them on Saturdays and Sundays. It turned out to be a fifteen-hour-a-day job. When I finally appeared before the Ways and Means Committee, and the Senate Finance Committee, the members were very considerate and sympathetic and helpful, in particular Senator Russell Long, chairman of the Senate Finance Committee, and Congressman Wilbur Mills. The appearance went well.

I had no sooner taken office than we had to confront a very volatile international monetary system. The Bretton Woods agreement—so named because it had been made at Bretton Woods, New Hampshire, toward the end of World War II— established a system of international monetary controls, of fixed exchange rates, in which the major trading nations of the world agreed what the value of their currencies to each other would be. In the aftermath of the war, the U.S. dollar supplanted the British pound as the reserve currency of the world; simply put, every other nation of the world pegged the value of its currency in relation to the dollar.

Throughout 1971, the U.S. economy was in such distress, and the world monetary picture so volatile, that comparisons were being made to 1933. That was the pivotal year of the Great Depression, as Franklin Roosevelt came to office in a climate of domestic and worldwide collapse. The dollar was gradually devalued—in fact and, later, in law—and its convertibility to gold was suspended. In both years, what was at stake was nothing less than the American role in a stable world society.

In the spring and early summer of 1971, the industrialized nations were being brought together in a fellowship of pain, and the real fear of an economic panic. There was wide fluctuation in currency rates, calling into question whether fixed exchange rates could continue to serve the interest of the respective nations. At home, the opposing theories were represented by Arthur Burns, the chairman of the Federal Reserve Board, and George Shultz, then the director of the Office of Management and Budget. Burns was in favor of fixed rates. Shultz insisted that floating exchange rates were the only answer to these changing conditions.

I agreed with George Shultz. In the first meeting of the Group of Ten, the ten largest investor nations in the world, in London, I tried out the idea of a floating exchange rate. I got no support whatever, notwithstanding that Canada, one of the Group of Ten, was then floating the value of the Canadian dollar against the U.S. dollar.

The turbulence continued unabated. In August, I had come back to Texas for a weekend and had just landed at Kelly Air Base, in San Antonio, when I was told that Paul Volcker needed to talk to me urgently.

When I got him on the phone, he said that we had received word that on Monday (this was a Friday) the United States would be asked by Great Britain to convert three billion dollars into gold. In the past, we had converted small amounts of dollars into gold for various countries, primarily Third World countries, and usually in the amounts of five, ten, or fifteen million. This was the first time we had been advised we would be asked to convert a large amount of gold.

We had historically allowed dollars to be held in official hands with the assurance that those dollars could be converted into gold at any time. Yet we had reached a point where so many dollars were held by governments around the world that we couldn't possibly cover the demand if there was a run asking for conversion. For every dollar in gold that we had at Fort Knox, at the then price of $35 an ounce, $7 were being held in official hands by governments around the world. We knew if we converted three billion dollars for one country, it would set off a chain reaction among other nations to get their dollars converted while we had gold left.

I asked Paul to call the White House and tell President Nixon I needed to see him. That was the beginning of the meeting at Camp David of August 15.

It was a wide-ranging meeting. Dr. Burns was there for the Fed. The full Council of Economic Advisers was there, Paul McCracken, Herb Stein, and George Shultz, along with Pete Petersen and Caspar Weinberger. Bob Haldeman and John Ehrlichman, of the White House staff, were also in attendance.

We all understood that we were seeing the beginning of a run on the bank; that is the closest I can come to describe what I thought was going to occur. The meeting at Camp David with President Nixon turned into a very heated discussion. I was taking the position that we had no choice but to close the gold window; that we must announce to the world that they could hold the dollars, but they would no longer be convertible to gold.

Burns vigorously opposed that position and said, "If we take that action, it will create panic in the world markets. The Dow-Jones averages will plummet to five hundred, losing most of its value. We will set in motion an economic depression throughout the world."

At the time, the President was very concerned about the rate of inflation, which was then only running about 4 percent but was considered much too high. Many of us were concerned about the trade imbalances. So I was the principal advocate for strong action on a number of fronts—specifically, that we should close the gold window, and impose a 10 percent surcharge on all items imported into the United States to correct the unfair trade balances. I readily admitted I was not in a position to dispute Burns's dire prediction that there would be considerable concern in reaction to closing the gold window, or in the impact on the stock market or world conditions. But if indeed he was right, we ought to impose wage and price controls in the United States to be sure we sent a message to our own people, as well as the rest of the world, that we were going to insist on economic stability in our own country.

The debate grew more heated. The President did not like the idea of controls, having had some experience with them during World War II. George Shultz was philosophically opposed to them, and proceeded to say so. The members of the Council of Economic Advisers also pointed out the difficulties surrounding the actions we were taking. Arthur Burns asked to see President Nixon in private, arguing vociferously against closing the gold window. But in the final analysis, the President decided that we would close the window, set a 10 percent surcharge on all imported items, and impose wage and price controls in the United States.

The question then arose as to how we were to proceed. Paul Volcker and Arthur Burns were primarily designated to call our principal trading partners, the Group of Ten, to advise them Monday morning of the actions the President was taking. I was designated as the spokesman to hold a press conference Monday morning, outlining the actions and the justification for the actions that the President had decided upon.

The press conference was nationally televised for about an hour in one of the most demanding appearances I have ever made. All the world press was represented, reflecting the interest manifested in the actions. We expected to be criticized for not consulting our principal trading partners before the action was taken, and we were. The words "shock" and "bombshell" were given prominence in most of the news stories. Obviously, there certainly could not have been any advance notice given to anyone because it would have immediately resulted in stock and currency manipulations around the world. So notwithstanding that the actions of this country did come as a surprise and perhaps a shock to many, it was nevertheless the only fair and logical way that the matter could have been handled.

Clearly, we were breaking new ground and smashing some long and dearly held protocol. But the economy could not get much worse in 1971, and I had at least two distinct advantages: I was not limited by the old diplomacy or predictable (knee jerk) thinking. In the early dialogues among the members of the Economic Council, I kept hearing that we had to be careful not to offend or anger our foreign partners.

I disagreed. I thought we had a right to expect and even demand fairer trade arrangements, and more help from our allies in bearing the cost of their defense. All too often, those in government spoke in a language that had to be decoded, that could be interpreted in various ways. I didn't believe you alienated people simply because they understood what you meant.

The wage and price freeze wasn't popular, but it was bold and it was the quickest and most dramatic way to curb the twin devils of high inflation and high unemployment. It seemed a mockery of Richard Nixon's values, and mine, but we built some elastic into it. We set up wage and price boards, the machinery that would force the representatives of labor, business, and the consumer to agree on the rules and how to enforce them. We created a kind of social compact, setting goals and deadlines and a process for appeals.

We divided the plan into Phase I, The Freeze; and Phase II, The Structure. George Shultz and Herb Stein hammered out the hard details, and the joke around the White House was that the plan was certain to work because it had been designed by people who did not believe in controls. There was actually some logic there.

If I have learned anything in my political lifetime, it is that you seldom go wrong by getting the people involved. There were light moments aplenty to prove the point. In Detroit, a newspaper reporter alerted federal agents that the Sheraton-Cadillac Hotel was replacing ten 10-cent locks on its men's room pay toilets with 25-cent locks. The hotel manager, embarrassed when the word of his overpriced plumbing leaked out, had the old 10-cent devices reinstalled.

In hindsight, the wage and price controls imposed in 1971 were a mistake. They will not work, and have never worked, over a protracted period of time. They should be applied only in case of war or an emergency.

We used them in 1971 because the President needed to take a bold and sweeping action. It was obvious that the fixed exchange rates were not going to hold. We were on dangerously shifting ground. A number of economists warned the President that the result of his moves would be a worldwide depression even worse than in the 1930s. None of us knew for certain. In my view, the primary motivation for controls and the ninety-day freeze was to give the country, as well as the rest of the world, time to reflect and to stabilize.

None of us thought that wage and price controls were the road to Utopia. They are the easiest system to get into, the most difficult to administer, and almost impossible to shed. The longer the controls are kept, the greater the inequities. The final result is nearly always an eruption worse than the situation that prompted them.

Still, the decisions made at Camp David not only changed the economic game plan, they changed the rules of the game. In the euphoria that nearly always results when great risks are taken, we thought the rules might have been changed forever. At the least, Republicans and Democrats alike would have to reevaluate how they thought about their economic gospel.

But all the projections, the charts, the hopes, and much of what might have been accomplished would be lost when Watergate blew out the windows.

Still, we had made a major departure from established policy, with far-reaching implications. Arnold Webber, an economics scholar, was brought in from the University of Chicago to direct the Wage and Price Administration. I chaired the Cost of Living Council, with Donald Rumsfeld in charge of the day-to-day operation. And we began the arduous task of trying to administer the controls.

Were they necessary? Probably not. But in the aftermath of

the announcements, there was greater stability not only in the United States but around the world. Possibly we could have done just as well by closing the gold window and imposing the 10 percent surcharge, which was not viewed as a permanent matter. Indeed, after about ninety days the surcharge was lifted, but the message was clearly sent to other countries that we were prepared to take strong action to assure that there would be equitable treatment in the markets of the world, that we believed in fair trade and free trade if it was fair.

In the fall of 1971, I accompanied President Nixon on a trip for a series of meetings with Ted Heath, the British prime minister, and the French President, Georges Pompidou. Nixon saw to it that I was seated next to Pompidou at a state dinner so that we could discuss international monetary affairs. The French President, he said, considered himself an expert in this area.

We did discuss the matter at length without reaching any conclusions, and the same was true of President Nixon's meetings with other world leaders. We all recognized that we were in difficult and frenzied times, but the conference in London broke up without any resolution and with the other nine members saying the United States should devalue the dollar. It was the U.S. position that the dollar was overvalued and therefore working to the detriment of our economic well-being by making our goods and services too expensive and non-competitive. All the other nine countries, however, were unwilling to talk about revaluing their currencies. They just wanted to devalue the dollar—primarily, I think, as a means of embarrassing the United States.

I could well understand that sentiment. The U.S. had come out of World War II intact, its economic machine functioning smoothly. We held substantially all the gold reserves of the world. Our industry was humming, whereas the other industrial nations had spent twenty-five years trying to rebuild out of the wreckage of World War II. We had become the dominant economic power on earth and, understandably, the other nations couldn't help but resent the degree of prosperity we enjoyed.

So I think the persistent cry that the U.S. should devalue was partly the desire to see the United States humbled. I kept President Nixon informed of how volatile the situation was. I asked him if he had any problem, politically or otherwise, in the U.S. devaluing the dollar. He asked, "Do you?"

I said, "No, not in the least. Wouldn't embarrass me at all." He said, "Neither do I. Do what you think needs to be done." I asked if he had a feel for how much we should devalue. He said, "No, you're authorized to take whatever action is necessary."

So I had this authority as the meetings of the Group of Ten moved to Rome, the last week of November, 1971. I also knew that none of the finance ministers had the same discretion and neither did their central bankers. Again in Rome, we were confronted with a chorus of sound from the other nine countries: the mercurial condition of the international markets was largely the responsibility of the United States, and we had to correct it by devaluing the dollar. One after another, the representatives of each country rose and repeated the refrain.

Most of this maneuvering was taking place behind the scenes. There was some news coverage, but little understanding of the issues. It was not all that complicated, no great mystery. If your currency is overvalued, you are at a competitive disadvantage in marketing your goods and services. Every country prefers to be undervalued. For my purposes, we were trying to establish a relationship among the currencies on a so-called level playing field.

Over the course of the meetings, I grew impatient with Arthur Burns for the first time. He kept saying to me, "Why don't you let me get together with these central bankers? We can solve this, we can work this out."

He made three or four runs at me, and in a rather testy fashion I finally turned to him and reminded him that he was the only central banker there who was not under the direct supervision of a finance minister. He was, in fact, an independent agent and under no obligation to me. But, in short, we were dealing with people who had no authority to do anything. Before any solution to this problem was reached, all the finance ministers were going to have to report back to their heads of government. More talk, more messages were not the answer. The political importance of the issue demanded action, and I happened to be the only one there with a mandate from his government to make a decision.

I suspect these remarks upset Dr. Burns, but nevertheless it stopped his continued requests that he meet privately with the central bankers. While the Group of Ten was meeting, we stood in adjournment half the time so that the Group of Six, the European finance ministers and bankers, could meet among themselves. They were more interested in trying to work out the relationship between their own currencies because most of their trade was within this inner circle. Still, they were unable to agree.

After a prolonged discussion, in which each of the nine countries reiterated that the only solution was a dollar devaluation, I finally said: "We think we need to solve the problem and the United States is willing to do its part. I am able to announce today that the U.S. is prepared to devalue the dollar ten percent." A hush settled over that room. No one said anything for a long, long period. Finally, there was muted discussion between the bankers, ministers, and their staffs, Then Anthony Barber, of Great Britain, spoke up: "We can't accept that."

I said, "What do you mean, you can't accept it? All we've heard for weeks and weeks is that the U.S. needs to devalue and we've agreed to devalue ten percent."

He said, "We can't accept that. It's too much."

I said, "It's not enough, but we'll agree to it if the other countries will revalue theirs."

Barber said, "We're prepared to accept a five percent devaluation."

I said, "That's not a sufficient devaluation to solve the problem and we might as well adjourn." And we did. Anthony Barber spoke up because he knew Giscard d'Estaing, the finance minister of France, would also object. At that particular time, Great Britain was concerned about the position France would take with respect to Britain's entry into the Common Market. And Tony Barber wanted to do whatever he could do to ingratiate himself with France. So he became the spokesman against whatever proposal we offered.

In the midst of these tensions, in this Babel-like atmosphere, we had dinner one night at the prime minister's palace atop one of the Seven Hills of Rome. We walked through a series of four drawing rooms, each elegantly furnished with elaborate tapestries and timeless paintings. We passed a magnificent work by Michelangelo.

Turning to our left, out onto the loggia, we were led to a table covered with white linen and settings to accommodate one hundred for dinner, fifty on each side. Floor-to-ceiling windows overlooked marble columns by Bernini and breathtaking statuary arranged among the gardens. I was inspired, by the might-have-been actor in each of us, to reflect on the history of our surroundings. I touched upon the "civilizing mission of the Roman leaders," who perhaps had often met at the spot where we were dining, and their legacy of law and learning and a common currency.

A motive needs to be ascribed to every act, and every denial makes the motive more plausible. But I was not trying to dispel my image as one who shot from the hip. I was simply moved by the grandeur and majesty all around us. I had no notes, had planned no speech, had no exact notion of what awaited us. But I have never underestimated the power of words to move men.

Paul Volcker, who was then my deputy, would write later that my speech may have been a step in our breaking the impasse, although I certainly saw no immediate sign of it. Paul thought he detected among his fellow ministers a "sneaking admiration" that I had somehow placed our mundane challenge "into the sweep of western civilization, going back two thousand years." I believe it is frequently helpful to give a political act historical cover.

In mid-December, we convened the Group of Ten for the third time to see if a solution could be reached with respect to exchange rates. These meetings were held in the Smithsonian, in Washington. It was still my objective to persuade our trading partners that it would be in the best interest of all to adopt a floating rate.

On Friday, Anthony Barber, Britain's chancellor of the exchequer, and Giscard d'Estaing and Karl Schiller, the finance ministers of France and Germany, came to me and said they were unable to work out an agreement among the Group of Six. If there was going to be any solution, they said, I was going to have to work it out. That put the problem directly in my hands.

I started immediately meeting with each of them individually. I told Giscard that the French had to revalue the franc about 9 percent, and I assured him that the Germans would revalue the deutsche mark even more. When I sat down with Schiller, he wanted to know what I had asked of the French. I told him they would revalue by 9, and the Germans must revalue by 13 percent. He asked if I had talked with the Japanese. I said no, but the Japanese would revalue the yen by 17 percent.

I said, "They really should revalue by twenty-five percent, but I talked to Prime Minister Sato some time ago and, politically, they can't take that big a bite."

Schiller said that Germany would agree if Britain, France, and Japan revalued their currencies to the levels I had indicated. It was understood that Italy would stay where it was. The Italian lira was somewhat in parity with what the changes would be. The governments of the European nations were waiting up until three in the morning, their time, to hear from their finance ministers and to approve the plans, which they did.

Now everything depended on getting an agreement with the Japanese, setting the stage for an odd footnote to the record of global politics. I asked to see the Japanese finance minister,

Mikio Mizuta. He had not attended that day's meeting and I was told by his deputy that, unfortunately, he had been taken ill.

It was now after 10 P.M. in Washington. I told Mizuta's aide that we were going to reconvene at nine in the morning. He was to tell the minister that I expected the Japanese to revalue the yen by 17 percent and I wanted his answer by ten o'clock. I said, "I'm sorry he's not well, but he can send his answer with you. But he needs to understand that I have an agreement from the other countries. If his answer is no, then I will adjourn the group and call a press conference. And there I will announce that we were all in agreement except Japan, and that our efforts had failed because of the intransigence of the Japanese government. I want him to understand where we are."

He nodded and said, "Yes, I will tell him." The next morning, we were preparing to reconvene the meetings at the Smithsonian. I was acting as chairman, since it was the turn of the U.S. to head the group. I was about to take my seat when the deputy minister of Japan beckoned to me from the back of the room by crooking his finger.

We walked into the hall and he said, "Minister Mizuta cannot accept a revaluation of seventeen percent." I said, "Thank you very much," and turned to walk away. He literally clutched at my coattails and said, "Wait, wait! You do not understand."

I said, "I understand quite well. I told you to tell the minister that if he could not agree to revalue the yen, in parity with the other countries, I would hold a press conference and lay the responsibility for the failure of these meetings at the door of the Japanese. That is what I intend to do."

Again he said, "No, no, you do not understand. In 1930, the finance minister of Japan revalued the yen by seventeen percent. The economy went into a deep depression. It was a catastrophe for our country, and the minister committed suicide. Mr. Mizuta cannot accept seventeen percent. Please, give us some other percentage."

Startled, I said, "All right, sixteen point nine."

247

He said, "Yes, yes, we can agree to that."

And that was how the agreement was reached, in the final days of 1971, to revalue the major currencies of the world. As verified later, Japan's finance minister in 1930 had been killed by an assassin, possibly a disgruntled investor. Still, the moral of the story was unchanged.

I called President Nixon at Key Biscayne and told him I thought the announcement was a significant one, and he might want to fly back to Washington to congratulate our trading partners and announce the success of the conference. Which he did.

The negotiations had been long and tedious and at times arduous. I had been criticized by many of the European leaders, who used every device they knew, including their banking connections, to bring pressure to bear. They had gone through Chase Manhattan, whose chairman, David Rockefeller, had called me to express his concern that we risked losing our friends. The Europeans complained that I had been difficult, too blunt, too tough. Others had fed this to the press. There were references to "this cowboy from Texas with the six-iron on his hip." The object was to soften me and thus soften the position of the United States. This went on for many months.

I was untroubled by such tactics because I knew I had the backing of the President, which allowed me to hold my ground. I didn't believe I had been discourteous or brusque. But I was keenly aware that we were a lone voice, and in the mere repetition of their demands the other nine countries had the ability to block us.

In the end, Guido Carli, the central banker of Italy, said in an interview that he thought the agreement was as fine an example of international negotiations as he had seen, and he had seen many of them. He added that the results would not have been possible without the tact and fairness of John Connally. I was heartened by this compliment from one of the most respected figures in the banking world.

Fixed rates would not solve the problems of the monetary

system over a protracted period of time. The volatility continued even among the six European partners and finally, in 1973, when George Shultz was Secretary of the Treasury, the industrial nations adopted the floating exchange rates, which prevail to this day. This was the only logical and workable thing for them to do. This action came as a result of the Arab oil embargo of that year.

During my time as Secretary of the Treasury, we had attempted to get a revenue-sharing measure passed in which the federal government would share revenues with the states in order to try to alleviate their ever-increasing burdens. However illogical this sounds, there was ample justification for it, because President Nixon felt that the federal government was going to have access to increasing revenues. If considerable money was not diverted to the states, which desperately needed it, the federal government would spend it anyway.

Wilbur Mills vigorously opposed the plan, and we were unsuccessful in getting it passed.

Another matter arose during my tenure there that required an enormous expenditure of effort, and that was the Lockheed loan program. Lockheed was at that time the largest defense contractor in the United States, with 72,000 employees and sales of $2.5 billion. Cutbacks in the defense budget had plunged the company into a financial crisis, with the immediate prospect of having to lay off nearly half its work force. Nixon had declared himself committed to full employment; the loss of 30,000 jobs was intolerable. The banks had refused to extend any further credit, and without some government assistance Lockheed was on the verge of going bankrupt.

The President gave me the task of trying to get legislation passed guaranteeing a loan of $250 million to assure Lockheed's economic viability. Part of the impetus for the move came from the British. Lockheed was in the process of building a new plane powered by Rolls-Royce engines. The British were extremely interested because of the impact on their economy and the jobs involved.

The chairman of Lockheed, Dan Howton, worked harder, with greater patience and perseverance, than anyone I had ever seen at overcoming obstacles in getting this loan. I had to appear before committees of the House and the Senate to justify it. We were not appropriating any money; it was only a guarantee for additional bank credit. We insisted that the banks subordinate their claim against Lockheed to that of the government, and we finally passed the Lockheed loan by one vote in the Senate and three in the House. In the aftermath, the United States did not have to put up a dime, the Treasury earned $32 million in standby fees, and the guarantee was never called upon. Lockheed survived the crisis and went on to produce the aircraft. This was a case that was very controversial; a number of members of Congress opposed it on philosophical grounds.

The battle had been hard fought, and coincidentally had a considerable impact when the Chrysler Corporation many years later went before the Congress for its loan. There was, however, a marked difference in the cases because Lockheed, at the time the loan was made in their behalf, was the largest military contractor to the U.S., and all of that work would have been in jeopardy if the loan had been disapproved.

I had a testy exchange, not the first or the last, with Senator William Proxmire, the Wisconsin Democrat, who questioned whether the Lockheed loan guarantee would not set a precedent.

"I think it will set a precedent," I retorted, only in part facetiously, "for all the companies that employ in excess of seventy thousand people, that have thirty-five thousand subcontractors . . . that are the largest defense contractors in America."

There were valid issues in this debate that touched upon a free market system, and the historic aversion of conservatives to anything that smacked of a government handout. Proxmire tried to turn that philosophy against me by suggesting that such loans would weaken the system.

I didn't think so. "As a matter of fact," I argued, "we have a pretty regulated society. We sometimes kid ourselves that it is a free enterprise system, but it is not all that free. Much of it lives under regulation. Much of it lives under subsidy. The government takes many actions to encourage various businesses of all kinds for various social purposes. So I don't think it is all that much of a departure from what we have known in the past."

I had headed the Treasury Department for nearly a year and a half when my agreement with the President was violated. We had a clear understanding that no principals would be named without my first being consulted. I felt this was only fair, since I was a Democrat being asked to take over a department whose positions were already filled with Republicans. I was basically at the mercy of those appointees and their staffs.

Nevertheless, I read in the newspapers that Romano Bañuelos had been named to the position of Treasurer of the United States. There was nothing personal in my reaction. She was an outstanding lady from California, but the agreement had been broken. I called Haldeman and asked why I had not been informed. He said it was a mistake, and offered to withdraw the name. I said, "Oh, no. Then it will be leaked that I objected, and I objected because she was Hispanic. Just know that if this happens again, I'll be gone."

In the latter part of March, 1972, I learned that John Ehrlichman had been calling Eddie Cohen, one of my assistant Secretaries, and having him over to the White House to develop tax policy without consulting me or even letting me know it was going on. Although it may sound inconsequential as I recount it, the incident went to the heart of control of a government agency and the clear understanding I had about the way the department would be run. "If it gets to the point where I can't run it, or you don't want me to run it," I had told Richard Nixon, "I will gladly leave, in good grace, without expressing any criticism. But as long as I'm there, I'll run it."

Ehrlichman was planning a tax policy that was clearly within the jurisdiction of the Treasury Department, asking my top tax assistant over to the White House without advising me this was going on. I called Haldeman, described the conversation between Ehrlichman and Eddie Cohen, and said, "Bob, I hope you have a new Secretary of the Treasury in mind."

Haldeman was apologetic. He stressed how upset the President would be and asked me to reconsider.

I said, "No, I don't make idle threats. I told you next time there was interference by the White House staff you'd better find a new Treasury Secretary—I'll be gone. And I am. We had an agreement. It was violated twice."

Aside from the fact that promises had been broken, I considered the most urgent part of my work to be finished. My interest was in problem solving, not longevity. I had already stayed beyond my original commitment.

I agreed to stay on for several weeks because the Vietnam peace negotiations were at a delicate stage. Within the administration, the strategy for ending the war was undergoing fierce debate. The talks in Paris had broken off again, and the North Vietnamese had renewed their offensive. The President was considering a major new escalation: bombing Hanoi and mining the harbors of Haiphong. It was feared that this action would jeopardize a summit meeting Kissinger had arranged for Nixon with Brezhnev in Moscow.

We were facing a difficult period in May. On the fourth, the President sent Haldeman and Kissinger to my office to brief me on the options, and to get my views on the political implications. If the order was given for a bombing strike, Kissinger felt we should cancel the summit rather than leave that initiative, and the propaganda advantage, to the Russians. I didn't think we should try to outguess the Russians and neither did Haldeman.

On May 8, President Nixon announced his decision to mine the harbors of North Vietnam, cutting off the uninterrupted flow of war matériel to the enemy.

On May 16, I announced my resignation as Secretary of the Treasury and my plans to return to the practice of law in Texas. As promised, I would leave without rancor. Until now, I have never told anyone precisely why I left the Treasury.

On May 20, President Nixon and Henry Kissinger flew off

to Moscow for the summit meeting with Brezhnev. There would be no cancellation.

On June 6, at the President's request—and to squelch rumors that we had "fallen out"—I left on a good-will trip to fifteen nations, starting in Venezuela. Eleven days later, five burglars would be arrested for breaking into the Watergate offices of Larry O'Brien, the chairman of the Democratic National Committee. Within hours, it was known that the men had been employed at the Committee to Re-elect the President. It didn't help that they had worked as a unit, and were called "the plumbers" because they supposedly fixed leaks.

It was on June 19 that Ron Ziegler, the White House press secretary, dismissed the break-in as a "third-rate burglary attempt."

I would return from my trip abroad on July 14 to hear for the first time the implausible details of the case. The White House staff was hoping that the strange episode would just fade away. I called Bob Haldeman and said, "I don't know the details, but the break-in obviously was politically motivated. It needs to be resolved in a political environment, meaning before the election. The President is going to win big, and you don't want this hanging over his administration at the start of a new term. It should be settled right now."

Instead, for reasons that elude me, it was decided that a full disclosure to the nation would have been hazardous to his reelection. After November, the President let matters slide, perhaps hoping it would somehow clear itself up. For nine months—from June, 1972, to March, 1973—nothing was done that did not deepen the problem.

NIXON

All of his public life, Richard Nixon suffered from the impression that he was too stiff, too formal, too austere. Of course, the impression wasn't far off the mark. But I have seen the unmarked side of him, a hunger to please that was at war with a lifetime of shyness.

In June of 1973, after I had returned to practicing law in Texas, President Nixon invited me to join him aboard Air Force One for a flight to San Clemente. A third passenger was to be his houseguest there, Leonid Brezhnev, the Soviet premier. Nixon did not tell me, but later confided to others, his reason for the meeting: "I still believed that Connally might be dealing with Brezhnev as President and I wanted them to take the measure of each other. I wanted Brezhnev to know him and understand him."

As we flew over the Grand Canyon, the three of us talked about matters relating to the rearrangement of the universe.

I did not remain for the full stay, discreetly leaving the leaders of the two world powers to their own agenda. But an incident occurred that did, in fact, enable me to take the measure of the premier, and to gain a fresh insight into the temperament of Mr. Nixon. The President was clearly bemused one morning, although not affronted.

Brezhnev had insisted in staying in the Nixon home, which the President described as "not that large. We put him in Trish's room, which was decorated in pink."

Brezhnev's insistence on not checking into a nearby hotel reflected his Russian sense of hospitality. Still, it raised an awkward moment or two because during the night there was what the President referred to as "a parade of pretty girls to the premier's bedroom." They were hostesses with Aeroflot, the Russian airline.

When they had moved their discussions to Camp David, on the same trip, Nixon went to Brezhnev's cabin one evening to take him to dinner. A tall, very attractive brunette answered the door, and as the President stepped inside, he shook hands with her. After she walked away to inform Mr. Brezhnev of his presence, he noticed a fragrance that lingered in the room. As he told the story, he raised the back of his hand to his nose and sniffed. "I recognized it immediately," he said. "Arpège. It was Mrs. Nixon's favorite. A very fine perfume. I could still smell the scent on my hand hours later."

He asked Brezhnev who the lovely young lady was, and the premier said, in his heavy accent: "She is my massoose."

The President went on to observe that "Brezhnev was a ladies' man, as many leaders are, including some of our own. I didn't feel prudish about it. In retrospect, I was glad that he felt at home enough that he could trust us and go ahead and live his usual life. So there she was. I bet he had himself a good massage."

I imagine that of the legions who have studied Richard Nixon, academics and politicians, few have seen him in his lighter moments. I am sure some of his critics felt that he was incapable of having any.

I came to respect him mightily as a scholar and for his instincts in the arena of foreign policy. I also glimpsed his compassion and neediness, qualities that he believed made him vulnerable. He concealed them by developing a hard shell.

There is a fascination with Nixon on the part of historians

and the press that goes beyond his ability to survive. He came to the office as one of the most unlikely Presidents in the history of the nation. Defeated by John F. Kennedy in 1960 in a razor-close election, he returned to his home state, California, to run for governor and resurrect his career. Instead, he was defeated again.

Moving to New York, he set about to build a new base of support. And so he did, undaunted by two defeats that would have fatally discouraged the average political figure. But whatever else he has been, Nixon was never average.

In a world where charisma is regarded as a priceless asset, and extroverts are the rule, he has been an anomaly. Basically a humorless man, and extremely private, almost antisocial, he nevertheless went against the trend and the grain. He has outlasted many of his enemies, and his contemporaries, rising again and again in an industry that rewards wit and social warmth and the kind of magnetism that attracts and aligns unrelated forces.

When he succeeded, he did so without the normal trappings of a political warrior. He became President of the United States while surrounded by an atmosphere that destroys privacy and magnifies all weaknesses. His ambitions were undone, but he never lost his ability to bring to a task his fierce determination. His knowledge and judgment in foreign affairs may have surpassed that of any other President in this century.

He had a distrust of academia, and an insecurity that led him to be secretive and devious. He has been viewed by many as cold, hard-hearted, and uncaring. Those were but shields for a man with a soft center. He disliked confrontation, except in the foreign arena. I observed a man who was unwilling to fire anyone, and incapable of uttering a harsh word to his staff or cabinet officers. Yet in what he believed to be the privacy of his quarters, he could rail in the most profane terms against friends as well as foes.

It isn't unusual for public officials to use foul language, but they don't generally tape-record it. Members of his staff understood that his threats and blustery behavior were the venting of his anger and frustration. They dealt with it most of the time by ignoring orders given in the heat of the moment. Watergate turned out to be the terrible exception. Still, I believe the long reach of history will treat him favorably as a President who confronted problems, both domestic and foreign, with intelligence and courage.

I never really understood what kept people from seeing his kind and sympathetic sides. The two great political traumas of my lifetime, not including war, were the Kennedy assassination and Watergate. Nixon lost to Jack Kennedy, but admired him and envied his easy self-assurance.

In one of history's footnotes, it developed that Richard Nixon was flying out of Dallas on Friday morning, November 22, 1963, an hour or so before the plane carrying myself and President Kennedy and our wives landed at Love Field. Nixon had appeared at a convention, and was flying back to New York. Like everyone else old enough to remember the day, the events are fixed in his mind: "Preparations were already under way for the arrival of the President. On the plane, an associate mentioned to me that for want of a few thousand votes here and there, it might have been me coming into Dallas that day. I remember mentioning that I try not to think about things like that, and the flight proceeded routinely.

"On arrival in New York, we caught a cab and headed for the city. The cab had no radio on. As fate would have it, the cabby missed a turn somewhere and we were off the highway, somewhere in Astoria, Queens, I think. We were stopped for a red light when a woman came out of her house screaming and crying. I rolled down the window to ask what the matter was, and when she saw my face she turned pale. She told me that John Kennedy had just been shot and killed in Dallas. We drove the rest of the way in silence."

During my service as Treasury Secretary, one Washington reporter said I was on a "feet-up basis" with Nixon, a closeness limited "to men he feels most at ease with. In all the country there are maybe ten."

I may or may not have been among them, but the number of people whom Nixon felt truly comfortable with was indeed limited. A case in point was Bob Haldeman, his former chief of staff. Haldeman, of all those around him, understood the President best and was entirely devoted and loyal to him. I think that has been proved in all the years since Watergate; you have never seen Haldeman quoted in any way that could be judged critical or disparaging of Richard Nixon.

By the same token, the President trusted Haldeman with his innermost secrets and felt totally secure in dealing with him on a day-to-day basis. Yet, strangely enough, he never made Bob Haldeman one of his confidants in a social or personal setting. He went outside of his administration for companions with whom he could relax or enjoy his leisure moments.

To my knowledge, only two people fit into that category: C. G. ("Bebe") Rebozo and Robert Abplanalp.

In what qualifies as a paradox, Nixon confided in Rebozo information that he did not share with any other human being. This fact notwithstanding, Bebe had been a close friend of Lyndon Johnson and John Kennedy before him. I knew him through those same years, and he has never used his Presidential ties for any personal gain. He never divulged to anyone the secrets entrusted to him, and some were intimate indeed. What Bebe saw, he kept to himself.

I was invited to join them for a night at Bob Abplanalp's island in the Bahamas. The mere fact that I was included was confirmation that the President trusted me. Bob would not have presumed to invite me, nor would Bebe. I was there because the President had asked for me.

Yet I had the distinct feeling that Nixon was less at ease, partly because he and the others had a couple of drinks and I did not. I have found that this inevitably creates doubts in the minds of people who tend to be suspicious anyway. I felt it and regretted it, but I still had no desire to drink. They didn't overindulge, by any means. They were relaxing in their traditional way and here I was, a new presence in their midst, not conforming.

I realize not everyone will see this as a compliment to either of us, but I had much in common with President Nixon. We both put a high value on discipline, of the mind and manner, and are wary of those who lose control. We both came from families that were large and poor, and had fathers who worked at a variety of jobs. We excelled at debating and began our political careers in college in the 1930s. We each met our wives in an amateur theater group, married in the same year, and served as naval officers during the war.

But until I served on the Ash Council, and later in Nixon's cabinet, most of what I really knew about him came from Sam Rayburn and Lyndon Johnson, who had the kind of dislike for him that lasted a lifetime. Johnson's attitude was unrelated to any personal rivalry. He thought Nixon was an unscrupulous campaigner—ironic, considering that the same had been said of Johnson—and held him responsible for the ruined careers of several Democrats who were painted as soft on Communism.

Nixon must have known this, but it did not prevent him from being objective, even generous. "My opinion of Johnson," he said, "is a helluva lot higher than that of many others. He got a bad rap because of Vietnam."

In 1972, I was not yet a Republican, was still sending in a monthly contribution of $100 to the Democratic National Committee (Robert Strauss, treasurer), and was three elections away from running on my own for the nation's highest office. There was a role I could play in the 1972 campaign and I played it gladly, but not without mixed feelings. I told my staff that sometimes I felt like a donkey and sometimes I felt like an elephant, and you know the problem with hybrids—they have no pride of ancestry and no hope of prosperity. I was never naïve enough to think that my support for a Republican President carried no risk.

In late April of 1972, Nellie and I planned the first of two visits by the Nixons to our ranch, Picosa, where they would be introduced to two hundred of the most important people in Texas. Santa Gertrudis cattle crowded the fences, and the coastal Bermuda grass was green and lush.

Many were Democrats, some of them larger than life, drawn to the scene by the promise of a good party and their own curiosity about Richard Milhous Nixon. Because their conservative views were more closely attuned to Nixon's policies than those of George McGovern, his opponent in the coming campaign, they were potential contributors.

The list included oilmen, bankers, lawyers, and publishers. Nelson Bunker Hunt, the third and most colorful of H.L.'s sons, was one of the few who had met the guest of honor and considered himself among Nixon's ardent supporters. But he was not alone as an envoy from the oil patch. Perry Bass, the nephew and partner of Sid Richardson was there, and the Murchison brothers, Clint, Jr., and John.

Their planes circled the old Spanish land grants and touched down on the runway 800 yards from the ranch house. The Nixons were flown by helicopter from Randolph Air Force Base. When the President ducked out of the chopper, his first words were, I thought, typical of him. "I'm sorry we scared your cattle," he said.

The crowd included the second generation of men who had helped build Texas: Amon Carter, Jr., from Fort Worth; James A. Elkins, Jr., whose father founded the First City National Bank of Houston as well as the law firm—Vinson and Elkins— where I was now a partner; Robert J. Kleberg, Jr., head of the King Ranch.

A former Texas governor, Allan Shivers, moved through the receiving line, along with the daughter of a former governor, Miss Ima Hogg. The gathering might have been described as eclectic. Anne Armstrong, a former ambassador to England and now a Nixon adviser, was one of the state's most influential Republicans.

There was a relative newcomer named H. Ross Perot, who made his fortune not in oil or cattle, but by starting a company that helped make data processing a growth industry. He had gained a reputation as a maverick and a philanthropist by trying to locate and free prisoners of war in North Vietnam. He was someone to watch.

They all drank a toast to the President's health; among them was a lawyer I had appointed to a Committee on Public Education when I was governor. He was then a senior partner at a rival Houston firm; his name was Leon Jaworski.

In their syndicated column, Rowland Evans and Bob Novak had written that the party had been arranged to "kill speculation of a Nixon-Connally rift." There was no rift. If there had been, we surely wouldn't have needed to invite two hundred witnesses.

The festivities were designed for the most basic of political and social reasons: to give the President and First Lady a showcase where they could unbend and feel at ease, and in this setting expose them to the movers and shakers of Texas. He would need their support, and their money, if he was to carry the state in November.

The menu featured barbecued beef tenderloin, corn on the cob, black-eyed peas, tossed salad, and hard rolls. Nellie had worked for ten straight days to get the ranch ready for the Nixon visit. She helped the hired hands wash lettuce and shuck corn, and she tramped the fields to gather a bouquet of wildflowers for Mrs. Nixon. She arranged bluebonnets, Indian pinks, fire wheels, and tiny white and yellow daisies in an antique glass basket, put them in a room to stay cool—and, in the excitement, forgot to give them to Pat.

The timing of this event was of no special significance, but it came during a period when a series of personal and global decisions surrounded us. First, there was the matter of the Vice-Presidency, which had become a source of continuing speculation in the press.

I could hardly be unaware that the President had been quoted, at seemingly every opportunity, as saying that "John Connally can handle any job in government." He had discussed with Bob Haldeman, I would learn later, dropping Spiro Agnew from the ticket and replacing him with me. There was talk that Agnew might be offered an appointment to the Supreme Court. Without mentioning a successor, the President raised the subject in the privacy of his summer home in San Clemente.

It was clear to me that he was probing for any personal interest on my part. I told him I thought the move would be unwise and unnecessary. He was going to win the election by a comfortable margin, and any effort to remove Agnew would be badly received by conservatives, who were solidly behind the Vice President.

Much has been written and whispered about the deal Richard Nixon and I had supposedly cut. That suspicion ignored a long tradition of Presidents reaching out to the opposition for cabinet officers, as Roosevelt, Eisenhower, and Kennedy had done. You can make that bipartisan leap if you are willing to put loyalty to the President ahead of your party. That was all there was to it, really, when I had accepted the job of Treasury Secretary in December of 1970. I wasn't trying to declare my independence, or trying to escape from Lyndon Johnson's shadow—I thought I had done so long ago. I wasn't being groomed for a spot on the Republican ticket.

Nothing was as clear then as it seems now. I played a role—but not a critical one—in the 1972 campaign by organizing the Democrats for Nixon.

George Christian, who had been my press secretary and moved to the White House with Johnson, coined the name. The idea of forming a separate apparatus was mine. Again, the motives were not very complicated. I was still a Democrat and had not yet abandoned hope that the party could be recaptured from the far left and the peace-at-any-price crowd. That phrase sounds dated now, but they were fighting words in 1972.

Of course, everyone understood that it would be more damaging to have Senator McGovern opposed by members of his own party. Even so, I insisted that certain ground rules be observed. The White House staff kept asking me to send out press releases over my name, taking on McGovern on a series of issues. I refused. I didn't come aboard for the purpose of cutting up Democrats.

I knew that I would lose some friends and catch hell among Texas Democrats. One of the more cutting lines came from Liz Carpenter, the former press secretary to Lady Bird Johnson, who said of myself and my fellow defectors: "I'm just glad we didn't have to count on them at the Alamo."

Richard Nixon had been in close contact with Harry Byrd, the senator from Virginia, and other prominent Democrats. He believed, as I did, that an exodus would have taken place after the election if not for the lengthening shadow of Watergate.

The scandal could and should have been dealt with in the first week after five burglars were arrested for breaking into Larry O'Brien's offices. It is inconceivable to me that no one on the President's staff had enough political judgment to realize instantly the dangers.

In May of 1973, I was in my law office in Houston when President Nixon called from Key Biscayne and asked me to come see him. As was the custom, I didn't go directly to the President. I was met by Bebe Rebozo, an old friend of mine before he even knew Nixon.

Rebozo told me in effect what the President wanted. Bebe told me that he was going to ask me to come back to his cabinet again, as Secretary of the Treasury. I was dumbfounded. I said, "Bebe, I can't do that. It doesn't make sense to me." He left, came back, and said the President was ready to see me. That was, in fact, what he wanted. He asked me to come back.

I said, "Mr. President, what are you going to do with George Shultz?" He said, "Oh, George will be pleased to go back on the staff." I said, "Mr. President, I don't believe that. In any event, I can't do this. I'm back practicing law. I want to help you, I've tried to help you." I recounted my support of him, and repeated that I just could not do what he asked. He accepted that fairly readily. Bebe had already prepared him for my answer. He said, "At least, you can come and be a special counsel."

I agreed, but on the condition that I would not leave my law firm, and would serve with no pay, no title, and no one cutting off my access to him. I believed that he was prepared to take the harsh and painful actions that would be necessary. The tapes had not yet been made public. I thought there was still time to separate him from the scandal.

I was convinced that he needed to make the fullest possible disclosure. Nearly everyone around him needed to resign, and I didn't hesitate to say so. I told Ron Ziegler that he had lost credibility. "If I were in your shoes," I said, "I wouldn't stay around here."

Ziegler had been hired by Haldeman to deal with the press for the very reason that he had no previous experience in dealing with the press. He had never worked in journalism, or in government, and had been to Washington only to visit. Haldeman explained the choice by saying the Nixon administration did not want "another Jim Hagerty" as press secretary, referring to the crusty, hardened old newsman who was much too visible, some Republicans thought, in the advice he freely gave to President Eisenhower.

Every administration in the last forty years has claimed it would bring in people who had not inhaled too deeply of the vapors of Capitol power and punishment. So it was that Nixon established John Mitchell, a bonds lawyer, as attorney general, and prompted Senator Goldwater to dismiss the White House staff as "a bunch of amateurs."

I can't help but believe that if a Jim Hagerty had been somewhere on the scene, history might have taken a different turn. The people around Nixon would have known well before the '72 election that he was headed for a landslide victory, and there was no need to take foolish—much less illegal—chances.

The government is crippled when a moral or legal taint is attached to it. Nixon's authority was weakened once a majority of the public came to believe that his election was rigged by secret funds and dirty tricks. In some respects, the moral cost is even more fatal; the ability to govern rests on a dialogue of trust—between the President and the people, and between this and other governments.

I did not suspect Haldeman was involved, but when I told him that whoever was responsible ought to walk the plank, he avoided a direct answer. I drew no conclusions from the vagueness of his response. But nothing was done. The staff continued to hope that the case would disappear, even as it dragged on and on, becoming, in John Dean's words, "a cancer on the Presidency."

I respected Haldeman for his service to the President and his calm, diligent approach to his work. It would become my unpleasant duty to tell Bob Haldeman that the President wanted him to resign.

After six weeks, I concluded I had given all the advice I had to give and I went back to Houston. You can offer advice, but you can't force someone to take it. Nixon's penchant for delegating authority and responsibility had led him into this calamity. That had been his style of operation. You accept him for what he is, as with any President.

I had been given an office and a secretary, and I caught up on my reading. There were no hurt feelings on my part, but I obviously wasn't performing any useful function. My appointment was simply a cosmetic one. There had been initial hints that I might be helpful to him, given the constantly decaying political environment. But no one ever explained what his expectations were, or what my role was. I was left to just conjecture on the vagaries of fate.

Nixon would win big and lose bigger than any President in American history. I do not defend or excuse what happened in the Watergate scandal, but I believed, then and now, that he had no part in the break-in. His downfall was in believing that he would not have to give up the tapes, and the scandal could be covered up and contained.

I have my own theory about what caused Watergate.

Questions had been raised in the press about a $100,000 contribution Howard Hughes had made to an earlier Nixon campaign. At the same time, the President knew that Hughes had been paying Larry O'Brien a $100,000 annual fee—Hughes seemed to be partial to that number—while Larry was chairman of the Democratic National Committee. My conclusion is that Nixon complained to his staff, demanding to know why this information wasn't getting out, why he was always the one under attack.

It takes no leap of imagination to see someone interpreting that message as a call to action. And one false step begat another, until the Watergate ordeal had run its course.

No one has ever told me that this prompted the burglary, but I'm convinced that they broke into the Watergate offices to try to find confirmation of the payments to O'Brien, to embarrass the Democrats during the campaign. I don't think the President knew about this particular espionage, but he was prodding his staff to get the information and slip it to the media.

The President then made a fatal mistake in trying to protect his people. He believed, wrongly, that the shield of the Presidency could keep them from facing court action and keep them from being punished. Even later, when the matter became public knowledge and very much a daily news diet, after Alexander Butterfield had acknowledged the existence of the tapes, he persisted on this path.

After the court had subpoenaed seven tapes, I immediately called Haldeman and said, "For heaven's sake, tell the President to go on and burn the rest of those tapes. Get rid of them. He has to preserve those seven, can't destroy them, but he can burn the rest. And don't be secretive about it. Have a bonfire on the south lawn."

Of course, he ought not to have recorded them anyway. Every head of state, every cabinet officer, every friend—every outrageous thing any of them said had been filed away.

I have heard speculation that he didn't destroy the tapes because another copy existed somewhere else. I don't believe that, but nevertheless he kept the tapes and that was his downfall.

Nixon prided himself on having survived his crises. He looked back on them as the divisions of his life; almost as if life were a pilgrimage, almost as if they were like stations of the cross. But though in all the past crises he had been able to extricate himself, there had always been another race to run.

The media wrote his political obituary three times, at least: after his loss to Kennedy in 1960; after he was beaten by Edmund Brown in the governor's race in California; and, finally, during and after Watergate. His career is a tangle of contradictions best left not to the historian but to the dramatist.

No matter how long you survive in public life, you never get used to the speed with which politicians abandon those in trouble if there is a risk of the trouble rubbing off. I saw it happen with two Presidents. In the years since they left office, the Democrats have rarely mentioned Lyndon Johnson, nor the Republicans Richard Nixon, at their national conventions.

To begin with, the party out of power nearly always runs against some form of "the mess in Washington." This has been true since the time of Dwight Eisenhower, who made Adlai Stevenson carry the burdens of the Truman years, to Bill Clinton, who ran against the excesses of the Reagan and Bush terms. It was a lesson in practical politics to see how quickly the party leaders tried to establish that any connection between Richard Nixon and the Republican Party was purely coincidental.

The loss of trust in government was immeasurable and, for the most part, irreversible. In 1970, some 1,700 persons, interviewed in six cities, said they did not accept the story that U.S. astronauts had walked on the moon. A man in Macon, Georgia, asserted the novel view that television pictures of the moon walk had been filmed in a "petrified forest" in Arizona. In some cities, as many as 19 percent did not believe that America's spaceman had landed on the lunar surface. Asked why such an enormous hoax would be perpetrated, they generally replied that the government had done it either to fool the Russians and the Chinese, or to justify the great cost of the space program.

There is something uncanny about the twists and accidents

of Watergate itself: the piece of telltale white tape placed the wrong way on a door; the almost casual discovery, in a throwaway question by a minor attorney, that the Oval Office had been bugged and the conversations recorded; the appointment of two stern, unforgiving Republican judges to hear the cases—John Sirica and Gerhard Gesell; and, of course, the astonishing decision to raise, launder, and conceal campaign funds that were not really needed.

Consistently, the President and his men seemed to create the things they feared the most by assuming the worst in everybody. Nixon's intent, as he contended, may well have been to protect and strengthen the Presidency, but the result was to revive the confidence and authority of Congress.

He set an electronic trap to gather material for the books to be written later, and produced instead evidence that threatened to impeach him.

He campaigned for the Presidency on a platform of law and order, appealing for the end of permissiveness, and was brought down by the disorder, lawlessness, and moral squalor of the team around him. I think he believed to the end he had told the truth as he knew it, and that his enemies in the press and in Congress were hounding him. But he was brought down by a Supreme Court that included four of his own appointees.

Out of such agonies, the nation has grown. It took a civil war to get rid of slavery, and a wasting economic depression to reform the social structure of America. But almost twenty years later I find it difficult to find anything positive that came out of Watergate. Surely no one can examine the Iran-Contra scandal, or our schizoid dealings with Iraq and believe that Presidential excesses have been eliminated, and that campaign financing has been reformed and the privacy of the people protected.

Nixon was not as bad as he came to appear, caught in the web he could not stop weaving. It was a sad time for the country, and the wrong time for people—journalists or politicians—to preen or gloat over a President's disgrace.

For a long while, I doubted that the President ever received my message about burning the tapes. Then I learned that my advice—and I was dead serious—had reached him in the hospital, during his bout with viral pneumonia. Alexander Haig, among others, had convinced him that to burn the tapes, as I had urged, might create a horrendous public-relations problem.

Years later, he said wistfully, "Connally could have convinced me to go ahead and burn the tapes. But I wasn't having any visitors. My aides were keeping people away so I could rest. I wish he had come to the hospital anyway, and banged on the door."

It might have been otherwise, but in the end our political fortunes did not prosper and we were of no lasting help to each other. Richard Nixon went back into retirement, and I went to a courtroom.

THE TRIAL

Even now, nearly twenty years later, I am out-raged and incensed at the thought of it: that anyone could accuse me of accepting a bribe for political fa-vors—and that anyone would believe it.

But that was what happened in the summer of 1974, when I was forced to defend myself against what I believed then and can document now, at least to my satisfaction, was a politically inspired persecution.

Nellie and I were vacationing in London, and were accom-panied by a film crew from CBS, headed by Dave Buksbaum and Bill Gill. We actually got the news from them that a story had been leaked out of the Justice Department that Jake Jacobsen had involved me in what came to be known as the Milk Fund scandal.

Jake Jacobsen? He had the personality of an eel, but a friendly eel. I had known him for decades.

I was astounded and totally unable to make sense out of the report. We completed our vacation and returned to the States. Shortly afterward, I received a summons to appear before the grand jury in Washington, D.C.

—

I had recently reached a quiet time in my political evolution. I had been Secretary of the Treasury, had organized Democrats for Nixon, and then made a swan dive into the Republican Party. During my year and a half at the Treasury, I still maintained my taste for Texas politics—news from home. And here an old, if not close, Texas connection resurfaced and now had returned again to haunt me.

In the fall of 1971, Jake Jacobsen, an Austin lawyer who had first been an assistant to Senator and then Governor Price Daniel, and later served President Johnson in the White House, began calling on me each time he came to Washington. He had an interest in several banks and at least one savings-and-loan, and made frequent trips to Washington to see Bill Campbell, the Comptroller of the Currency, which is a division of the Treasury Department. On most of these visits, he would drop by my office and keep me abreast of what was happening in Texas.

This was a period in which the Sharpstown bank scandal began to take shape, a Texas-size story of failed banks, insider stock trading, and ruined careers. Also, my younger brother, Wayne, was preparing to make a race for lieutenant governor the following year. Although I had little time to devote to state politics, I was extremely interested in the ebb and flow of events there.

In the course of his visits to me, Jacobsen confided that he thought the Justice Department was pursuing him. He suggested that the investigators were trying to pin something on him simply because it might be embarrassing to President Johnson. He asked me if there was any way he could be sure he was not being "set up" for political reasons.

I called Dick Kleindienst, the deputy attorney general under John Mitchell, and gave him the few facts I knew: that there were people in the Justice Department who might be pursuing Jacobsen. If they were investigating Jake, I asked if he would look into it and determine whether it was for other than political reasons.

I didn't hear any more until the spring of 1972, after another visit from Jacobsen, who was growing more and more concerned. Again I called Kleindienst. He said to me, "John, we have Jacobsen cold, he's guilty as hell, leave it alone." I said I certainly will, thank you very much, and did not mention the matter to anybody. Nor did I tell Jacobsen what Kleindienst had told me.

This was the background behind the visits that were dragging me into the post-Watergate whirlpool.

When I walked into the grand jury room, I was advised by a prosecutor for the Justice Department, Frank Tuerkheimer, that I was, in fact, the subject of an investigation. Up to that moment, I was so convinced that there was absolutely nothing to the rumors that I had not troubled myself to analyze all the legal ramifications. Nor had I retained an attorney who would ultimately represent me.

I did take with me Richard Keeton, one of the partners in our Houston-based firm, Vinson, Elkins, Searls, Connally and Smith. His father, Page Keeton, was dean emeritus of the University of Texas Law School, and had befriended me in my student days.

Of course, Richard was not permitted inside the grand jury room for the interrogation. I always regretted that in my sporadic career I had not practiced trial law and gained exposure to the courtroom. This was not the recommended way to acquire some.

Even for a lawyer, testifying before a grand jury can be an unnerving experience. You have no idea what you are going to be asked, or why. You are sitting before a large number of people, eighteen or twenty of them, lounging about in chairs, some reading, some totally indifferent to what is going on, others seemingly half awake. It is a disconcerting scene to think that these people are going to pass judgment on you, until you realize that they are basically window dressing.

Any prosecutor will tell you that he can secure an indictment 99 percent of the time, whenever he wishes. The grand jury
system is really a sham behind which the prosecutor willingly
hides.

It developed that Jacobsen, a lobbyist for the dairy producers, had plea-bargained his way out of forty years in prison by
claiming to have delivered $10,000 to me in 1971 after I advised
President Nixon to raise federal price supports on milk.

I was completely open and frank in my testimony—not that
it mattered. The environment in Washington was poisoned by
Watergate, and while this case was not related to Watergate, it
was viewed as part of that whole episode.

Once the indictment was brought, in August of 1974, I
went to the office of Edward Bennett Williams, and he agreed to
defend me. He picked for his co-counsel a bright, young lawyer
in his office aptly named Mike Tigar.

I told the two of them the entire history of my dealings with
Jake Jacobsen; that he had indeed discussed making available to
me money, initially the sum of $10,000, that I could distribute
on the Hill, winning points by helping in the members' congressional campaigns in 1972.

Obviously, Jacobsen knew there was no way that he would
dare suggest that I would take money for my personal benefit.
He knew that as governor of Texas I had refused contributions
when they weren't needed, had asked contributors for less than
some offered, and had served three terms as governor without a
single scandal involving me or any of my appointees. I very
jealously guarded the integrity of my office and the integrity of
everyone around us. I would not have condoned for one minute
anything of questionable character, much less anything illegal.
What he suggested was that this money was available, and I
could control who received it to enable me to gain some influence with Congress. I told Jake when he brought it up I couldn't
do that, and wouldn't. I was a Democrat in a Republican administration. I didn't want to be out raising money for the Demo-

crats while I was Secretary of the Treasury, and at the same time I didn't want to be raising campaign money for the Republicans, or against members of my own party.

That was all there was to it. Jake concocted an elaborate story of how he brought the money to me; how I took the wrapper off and flushed it down the toilet. It was a sordid, sleazy story he offered up in return for his immunity. Pure fabrication. While the charges, and the trial, were hard on Nellie and the children and my friends, they were all totally sympathetic and supportive, as was my law firm, which paid half my legal fees. I paid the other half.

I came to have a very strong attachment to Ed Williams and Mike Tigar. We debated at some length whether we should ask for a change of venue, recognizing that the jury in Washington would be primarily black. We would have to be fools not to recognize how they would see me, a politician who had "just switched parties" in 1973, and looked the part of a rich white Republican appearing before a panel of predominantly black jurors.

But I said to Ed Williams, during one of the final discussions, that I thought we would be better off staying in Washington. I trust the instinct of black people for justice, and for determining who is telling the truth and who is lying. I would trust my life and future in their hands. Williams said, "I agree with that. We'll stay right here if that's all right with you, and I think we'll be in good hands."

I readily understand that there was no little irony in my choice of Edward Bennett Williams to represent me. He was a charter member of the infamous Nixon Enemies List ("We're going to fix that son of a bitch," the President was heard saying to Haldeman on one of the tapes).

A Washington fixture, Williams had been the special counsel to *Newsweek*, the *Washington Post*, the Democratic Party, and Jimmy Hoffa. He was also owner and president of the Washington Redskins. Of immediate importance to me, he was one of the finest trial lawyers in the country, and a hero to young attorneys all over the East Coast.

Williams was a large, very attractive man, about six feet tall, weighing over 200 pounds, with a robust sense of humor. He had a reputation for getting thoroughly enmeshed in the case on which he was working to the almost full exclusion of everything else. He studied the facts, memorized them, tried to know everything possible about his client and about his case.

I had not known Williams except by reputation prior to the time I retained him. But it was quickly apparent to me that when he took a case, he examined it from every possible angle. He wrote on a yellow legal tablet, and made voluminous notes on all the witnesses, as well as questions he planned to put to his client. For the most part, he questioned the witnesses without any sarcasm or biting humor; he did it in a quiet, workmanlike manner. Occasionally, however, he would engage in a bit of playacting.

In the end, of course, the verdict in my case would come down to whether the jury believed Jake Jacobsen or John Connally. Williams ridiculed Jacobsen's testimony about a cigar box in which I was supposed to have handed him some money to replace the cash he had given me. At this point, Williams did a little playacting in the courtroom, sneaking around, wearing rubber gloves, carrying an imaginary cigar box surreptitiously in his hands, discrediting Jacobsen, who couldn't remember if there had been one glove or two, or what color they were, if any.

But for the most part he avoided histrionics. He was not a flamboyant questioner, as some trial lawyers are. He didn't win his cases by theatrics in the manner of Perry Mason. He won them, as I've said, with a tireless attention to detail.

He was fine company, with a great sense of humor. On one of his trips to Texas we were talking about the case. We had driven from Houston to Austin, and someone asked him how far it was. He said, "I don't know how many miles it is, but it's three Dairy Queens from Houston to Austin. That's John Connally's measurement of the distance." In truth, I am an ice-cream fan. Williams was more interested in a case of scotch.

Nellie and I came not only to admire him but to have a feeling of affection for him. At a conservation meeting in San Antonio, I had bought a beautiful painting of a pride of lions, and on his trip to Houston we presented it to Williams. Nellie started calling him Simba, which is Swahili for lion. It was symbolic that the lions in the picture are taking precautions to safeguard their pride, just as he, as a lawyer, kept a constant vigil to perceive any danger to his clients.

Mike Tigar, whose work I observed with admiration and gratitude, did a superb job of briefing the case from the standpoint of the legal points. He was also a superb trial lawyer, one of the best in the country. He made the impression of being a country lawyer, wearing boots, shuffling along in a tweed jacket with an odd-matching pair of pants. He had a warm, friendly smile, and straight brown hair that fell over one eye. Nomadic by nature, he was a graduate of Berkeley, where he had been a brilliant student and, later, a teacher. He had been on the defense team for Angela Davis and, along with Bill Kunstler, had defended the Chicago Seven, the self-styled "Yippies" who were largely responsible for the chaos in Grant Park in 1968.

Tigar had then joined Williams's firm for a period before leaving to go to France, where he spent a year or two studying. He had just returned to the firm when my case arose, and was chosen to work in my defense. Later, he went back to the academic life and is now a professor of law at the University of Texas.

I was aware that Mike had participated in several cases where our philosophies were widely separated, yet we never discussed them. I was more than willing to accept him at face value for his ability and capacity, and neither of us ever let any supposed philosophical differences have an effect on our professional relationship or our personal feelings.

The trial itself was an ordeal, draining and humiliating. The only witness against me was Jake Jacobsen. The indictment was even more puzzling when you consider that in the federal jurisdiction of Washington, D.C., there is a rule that no case will be brought on the basis of uncorroborated testimony by one individual.

Dick Kleindienst had told me two years earlier that they had Jake cold, on charges of fraud, embezzlement, and perjury involving the San Angelo Savings & Loan. In order to bring an indictment against me, they bought his testimony by giving him immunity not only with respect to his alleged bribe attempt but also in the San Angelo case.

To make my situation even more perplexing, it was revealed in transcripts previously sealed by the court that Jacobsen had first offered to testify against President Johnson about alleged gifts from the milk producers, but that John Mitchell, the attorney general, had said absolutely not. He quashed round that Jake's testimony would amount to an "inevident exploration," which loosely translates as a fishing expedition. But, clearly, Jake was prepared to offer up a former President to save his own skin.

When that ploy didn't work, he turned to the prosecution and offered testimony against me. Between the indictment and trial, months passed, during which time I continued to practice law in Houston. Obviously, it was an incredible burden to bear each day as I went to the office, saw old friends, and felt the curious gaze of strangers. I always assumed that they were wondering, Is he guilty or not? Did he do it or didn't he? How did he get involved with a shadowy guy like Jacobsen?

All these thoughts ran through my mind at a time when most people—almost without exception—were totally sympathetic, and expressed anger and disgust that such a charge had been brought against me.

I was aware of the street talk. A great many people disposed of the matter by saying that it was ridiculous, the very idea that you could buy John Connally for ten thousand dollars; maybe a million, but no way would he be involved in something like this. My real friends, of course, felt that under no circumstances, regardless of the amount, would I be engaged in a criminal act.

The thing that hurt and disturbed me the most, and that I still live with, is the stain all this left on my character. It was untrue, and so totally uncharacteristic of my life, which I have tried to live in a scrupulously honest way.

I attempted not to let the prospects of the trial overwhelm me, and so I carried on my legal activities, advising clients and maintaining as normal a routine as possible. I was greatly helped, of course, by Nellie's attitude and that of the children, who appeared to be taking it in stride.

The tension was interrupted by one somewhat comic incident that occurred outside of the courtroom. We were staying at the Mayflower Hotel, and Nellie had cautioned the children and their spouses to be very quiet, given the great strain I was under. They took the advice to heart, and one particular night our daughter Sharon and her husband, Robert, had gone next door to visit our other children. Robert was dressed only in his shorts, and when they walked back into their room, they saw what appeared to be a maid rifling through their clothes and possessions.

They started to give chase, quietly, and followed the maid down the hall, Robert in his shorts, trying to catch this thief who had stolen what money they had, which was very little. Though the children joined the pursuit, while trying not to make any noise, the culprit—actually a professional thief impersonating a maid—made his escape. I knew nothing about it until several days later.

The courtroom drew a full gallery of spectators every day, including a number of law students. I will never forget the two United States senators who came and sat in the courtroom— part of the trial—to show their support. One was Cliff Hansen of Wyoming, and the other was former Governor and then Senator Henry Bellmon of Oklahoma. I shall always be grateful, not only to those who testified as character witnesses, but also to these two senators, as well as to Congressman Jake Pickle, who appeared at the courthouse steps, shook my hand, and put his arms around me. It was a manifestation of friendship and confidence that went back to the middle 1930s, and to 1940 when he stepped in as best man at our wedding in Austin.

There were ugly moments, as well, such as the deliberate leaks out of the Justice Department before the trial, leaks primarily to Jack Anderson and Daniel Schorr, both of whom used them in their columns to try to poison the atmosphere against me. Of course, other newspapers picked up the stories and carried them.

There were headlines all over the country, particularly in my home state of Texas. I was helpless to counteract leaks of this type, made for the purpose of prejudicing public opinion. We were certainly not in a position to launch any full-scale denial and have the details of a full-blown trial in the press. The lawyers felt this was unwise; ultimately we were concerned with what was presented to a jury of twelve people, a fact you can't lose sight of no matter how many damaging stories appear in the press.

I had great confidence in Ed Williams and Mike Tigar, and although we discussed the strategy, I made no attempt to tell them how to try the case. We agreed early on, almost from the first conversation we had, that I was guilty of nothing, and under no circumstances would I plea-bargain for any diminution of the charges. After that basic decision was made, there was nothing left but to try the case.

During the trial, the prosecution produced a tape of a conversation I had with President Nixon in the Oval Office regarding the milk price supports. At the time, this was a major issue in the Congress. I had become the focal point within the administration for the Democrats to express their support for price supports. Wilbur Mills was extremely interested, and former Vice President Hubert Humphrey called, beseeching me to convince President Nixon it was in his interest and the interest of the country to increase milk price supports.

After talking to these two and other Democrats, it was clear to me that they were going to pass an increase in the supports if the President didn't act, and that they had the votes to override a veto if he was inclined to do so. I thought that politically it would be unwise to oppose the increase.

After a cabinet meeting, I went into the President's office to relate my conversations with Mills, Humphrey, and other Democrats who favored the milk price supports. Since Mills now controlled all the taxes, I pointed out that now would be the appropriate time for the President to make whatever tax deal he wanted to make with Wilbur. The price increase was going to pass anyway, and he could get a great deal in return for his support, both in the House and in the Senate.

The prosecution took the tape, the quality of which was poor, scratchy, and all but unintelligible, transcribed it, and showed it to the jury over our protests. In their interpretation, I had attempted to influence President Nixon to support the increase in price supports; when he did, we could take care of him with "a substantial allocation of oil in Texas."

Obviously, this was a deliberate and total misinterpretation of what was on the tape. Could any sane person believe that I would, or could, make a gift of a couple of oil wells to Richard Nixon? What they had understood as "oil in Texas" was a reference to Wilbur Mills, and a reminder to the President that Mills controlled "all the taxes," which he did in the House.

Their interpretation would clearly indicate that I was involved in a bald and even bizarre conspiracy to bribe the President for his support of the milk price increase. The judge allowed the jury to listen to the tape, but withheld the transcripts cooked up by the Justice Department. I listened to the tape and, try as I might, I could not clearly distinguish what was said. But I had the advantage of knowing that I told the President he was in a perfect trading position with the chairman of the Ways and Means Committee, if indeed he made up his mind to support the price increase. But without that knowledge, even a fair interpretation would conclude that the tape was unintelligible.

For all the digging the government did, it could not rely on faulty tapes or justify the time and millions that were spent checking every bank in Texas to see if I had any hidden accounts. They even canvassed all the jewelry and department stores in Washington to see if I had made any significant purchases. They found nothing.

The government's case consisted of Jake Jacobsen. Just before Jake took the stand, my brother Merrill leaned over and whispered in my ear: "John, now don't lose your composure when that man starts testifying." I had to stifle a laugh. "Don't worry," I whispered back. "I've known so many lying sons of bitches that one more won't crater me."

We had a parade of blue ribbon witnesses who spoke to my character: Bob McNamara, Dean Rusk, Billy Graham, Barbara Jordan, and Lady Bird Johnson, who said simply: "John is a man of integrity, a man of honor, and so known."

Barbara Jordan, who disagreed with several of my political beliefs, got up and in her magnificent voice said I had a reputation for honesty and integrity.

All earned my undying gratitude that they would come and bear witness for me.

A jury brought in a verdict of not guilty.

That night my family and friends gathered in Bob Strauss's apartment in the Watergate Hotel for a celebration. I assure you we were a happy bunch, fielding a steady flow of calls from friends congratulating me on my acquittal. It was an unbelievable relaxation of the tension that had built over many weeks and many months. I realized now that I could indeed go back to my normal living and the practice of law.

One of the galling things about the aftermath of the trial was that the press, five years later, in my quest for the Republican nomination for President, constantly alluded to the trial. It was almost the first, last, and the in-between question at every press conference, an obvious attempt on the part of the press to keep the issue alive, to bring it into the forefront of the minds of people. The damning thing about an indictment and trial is that forever after in the minds of a segment of the population, you are not quite innocent.

Or, even if they know you were found not guilty, they still remember that there was something negative that reflected adversely on you. I was acquitted, as I should have been, but the stain was left.

In the end, I believe that my trial had less to do with Watergate and the Milk Fund than what others perceived as my ambitions to hold high office.

Earlier, when the crisis in Watergate came, I was back in my law office in Houston, with no hint yet of the charges that would be leveled against me. Spiro Agnew had resigned, and I got a call from Al Haig, at the request of the President, seeking my opinion about the naming of a new Vice President. We talked briefly, and Haig clearly indicated to me that the best choice was Gerald Ford.

I readily agreed with him, and said he ought to tell the President he should appoint Ford. If he appointed me, I knew it would touch off a big battle in the Congress. I would be confirmed, but I felt the confirmation would be delayed for a considerable period of time for political purposes.

The President was under great pressure, and my opinion was that if anyone could help him, it would be Gerald Ford. A speedy confirmation of the Vice President was essential, and Ford was the wisest and safest appointment he could make. I asked General Haig to convey those thoughts to the President.

After Ford was confirmed, he told me of his conversation with Nixon. He was extremely candid, and volunteered that once he had been offered the Vice-Presidency, Nixon made a point of saying that he would not support him for President in 1976 because he intended to support John Connally. Ford said he understood, and hadn't considered running in any event. He said that I should, and he would support me. I was gratified that he made such a statement, but was not convinced that things would turn out that way. Indeed, when Ford became President, I knew he would be under enormous pressure to run. He was, and he did. I don't fault him for that, and did all I could to support him.

I was troubled, however, by the way his campaign was being run and so was Nelson Rockefeller, who had been chosen by Ford to fill the Vice-Presidency after Nixon had resigned. Rockefeller and I flew to his lodge in Vail, Colorado, to meet with Ford and Bob Dole. Nelson, who knew more about the people around him and the inner workings of the Republican Party than I did, said flat out that the campaign was being run by third-raters. Our criticisms could not have made either one of us very popular, but we believed that it was in Ford's interest to hear them.

We argued that Ford had to have better advice if he was going to win the election. Naturally, this didn't endear Nelson or me to any of the staff once the word got out, as it usually does. Nonetheless we were concerned that Ford's prospects were in danger. I must say he listened attentively, but we saw no substantial change as a result of our visit.

All along, there had been a hidden effort directed against me by the inside staff at the White House, and also against minority leader Howard Baker, both of us having been seen as threats to run on the ticket with Ford. Without his knowledge, I'm convinced, people around him conspired: Mel Laird, the Secretary of Defense under Nixon; Philip Buchen, the counsel to the President; Dick Cheney, Ford's chief of staff and Secretary of Defense under Bush; Donald Rumsfeld, who had been with Nixon and now Ford; and Bob Teeter, Ford's poll-taker. They brought in others as well, including Bob Griffin, senator from Michigan, who made the statement that if I was on the ticket, he, Griffin, would be defeated as a candidate. Of course, he lost anyway. But they convinced Ford that it would be a great mistake to name me as Vice President. It amounted to an exercise in wasted energy. I wasn't seeking it, didn't want it, under him or anyone else.

In the meantime, I found myself indicted on the Milk Fund charges and, as a practical matter, withdrew from the national political scene. This is something that I still bitterly resent, all the more so because in time I learned that these events were at least loosely connected.

I thought then and I think now that it was largely a case of collusion between disgruntled Democrats and Republicans in and out of the Justice Department who wanted to taint my name. Unbeknownst to those conspirators, I was getting inside information about what they were doing and what they were saying. These adversaries went to great lengths to try to make sure that under no circumstances would Ford choose Howard Baker or John Connally as his running mate. Rockefeller was out as Vice President in 1976, and the opening was there.

In a campaign orchestrated by Dick Cheney, rumors about me were circulated among major Republican organizers and contributors. Bob Teeter, Ford's official pollster, distributed polls showing how damaging my presence would be on the ticket. At the same time, a memorandum attributed to Cheney attacked Howard Baker with malicious gossip directed at Baker's wife, Joy.

In another memorandum, a White House staffer quoted Cheney as telling an aide that more dirt was needed "to convince the dumb shit [Ford] that Connally is poison."

My source for the details of the dirty tricks campaign was a holdover from the Nixon staff, only slightly brushed by the Watergate fallout. He was then working for Ford and engaged to a secretary in Cheney's office. Since both may be still involved in Republican politics, I won't identify them by name. I don't know if they were boosters of mine, or upset by the tactics they saw being used.

If this sounds gross and appalling, it surely was; this is the way the hit-and-run artists play the survival game. Later, when Cheney was Bush's Secretary of Defense, he was mentioned as a Presidential hopeful himself.

It was this attitude that prevailed around the Ford White House, and in certain other quarters, at the time the indictment was brought against me. Nor did I believe it to be a coincidence that Leon Jaworski was the Watergate special prosecutor at the time, and in effect still had jurisdiction on my case.

Jaworski was on leave from his role as a senior partner in a rival law firm in Houston, Fulbright and Crooker, later re-named Fulbright and Jaworski.

As time passed, and I was acquitted, and both my reputation and political fortunes were partially retrieved, I became, in 1980, a candidate for the Republican Presidential nomination. Years later, I received a copy of a report that described a visit with Speaker Tip O'Neill by Leon Jaworski and Jim Wright in January of 1979.

The meeting was held the day after I declared my candidacy, and was tape-recorded by an aide to Speaker O'Neill. A confidential summary of that meeting shortly made its way into my hands. Jim Wright opened the conversation by declaring that my election would have "a more catastrophic effect on the country than did the Civil War." I am not sure how one should react to a comparison of such historic scope. But the thought must have exhausted Congressman Wright, because from that point on Leon Jaworski did nearly all the talking.

Jaworski tried to persuade O'Neill to start an investigation of whether I had been guilty of fraud, had manipulated the commodities market, and had illegally procured and sold bank loans—all of which was total nonsense. I had never in my life bought or sold a commodity of any kind, nor had I arranged a fraudulent bank loan for myself or anyone else.

When O'Neill wondered why Jaworski didn't simply submit his evidence through the Justice Department, he replied that "the current political climate was wrong." I found the statement baffling. I was under the impression that a nice, raw corruption case can nearly always find fair weather in Washington.

O'Neill asked his visitors to submit a bill of particulars. None was ever produced or delivered.

The charges were the strange fiction of a man who seemed

to have a vendetta against me that was consuming him. Oddly enough, I never had a cross word with Jaworski in my life and always thought of him as a fine lawyer.

When Jaworski was appointed special prosecutor, President Nixon asked me about him. I told the President he had a great reputation, wide experience, and I thought he would do a very capable job. To this day, I am at a loss to explain the animosity that he felt against me, other than the rivalry between our competing law firms. The big Houston firms had been for years part of an interlocking network. We were affiliated with Methodist Hospital, they were affiliated with Baylor. They were affiliated with Bank of the Southwest, we were with First City. If we clashed on any personal level, I was unaware of it.

There was one other possible explanation. A number of people had gotten close to Lyndon Johnson in their public lives, and in some way competed for his attention. This had caused one prominent Austin lawyer, Ed Clark, to develop an animosity toward me, and Clark and Jaworski were close friends. I never resented anyone jockeying for position with Johnson, for his favor and friendship. My own position was what it was. No one was ever able to endanger that relationship or alter it at all, but that could well have been part of the problem.

Given the attitudes of Jaworski and the Ford staff, one could well understand how the indictment was brought and the attempt made to destroy my viability as a political figure.

A RUN FOR THE WHITE HOUSE

Near the end of 1978, I began to think seriously about running for President. Later, two television images propelled me in that direction and reinforced my resolve. One was Jimmy Carter telling the American people that the country was suffering from a crisis of confidence. I didn't see it that way. I thought the people had lost confidence in Jimmy Carter, not in themselves.

The second was the long, morbid face of the Ayatollah Khomeini, with his flowing white beard and the eyes of a mystic, his words inciting all of Islam against "the Great Satan."

The 1970s had given us a newsreel that included Kent State, where nervous National Guardsmen fired into a crowd of students and took four lives. Murder came to the Olympics as Israeli athletes were massacred in Munich. Members of a religious cult drank Kool-Aid laced with cyanide and committed mass suicide in a place called Jonestown. Watergate brought down the Nixon Presidency. The U.S. presence in South Viet-

nam ended with the last flight out of Saigon. Iranian "students"
seized our embassy in Tehran, taking sixty-three Americans hostage. These were years of turmoil interrupted by an occasional
bright note: Israel and Egypt agreed to a peace treaty at Camp
David. The Vatican elected the first Polish Pope. But to many,
the world had never seemed more unsafe or unstable. With the
threat of hijackings, passengers were required to walk through
metal detectors at every major airport.

It was against this background that I weighed my decision
to run for President in 1980. I could expect the press, and my
rivals, to pound away at several points: the Texas wheeler-dealer
image; my recent Republican status; my defense of two Presidents, Johnson and Nixon, whose reputations were now in disfavor. I knew I would be accused of this and much more if I ran
for President.

Twice I had avoided the Vice-Presidency: when Nixon considered dropping Spiro Agnew in 1972, and again, a year later,
when Agnew's legal woes forced him to resign. Before the President named Gerald Ford, the Democrats had held out for a
caretaker, one who would not run for the Presidency in 1976.
That restriction seemed aimed at me, and when I was pressed for
a comment, my answer was "I am flattered by the apparent fears
that some have of me and my prospects."

Not then or any other time, not in public or in private, did
I express any serious interest in being the Vice President. All it
could have done for me in 1973 was provide my political opponents with an easy target for three more years.

So why in the name of Millard Fillmore did I decide to
become a candidate eight years after I had last served in the
federal government, twelve years after I had last held an elective
office? I had survived an assassin's bullet, a federal trial, and a
switch of political parties.

How could I not run?

I had served in the cabinets of John Kennedy and Richard
Nixon, had managed most of the campaigns that led Lyndon
Johnson into the White House. I had seen how they made

sausage, and I had no illusions. There was nothing in my disposition that drove me to make the race. I never felt afflicted with Potomac fever. I could have spent my entire life happily as a pretty fair cattleman, or even as a corporate lawyer.

Now, it is true that few politicians sound sincere when they are trying to be modest. All I am saying is that the Presidency was not my obsession. From the time I was elected governor of a state with 24 electoral votes, my name was dropped here and there. My problems had little to do with my party affiliation. I believed I could be elected *if* I won the nomination. The timing was never ideal, and I would always face an uphill battle to be nominated.

In 1968, with Lyndon Johnson a target of anger and derision, a Texan was not going to lead the Democratic ticket, not then, probably not again in this century. In 1972, I was working for the re-election of President Nixon. In 1976, I had been a Republican less than three years and too little time had elapsed since my acquittal in the Milk Fund trial.

If there had been no Watergate scandal, there would have been no Milk Fund trial, and Nixon—had he completed a second term—believed he could "deliver the convention to Connally," or so he told Haldeman, Ford, and others. I don't look back. What would have happened is what did happen.

But the 1980 race appeared to be wide open, and if I was ever going to run, now was the time. I would have stayed out if there had been a candidate in the Republican field I felt had the wealth of experience I could offer on a state, national, and global scale. Before Reagan announced, there were ten, including Al Haig, Bob Dole, George Bush, Howard Baker, John Anderson, and Philip Crane.

Nellie and I made the decision together. She could have ended it with one shake of her head. But what she said was "We'll both be happier if you're content. And you won't be content if you don't do this." Then she added, in what I took to be a totally unbiased remark, "Besides, there is no one out there more qualified than you."

We sounded out a number of key Republicans from Maine to California, and I was encouraged by their offers of support. But in a curious way, the ones who were the most vocal were my longtime Texas friends Bob Strauss, Ben Barnes, George Christian, Mike Myers, and Larry Temple, Democrats who urged me to run—as a Republican.

Before I announced my candidacy, I tried unsuccessfully for months to learn whether Ronald Reagan planned to declare himself. I talked twice to Reagan, then governor of California, and on other occasions with Michael Deaver, his deputy. If Reagan intended to jump in, I was going to pass. I recognized fully that if he ran he would be nominated. I had seen how close he had come to taking the nomination away from a sitting President in his own party in 1976. He had been in the movies for twenty years, on radio for the last fifteen. People believed what they thought he was saying.

He insisted that he hadn't made up his mind, and I thought there was a chance his age might keep him out. At any rate, he could afford to delay because of his standing among the Republican Party workers throughout the country; I could not.

So I announced in January, 1979, at the National Press Club in Washington. Even though he was not yet a candidate, the polls showed Reagan's support at 40 percent. I was the choice of 6 percent of those surveyed, but I had faced those odds before and felt no terror. In my mind, Reagan had been preparing for this race since 1968.

If my decision seemed to contradict my earlier disavowals about the Presidency, I now felt a sense of fitness. Perhaps many politicians could relate to Henry Kissinger's wry observation: "The longer I am out of office, the more infallible I appear to myself."

I doubted that the country could endure four more years of Jimmy Carter's policies. I felt confident that I could provide the leadership he seemed so painfully to lack. I was appalled by his handling of the convulsions in Iran: the overthrow of Shah Mohammed Reza Pahlavi; the taking of the American hostages;

the failed rescue attempt. I was saddened by the spectacle of the Shah, who had ruled Iran for thirty-seven years, reduced to begging countries to admit him so he could be treated for the cancer that would shortly kill him.

I immediately tackled the questions that were certain to follow me. A reporter in Chicago asked how I answered the charge that I was a wheeler-dealer. I said, "If you mean someone who knows how to deal with congressmen and senators, then I plead guilty. If you're talking about someone who can negotiate with world leaders on an equal basis and not be a tail-end Charlie, then I'm a wheeler-dealer. If you're talking about someone who is smart enough to go into a horse trade with a good, sound horse and not come out with one that's one-eyed and swaybacked, then I'm that."

I didn't resent references to my having an ego; the ego of man gets big things done. I knew I would be accused of this and much more. I would not be defeated for reasons of insecurity, which can be fatal to the Presidency. It kept Johnson in Vietnam, drew Nixon to Watergate, and rendered Carter politically paralyzed.

In politics, image has a way of becoming self-fulfilling. We now know that Carter's image and his record were distorted—by the press, by his opponents, and by the times. He may have been the most humble of twentieth-century Presidents, and almost surely the least flawed in moral terms.

Yet few saw him that way. He was labeled soft and pious. He declared that he would "never lie" to the American people. He meant it, and in his heart he may have succeeded. Certainly he tried, but you can't give the news media a challenge so open. He left himself no margins; he could not make a mistake, or change his mind, without having his truthfulness questioned.

I disagreed with his handling of the economy and felt he was incapable of inspiring confidence. But I also recognize that he suffered from almost unending bad luck. From his first days in office, he tackled a no-win issue: amnesty for the young men who defected to Canada to avoid being drafted during the Vietnam War. It wasn't clear, among the tens of thousands who fled, if they opposed in principle all wars, but there was no doubt that they opposed this one. For Carter, the choice wasn't between right and wrong. It had to be done, and he did so sooner rather than later.

During his administration, inflation and interest rates went into orbit. The rising cost of gasoline and the second Arab oil boycott created brutally long lines at the pump, and angry motorists blamed Carter. When the OPEC policies created an earlier shortage, under Ford, they blamed the Arabs.

He would be acclaimed for the Camp David peace accord between Egypt and Israel. But this accomplishment would be eroded by the fall of the Shah and the loss of Iran as an ally. Then came the hostage crisis after Iranian "students" occupied the U.S. embassy, and the failed rescue mission with American helicopter pilots dying in the desert. These were every President's nightmare.

His smile, his voice, his manner seemed to suggest anything but toughness, and this compounded his problems. He was a former naval engineer, and he found himself in an environment where his attention to detail worked against him. His sense of precision in an imprecise world made it difficult for him to deal quickly with the innumerable problems that beset any President.

If the economy had been less wretched, we might have appreciated his intelligence more. He was motivated by a care and concern for the less fortunate more than most Presidents. He reflected then and now a personal dedication to trying to improve the lot of those whose lives he touches. He would probably win with ease a contest to name the best ex-President. No President since Truman has shown less interest in making money.

But the Jimmy Carter of 1976 was a mystery, and the virtue that got him elected—he was a Washington outsider—in many eyes became a weakness. If Jimmy Carter didn't return a phone call from a senator, it was interpreted as a sign that he didn't know how to get along. If Lyndon Johnson didn't return one, it was interpreted as his way of sending the senator a message.

I had been curious about Carter, the former Georgia peanut farmer, ever since the primaries in 1976. Some of my old friends in the Democratic Party have persisted in telling me that I would have been the party's nominee that year if I hadn't defected to the Republicans. I don't believe it. Never did.

Week after week, I watched Jimmy Carter hold on during very trying times against as many as thirteen opponents. In a close election, he succeeded in defeating Gerald Ford, in part because the American people were still reacting to the wrongs of Watergate. At one point, I called a few of my contacts in Georgia, all Democrats, some of them active in politics, others in business or law, and asked them what they knew about Carter. Their comments were fairly uniform: they rated him not highly as a governor and unreliable as a person.

I expressed amazement that he was able to survive, and then it was explained to me that he had done so largely with the support of the born-again Christians and the Evangelical movement, which had not yet reached the prominence it would later achieve. Very few people were aware that this growing religious base even existed, but it was a factor in the 1976 elections and beyond. Pressure and financial support from the Evangelicals, who wanted to spread their gospel across Central America, helped persuade the Reagan administration to step up our aid to the Contras and widen the war in Nicaragua in the early '80s.

This was a very potent force, entrenched in the religious lives of millions of people in the South, and just beginning to take shape in the political arena. They would later deliver their votes in substantial numbers to Reagan.

As I analyzed my prospects, I knew I had to literally introduce myself to the Republican faithful, many of whom viewed me as a relatively recent convert. My best hope was to get as much of a head start as I could, before Reagan entered the race.

Much would be made of the fact that I raised $12 million and landed just one delegate. But while the contrast was worth a chuckle, it tended to overlook the more important point: the money was more than any other candidate collected. Some must have believed in me and the programs I advocated.

From the outset, my staff and advisers were concerned that I would be labeled the candidate of Big Business. I never saw it as a liability. I wasn't going to be their errand boy, but I wouldn't run from them, either. I have found that you can talk tough to business people and earn their respect—if what you tell them is true.

From Wall Street to Main Street, this is what I said: "If you're not willing to get into the political arena and defend your business, to defend your interests, to defend this economic system, then you're not worthy to head any corporation in America, in my judgment. And if you don't get into the political arena, you're not going to have a business to head."

Of course, everyone assumes you are talking about Big Business. I couldn't care less about Big Business. We have to quit thinking in terms of what government can do for us in this country and think more about what people can do for themselves. When I refer to businesses making this country tick, I'm not referring to General Motors or AT&T. I'm talking about the chicken farmer who is my neighbor in Floresville, and the trucker who hauls my cattle to market.

My chances of establishing a foothold and taking the nomination from Reagan were slender at best, but I had an early setback that may have been critical. I offered the job of campaign manager to Lee Nunn, brother of the governor of Kentucky, and widely respected among Republican campaign workers throughout the country.

When Lee declined, my second choice was Eddie Mahe, a veteran operator who had been recommended by several high-placed Republicans. Lee Nunn left me with a warning: if I put Eddie in charge, the campaign would be a financial disaster. Eddie was sincere and honest, but he had no concept of how to regulate the flow of money and was incapable of performing the role I asked him to perform. Lee's advice proved to be woefully correct.

Wherever we had a campaign office, I found we were overstaffed and ineffective in terms of utilizing the resources we had. I received criticism for trying to run the campaign by myself, but I think the opposite was true. I was on the road 95 percent of the time, making speeches and raising money. I paid too little attention and had too little time to monitor the inner workings of the campaign itself.

I felt like Edward Bennett Williams when he owned the Washington Redskins and had to adjust to the expensive ideas of his football coach. "I gave George Allen an unlimited budget," quipped Williams, "and he exceeded it."

Eddie Mahe's real value to me was in his long-term Republican connections, and in his knowledge of the other players. He projected that Bush and Howard Baker would be rejected as too moderate. Bob Dole would be eliminated because of his rocky showing as Ford's running mate in '76. That would reduce the field to a two-man race: Reagan and Connally.

Mahe also believed that Ted Kennedy would replace Carter as the Democratic nominee, and I hoped he was right. It was generally agreed that I matched up better against Kennedy than Reagan. Ted was the liberal torchbearer, and his name still evoked youth and style and a touch of Camelot.

Kennedy's other advantage was that he wouldn't have to run on Carter's record: runaway inflation, high interest rates, the Ayatollah cursing America nightly on television. That year, the Republican nomination was the prize.

We had adopted the basic strategy of building a broad base across the country. It wasn't going to be enough just to win Iowa or New Hampshire. We assumed that because I was still a relative newcomer to the Republican Party, I had to attempt to carry the campaign to all of the fifty states, and attract the support of the leading Republicans in various regions.

That was exactly what we set out to do, and I'm proud of

the quality of the support that joined us in the early stages. My press secretary was Jim Brady, a truly delightful, impish individual, who was knowledgeable about the federal government and how it worked. He knew his way around the Defense Department. Most remarkable was his unfailing good humor and his aura of gentility.

Outside of my close Texas friends such as Julian Read, Wales Madden, and Mike Myers, Brady was clearly the person I relied upon most. Nellie and I formed a real affection for him and referred to him as "Friar Tuck." It was one of the tragedies of our time when he was badly wounded, and left partially paralyzed, in the attempt on President Reagan's life in 1981.

By the time Reagan announced, I knew that South Carolina, whose primary came early, would be our best battleground. There we felt we would have an even chance with any other candidate. I had the endorsements of Senator Strom Thurmond, then seventy-seven and a popular former Dixiecrat, and ex-Governor Jim Edwards. Both had supported Reagan against President Ford in 1976.

Thurmond and his wife, Nancy, rode the buses with Nellie and me day after day, traveling to the big cities and over farm roads to the smallest towns. We had the backing of a number of mayors in the major cities. We had endorsements from the state's leading newspapers. We had the time and the money.

But when the final returns were in, I had received 30 percent of the vote and Ronald Reagan 55. George Bush trailed with 15 percent. Even though our organization was strong in Florida, and we figured to run well there and in Georgia, Alabama, and my own state of Texas, I knew that South Carolina had told us all we needed to know about the campaign.

It was simply that Reagan was going to be nominated. All he had to do was live.

Political money follows political odds. We were running out of funds, and I had no interest in hanging on in the hope of winning the second spot on the ticket. Our strategy had been to improve my standing in the national polls and block Reagan in the South. The scheduling came apart, and I learned an expensive lesson: you don't know how to run a Presidential campaign until you've run in one.

The day after the South Carolina primary, Nellie, our older son, John B. III, and a few of my close advisers flew home to Texas. The flight lasted five hours and we reached a decision with a minimum of discussion and not much anguish. Quite simply, I had been rejected by the Republican voters. There was no hope. We held a press conference at a Houston hotel and I announced my formal withdrawal from the race. It was not an easy thing to do. Nellie gently patted my arm as I spoke the words "I do not intend ever to be a candidate again."

I immediately threw my unstinting support to Governor Reagan. Nellie and I traveled with the Reagans on some of the remaining campaign stops, and listened sympathetically as they both complained about George Bush staying in the race when it was obvious he could no longer succeed.

There is nothing else in the world quite like an American Presidential election. It is one part running with the bulls in Pamplona, one part Mardi Gras in Rio, and one part Judgment at Nuremberg. It can be unproductive to try and look at the process with logic, or to make sense of all the deal-making and compromising.

With each passing day on the campaign trail, the Reagans were more infuriated with Bush. At one point, Nancy turned to me and snapped, "Why can't you get him out of the race? He's doing nothing but costing us time and money and energy."

I had to suppress a smile. I understood how she felt, but realistically I didn't think George Bush was going to be persuaded by anything I had to say. Still, I offered to call Jim Baker, adding a cautionary note to Governor Reagan: "I hope when it's over that you won't reward him with the Vice-Presidency."

Reagan shook his head. "Don't worry," he said. "I'll never do that."

Of course, at the convention, after an offer to Ford went haywire and almost turned into a co-Presidency, Reagan did exactly that. To his credit, he remembered our conversation and gave me the courtesy of a phone call. "John, I know what I said," he apologized, "but I have no choice."

I replied, "Do what you have to do."

He said, "I knew you'd understand."

I cannot erase from my memory bank the knowledge that this was the same George Bush who, during the 1980 campaign, kept circulating seeds of deception about remarks I had supposedly made on the Watergate tapes not yet open to the public. The thrust was that they incriminated me in some unspecified way. It reached a point where I telephoned Jim Baker and said I wanted it stopped. I thought Bush had gone well out of bounds. There was nothing on the tapes, and if there had been, he wouldn't have known because no one had heard them. If he persisted, the campaign was going to get rough indeed. Baker said he would talk to him, but the stories continued to come out of the Bush campaign.

In the end, amid the postmortems that always follow a political demise, a number of factors were identified as having prevented my campaign from getting on track. Some Republicans still disapproved of my ties to Lyndon Johnson, and others of my ties to Richard Nixon. I wouldn't apologize for either.

The Milk Fund trial was a handicap, but I countered it as best I could with my standard line: "I am the only certified non-guilty candidate in the race."

At the time, many of the pundits were inclined to believe that my candidacy had been crushed by the reaction to a major policy speech I had made in October on the Middle East. I knew it would be controversial. I thought the speech was balanced and reasoned. I had deliberated before I delivered it, at the National Press Club, knowing that most of my closest advisers had opposed my giving it, fearing the political consequences. I felt strongly that peace in the Middle East should be a subject of debate in the campaign. If a campaign is to have value, it should be used to encourage debate on what the candidates and their parties believe. The idea that an election can turn on personalities and sound bites leaves me cold.

So I undertook to inject the Middle East into the campaign. Without question, the speech angered the American Jewish community, and the immediate reaction was so negative that some of my supporters announced they were withdrawing from the campaign. But I was convinced that the points I made, the plan I outlined, needed to be said. I proposed that Israel give up the occupied lands, in return for which the Arabs would "forsake the oil weapon," assuring a stable supply of oil. I proposed that a Palestinian homeland be created, preferably within Jordan, as either a state or other entity. An overall peace treaty would protect Israel's right to exist and to have secure borders.

I warned that continued tension between Arabs and Israelis threatened further disruptions in the supply of Middle Eastern oil—"the lifeblood of Western civilization for decades to come." I questioned what was then Israel's policy of "creeping annexation" on the West Bank. I argued for a more forceful American diplomacy and a broad new policy in the Middle East. The United States could ensure Israel's security by stationing U.S. Air Force units in the Sinai and establishing a naval base in the Arabian Sea. Israel then, and only then, would be required to withdraw from its occupied territories.

Palestinians who renounced further violence could settle on the West Bank; unrepentant terrorists would be denied sanctuary anywhere. Regional stability would be assured by a military alliance that would include Israel, cooperating Arab states, Japan, NATO, and the United States.

The next day, I bought an ad in *The New York Times* to reproduce the speech, so people could read the full text and not just read or hear a few excerpts.

The reaction from Jewish groups and the Israeli government grew into a firestorm, and my political rivals tried to paint the speech as a cynical Connally swap: Israel's land and security for Arab oil. There was very little effort on the editorial pages to analyze in more than a superficial way the arguments I had made. And, yet, more than a dozen years later my ideas had moved into the mainstream, and are now being openly debated by Israel's leaders and the Arab states.

It was a personal hurt to be accused—unfairly, I thought— of being anti-Israel or anti-Semitic. The political fallout scarcely mattered. Although some thought my speech in October was a turning point in the campaign, I knew better. The turning point came in November, when Ronald Reagan entered the race.

After the election, Reagan called and offered me what would have been my third cabinet position under three Presidents—as Secretary of Energy. I declined it, mainly because Reagan had already said he planned to abolish that department. I did not see myself as a very good liquidator.

My encounters with Ronald Reagan left me with a lingering puzzle. On the day of his inauguration, I mentioned that I had an important matter to discuss with him involving foreign affairs. A meeting was arranged that afternoon, and he invited Al Haig, his new Secretary of State, and two members of the White House staff, Ed Meese and Michael Deaver.

I produced a paper that had been handed to me by a member of the parliament of the PLO, a man I trusted implicitly. The paper contained ten points proposed by the PLO to end the conflict between the Arabs and the Israelis. The plan was new in the sense that the PLO, in 1980, was offering to guarantee the existence of Israel and the sanctity of its borders.

The paper was unsigned, and I explained to them what had been told to me: that the missing name was Yasir Arafat's. If he had signed, and that became known, he would without doubt have been assassinated.

I assured them that my contact was a respected Middle East businessman, who devoted most of his time to trying to bring about a resolution of the Arab-Israeli conflict. After discussing the details with those assembled, the President asked me to give the paper to Haig. I never heard another word about the proposal. I checked with friends in the Middle East to see if any overtures had been made, and the answer was no. The whole matter had dropped into a black hole. I thought that Reagan missed an opportunity to advance the peace that had so long eluded the people of that tortured world.

I felt a bitter sense of disappointment at the outcome of the 1980 election. I don't like to lose at anything; as we say in Texas, you may not believe in beauty contests, but if you enter one you want the judges to vote you "pretty."

As immodest as this will sound, I didn't think Reagan would be as good a President as I would have been. And he wasn't.

I disagreed mightily with Reagan's devotion to the supply-side economic theory, which Bush had labeled, correctly, as "voodoo economics." It was almost the last independent thought Bush expressed. I disagreed with the lack of courage on both their parts in not trying to bring about debt reduction and a more balanced budget.

Reagan essentially promised these things to the nation: that he would change the attitude of the nation, restore confidence in and respect for the United States and the flag, upgrade the military, and lower taxes. He did all of them. A man of consummate charm, good humor, graciousness, and warmth, he reflected a kind of grandfatherly image that every American, regardless of age, could accept.

Unfortunately for the nation, he failed to confront the real problems of the country during his eight years, when he could have accomplished so much by expending more of his personal capital. His Presidency will be remembered not for what he did but for what he could have done and didn't. His Presidency also will be remembered because of his wife, Nancy, who understood the strengths and weaknesses of her husband, and who put herself on the line to ensure that he would always be cast in the best light possible.

She was severely criticized by many for her aggressive involvement in Presidential matters and in Reagan's decisions. I found her actions commendable rather than to be criticized. At least partly as a consequence of Nancy's support, he left office with a degree of popularity almost unequaled in modern history. And it will not be until historians evaluate the decade of the 1980s in its entirety that a final judgment will be passed on the Reagan Presidency, the debt and deficits he created. And that judgment will not be entirely laudatory.

BOOM AND BUST

Not long after I had filed for bankruptcy in 1987, a painful and depressing step, I was sitting unnoticed in the audience one day while several panelists gave their views on Texas politics.

The symposium was held on the campus of Rice University, in Houston, and the discussion eventually turned to the recent rash of failures among banks and savings-and-loans across the state. One member of the panel, Molly Ivins, the liberal newspaper columnist, said she thought the trend meant "the end of the good-old-boy system, where people like John Connally could walk into any bank in the state and get any amount of money he wanted."

A little later, as the speaker at a luncheon for those attending the program, I looked for her and said, "Molly, I wish those bankers hadn't been so generous to me. I wish they had been a little tougher." The room, and Molly, erupted with laughter.

I wish I could say that it only hurt when I laughed. But that would beg the questions that greeted the news that the former Secretary of the Treasury, the former governor of Texas, had been forced to take bankruptcy. How could such a thing happen? What led John Connally to this contradictory turn in what had been so often a charmed public life? It happened step by misstep, as big deals turned into no deals and good intentions chased lost money.

In 1982, I had reached the age of sixty-five, which was the age of mandatory retirement at Vinson and Elkins, the Houston law firm where I had been a senior partner since 1968. This had been the policy of the firm since the death of Judge James Elkins, who had been active until his death at the age of ninety-four.

Realizing that I did not want to retire—I don't believe in it, think it's a great mistake if your health is sound—I began to look around to see what other kind of activity might interest me.

I settled on a partnership with Ben Barnes, a longtime friend and, I believe it is fair to say, once a political protégé of mine. In 1965, at twenty-six, Ben had become the youngest speaker of the state House of Representatives in Texas history.

Barnes had been in the building and construction business since 1972, when he was a victim of the upheaval surrounding the Sharpstown bank scandal. He was never charged with any wrongdoing, but was defeated in his race for governor and departed from politics. By the time we teamed up, Ben had ten years' experience with Herman Bennett, a successful builder and developer in Brownwood.

The net result was that we formed a partnership to invest in real estate and construction. With Ben as the managing partner, we opened the offices of Barnes/Connally Investments in Houston and later relocated them to Austin, where several of our projects were under development.

One of them was the Barton Creek Country Club and Estates, now a club, hotel, and complex of luxury homes and condos. I remember standing on the site, gazing down upon the state Capitol and the Austin business district, and telling a reporter, "We're beginning an era of prosperity like America hasn't dreamed of, and Texas will be at the forefront of it."

I was wrong on both predictions. I could not have been more wrong.

We moved awfully fast in a period when we should have

been forewarned. Interest rates were extremely high, a hangover from the Carter years. That was one of the reasons I ran for President in 1980 in the first place. I thought the Carter administration had totally mismanaged the economy.

We found ourselves paying 18 percent to the banks. In a year and a half, we had no less than fifteen developments in progress, with a projected cost of $203 million. It was reported that we had hit the Texas real-estate scene "like a whirlwind," and the description fit. We were building in San Antonio, Lubbock, Alvin, Huntsville, Round Rock. We were putting up an office tower and strip shopping centers in Houston, and developing condos near the racetrack in Ruidoso Downs, New Mexico. We owned two hundred units on the beach at south Padre Island.

We were moving too fast, too far, and paying dearly for it. We also made the mistake of financing most of our projects with Texas savings-and-loans, taking on short-term debt instead of going to insurance companies for long-term capital. Our apartment projects were well constructed and had a high occupancy rate at the time we sold them. Most of them I believe we can take pride in; based on their quality, we certainly should have been far more successful.

But in our shopping centers the Wal-Mart stores were a key tenant, and before too long the small tenants were under pressure from their creditors. The other space in the centers soon ran into trouble. For most—if not all—the tenants, sales were off, their financing was collapsing, and we had difficulty maintaining the occupancy.

We struggled to find the funding to complete some of our biggest projects. Our development in New Mexico, which we called the Triple Crown, finished about the time the recession reached a peak. Sales were slow and then nonexistent, though the project was well built and beautifully located adjacent to Ruidoso Downs. I used to sit on the terrace of a condo I had built for my family's use, and watch the horses work out right under my balcony. At such moments, it was fairly easy to ignore the warning signs, the nagging whispers in my ear.

We were, plain and simple, victims of the economic times.

By the time we opened our South Padre condominiums and shopping mall, a first-class property, the peso had collapsed in Mexico and in South Texas the economy was hurting. We were never able to sell the units on a profitable base.

We were unable to sell or lease the office space in Houston, where builders were trying to coax tenants by offering up to three months of free rent. Even on that basis, there were few takers.

Our resources had dried up. We couldn't finish the plans for the Barton Creek Country Club, with a magnificent golf course designed by Ed Fazio. We couldn't refinance the debt to sustain these projects, and we couldn't operate them under such adverse conditions.

We had largely funded these projects on borrowed money. When the savings-and-loan industry, our primary lenders, started to crumble, we ran out of options. We were in a situation where the financial institutions could no longer lend any more money; they were trying to collect and call every loan they could. When they collapsed, inevitably, we collapsed with them.

Within another year or two, cities all over America would be suffering much the same financial shocks. In Texas, the boom had ended with the collapse of oil and gas prices, taking with them the real-estate market.

By the mid-1980s, the state's misery was reflected in a joke that made the rounds in certain social circles. Two well-dressed ladies were walking through downtown Midland when a frog hopped up to them and implored: "Help me, please. I'm not really a frog. I'm really a handsome Texas oilman. A witch put a spell on me. If one of you will kiss me, I'll turn back into a Texas oilman."

With that one of the women scooped up the frog, popped him into her purse, snapped it shut, and continued walking. "Aren't you going to kiss him?" asked the other.

"Of course not," she replied. "These days a talking frog is worth a helluva lot more than a Texas oilman."

We spent a year and a half doing everything we could. Ben went to the Far East, I went to Europe. By that time, frankly, Texas was redlined. No one anywhere would touch a Texas oil or real-estate venture. It wasn't a good time for cattle ranching, either.

We saw it coming. In hindsight, our mistakes were clear; we should have declared bankruptcy a year earlier. I would have owed not nearly as much, and considerably less interest would have accrued on what I did owe. Bankruptcy seemed absolutely inevitable to me eighteen months before it actually happened, in July of 1987.

I stayed awake every night. When I did fall asleep, I would wake up at two or three in the morning, worried, thinking about all that we stood to lose, unable to go back to sleep. I realized how embarrassing it was going to be, how the news might be treated. The man who once signed the nation's money had lost his own. I believed I could handle that, the gloating of any of my political critics who might be so inclined. But what was nearly intolerable was the feeling of having no control, of being helpless to avoid the crash you could see coming.

We would lose the homes we had owned in Houston and Austin. Under the law, we kept two hundred acres of land and the ranch house in Floresville, our homestead ever since it was built in 1963. That was the one fortunate move we had made, in retrospect. When we built the ranch house, we paid cash for every dime of construction. There never had been a loan of any kind on the house, or any of the land, so we were able to keep that much when I declared bankruptcy.

But that was little solace, really, in light of the torment we went through before we filed. In reality, the actual filing was a kind of relief. I had fretted, worried, and grieved for those eighteen months, knowing there was no way out and that the outcome was inevitable. I knew how humiliating it would be. There was no easy way to explain to people what Ben and I had ments. In fairness to all, we felt we had to file immediately. Failure to do so would have given the more aggressive lenders a higher priority, as opposed to a general creditor who had not yet filed suit.

In order to let all the creditors have equal access to whatever assets were available, we put the partnership into Chapter 7. At the same time, I filed for Chapter 11. It was obvious I was going to lose the personal property as well as the community property that Nellie and I had acquired over a lifetime.

We faced a somewhat different set of problems than the hundreds of other Texans facing bankruptcy. Not many people talk to Ted Koppel on "Nightline," as we did, while their most intimate belongings are auctioned off, all under the glare of TV lights. From the outset, we accepted the fact that our filing was going to be of public interest and elicit a lot of news stories.

Since we were going through the humiliation of bankruptcy to begin with, we thought out of fairness to the creditors we ought to get the last dollar our assets would bring. So instead of calling in private concerns or furniture dealers, and in effect wholesaling our personal assets, we talked to Jerry Hart, of the Hart Galleries in Houston. We decided to have a public auction. The house at the ranch was stripped. The house in Austin was stripped. The auction was advertised for January of 1988, and there were 1,700 items in the catalogue.

They ranged from a Picasso lithograph to the desk I used during my years as governor of Texas. There was an old statue of St. Andrew, five feet two inches high, that Nellie and I had purchased in London. It had stood outside Westminster Abbey for a hundred and fifty years. When the movers came with their truck to the ranch to ship our belongings, I asked them to pack that piece last. When there was nothing else left, I gave it a hug and walked into the house.

When it was over, almost three million dollars had been raised. This was not a large amount of money in terms of the debts we still had, but it made a statement. I did not feel that I should walk away with my possessions untouched when so many people who believed in me had lost so much. I wanted to repay what I could, and I wanted to leave no doubt that I shared in their distress. The auction wouldn't dissolve our debts, but it was the best we could do.

We sat on folding chairs in the second row of the gallery, for five days and evenings, as the auctioneer sold off the evidence of our lifetime. I kept a catalogue in my hand and recorded the prices of each of the items as they were auctioned off; I actually felt a twinge of irritation if they brought a figure below what I felt they were worth.

I felt sympathy for the people sitting in front of us, in the first row. Photographers leaned over them to take their close-ups. The event was covered by reporters from *The New York Times*, *Newsday*, *People* magazine, *Life* magazine, *USA Today*. The three television networks sent camera crews. I understood that they were looking for tears, and I can't say for certain that they didn't find some.

The first night, the auction attracted 2,000 bidders from as far away as London, Vienna, Hollywood, and New York. The gallery staff served complimentary wine and cheese. Someone suggested that we might have discovered a new social event, the Bankruptcy Gala. A reporter asked me how I felt and I said, "I don't really know. I think I'm kind of caught up in the excitement of the evening." It was an honest answer. The knowledge that these things no longer belonged to us would hit us later. Nellie joked that she could see herself being dragged across the stage, grasping a chair leg as the chair was being handed to the new owner.

It never occurred to us not to be there. Still, it was demoralizing to watch the things we had treasured, and spent a lifetime collecting, go under the auctioneer's gavel. There was hardly an item whose acquisition I could not describe: where it was acquired, under what circumstances, and roughly what we had paid. To see these pieces of our life tagged and sold and in such a public display was a soul-wrenching experience.

I consoled myself, and tried to console Nellie, with the

thought that these were just possessions; furniture, art, Oriental rugs, dishes, silver, personal mementos. I ultimately came to believe that they were, in fact, material goods. What was important in life was not the accumulation or enjoyment of things, but the love of family and friends and the pleasure that those associations brought.

There was a point, I must admit, when I didn't feel very philosophical. Nellie kept hearing the same questions and the same reassurances. "At first," she said, "I felt like it wasn't happening to me. Everybody said, 'They're just things.' And I thought, Yes, they're just things but they're *my* things, and it's just money but it's *our* money. I finally accepted it—that they were just things—and then it was easier to watch our possessions walk out the door."

We have been blessed over the years with many friends whose concern and affection meant so much to us. We were consoled by the knowledge that these friends not only stood by us, but grieved with us at our misfortune. We were able to mentally accept the adversity by reminding ourselves that we had started almost fifty years before with nothing. Our parents were people of very modest means, hers and mine. We had started life together living on $175 a month. We had struggled. We had saved. We had striven to succeed. If we were almost back to where we started, we had traveled a fairly glorious road.

I couldn't help but remember when we came back from Mexico City on our honeymoon in December of 1940. We were flying in a DC-3 and we flew into a violent storm over Tampico coming from Mexico City into Brownsville. Everyone on the plane was deathly ill except me, and I was green around the gills. I was the one holding the sack.

When we landed in Brownsville, Nellie didn't feel she could go on to San Antonio. So we got off the plane to spend the night. We had barely, just barely, enough money to pay for the room. It was seven or eight dollars.

So when I say we started with nothing, I don't miss it by much. We have known considerable sadness in our lives, but by and large we had a great deal to be thankful for. We were unhappy over our losses and embarrassed by the bankruptcy. But the future held no fear for us.

We had known all along we would have to sell everything. We had spent fifty years collecting things from all over the world, items not of great intrinsic value but appealing to our taste and senses.

Some of our friends questioned the wisdom of our taking part in the auction. There were no reserves on any of the items. If the highest bid was a dollar, it was gone. We felt so strongly about many of them that if people wanted to know why we bought something or what they were getting, we wanted to be there to tell them.

Before the auction, Nellie took a call from a woman she didn't know. She said she had been reading about "all those bills you owe," and she said, "It just breaks my heart. I know what it is to owe money. I have followed Governor Connally's career. Would you please send me a small bill under fifty dollars so that I can pay it for you?" Nellie burst into tears, and so did the woman on the phone. Of course Nellie said she couldn't let her do that, but it was wonderful people like her who made it easier for us to get through this period.

I had always told myself that to achieve big goals it is necessary to take big risks. Running for President in 1980 was a big gamble, and one I obviously didn't win. The venture into the real-estate market was another kind of gamble, and obviously we didn't win that one either. But we have won more than we lost. I am by nature an optimist. I believe if you work hard enough, if you plan carefully enough, you can succeed most of the time. The money is incidental. We did not have an extravagant life-style. Never needed one. We lived well. We acquired art and antiques and precious mementos, but we did so over many years by being frugal and discerning. We felt we had earned them and now they were gone.

During the five days the auction lasted, over four thousand people paid fifteen dollars to crowd inside the Hart Galleries.

The money from the admissions went to charity. We put the auction and the bankruptcy behind us and set about in a modest way to rebuild our future.

Fortunately, we had friends who still felt that however stupid I may have been for making the decisions I had made, I still had some knowledge that was worthwhile. Friends like Oscar Wyatt, of the Coastal Corporation, and Charles Hurwitz, of the Maxxam Corporation, asked me to join their boards and serve as a consultant to their companies.

You could hardly find two men less alike: Oscar is a bull-dozer of a man. Charles is quiet and reserved, the kind of man who will introduce himself to someone he has met before, as if there were little reason to remember him. Coastal trades oil and gas around the globe. Maxxam is a holding company for Kaiser-Tech and Pacific Lumber.

Nellie and I re-established our home in Houston, where we have a condominium with a sweeping view of the city. We have been able to refurnish the ranch house, which sat virtually vacant except for beds for over two years. From my office on the second floor of the ranch house, I look out over the land that I once owned but no longer do. The horses and most of the cattle are gone.

And yet I don't grieve about our misfortunes. No one is to blame but me for what happened. I made the mistakes . . . and I tried in an honorable way to pay for them.

Out of our bankruptcy and auction came more than one story to warm our hearts. My favorite had to do with Nellie's wedding silver—dating back to our marriage in 1940. When the newspapers reported that the silver would be included in the auction, it aroused considerable interest. On the night this item was offered, a stranger who had flown to Houston from Georgia bought the service, brought it over in a box, handed it to Nellie, and said, "No woman should lose her wedding silver."

He then flew back to Georgia, without our knowing who he was. We found out, wrote and thanked him as profusely as we knew how. We have not seen or heard from him since.

A number of friends also got together and formed a pool to purchase some of the possessions we most treasured. Some individuals, on their own, bid for, acquired, and returned to us some of the most precious items in the auction. All told, approximately twenty-five different items that were bought by friends, either individually or as part of the pool, were restored to us. And for those we are profoundly grateful, as we are for all of those who thought enough to write letters or to call with expressions of sympathy and with words of encouragement. The calls and letters we received made it almost impossible to keep the tears contained in reaction to the kindness and understanding of people, many of whom were undergoing the same misfortunes.

In spite of the disillusionment of our business arrangements, Ben Barnes and I remain friends, although I doubt that either of us would go back into business with the other.

For myself, I came away with one resolution: I would never again get deeply involved in a venture where I did not have complete control.

Finally, I console myself with the knowledge that surely it is true that nothing ventured, nothing gained. You cannot expect to live a risk-free life and accomplish much. If you are prepared to take risks, then you have to be prepared to suffer losses. If I have advice to pass on to anyone who suffered the same fate I have, I would simply say: don't quit; start over and don't look back. To lose is no disgrace; the failure to try is. If you suffer failure, don't be fearful, don't run and hide, any more than you ran and hid when you were accepting the accolades of those who applauded your achievements.

The bankruptcy brought me to terms with the labels we tend to place on our jobs and our lives. Failure? I think failure is quitting. Failure is being unwilling to try.

MISSION TO
BAGHDAD

Oscar Wyatt was on the phone. Outside of
Texas and the energy industry, Oscar isn't
widely known, which is the way he wants it. But he is a major
player among international oil and gas traders.

He is a throwback to the independent oilmen of another
era, the ones who dug out a fortune virtually with their hands
and fought to protect and expand it. Wyatt drilled his first wells
in South Texas, financing them with eight hundred dollars he
raised by hocking his '49 Ford. In 1955, he founded what is now
the Coastal Corporation and built it into a company with holdings worth billions. Often blunt and sometimes profane, he is a
man capable of surprising warmth and sentiment and charity. I
have known him for thirty years; I have been on his board at
Coastal since 1988.

One day, without any chitchat or preamble, Oscar said to
me, "Do you want to fly to Iraq?"

"Where?"

"Iraq."

"What the hell for?"

"To get the hostages released."

"Are you going?"

"Yeah."

Wyatt doesn't like long pauses. As we say in Texas, he isn't the kind of fellow who has to look at a horseshoe all day before he pitches it. I said, "Well, if you're crazy enough to go, I'm crazy enough to go with you. When do we leave?"

"Next Saturday."

That meant the first day of December, 1990. "Can we get ready?" I asked. "Passports, visas, all that?"

"I'll take care of it," he said, adding, "We'll be bringing lots of medical supplies with us . . . about fifteen tons."

"Do we have any hope of bringing out any hostages?"

"I think so," he said.

You try to imagine what each day must be like for the hostages. You recall scenes of airplane hijackings: one psycho with a machine gun walking up and down, demanding, "Let's kill them now." And another psycho saying, "No, let's wait a while." From all accounts, the hostages held by the Iraqis were not bound and gagged, were not subject to hourly threats or physical abuse. But the grim reality was, they were being held against their will, most of them under armed guard, and no one could predict when or how their treatment might change.

The plight of the hostages had caused anguish in countries around the world for four months as one act escalated into another. Iraqi troops had crossed the border into Kuwait on August 2. Within the week, the American-led coalition had begun the massive deployment of troops and weaponry to Saudi Arabia. And Saddam Hussein responded by sweeping up some 11,000 foreigners, including 3,000 Americans.

They were civilians working in the oil fields and on construction jobs, teachers and tourists and their families. Many of them had been moved to strategic locations in Iraq, as "human shields" in the event of U.S. bombing raids. I don't know who used the description first, Hussein or the press, but the phrase was chilling.

We were under no illusions about the seriousness of the trip. In the fall, Wyatt had talked with Jesse Jackson and Muhammad Ali and, working through back channels in the Middle East, helped arrange their trips to Baghdad. The State Department was on record as discouraging efforts by private citizens. We didn't expect any support from our government, and we asked for none.

The trip had been initiated with a phone call to Oscar from Charlie Wilson, the congressman from Lufkin, Texas. A flamboyant sort, Wilson—known to his constituents as "Good Time Charlie"—had been active on behalf of the rebels in Afghanistan. He made news by traveling to the war zone accompanied by a former beauty queen.

Wilson wanted to free six hostages who were employees of companies in his district in East Texas. "Is there any way you can use your contacts inside Iraq," he asked, "to get those people out?"

Oscar worked his sources, starting with Samir Vincent, a geophysicist based in Washington, who had attended Jesuit High School in Baghdad with Nizar Hamdoon, the foreign minister of Iraq. The word came back to him from Hamdoon: "If you want them, come get them."

At that point, Wilson begged off. He had received a call from Lawrence Eagleburger, the deputy Secretary of State, urging him not to go. Eagleburger said that he was speaking for President Bush. "When you get a request from your commander in chief," Wilson told Wyatt, "you honor it." As far as he was concerned, the trip was canceled.

Privately, Oscar was seething. People in top positions of the Iraqi government had put their necks on the line to help him. He decided to go ahead. "You know," he warned me, "if you come with me, it is going to upset the White House, and it is going to offend the Kuwaitis and the Saudis." Those were risks I accepted. Before we left, Coastal's attorneys gave us an extensive briefing on the Logan Act, and the sanctions that were now in effect against Iraq. We could conduct no commercial operations with the Iraqi government. We could not convert dollars into their currency. We could not spend a dime on anything without violating the boycott.

The week of our trip, public-opinion polls were still divided. Was the liberation of Kuwait worth fighting for? The polls revealed 49 percent said yes, 42 percent said no. The numbers were sharply against the President acting without the authorization of Congress, 68 percent to 29 percent. On the question of what our objective was in the Middle East, 51 percent believed it was to protect the oil supply, 34 percent said to stop aggression.

The White House had been groping for reasons to rally support for the showdown to come. The suggestion that we would be fighting for democracy didn't work; Kuwaitis live in a feudal and repressive society where women have almost no rights.

The first 100,000 troops were airlifted to Saudi Arabia for defensive purposes, the operation called Desert Shield. The goal was to defend the Saudi oil fields and to prevent an Iraqi madman from controlling the price of the world's oil. Yet, on the eve of the war, Sheik Zaki Yamani, the former Saudi oil minister, perhaps the most respected of all Arab diplomats, was asked what the chances were of Iraq invading his country. "Zero," he said. What were the chances of Saddam burning the Saudi oil fields? "Zero."

It would have made more sense to draw the line in the sand in Saudi Arabia rather than Kuwait. In the weeks after Iraqi troops crossed the border, Wyatt checked his contacts. "Almost all of the Kuwaiti casualties thus far," he said, "have come from auto accidents of people fleeing the country."

After the midterm elections in November, another 380,000 troops were sent in to provide an offensive option, meaning enough force to drive Iraq out of Kuwait and destroy their ability to wage war. We had moved into another phase: Desert Storm.

When we added to the mix the need to wipe out Iraq's nuclear capability, the public-opinion tide began to turn. There was some irony in the fact that the Reagan and Bush administrations had doubted this capability would exist before the next century, if at all. President Bush had continued to provide Saddam with billions of dollars in credits and weapons sales, almost up to the week of the invasion. There was the now famous cable relating the U.S. ambassador's message to Saddam in July: that the U.S. had no position on his "border disagreement" with Kuwait.

No one doubted the Iraqi dictator's capacity for cruelty. Now it was necessary for Bush to demonize him further. In nearly every public utterance, he compared him to Adolf Hitler. He was a war criminal. A mass murderer. A lunatic. Bush also resorted to a somewhat petty habit of his, toying with his foe's name. He alternated, calling him "Sodom" and "Sa-DAM" among other variations.

Oscar Wyatt and I were in agreement: President Bush had made up his mind to commit the troops to war in the Persian Gulf. It was difficult then—and, to a lesser extent, it still is—to express a viewpoint opposing the war and not come off as being unpatriotic. I wasn't pro-Iraq. I was just against the war. "In nineteen years of trading with the Arabs," said Wyatt, "the one and only thing I've learned is to stay out of their chickenshit conflicts."

The need was more pressing than ever to remove the hostages from harm's way.

On December 1, we boarded a Boeing 707, owned by Coastal and equipped with tourist seats, for the flight to Baghdad. It would take twenty hours. We stopped in New York and picked up the medical supplies and the missionaries who were going to distribute them. We landed in Amman, Jordan, and unloaded our cargo.

Two Iraqi officials were waiting for us with Iraqi Airways tickets; we were not allowed to fly directly into Baghdad. When we arrived, I was impressed with the size of the airport, the beauty of it, and the emptiness. There was no traffic and no passengers. We were virtually alone as we walked through the almost vacant airport.

The highway leading into the city was four lanes of divided road, with flowers and shrubs planted in the median and on each side. We checked into our rooms at the Al Rashid Hotel, which was less than five years old. There were cut-glass crystal chandeliers in the lobby, and marble everywhere. Each of us had been assigned a suite, which was more luxury than we needed. Still, I knew we were not depriving anyone else of accommodations, because the hotel was almost unoccupied. We were now guests of the Iraqi government, which paid for our hotel bill, our meals, and the fuel to take us home. As Oscar put it in his delicate way, "We didn't furnish anything but our hat and our ass."

Samir Vincent kept the list of the American hostages we hoped to bring out. In the days before our departure, he had been given names from senators, congressmen, corporations, and the Kuwaiti underground. The list kept growing, 10 names, then 20, then 30, not one of them employed by Coastal.

Oscar Wyatt had met Saddam Hussein nineteen years before, when he first arrived in Iraq to buy crude oil for his refineries. Saddam was then the country's second-in-command, and he walked into a meeting Oscar was having with the oil minister. He recalls his first impression: "He was tough, efficient, rigid—the kind of guy who was willing to go to the wall for what he believed in."

He was struck by a gesture Saddam made. He cupped his palms several times, indicating, Oscar thought, that the future of his country was in this earthy Texan's hands (and others like him). "We can't build our country without money," Saddam said, "and oil is all we have to sell."

Until the embargo, Coastal was buying up to 250,000 barrels of crude a day from the Iraqi government. No one, and no threat of war, could make Oscar feel defensive about his dealings with the Iraqis. Exxon and Texaco and the other major American companies have traditionally done business with the monarchies. Oscar prefers not having to go through members of the royal family. He prefers his deals straight up, one price, take it or leave it. "The Seven Sisters like the Saudis," he says. "Guys like me like Iraq." Now we were relying on that good will.

Oscar didn't invite me along to keep him company. He knew I was familiar with the Middle East, had studied it for over fifteen years. As a former governor and cabinet member, I had credentials without strings. He thought I could be helpful in whatever negotiations might be needed to obtain the release of the hostages. And he well recognized that diplomacy is not his strong point. His critics—and, for that matter, his friends—have often described him as blunt and abrasive. At times, he is capable of making Ross Perot sound like the late Cary Grant. Once, working on a deal in Singapore, a Japanese oilman invited Oscar to visit his country. "I've been there," Wyatt told him. "In 1945, I was dropping bombs all over you bastards."

He was flying a cargo of munitions out of Okinawa in 1945 when his plane caught fire and he had to crash-land. His flight suit was burning. He couldn't see. Both his legs were crushed, his jaw was broken, and he had seven fractures in his head. He crawled back and forth to the plane until he had dragged out his five crew members, all of them alive. Wyatt has powerful feelings about war, and he did not get them secondhand.

We stayed close to the hotel, awaiting word from the foreign office about our hoped-for meeting with Saddam Hussein. On Monday, December 3, Wyatt and I met with Saddam's son-in-law Hussein Kamel Hassan, who gave us no assurances.

On Wednesday morning, we received word to expect a call in twenty minutes and please stay in our rooms. The call came, advising us the President would see us at eleven o'clock. We were driven to the palace, taking a rather circuitous route of one-way streets and U-turns. People were moving about on foot and in cars in a relaxed, leisurely atmosphere, reflecting none of the signs of a country about to be at war with a sizable part of the world.

Once inside the Presidential compound, we saw as many as five soldiers or more at each intersection, at least one wearing a gas mask. Those were about the only armed troops that we saw. As we approached the palace itself, we were met by protocol officers but no military guards.

We were led into a large, formal reception room, furnished in French ("medium French," Oscar described it), and were seated on a brocade sofa, white on white. The palace had been built by the last king of Iraq, shortly before his overthrow in 1958.

The room was enormous. I guessed the dimensions to be approximately 65 or 70 feet wide by 90 to 100 feet long, with a 40-foot ceiling. We were joined by a translator, an interesting young man who had studied in London for eight years, taught seventeenth-century English literature at Baghdad University, and was a Shakespearean scholar.

After a wait of perhaps fifteen minutes, we were led into a smaller room, furnished in the same fashion as the reception hall. As we entered the room, Saddam Hussein rose and greeted us with a handshake and a very solemn expression. He was dressed in his informal military garb, including a webbed belt, holster, and pistol.

He introduced us to three members of his cabinet, who sat side by side along one wall during our conversation. Saddam sat toward the end of a couch with the interpreter on his left. I sat on his right, with Oscar to my right.

We went through the preliminaries: thanked him for his willingness to see us; stressed that we were there as individuals— we were not representing nor had we communicated with our government. We were proceeding entirely on our own, on what we regarded as a humanitarian mission, in the hope of bringing back specific hostages. Oscar handed him our "priority list," the one Samir Vincent had been working on when we left New

York, and a second list containing the names of people we had heard about in the three days that we had been in Baghdad.

Now it was time to make our case. I spoke first: "Mr. President, the average person in the United States or elsewhere knows little of your disagreement with the Kuwaitis. They feel no great sympathy for the emir and the royal family, but they are incensed and outraged when they know Americans are being held here as hostages." The translator interrupted and said nervously, "Call them guests."

"You call them guests," I went on, "but nonetheless they are people held against their will, they are not free to leave. In the minds of most people, this is an emotional revulsion to the point that you are being painted as a modern-day Hitler in the American press." Hussein ducked his head and grimaced in reaction to that reference, but said nothing.

"This month Americans will celebrate the Christmas season, our holiest day. You can show an act of compassion by releasing the hostages before Christmas."

We had been talking to him for ten minutes or so when he reached down, unbuckled his webbed belt, wrapped it around his pistol and holster, and gently laid it on the coffee table in front of us. I thought the gesture was significant and hopeful. He was telling us he trusted us. It may not be reaching too far to say that it meant he did not want a war with the United States.

We had said we hoped to speak frankly. Now it was Wyatt's turn. "Mr. President," he said, "we think you are on a collision course with President Bush. Unless something dramatic happens to stop it, there is going to be a shooting war. Think about how difficult it will be to handle all these detainees if war breaks out. For every two of them you've got, you're going to have at least one soldier guarding them. You will have to feed them, clothe them, and house them, and all the time you've got a war to fight."

Saddam asked, through the interpreter, if the presence of the detainees would discourage Bush from attacking Iraq. "Absolutely not," Oscar snapped. "If the President reaches the point that he believes an attack is necessary, a few hundred hostages won't deter him for one minute."

Saddam said he had no argument with the American people, only with President Bush. Wyatt repeated that holding the hostages would gain him no advantage. World opinion would harden against him unless he let them go.

At that point, his minister of information said he understood that this morning the House of Representatives had indicated it would oppose the use of force in the Middle East. The remark surprised us. We were out of touch with that day's news. "Don't be deceived," I said. "If the President launches an attack or asks for support, he will undoubtedly get it. Congress will back him in whatever action he takes."

With a nod, Saddam told me that he knew this to be so. He listened attentively to what we had to say, said little himself, rarely changed expression. When he did speak to his interpreter, it was in a voice so soft I could hardly hear him, even sitting as near as I was to him.

There was no bombast, no menacing gestures. He was calm, deliberate, restrained, and gave the impression of being totally in command of himself. He was bigger than I expected, about six feet two and around 200 pounds. He appeared to be in excellent physical condition.

Wyatt reminded him that he had been trading with Iraq for nearly two decades, and he regretted that our countries were on the brink of war. "My plane is waiting in Amman," he said, "and it is my hope that we can take as many Americans home with us as we can." He mentioned that fifteen tons of medical supplies had been unloaded and turned over to an Arab relief organization.

"Thank you for your generosity to our needy people," said Saddam.

I added, "You have our two lists of names. The plane has room for up to one hundred and fifty people."

We had been with him for just under an hour. We all stood to say goodbye. Saddam Hussein smiled for the first time. He shook my hand and then reached for Wyatt's hand and covered it with both of his. When we first walked into the room, Oscar said later, he wasn't certain Saddam remembered him, his face was so blank. Now he knew. Saddam said, "Your plane will not go home empty."

When we returned to the hotel, the scrambling began. Five hours after the meeting, the phone in Oscar's room rang: Saddam Hussein had decided to free not only the hostages we had sought, but *all* of them.

On Thursday, December 6, we heard for the first time from the U.S. embassy. They had ignored us, as we had them, but now they had an urgent request. Could Wyatt slip three of their employees onto the plane? We knew they were "hot," possibly with the CIA, and they needed to get out of the country. "Okay," Wyatt told them, "but only if you get your ass moving and clear some of these other civilians for release."

Around noon on Saturday, December 8, an Iraqi government official called and said, "We think you should get your people on the airplane and leave immediately. Just hurry." Five minutes later, an Iraqi friend called and gave us the same message: "Leave the hotel and leave the country as soon as you possibly can." We were confounded by the two calls, but we certainly took them to heart.

There were hints that our efforts might be undermined by an official at the U.S. embassy. There were rumors that American bombing raids could begin at any time. We left the hotel in half an hour, then stalled for seven hours while Oscar's contacts tried to round up the hostages. Some were stuck in remote villages. Some still needed exit visas. One hostage came aboard at the last minute with no passport, no papers, no money, and wearing a T-shirt and blue jeans.

So far, we had collected twenty-four hostages. The Boeing 707, which had taken on a full tank of Iraqi fuel, had room for six times that many. Oscar kept pacing the tarmac, squeezing the clock, hoping for late arrivals. Finally, we were out of time. At eight o'clock, the plane lifted off the ground. Inside, the cabin shook with cheers. Some of the crew began to cook chili in a crockpot. Soon Oscar announced over the intercom: "Welcome home. But don't cheer too loud until we get over the Mediterranean Sea. Then we'll be safe."

Twenty hours later, with a refueling stop in Ireland, the plane landed at Houston's Hobby Airport. We hadn't slept in nearly two days. Nellie was waiting with Oscar's wife, Lynn. Both were crying. There were hugs all around, but it was Ryan Parker, the grown son of hostage Bobby Gene Parker, who brought Wyatt to tears. He handed him a single red rose and said, "Thank you, sir, for bringing my daddy home."

We had been able to evacuate nearly all of those on our priority list, though that success was tempered by our disappointment over the ones we were forced to leave behind. Once the Iraqi government announced that all the hostages were to be released, every affected country was calling and firing off cables, wanting to send in planes to pick up their citizens.

All we knew for certain was that our efforts had secured the freedom of the six Texans whose names we started with, and eighteen others, including the three the U.S. embassy needed to get out of the country immediately. Whether our arguments helped persuade Saddam Hussein to release all the remaining hostages, we could not say. Nonetheless, we looked upon it as more than a happy coincidence.

Not until our return were we made aware of a curious statement by President Bush, who had been asked if Saddam Hussein's concession to common decency had changed anything. The President said: "I think you can make the case that this facilitates the tough decisions that might lie ahead . . . when you don't have Americans there, and if force is required, that's just one less worry I've got."

That statement would have been dangerous enough if he had made it *after* all the hostages were safely out of the country. But he said it before any of the mercy flights had departed, including ours. In short, he was telling Saddam that his release of the hostages made it more convenient for us to drop our bombs.

I had felt no hesitation about joining Oscar Wyatt in the rescue attempt. Nor was I unaware that by doing so we would be likely to incur the wrath of the White House. Our motives and indeed our patriotism might be questioned. There were strings of negative letters in the Houston papers, including one that referred to me as "the Ayatollah Connally."

I would have stopped the war if I had the power. I did not. I had said in December of 1990 that we would win the battle and lose the peace, and I believe time has proved it so. History has shown time and again that there are no little wars, only long or short wars, unavoidable or necessary wars.

The combat in the Persian Gulf, which lasted sixty-three days, six of them on the ground, may have been the most tele-vised and reported war of all—and the least revealed. With few exceptions, the nation's press accepted a censorship tighter than that imposed in World War II, in the process reporting stories that were false or misleading, and in some cases fabricated. Few of the nation's politicians debated whether the war needed to be fought, or whether so many Iraqi civilians—100,000, by some accounts—had to die to punish Saddam Hussein, who remains in power.

Long after Iraq surrendered, the truths of the war have slowly come out, like water dripping on a rock. More than two years later, they continue to do so, wearing away the monument the victory initially represented.

The Coastal plane touched down in the predawn of Sun-day, December 9, 1990. That day the exodus began, with at least seventy-five Americans emerging from their hiding places in Kuwait. In such times, you try hard not to be paranoid, not to imagine shadows and schemes. But there would be ample reason to suspect that the administration was less concerned with the security of the hostages than in using them to inflame American public opinion. That charge is not one I would make lightly, or without substance.

I thought back to the repeated calls by the President and the Secretary of State, in every public forum, for the release of the hostages. Yet when we returned, we heard nothing from President Bush, except indirectly that he was furious, and that the Justice Department was investigating us to determine if we had violated the Logan Act.

Oscar Wyatt and I were the last Americans to speak with Saddam Hussein before the air war began, and we engaged in nearly an hour of frank and intense dialogue. Yet no one from the State Department or the CIA ever debriefed either of us about his frame of mind, what questions he asked, how he looked or acted. From a source inside the State Department, we did learn Jim Baker's reaction when he heard our plane was leading the final evacuation of the hostages: "Oh, shit!"

I thought back to Charlie Wilson having to beg off from the trip at the last moment, under pressure from the deputy Secretary of State, acting on orders from the President.

I thought about a phone call from a retired Air Force general, who had been an advocate of the Stealth bomber. He had left a meeting on the night of January 10 convinced that there was little enthusiasm among the Joint Chiefs of Staff to recommend the use of military force against Iraq. They were told by Brent Scowcroft and Colin Powell: "The President wants this war." Six days later, the U.S. launched the biggest bombing raid in history.

This would turn out to be the first American war promoted by an advertising agency, the first in which the politicians and generals were the heroes. Millions of dollars were funneled through Hill & Knowlton, the public-relations and political-consulting firm, to help sway public opinion.

One of their clients was "Nayirah," the fifteen-year-old Kuwaiti girl whose testimony shocked the country, and especially the Congressional Human Rights Caucus. In October, she testified that she had watched as fifteen infants were yanked from incubators in Al-Adan Hospital in Kuwait City by Iraqi soldiers, who then "left the babies on the cold floor to die."

The public was told that Nayirah's identity was kept secret to protect her family from reprisals in occupied Kuwait. There turned out to be a better reason: she was the daughter of the Kuwaiti ambassador to the United States, Saud Nasir al-Sabah. At the time of the atrocity she described, she wasn't in Kuwait. She was in school in Washington, D.C. The CBS program "Sixty Minutes" turned up copies of a check paid to her family by Hill & Knowlton. The amount on the face of the check was $10,000,000. If it is true, I find that astonishing. No one ever explained the check. The story was short-lived.

Yet her testimony was cited by seven senators who changed their minds and voted in favor of the resolution to authorize military action against Iraq. The resolution passed by six votes.

Later, the accounts of the murdered babies and the stolen incubators would be contradicted by the testimony of the Kuwaiti doctors who were at the hospital. It had been the most gruesome of the atrocity charges leveled against Saddam Hussein's troops, but one puzzled doctor asked the question the media essentially ignored: "What would they want with incubators?"

During the air war, the Pentagon claimed that we had hit 80 percent of our Iraqi targets. All of us had seen the so-called "smart bombs" plunging down chimneys, entire convoys reduced to burned-out shells. It was so fast, so clean, that we were quickly caught up in the surge of pride in our fighting men and their Star Wars technology. Watching the footage on the nightly news was like walking through a video arcade.

Oscar Wyatt scoffed at the Pentagon numbers. "That's bullshit," he said. "The Russians say it's more like twenty percent, and my sources in the Middle East tell me the Russians are, for once, telling the truth."

It may be that the worst thing to happen to American

foreign policy in the last twenty years was England's swift victory in the Falklands War. The government sent its fleet and modern jet fighters halfway around the world to devastate the poorly equipped, poorly led Argentine military. In the White House, Ronald Reagan sat enthralled in front of a television screen as the British welcomed home their ships with bands playing and crowds shouting and waving flags.

The air-sea battle resulted in the sinking of ships and serious casualties on both sides. But the retaking of the islands while shepherds tended their flocks was compared in the media to a Sigmund Romberg operetta. That war may have been the model for America's invasions of Grenada and Panama.

Later, when both leaders happened to meet in Colorado, Margaret Thatcher made the connection for George Bush. "George," said the British prime minister, "I was about to be defeated in England when the Falkland conflict happened. I stayed in office for eight years after that."

In 1992, the Pentagon released the final, adjusted figures: 7 percent of the smart bombs had hit their targets. The convoy so many of us saw, the vehicles blackened by fire and on their sides, turned out to be mainly civilian cars and trucks, families with their possessions, refugees trying to reach Jordan.

The Census Bureau assigned a twenty-nine-year-old demographer to update the U.S. estimate of Iraq's population. The casualty figures for the Persian Gulf War—so sensitive virtually no one had analyzed them—were essential to her task. In the spring of 1992, her figures became available. The Iraqi dead included:

86,194 men
39,612 women
32,195 children

They died from the bombings of the American-led coalition, or during the domestic rebellions that came later, or from the deprived and polluted postwar conditions. The census worker who assembled the figures, Beth Osborne Daponte, was fired.

American pilots and ground forces and support troops were magnificent in their performance. George Bush and Colin Powell deserve credit for their strategy of massive bombing raids, reducing the enemy's will and capacity to fight back, and making it possible to end the ground war after just six days. Their triumph in the air made it possible to avoid a bloodbath on the ground, and limited the number of American deaths to under four hundred.

Before the January 15 deadline, the White House was masterful in turning around public support for the war. No question, Americans rallied behind the President to a degree that had been unseen since December 7, 1941. The Pentagon briefings held us rapt, and the footage of clean-cut soldiers and Marines and airmen briskly going about their business sent spirits soaring. We went through a frenzy of yellow ribbons and homecoming parades.

Yet it is my belief that the Persian Gulf War didn't help George Bush's chances for re-election. For all their preoccupation with the economy, most Americans now sensed that the war had been less noble, less pure and antiseptic than we thought. It became a subliminal issue, an uncomfortable and unspoken one, and this was borne out by Republican research with focus groups. George Bush scarcely referred to it during his losing campaign against Bill Clinton. What irony! President Bush could not bask in or celebrate what had been his greatest foreign policy victory. In late January, 1990, the President was sitting with a favorable rating of 88 percent in the polls.

In a way, he became a captive to the war, unable to exploit this huge advantage over a challenger who had never served in the military.

I believed then, and now, that the administration thought the war would address several problems: divert attention from the sagging enemy; justify the continued, almost uncontrolled spending on the defense budget; remind Americans that even in the era of *glasnost* the world was a dangerous place. There had to be a reason for maintaining nearly half a million troops in Europe. The Persian Gulf War did, in fact, demonstrate how well the U.S. was equipped to deal with situations that require the rapid deployment of maximum force.

But, in the end, the war turned out to be something less than history's longest-running campaign commercial.

A POLITICAL
PASSAGE

As the 1990s unfold, spinning toward a new century, we are witnesses to one of the most astounding changes in modern history. Whatever his shortcomings, however fleeting his time on the stage, Mikhail Gorbachev literally changed the world—not just the Soviet Union, but Germany, Western Europe, the United States, and indeed the rest of this wrinkled prune of a planet.

Few actions by world leaders have had such a profound effect in so short a period of time. His one great failing was to assume that he could bring about massive changes in the structure of his government and his society within the framework of the Communist Party, which he never renounced.

His successor, Boris Yeltsin, however, did renounce Communism and its philosophy, and he fully embraced the free-market capitalist system. Whether he can survive for a period of time sufficient for Russia to make the transition remains very much in doubt. Russia's destiny depends to a large degree on the amount of aid, in all forms, that Yeltsin receives from Western Europe, the United States, and Japan.

The U.S. came late to the cause of Gorbachev, and too lightly when he teetered on the brink. President Bush responded that he did not have a blank check with which to provide assistance. He was correct, largely because under two Republican Presidents, spanning twelve years, this country had incurred an external debt of approximately four trillion dollars. The irresponsibility of the Congress and the Republican administrations now restrain the United States in terms of what it can do to provide aid and support to other nations around the world, large and small.

Since World War II, military power has been the standard that nations have been judged by in terms of their ability to provide leadership. Gorbachev changed that standard. Military power will no longer be the sole criterion of the strength of a nation and its ability to provide order and direction for much of the rest of the world. Rather, economic power is going to be the beacon that nations are guided by in seeking to meet the needs of their own domestic economy, yet provide sufficient strength for external purposes.

America today lives in a changed world. I think it is fair to say that up until 1960 the U.S. was little concerned with the economic affairs of other nations. As a people, we had grown inwardly from the founding of the country until about the beginning of the Kennedy administration.

It was only in the waning days of the Eisenhower administration that Robert B. Anderson, Secretary of the Treasury, warned Eisenhower about an impending trade imbalance that was worrisome. But these changing conditions did not manifest themselves in any change of policy within the government.

This nation was founded by people suspicious of government, and the government was devised to try to restrain and counteract any and every branch of itself. That philosophy has permeated the thinking of our society. The passage of legislation is designed to restrain, to break up, to retard, and to place government reins on all types of businesses for the ostensible purpose of protecting an unwary public.

Government, business, and labor have always found themselves in adversarial positions. We have acted and reacted as if we had no concerns about the effect that our laws, regulations, or culture would have on external forces, but were concerned solely with their impact on our domestic economy.

In the aftermath of World War II, other nations rebuilt and restructured, not only with new and modern plants, many of which were made possible by our generosity and largesse, but with the full understanding that their well-being depended on their ability to compete in the marketplaces of the world. Their internal relations were designed to foster and promote such production and trade.

We, on the other hand, have followed a policy that inevitably weakened America's ability to compete for international markets. Our tax laws were designed to tax productivity and savings. Our antitrust laws were designed to prevent American companies from combining forces for research and development, production and marketing, or to be more competitive in world markets. Our regulatory markets, through the Securities and Exchange Commission, the Environmental Protection Agency, and countless other arms of the government, acted to inhibit American business from competing.

We no longer live in a world where our growth can be all internal, where international trade means nothing to us. We live in a world where every major industry in America is in trouble and is laying off workers. This is true of steel, aluminum, and high-technology companies, including IBM, Digital Equipment, Hewlett Packard, and Texas Instruments.

Our banks and savings-and-loans have been devastated and are in a critical position even today. We have no energy policy worthy of the name, and the oil and gas industry grows weaker by the day. A decade ago, there were 4,500 rigs exploring for and developing oil and gas; today there are fewer than 600. The industry is on the rocks.

Retailing is at one of the lowest ebbs in the history of this country. The automobile industry is in a downturn, and approximately one in six jobs in America is related to the auto industry. Housing starts are at one of the lowest points in modern times. Agriculture is declining; fewer and fewer people are able to eke out a living following agricultural pursuits. We're under siege from countries large and small—industrialized and Third World countries—in terms of their exports to the United States. We find it difficult to compete in price and, in many cases, with the quality of imported products. And yet government, for the most part, sits idly by, unaware that it has a role to play in a restructuring.

We are only now beginning to realize that we cannot maintain military forces as we have in the past. If we cut our defense budget by half, to $150 billion a year, we would still outspend the rest of the world combined. We cannot provide foreign aid to nations around the globe, as we have habitually done, or bear the burden of world leadership, because our economic base has weakened to the point where we can no longer afford it. We are not in the desperate straits in which Gorbachev found himself and the Soviet Union, having committed to the maintenance of a military force that the nation could not sustain. He had no choice but to change.

The American people are today making it clear that they are unwilling to commit the resources available to maintain a military establishment and to continue providing foreign aid when both are basically being done with borrowed money while the country's economic security is threatened.

The private sector realizes full well that dramatic changes are occurring; businesses large and small are restructuring to meet changed conditions. They are attempting to become "lean and mean" in order to survive. Yet government at all levels has failed to react in concert, and has instead competed to pursue policies that are unresponsive and detrimental to the changing economic situations.

We should thoroughly undertake a major restructuring of

government itself and its method of providing services to the American people. In 1993, with a new administration striving to come of age, I find myself advocating a number of changes at the federal level, the listing of which will probably do nothing but satisfy myself. Still, they need to be made.

—The State Department needs to be completely reorganized, with many of our embassies curtailed or abolished. New technologies have rendered the ambassador corps overstaffed and, in some cases, unnecessary.

—The Special Trade Representatives should be abolished and the duties, if any, assigned to one of the cabinet posts. Congress created this authority because it did not trust our embassies to negotiate on behalf of U.S. interests. At the same time, the Council of Economic Advisers should be eliminated. The President has available to him at a moment's notice all the economic advice he could want or use. In addition, he has tremendous resources available to him within the government.

—I would like to see President Clinton demonstrate his trust and confidence in the cabinet, having appointed officers he knows and will use. This would be a departure from recent tradition. The tendency has been to name cabinet Secretaries for political reasons and then to create a huge White House staff to more or less supplant them and the areas they represent. In a government such as ours, power by legislation, and otherwise, is embodied in each of the departments and agencies. It is assumed that the Secretaries have substantial influence and leverage in Washington and in the Congress. If a President actually appointed officers he liked and in whom he was willing to confide, we could contain one monster: the White House staff, which inevitably engages in turf building and turf guarding to the detriment of the President, who becomes ever more isolated.

—Secret Service protection for former Presidents should be reduced, and eliminated altogether after a reasonable period of time. In the first week of December, 1992, two ex-Presidents, Richard Nixon and Ronald Reagan, were in London at the same time, both staying at the Claridge Hotel. Nixon had with him one aide and one security guard, whose salaries he paid himself. In contrast, President and Mrs. Reagan arrived with five aides and sixteen Secret Service agents, all paid for by the taxpayers. Drastic changes should be made, and the provisions for former Presidents should be limited to a maximum of four years after leaving office.

All of this, incidentally, started under President Truman. One of his close friends approached Speaker Sam Rayburn and said that Truman did not want to exploit the Presidency by selling his services in the private sector. He had no means of livelihood unless the government provided help. Whereupon, Speaker Rayburn set about to establish a means of modest support for former Presidents, which, like everything else in Washington, soon got out of hand. In 1993, with five former Presidents still active, the tab runs to nearly $50 million annually in pension, salaries, travel, and office expenses.

—Secret Service protection for Presidential candidates should be abolished. For all the concerns over safety, the agents are used primarily as additional staff people for the campaigns, providing communications as well as security. In 1980, I was the only candidate to decline mine, a point that attracted almost no notice. I found it interesting that my political adversaries have so often accused me of being arrogant and egotistical. Yet one of the most ego-building things in the world is to have a squad of Secret Service agents forming a cocoon around you, making you feel important.

These observations fall into the category of Obsolete or Unnecessary Trappings of Power. There are other, more complicated issues that beg to be addressed, amounting to an overhaul of the way we govern. American citizens are aware that drastic action is necessary. They have been attempting by various means to inform those who run the government that they want changes made. The government, particularly at the national level, has failed to get the message.

California passed a Proposition 13, affecting the ability of that state government to further impose taxes. Other states have adopted similar measures. For the last dozen years, I have strongly recommended limiting the terms a senator and a representative can serve. State after state is now putting that measure on the ballot, and when it is put to a vote, it is almost universally adopted by huge majorities. People are reacting in the only way they have to try to restructure government and to make it more responsive.

We should seriously consider the total elimination of the individual income tax and the corporate income tax as revenue measures. These taxes discourage savings. They discourage investment. They diminish growth and productivity. We desperately need more capital. We are one of the few nations that tax capital as we do. The revenue stream should be replaced by a consumer tax—either a national sales tax or a value added tax. According to the breakdown of U.S. tax revenues for 1989, the total income produced from personal, corporate, estate, and gift taxes amounted to $558 billion.

I realize the difficulty of trying to grasp such numbers (it is hard enough accepting the salaries of baseball players). But assuming a gross national product of $3.5 trillion, which is conservative, it would require a sales tax of about 16 percent to produce $558 billion in revenues. Even allowing a rebate for households earning less than $13,000 per annum, and with an exemption for food, the sales tax would only increase to about 18.5 percent. Again, in the year 1989 there were approximately 113 million income tax returns filed. Under a national sales tax, for example, that number would be reduced to approximately 10 million. Thus we eliminate 103 million returns, the billion man-hours necessary to prepare them, and the enormous effort involved in just handling them.

Obviously, the argument will be made that the sales tax and the value added tax are regressive. But the inequities can be eliminated without unduly burdening the system. There would be no national mental breakdown as April 15 approaches, no paper blizzard burying every mailbox.

Our antitrust laws should be amended to permit greater

cooperation and research and development in the production and marketing of exports.

We should again devise a so-called "disk," an international sales corporation that enables the United States to sell in world markets without reporting income until the proceeds are repatriated to the United States. This program was repealed in the past because labor opposed it as a giveaway to business, but its true purpose was designed for the creation of jobs in America, and the greatest proponent of it should be organized labor in this country.

We need to develop an energy policy and restore the incentives for the exploration of oil and gas instead of continuing to rely on imported oil. We should put a ten-dollar-a-barrel tax on imported oil, which would amount to $30 billion a year at present levels, and we should dedicate those funds to a restructuring of the educational system in the country on a per capita basis, or some similar means of distribution. This increased cost would result in a rise in the price of gasoline by consumers, but we would still have the cheapest gasoline prices of any industrial nation in the world.

The public-school education system in America should be revised; foreign languages should be taught in kindergarten, and school terms lengthened to ten and half or eleven months a year. No more schools should be built unless, or until, the existing facilities are fully utilized, even if it means starting classes at seven in the morning and running them until noon, and another series starting at one and running until five or six in the afternoon. Such measures unquestionably would result in enormous opposition, but the educational system has to change. That it is not meeting the needs of the students is becoming more apparent every day. The curriculum of the public schools has to be constructed to deal more intelligently and fairly with the approximately 35 percent who never go beyond high school. We also have to recognize that the false standard that saturates education today—that to be a success you must have a college degree—has to be abolished.

We should immediately begin planning to reduce expenditures for the military by at least a third, cutting $100 billion a year out of the defense establishment, with a large portion of that being dedicated to rebuilding the infrastructure of the country—the roads, buildings, and bridges.

Today, America devotes approximately 14 percent of gross national product to health care in all forms. This is substantially higher than any other nation in the world. Most industrial nations spend approximately 6 to 7 percent for health-care benefits and provide them on a much broader basis than we do. There have to be major innovative changes in order to meet what has become a universal demand for health care. A more efficient delivery of government benefits in the welfare area should be considered. Imagine the savings that would be achieved in eliminating the bureaucracy administering the system by first determining those who truly are entitled to welfare, then mailing them a check every month without going through the red tape that prevails today.

I recognize full well the first criticism of such a plan: that there will be cheats and some recipients who are not entitled to it. My answer is that there are cheats today and many receive benefits who are not entitled to them. No perfect system has been or will be devised. We have to recognize that cost-effectiveness must be considered, rather than attempts at devising a perfect system of distribution that is not achievable.

In the health-care field, if necessary, legislation must be passed to limit the exposure of doctors to malpractice suits by avaricious lawyers. The same remedy is needed to prohibit greedy lawyers who file product liability cases that retard research and development, innovation and distribution of new products, new devices and new inventions.

The court system is going to have to be modified to restrain federal judges, who dictate what states can do in their present prison and educational systems. The lifetime appointments of federal district judges, if these abuses continue, should be altered so there is a reconfirmation, not reappointment, of federal district judges every ten years of their service. It is unconscionable for a federal judge to assume that he should be the sole arbiter of how a prison system should be designed and built and how prisoners should be treated, usurping the authority of both the legislative and the executive branches of government. The same is true where judges are involved in the educational system.

Without a fair, accessible, impartial judiciary, every freedom, every right, every privilege we have will be in jeopardy. I am disturbed when I see the RICO statutes, created to attack organized crime, used today in cases never intended to be covered by those statutes.

I am disturbed when I see the Supreme Court of the United States ruling, as it did in the spring of 1992, that a prosecutor does not have to offer evidence to a grand jury that tends to prove the innocence of the accused; that the prosecutor is free to tell one side of the story in order to obtain an indictment. The vote was five to four, and I find this split decision unbelievable and distressing. It totally overlooks the fact that an indictment leaves an indelible stain on any individual regardless of a verdict of not guilty by a trial jury.

There are two other major changes that beg to be made in our legal system, and I address them as one qualified by first-hand experience.

I believe it is time to eliminate the grand jury system, which dates back to the early history of this country. You were first judged by your peers—literally, people assembled from the neighborhood—who were familiar with the circumstances under which you were accused. They had the power to indict or not to indict.

Over the decades, the system has evolved to a point where the grand jurors know nothing of the facts of the case other than what they are told by the district attorney or the prosecuting attorney. This means they have no other basis for forming a judgment as to whether a criminal act has been committed. When it is announced to the press that the grand jury has indicted so-and-so for such and such, the prosecuting attorney is, in fact, responsible.

An attorney is not allowed to accompany a client into the grand jury room—in theory, to avoid heightening the appearance of a trial. Meanwhile, the prosecutor has unrestricted access to a witness without restraints—supposedly to draw out a complete picture from the witness, unhampered by the interference of a defense attorney.

Unlike the occasional courtroom trial, there is no sense of circus in this somber chamber. There is, rather, the air of inquisition, which does not seek the truth but seeks to have the jurors accept as truth what those in power, or seeking power, would have them believe.

The prosecution is always poised to take advantage of the intimidation of a witness, and the confusion of a witness. This is human nature: when a witness is telling what he thinks is true and is confronted with an inconsistency, he feels compelled to explain the contradiction. He quite honestly calls on his imagination to fill the void his memory has left. Whereupon the prosecutor can tear the witness apart, his questions larded with heavy sarcasm, making the improvisation into a calculated lie. Inevitably, as a result of the uncertainty of facts, dates, and places, witnesses lay themselves open to the charge of perjury, which can lead to indictment when other grounds may be lacking.

It would be far fairer to abolish the grand jury system and let a prosecuting attorney file a bill of information, and indict by that means. At least then the defendant would know and the public would know who was responsible for bringing the case to court. And to what extent the prosecuting attorney would be accountable.

The second change I believe would restore more fairness to the judicial system is to severely restrict, if not eliminate, plea bargaining. In my particular case, if I was guilty of accepting a bribe, then Jake Jacobsen, ipso facto, was guilty of giving one. But in an effort to convict me, the prosecutors granted Jacobsen total immunity with respect to his alleged bribery—and other, unrelated, serious, and provable criminal charges. This happens time and again when the government, in effect, buys the testimony of a suspected felon through the device of plea bargaining.

As one looks at today's problems, the issues that inevitably come into focus are: crime, drugs, health care, the environment, and education. All of these can be an enormous drain on the resources of the nation, and none except education will contribute to the increased productivity and competitiveness of American life, regardless of how desirable and noble they are in terms of societal needs and the quality of life.

But to reduce crime and drug abuse, I know of no better answer than to pass a universal service law. Every young person would be required—upon graduating from high school or reaching the age of eighteen, whichever occurs last—to enter into two years of public service, in the Army, in hospitals, in the parks, or in some other branch of government. I advocated this proposal ten years ago; there was much criticism and concern about government domination of lives, but in truth I strongly believe that two years in such programs would provide maturity, discipline, a sense of responsibility, an awareness of competitive life in America, and would be enormously beneficial to every individual who participated, as well as to society as a whole.

Many of these ideas and changes, such as universal service, have been recycled by the new President, Bill Clinton. I support his efforts to appeal to the best instincts of young Americans, their pride and unselfishness.

It will be fascinating to watch how Clinton adapts to the office. Some older Republicans feel threatened by him and by his wife, Hillary. I would caution my friends in my adopted party to soften their cries of alarm over the role of the First Lady. With no disrespect intended, I believe Ford, Reagan, and Bush have wives who did not suffer intellectually by comparison to their husbands.

I am also struck by the fact that, in my experience, world leaders who are women are almost universally tougher and more decisive than their male counterparts. I think this was true of Golda Meir, of Israel; true of Margaret Thatcher, of Great Britain; and certainly true of Indira Gandhi, of India.

In his first few weeks in the Oval Office, President Clinton demonstrated political courage by tackling the problems of the deficit, the national debt, and health care, along with a few other issues that made many people even more uncomfortable. In his four-year term, he has a chance to be recognized as a great leader, a Franklin Roosevelt for the '90s. If he fails, in four years he has a chance to be fifty-one.

During the campaign, then Governor Clinton started with little hope of success and carrying a truckload of baggage, all of which surfaced. That he was able to overcome it became a story of amazing perseverance. He conducted a campaign that was about as faultless as any I have observed in over fifty years of watching American politics. He continued to fight against the charge of womanizing, and the troublesome draft status problem that confronted him almost daily. He overcame them, showing vitality and a quick, resourceful mind. I believe he represents a model of Democrat not recently seen, a true centrist. There is a danger here; on the far, far left and right, the moonies, loonies, and goonies will always be angry with him.

I suppose this is as good a place as any to deal with a question that I no longer have any reason to avoid. I have run my last race, and have probably equally offended important figures in both parties.

I am often asked if I regard my switching parties as a mistake. In terms of making a difference, of changing the country or even the Republican Party, I have to say that it did not. Some of my friends still entertain themselves by speculating that I could have been elected President as a Democrat. I do not subscribe to this theory for reasons that by now need no repeating. One excuse works as well as another, but I feel certain that the Democrats were not going to nominate a Texas conservative in my time. In politics, something is always wrong: the year, the opponent, the issues. Think of how few people actually run for

President; only one gets elected every fourth year. For most, it is like a romance that is never in sync: one of the parties is always free when the other is married.

In any event, my switching had nothing to do with Presidential ambition. At the time, in 1973, I was just a wild card. I was too long a Democrat, too soon a Republican, to hold any such lofty ideas. But it long ago became clear to Nellie and me that we were at least as comfortable among our old friends as our new ones. "I think you have to be born into the Republican Party," said Nellie, "before they will accept you at something other than entry-level."

To me, the Republican Party makes a grievous error in relying so much on the impersonal communications of phone banks and fax machines, and direct mail, which tend to isolate people from the party. I grew up as a Democrat, where we thought it essential to "press the flesh." I have always believed in personal campaigning, hand to hand, eye to eye.

Republicans like to rely on machines, the Democrats on people.

In any event, my philosophy has not changed. My party affiliation has, but in many ways I view that as immaterial. I dislike labels and litmus tests. I am pro-choice. I believe the government has an obligation to help create jobs. These are Democratic positions. I have never considered serving a political party as an end in itself. Serving your country is.

In 1979, the year before I ran for President, I spoke at Republican fund-raisers in forty-six cities. I campaigned once for Ronald Reagan and supported him twice, but I conclude with regret that in twelve years Reagan and Bush turned the clock back and wasted their separate mandates to improve our society in a profound and lasting way.

In the summer of 1991, as a result of Desert Storm, the popularity of George Bush remained at an all-time high. In the years since science was introduced into polling, I doubt that any other President could boast of an 88 percent approval rating in the third year of his term.

I was among an almost invisible minority who believed this support was transitory and illusory. I thought his numbers would drop like a rock down a rain pipe, and his support would erode and fade as quickly as it had soared. I expressed that opinion to a number of people, although I am not sure I convinced any of them.

One in particular who rejected my forecast was Lloyd Bentsen, the senior senator from Texas, who had gained enormous respect across the country as the running mate of Michael Dukakis. He won praise despite the defeat of the ticket and the campaign strategy of Dukakis, which was virtually beyond comprehension.

Well before the 1992 campaign began, I sent word to Senator Bentsen that I thought Bush would slip, and on three separate occasions I urged him to announce his candidacy. Like many Democrats at the height of the Desert Storm celebrations, he thought they needed to worry about retaining control of the Senate. Through the summer of '92, as Bush's popularity shrank and the Clinton campaign gathered momentum, I wondered many times what might be going through Lloyd Bentsen's mind.

With the possible exception of the race by Dukakis, the Bush campaign in 1992 was probably the weakest, dumbest, and most out-of-touch campaign waged in modern times. My own view is that it was worse than the Dukakis effort because Bush was an incumbent President and had every conceivable advantage.

I think I have the capacity to be objective in looking at a political operation, but I must admit to some prejudice as far as the Bush campaign is concerned. I never thought that he had the vision or the wisdom to be President in the first place. What he had was a great résumé, largely because Presidents Nixon, Ford, and Reagan appointed him to positions that kept him alive politically. Then, largely on the coattails of Ronald Reagan, he succeeded to the Presidency. But any careful analysis of Bush's background as U.N. ambassador, envoy to China, head of the CIA, and head of the Republican National Committee will show that he was a man who left few footprints.

Out of the blue, the '92 campaign took a turn so strange and improbable it seemed to mock the classic movie *Mr. Smith Goes to Washington*. The Perot movement, so called, was not really launched by the Dallas billionaire, no matter what the cynics think. In one of the remarkable moments in American political lore, Ross Perot appeared one night on CNN's "Larry King Live" and casually announced that if the people wanted him to run for President, he would. The response was overwhelming.

Ross began buying time on television for his pie charts and taking phone calls. In his homespun way, he talked a language that the average American hungered to hear. He simplified the problems. He talked about the deficit and the debt and the creation of jobs. He not only told them things they could believe, he told them things they could understand. When Ross said, "That's as clear as cow pies in the moonlight," he made it seem so. The same applied when he caught the Bush campaign misrepresenting something he had said: "You can stick a boot in the oven, but that won't make it a biscuit."

His words reached such receptive ears that before he withdrew from the race, polls were indicating that he was pulling even with the Republican and Democratic candidates. Then, by withdrawing from the race, he committed one of the greatest mistakes in political history.

I can't say what went on in the voting booths, but I do know Perot did not hesitate to seek or receive advice from prominent Republicans. Messages went back and forth, through intermediaries, between Ross and Richard Nixon. Although his loyalty to the party is such that I do not doubt that Nixon supported Bush, I have gotten the impression over the years that he felt slighted by a man whose political fortunes he had often rescued. He considered it a personal snub when Bush sent Jimmy Carter on a mission to Latin America.

It is not exactly clear to anyone—except, possibly, Perot—what his eventual goals are. But for the short term, he is content to be the hornet buzzing around the do-nothing or retrograde politicians, ever ready to sting their backsides.

One way or another, the winds of change will sweep across this land because Ross Perot, who altered the rules of the game, will still be around. If anything, United We Stand, the organization he established—it may be fairer to say they found each other—will continue to be a major new force. The zeal that existed among his supporters still remains. His millions of volunteers are still there, still legions of discontented, and he can lead a formidable third-party movement by whatever name he wishes. He can decide elections in Congress and the Senate—if he so chooses.

Whatever his future role, his presence has changed American politics. His appearances on the talk shows, his 800 numbers, his pep rallies have introduced a new element to the political landscape. More and more, you will see the candidates talking directly to the people, responding directly to them, and going over the heads of anchormen and White House correspondents. That approach is an end run around the political experts and analysts, who in the past have always considered it their right to interpret the candidate, the meaning and nuances of his words, for the American voter. The most interesting part of Perot's campaign was the confrontational mode he adopted with respect to the press. He dominated almost every interview. He dared to say, "I'm not going to talk about that," or quickly dismiss a question with a favorite retort, "That's irrelevant."

This style will be part of the American scene for a long time to come—a prospect that may not inspire the media to do cartwheels off the nearest curb, but they will learn to live with it. Perot demonstrated that a candidate doesn't necessarily go in harm's way by taking on the press. Many have tried.

The problems we have are problems we will always have. The government has to be a part of the solution to these problems; it should not be indifferent, overbearing, domineering. But it should provide leadership in times of stress and change in the nation as a whole. A government of omission is frequently much worse than a government of commission.

Above all, if we are going to be linked to world conditions, as inevitably we are, then the leadership of this nation, private and public, is going to have to be courageous enough to anticipate changes, sense the mood of the people, and act decisively to suggest reasonable and rational changes in our method of governing ourselves. One thing is certain. We will be living in a forever-changing world.

Epilogue

A Long and Winding Trail

An old friend visiting Picosa one day remembered an escapade that may have dated back to our early, untamed college days. We laughed and then, a little sheepishly, he turned to Nellie and assured her, "Of course, John has mellowed after all these years."

"Oh, no, he hasn't," she responded quickly. "He's still vain, arrogant, and conceited . . . the three things I always wanted in a man."

I am not about to contest Nellie's judgment at this late date. If I have exhibited all of these qualities across the long span of years, I suppose it speaks well to my consistency. I must confess now to feeling more than my ration of mellowness. It is pleasant indeed to look back, but not as inviting as looking ahead.

One of the side effects of growing older is that the memory has its own cemetery, a quiet, respectful ground. I am thinking of Grandpa Haddox, my maternal great-grandfather, who was born in 1836, the year Texas won its independence from Mexico. He lived to be one hundred and two. My grandmother, his daughter, lived to be ninety-four. My own mother lived to be ninety-two. Nellie's mother is ninety-three and still going strong. My mind and my heart swim with thoughts of what has been and what still might be.

Of my six adult brothers and sisters, only Golfrey is no longer with us. The others are not only alive and active, they refuse to retire. Stanford, the eldest at eighty-two, owns an antique shop in San Antonio. Merrill and Wayne are ranchers in Floresville, and Carmen is married to one, Speedy Hicks. Blanche works in an office in Dallas. Ours is a family that does not countenance quitting.

And then I think of my father, who died young for a Connally, of a heart attack at sixty-two. The year was 1950 and he was never to know that I would be Secretary of the Navy, governor of Texas, or Secretary of the Treasury. Nor would he see the house that Nellie and I built or the improvements we made to land that he once plowed. All that we have, or had, resulted from the inspiration he and my mother gave us.

Our generation is passing from the stage now. No veteran of World War II will ever again be elected President. And there are fewer sons and daughters to remember the parents who were not far removed from the frontiers of America. They provided for their families, as mine did, with back-breaking, dawn-to-dark physical labor that was an extension of the harsh and demanding rural life they led. There were no luxuries and no options—no other way to rear a family of five boys and two girls, to educate and prepare them for the world of opportunities that beckoned to them, a better life than my father, an eighth-grade dropout, had ever known.

In a more innocent time, before capital gains taxes and even Social Security, this was called the American Dream.

When I became governor in 1962, Texas was less than fifty years away from its frontier. Texans had ridden against Pancho Villa, the Mexican revolutionary and bandit-hero, less than fifty years earlier. That was history pretty close by.

By the end of the 1960s, American astronauts walked on the moon, their flight plan calculated by scientists working at NASA, outside of Houston, in the state I governed.

Now we are approaching the end of this century, and the wonders of it could reach from here to the lunar surface itself. I think of loved ones and friends long gone, and what I feel isn't maudlin. As these words are written, I am seventy-six and still trying to find my potential.

In early April of 1993, Nellie and I drove along Interstate 10 between San Antonio and Houston. Through our windows we viewed the kaleidoscope of spring flowers that brighten the highways of our state.

Nature painted the colors of the Texas countryside, but Nellie Connally gave her a hand. When we occupied the governor's mansion, Nellie set about to redo and beautify the grounds through private donations. Thirty years later, they remain much as she created them. She also inspired a greater interest in spreading the growth of wildflowers, a cause Lady Bird Johnson happily picked up and turned into a national movement, one that continues to this day.

In the process, we all but cornered the bluebonnet market. We designed special little blue packets containing a few seeds, with instructions on how and what time of year to plant them. We sent them out by the tens of thousands to our Christmas card list, as a way of sharing and expanding the joy Texans feel for their state flower. Today the highways of southern Texas appear to be bordered by blue seas, the bluebonnets grow so thick and so vivid. They seem like lakes of sky-blue water.

We prefer to travel across the state by car, competing to call out the names of the distinctive flowers we see around us: Indian paintbrushes, white primroses, thistles, and scores of unidentified growths. I did not mean to detour into the "Home and Garden Hour," but I cannot take a trip across the years without describing the bouquet of spring.

Nellie and I were returning to Houston from the ranch. I had spent five hours on a tractor shredding one of my pastures,

The major changes would have been in the management of the Vietnam War and the Presidential succession. If Kennedy had lived, Lyndon Johnson would have run again in the second spot on the ticket, and he would never have been elected President. By 1968, his health and age—and the diminishing effect of eight years as Vice President—would have eliminated him.

The intriguing question relates to Robert Kennedy. He could have been nominated to succeed his brother, and would have been elected. But while this country may lust after royalty, and might not have been troubled by the idea of a dynasty, I believe Bobby Kennedy might have been. I think he would have wisely resisted the kind of rock stardom that was building around the brothers. He could easily have waited four years or eight.

My guess is that Jack Kennedy would have withdrawn American troops from Vietnam shortly into his second term. Although he did hesitate to raise the ante, he was less charmed by the generals than Johnson and less susceptible to their pressures. I believe he had already concluded that the war was unwinnable, and had found his pitch: we wanted to help, but in the end the sons of South Vietnam had to fight for their own country.

The country would have swung neither wildly to the right nor to the left. The Peace Corps might have played a larger role in helping underdeveloped nations, and more young people would have been drawn into public service. Jack Kennedy's appeal to minorities might have spared us summers of urban violence. We might have become the kinder and gentler nation we are still looking for thirty years later.

If Kennedy had lived, I assume my own attitude would not have changed, and it is conceivable I might have presumed to run for President myself in 1968. My political ambitions would almost certainly have taken on more steam. If not the Presidency, I would have run for a fourth and even a fifth term as governor of Texas, perhaps for no other reason than to set a record. That goal is one I now regard as ignoble, but there is a time in your life when records matter.

The skepticism I have so long encountered over my desires about being President stems from this period. In the weeks after the assassination, the weeks spent in Parkland Hospital, my temperament changed. John Kennedy's death gave me a different perspective on life, its frailties and its meaning. It made me impatient with trivia and egos and self-aggrandizement. The fires of ambition had been considerably banked by the tragedy. Not out of personal fear, but out of a new awareness, I no longer had an irresistible desire to subject myself or my family to a continuing political career.

It is true that I have never found a satisfactory answer to the question of why my life was spared. And so I made my run, and had a last hurrah, in the 1980 primaries. Having lost, I decided there was much more to life than what I could see in the crystal ball of a political arena. And today I have no regrets that there was never a President Connally.

As I neared the end of these pages, I returned to the Warren Report to verify a passage of my testimony. And a feeling of awe welled up inside me. So much was changed, so much destroyed, in so few ticks of time. I looked up from my desk, and through the windows of my office I could see the roofs of a tree-shaded neighborhood in Houston. Here we are, I thought, thirty years later, still speculating about what did or did not happen. And no one will ever know the complete truth.

I cannot say that I think about the assassination every day, but I don't miss by much. There is an endless stream of letters, and questions from students, occasionally from strangers and even friends. Richard Nixon has asked people around me about that day in Dallas, but never put a question to me directly.

The long-term effects of my injuries have been mixed. I have a slight rigidity in the right wrist. I am now plagued by a pulmonary fibrosis, which results in shortness of breath whenever I undertake any physical exertion; my doctors attribute this condition to the assassin's bullet that damaged my lung.

In 1992, for the first time since I was a junior in college, I did not take an active part in a national political election. My interest has not lessened, however. The phones still ring, the mailman still comes around, and I remain as consumed as ever by the twists and turns of the unique brand of politics at home.

As I survey the political scene in Texas today, my thoughts somersault back to my childhood, when Texans elected their first woman governor. I remember so well my first contact with bumper stickers, although at the time I saw more of them on horse-drawn wagons than on automobile bumpers in the streets of Floresville.

This was in the aftermath of the impeachment of Governor Jim ("Pa") Ferguson, who then successfully ran his wife in his place. The rural communities were enlightened and informed by the *Ferguson Forum*, a political propaganda sheet published by Pa Ferguson and his wife. It was supplemented by the novel production of the bumper stickers, which said simply "Me for Ma." They soon adorned the tailgates of wagons, buggies, pickups, and the few cars that were on the streets.

Today, Texas has another woman governor. Unlike Ma Ferguson, she is bright, witty, personable, very much an extrovert who has achieved the highest office in the state on her own, without the help or support of a crafty, wise, and corrupt husband, as Ma Ferguson had.

Governor Ann Richards is today inheriting the whirlwind of growth that has resulted from a migration into Texas from around the world. She inherited an exploding student population, an alarming expansion of prison inmates, street crime, and drug trafficking—all the problems of a complex industrial state of over 17 million people.

I wish her well. I think she has the brains and the capacity to cope with the problems. If she succeeds, she will indeed be the forerunner of other women who will be instrumental in transforming our society, turning old ways into a new future.

The state Ann Richards presides over is different than the

one I governed twenty-five years ago. It will be different ten years from now than what it is today. The real question for us in Texas, as in the nation, is whether or not we have the insight and the courage to restructure our government in time to meet the changing conditions that will touch each of our individual lives.

If we have the courage to make dramatic changes, then our democracy will survive and expand, our personal rights and freedoms will be assured. If we do not react in a timely fashion, reshaping the government at every level to meet the tests of a reinvented world, then we run the real risk of forfeiting our individual freedoms, stifling private enterprise, and expanding a monolithic, bureaucratic blob until the country is, in fact, ungovernable.

When that time comes, if anyone needs to look for John Connally he will be with Nellie—back at the ranch.

CO-AUTHOR'S
NOTE

Powerful currents surged through John Connally's life, which ended, not without irony, on June 15, 1993, in Houston's Methodist Hospital. He had been confined for most of a month in intensive care with pneumonia. His condition was complicated by a lung problem believed to be related to the wounds he suffered during the murder of John F. Kennedy.

His death reopened old scars.

Three months earlier, I had helped him add an epilogue to his autobiography. In it, he dismissed almost lightly his medical file. He dwelled on the longevity of his family, including a grandpa who lived to be 102. John Connally thought it was not unreasonable that, at seventy-six, he might have another ten or fifteen years to enjoy the colors of the Texas countryside. He mused that he and Nellie, his University of Texas sweetheart, might yet retire to the ranch house they had built in 1963 but never slowed down long enough to make their permanent home.

Fate did not grant what turned out to be the last wishes of the man regarded by scholars as the strongest governor the state ever had, a man who helped elect three Presidents but could not do the same for himself. He would not see his book published. He would not see another spring "when the bluebonnets bloom like lakes of sky blue waters."

Those words were his, not mine; his description of the state flower that so pleased his eye reveal a curious softness in a character both macho and elegant—the Marlboro Man in a tux. He has a guaranteed place in the history and mythology of Texas, a land so proud of its capacity for producing giants, real or imagined.

To those who knew him, who had observed his restless nature and boundless energy, the news came as a shock and a mystery: how did he find the time to die? The question was not meant to be flippant. Six days before he was brought by ambulance to the hospital, Connally announced that he would head a new, $75 million thoroughbred racetrack to be built in Houston by the Maxxam group. It was not the title or the exposure or being around horses—although he loved horses—that excited him. It was the action. He had a need to be in charge, to compete, to operate on a certain scale.

Two days before he fell ill, he drove a tractor around his ranch, mowing a few green acres.

Politics gave him a way out of the rural life that molded him. He did not romanticize his roots and rarely spoke about his upbringing. Like his fateful connection to Jack Kennedy, he chose not to exploit it.

It was in John Connally, rather than Lyndon Johnson, that the great Texas paradox expressed itself. He brought blacks and Jews and women into the state government, rebuilt what had been an inferior system of education, and then resolved his differences with the liberal wing of the Democratic Party by becoming a Republican.

He resented and regretted the fact that he was seldom if ever given credit for his idealism. He accepted it reluctantly when his good intentions were treated as acts of opportunity. He had to declare bankruptcy, in 1987, to change the minds of some who had viewed him as cold or aloof or uncaring.

Yet he was among the kindest men I have known, considerate and courtly in the old-fashioned sense. He would walk a visitor from his office to the elevator. He would rise from behind his desk if the cleaning lady came in to empty the wastebasket.

He had a humor that could be cutting but not mean. We were of different generations, different worlds, different habits. The Governor still rose at dawn with the chickens, as he had all his life. My habits are irregular, and include the late-night weaknesses of a writer. The first night I spent at the ranch, I overslept. The Connallys had taken their Sunday morning coffee at seven. When I opened one eye, the clock read 10:30, and at that moment I heard a voice booming down the hall: "Nellie, do you want to see if Sleeping Beauty is up yet?"

In a eulogy his older son, John B. Connally III, said, "We felt both the sting of his magnificent temper and the balm of his sympathetic heart. He approached yardwork and homework with the same intensity that he brought to the international monetary structure."

The body lay in state for two hours while mourners lined up around the block for their turn to walk inside the pink granite Capitol. Nellie Connally, who had borne her husband's final days with strength and dignity, stood by the casket greeting them. The protocol people had tried to talk her out of it, but she insisted: "It's the last time I'll get to stand beside John Connally."

More than eight hundred mourners attended the services at the First United Methodist Church, where John Connally and Idanell Brill were married fifty-two years ago. Jake Pickle, his law school classmate and a longtime congressman, had been their best man. Pickle gave one of the eulogies: "He looked like a President. He acted like a President."

That was the line so frequently heard about Connally, that he looked "Presidential." And so he did: tall, tailored, with a sculpted face and thick, wavy white hair. He was "sometimes wrong," said Pickle, "but never in doubt."

Former President Richard Nixon, whose wife Pat would die a few days later, flew in from California. "In politics," he said, "when you win you hear from everybody. When you lose you only hear from your friends. I always heard from John Connally."

The Reverend Billy Graham helped conduct the service. He had been in the hospital room in Houston when Connally died.

It was Lady Bird Johnson, in her sweet, lilting voice, who provided the most vivid of memories. "We shared our youth, dreams and ambitions," she said. "We shared campaigns and unending work. We shared births . . . and deaths. We shared a war. There were times we even shared houses.

"John was always the young one. Always the strikingly handsome, energetic, can-do man—as Lyndon would say." She remembered an incident during the war, when the Texans were at a cafe in Alabama. There was a rush of patrons to the window, and Lady Bird asked their "somewhat crusty, middleaged waitress," what the commotion was all about.

"She said Clark Gable was stationed at Maxwell Field, and everyone wanted a glimpse of him walking down the street. She then turned to John and said, 'You-all don't have to go. You're just as handsome as he is.' "

Connally did not resist such flattery. But he had no illusions about his ups and downs. During the bankruptcy woes, a TV reporter asked if he thought his was the story of Texas.

"No," he said, grinning, "I don't think I'm the story of Texas. But I think I'm typical of a lot of Texans, in that I'm going to keep fighting back." Which he did, up until his last breath.

He was laid to rest on a green hillside in the Texas State Cemetery in Austin, a few feet from the monument to Stephen F. Austin, the father of what was once the Republic of Texas. An honor guard fired a 21-gun salute, a bugler sounded Taps, and a state trooper handed Nellie Connally the two flags folded into triangles that had covered the casket. Four surviving ex-governors paid their respects. "But John Connally," said Ann Richards, the current holder of the office, "was *the* Governor."

Inevitably, his death raised new cries from the conspiracy theorists and speculation about his wounds. In recent years, Connally suffered from pulmonary fibrosis, a rare disease that involves scarring of the lungs. His doctors emphasized that there is no known cause. The Governor had made no previous disclosure of his condition. He had one healthy lung and one that had been punctured by splinters of bone when a bullet tore through his chest and shattered part of the fifth rib.

The country lost one of its most astute political minds, and Texas lost an original resource the day John Connally died, possibly from a bullet fired thirty years ago.

—Mickey Herskowitz

BIBLIOGRAPHY

(AND NOTES ON SOURCES)

T he political events of my adult life, described in this work, cover a span of more than fifty years, from 1939 to the Presidential election of 1992. As those who took part and those who were witnesses depart from the scene, the events themselves are left to the custody of journalists, scholars, and political addicts. The latter function in somewhat the same role as the African elders whose oral recitals keep alive the tribal history.

No lines are drawn here. All record-keepers serve a purpose. But this book is my own. It is my story, my life, and in the end I have relied on my memory for the major portion of what appears here. I am comfortable with having done so, especially with respect to those long ago times for which documents are scarce or nonexistent.

In the process of assembling my memoirs, I referred to literally thousands of documents, most from my own files, but including the archives of former Presidents Lyndon Johnson, John F. Kennedy, Richard Nixon, and Gerald Ford. I reviewed books about them, in some of which I was a passing or distinct presence. Others compared for me their accounts and mine of the historical and controversial events that make up a political life. Some of the accounts vary wildly.

While I disagree with certain conclusions that were reached, I recognize that these books are now part of the historical record. In this category are:

William Manchester. *The Death of a President.* New York: Harper & Row, 1967.

Lyndon Baines Johnson. *The Vantage Point.* New York: Holt, Rinehart and Winston, 1971.

Congressional Quarterly. *Watergate: Chronology of a Crisis.* Washington, D.C., 1973.

Doris Kearns. *Lyndon Johnson and the American Dream.* New York: Harper & Row, 1976.

Richard Nixon. *RN: The Memoirs of Richard Nixon.* New York: Grosset & Dunlap, 1978.

Merle Miller. *Lyndon, An Oral Biography.* New York: G. P. Putnam's Sons, 1980.

Robert A. Caro. *The Path to Power: The Years of Lyndon Johnson.* New York: Alfred A. Knopf, 1982.

James Reston, Jr. *The Lone Star.* New York: Harper & Row, 1989.

Robert A. Caro. *Means of Ascent: The Years of Lyndon Johnson.* New York: Alfred A. Knopf, 1990.

Other books, written with what may be described from a more regional viewpoint, were valuable as a frame of reference for my deep Texas roots, my years in the governor's office, and for the often serpentine world of Texas politics. I was interviewed at varying lengths by the authors, and the tapes of those interviews were helpful in refining my thoughts and opinions through the years. These sources include:

Governor John Connally. Report to the Texas Legislature. 1969.

Jimmy Banks. *Money, Marbles and Chalk*. Austin, Texas: Texas Publishing Co., 1971.

Ann Fears Crawford and Jack Keever. *John B. Connally, Portrait in Power*. Austin, Tex.: Jenkins Publishing Co., 1973.

James Conaway. *The Texans*. New York: Alfred A. Knopf, 1976.

Frederick A. Birmingham. *John: The Man Who Would be President*. Hayward, Calif.: The Curtis Publishing Co., 1979.

In re-creating my years with Lyndon Johnson, I drew freely upon interviews I had given for the Oral History collection, headed by Joe B. Frantz, at the LBJ Library on the University of Texas campus. I also drew upon the transcripts of a symposium on the late President Johnson, which I chaired and to which many former Johnson staffers contributed.

Portions of the material related to John Kennedy's trip to Dallas have been vastly expanded from an article I wrote for *Life* magazine in November, 1967. My career was covered generously by *Time* and *Newsweek*, whose articles were useful in verifying dates and details of my national and international activities.

In the ongoing process of research, other publications, agencies, and news services that were consulted included:

Associated Press
Austin *American-Statesman*
Business Week
Dallas *Morning News*
Dallas *Times Herald*
Fortune
Houston *Chronicle*
Houston *Post*

Los Angeles *Times*
New Republic
New York *Daily News*
New York Times
President's Commission on the Assassination of President
    John F. Kennedy (Warren Commission Report)
San Antonio *Light*
Saturday Evening Post
Scripps-Howard
Texas Monthly
United Press International
U. S. News and World Report
Vanity Fair
Wall Street Journal
Washington *Post*

Index

INDEX